Sandra Hill

The Pirate Bride

AVON

An Imprint of HarperCollinsPublishers

AVON BOOKS
An Imprint of HarperCollins*Publishers*
10 East 53rd Street
New York, New York 10022-5299

Copyright © 2013 by Sandra Hill
Excerpt from *Kiss of Wrath* copyright © 2014 by Sandra Hill
ISBN 978-0-06-221044-9
www.avonromance.com

First Avon Books mass market printing: December 2013

Avon Trademark Reg. U.S. Pat. Off. and in Other Countries, Marca Registrada, Hecho en U.S.A.
HarperCollins® is a registered trademark of HarperCollins Publishers.

Printed in the U.S.A.

10 9 8 7 6 5 4 3 2 1

This book is dedicated to my longtime fans, who have been with me from the beginning. You know who you are. I won't mention you by name for fear of leaving someone out.

These are the folks who write me now, as they have over the past eighteen years, saying, "I have been reading all your books since the very first one." They tell me that they glom some of my novels multiple times. They buy e-book editions of novels they've already read in print. And when I meander off into other genres—time-travel, historical, contemporary, Viking Navy SEALs, Cajuns, and Vikings—they might at first say, "Whaaat?" But they always give me a try, and most times, follow that new series.

It's particularly appropriate that I dedicate The Pirate Bride *to those longtime fans because it is the eleventh book in Viking Series I, which began in 1994 with* The Reluctant Viking, *my very first book. In fact, Tykir, the father of Thork, the hero of* The Pirate Bride, *was a little boy in that first book. Boy, does time fly!*

Thank you, thank you, thank you!

CHAPTER ONE

When he was bad, he was very bad.
When he was good, he was still bad . . .

Thork Tykirsson sat in a bustling tavern in the trading town of Hedeby, brooding.

He'd tupped the ale barrel. A mere once.

He'd done another type of tupping. Once.

He'd engaged in an alehouse brawl. Once.

He'd told a ribald joke. Once.

He'd tossed dice for a vast amount of coins. Once.

Ho-hum.

His virtuous behavior—*Bloody hell! Whoever heard of a virtuous Viking?*—followed on his having quit pirating a year ago when that evil Saxon king Edgar had finally gone to his eternal reward. Everyone knew that Vikings were pirates of a sort. Not him anymore.

He could go a-Viking, he supposed. A respectable occupation that he enjoyed on occasion. He freely admitted to having plundered a monastery or two for gold chalices or silver-chased crucifixes. How many chalices does one church need, anyhow? You could say Vikings did the priests a favor, helping them avoid the sin of greed. And the

hated Saxons deserved everything a-Viking Norsemen sent their way. Same went for those arrogant
Scots and the foppish men of Frankland. But, truth
to tell, he had more than enough treasure.

The most appalling thing was that Thork was
actually considering marriage, something he'd
avoided with distaste for years. In fact, he had already made a preliminary offer to Jarl Ingolf Bersson for his daughter Berla. He planned to set sail
in the morning for the Norselands and his father's
estate at Dragonstead, where he had not been nigh
onto five years now. Barring unforeseen circumstances, he would return to Hedeby before winter
when a final betrothal agreement could be made.
That should please his father.

*But married? Me? I will become just like every other
man I know who succumbs to marital pressure. Wed-
locked and landlocked. No doubt I will soon have baby
drool on my best tunic, doing my wife's bidding like a
giant lapdog.*

"Bor-ing . . . I have become bor-ing," Thork exclaimed aloud with horror. "I was once deemed
the wildest Viking to ride a longship, a wordfame
I worked good and well to earn, and now"—he
shuddered—"I am becoming a weak-sapped,
sorry excuse for a Norseman, and I have not even
wed yet. What will become of me?"

"Methinks you are being too hard on yourself,"
said Bolthor, once a fierce warrior, now an aging
skald noted for his big heart and bad poems.
"Your father will be proud of you. That counts for
more than a bit of boredom."

And that was the heart of the problem: his estrangement from his sire, Tykir Thorksson, and

his determination to restore himself in the old man's good favor. At just the thought of his father, Thork instinctively tugged on the silver thunderbolt earring that hung from one of his ears. It had belonged to his father, and his father's father before him. There had been many a time in the past ten years when his father would have liked to take it back . . . if he could catch him.

Just then, there was a commotion at the door.

"The crew is missing," Alrek, the clumsiest Viking alive, said breathlessly as he rushed into the alehouse and tripped on some object hidden in the rushes, almost landing in Thork's lap. His blond hair, sun-bleached to almost white, stood up in unruly spikes, and his green eyes were huge with worry.

"What crew?" Thork asked.

"Your crew."

Thork crossed his eyes with impatience. "The crew of *which* ship?" He'd brought three longships here to the trading town of Hedeby to sell the amber he'd harvested in the Baltics these many months. And wasn't that respectable occupation yet another sign of dullness growing in him like a blister on a Saxon's arse?

"Oh." Alrek blushed. "*Swift Serpent.*"

Thork's smallest, but one of his favorite vessels. "Are you saying all of the *Serpent*'s seamen are missing?" That would mean about sixty rowers.

"Good gods, nay!" Alrek was momentarily distracted by the serving maid who smiled at him as she poured ale into the horn he lifted off the loop on his belt, making sure Alrek got a good look at her mostly exposed bosoms. Alrek blinked several times . . . with amazement, no doubt. It *was* a voluptuous view, although the maid's hand shook nervously as she refilled his and Bolthor's horns, as well. Odd that a tavern maid, dressed to entice, would be so nervous.

But that was neither here nor there.

Alrek shook his head to clear it and turned his attention back to Thork. "Only a half dozen."

"Only a half dozen," Thork repeated. "Alrek, the men are no doubt off somewhere wenching, or they are too *drukkinn* to walk back yet."

"But you told everyone to be on board by midnight so that we could set sail at dawn," Alrek persisted.

Bolthor jerked with surprise as the serving maid trailed a fingertip over his shoulders as she walked away. Not many women approached the old man, who had seen more than fifty winters, when there were younger, more comely men about. Not to mention the black eye patch over his one eyeless socket, due to an injury in the Battle of Ripon many years past. But then Bolthor said, "Alrek, Alrek, Alrek. When will you learn? A Viking man does not take well to orders, especially when bedsport is available."

Thork agreed. "The men will be there in good time, or left behind to find their own way home."

Alrek shook his head vigorously, causing ale to slosh over the lip of his horn. "Nay. Something is amiss, I tell you. There are strange people about Hedeby this night."

"There are always strange people in Hedeby," Bolthor remarked. "Why, I recall the time there was an archer from Ireland who could shoot three arrows at one time. Or the man who could touch his eyebrows with his tongue. And then there was—"

"Not that kind of strange. These men I see skulking about . . . they are small in stature and curved in the wrong places. Like those two over there staring at us."

Thork and Bolthor both turned to see the two men leaning against the wall, wooden cups in their hands. They were, indeed, shorter than average, and they had hips like a woman, if the tunics that covered them down to their knees over tight braies were any indication.

"By the runes! They must be sodomites," Bolthor declared.

"Sodomites?" Thork exclaimed.

"Yea. Sodomites are men who prefer men to women."

"I know what a sodomite is. One of my best friends was . . . never mind!" Thork said, waving a hand dismissively. "Alrek, surely you are not saying there are vast numbers of man lovers about this night, waiting to prey on innocent seamen. As far as I know, they seek like-minded males."

"They are not all like those two. Some are taller. Some wider. But they are shifty-eyed and move in a sly manner. And there were a goodly number near *Swift Serpent*."

Alrek ever was fanciful, and a worrier, besides. But Thork did not want to offend the man. No need to worry. Bolthor was launching into one of his awful poems. And Thork did not want to offend him, either, though betimes it was the only way to stop his poetic musings.

"Men are as different as night and day.
The gods molded them like clay.
But there is one part that is prized most.
The one of which they are most likely to boast.
Like homing pigeons those bloody things are
Seeking out whate'er nest is close by."

Bolthor is getting worse, instead of better, I swear.
"Well, best we get back to the ship ourselves. In truth, I am beginning to feel a bit shaky," Thork confessed, downing the rest of his ale, and attaching the horn to his belt.

Bolthor did likewise, swaying on his feet as he stood. Being the giant he was, no one wanted to be near when he fell, so Thork took him by the elbow and steered him toward the door. He noticed with seeming irrelevance that the two "sodomites" were gone.

Alrek followed behind them, muttering something about the bitter aftertaste in his mouth from the ale.

Most of the stalls were closed for the night as they made their way slowly along the raised board walkways that crisscrossed the well-ordered market town. Thork had erected his own stall earlier that day and sold all the amber he'd brought to market, saving one large, pale yellow stone with a tiny bumblebee inside to gift his mother, Lady Alinor.

Ahead he could see the palisaded harbor with the earthen ramparts that rose over Hedeby in a half circle. They approached one of two gates in the wall that regulated traffic in and out of the city. Hedeby was situated at the crossroads of

Slien Fjord and the Baltic Sea, from whence they'd come after harvesting the amber. In the daytime, it was a bustling center for commerce because of its strategic position linking trade routes of eastern empires with the west . . . the Norselands, Frankland, and Britain.

As they turned a corner, Bolthor lurched for a hitching post outside a stable, bent over, and began to heave the contents of his stomach over the side into a muddy trench. Thork leaned against the railing for support, his knees suddenly feeling weak as butter. Alrek had both hands on his stomach and was groaning at the pain.

Suddenly, Thork felt a hard blow to the back of his head. Even as he fell, he saw that Bolthor and Alrek were following his path to the ground, Bolthor with a loud thud that broke a few planks.

It was then that Thork gazed up woozily to see that they were surrounded by a *hird* of little men led by the two from the tavern.

They seemed to be discussing him, Bolthor, and Alrek, as if they were goods.

"How are we ever going to get them back to the ship?"

Ship? What ship?

"I forgot. *Pirate Lady* is at the far, far end of the wharf."

Pirate Lady? What kind of name is that for a ship? Ah, she must mean Pirate's Lady. *Still, pirate? I do not like the sound of that.*

"Drag them, I suppose."

Do not dare!

"Where's a horse when you need one? Ha, ha, ha!"

I'll give you a horse, you misbegotten dwarf of a man! Pirate or not, pirate's whore or not, when I get up, you will regret your sorry jests.

"Wrap them in ells of sailcloth and lift them up onto yon wagon. If anyone asks, we can say that they are graybeards who died of old age, and we are carrying them to the funeral pyres."

I am not a graybeard. I am only twenty and eight.

"I get the big one. Think of the bairns I could have with his seed."

Bairns? How do they expect to carry babes in their wombs if they have no wombs?

"The clumsy one is adorable. Did you notice his dimple?"

What about me? Thork thought, then immediately chastised himself for caring.

"We'll draw lots when we get back to the island."

Island? Uh-oh!

Just before he blacked out totally, Thork realized something important. The men's voices sounded female. Very female.

Oh, good gods! They were being taken captive. *By women!*

**The women went a-Viking . . .
a different kind of a-Viking . . .**

Medana Elsadottir, best known as Sea Scourge, had never intended to become a pirate. In fact, when she'd left—rather, *escaped*—her home in Rognvald, land of the Danes, ten years ago, she'd never even heard of female pirates.

And she'd certainly never intended to take other women with her, nor continue to gather recruits to her unlikely *hird* of sea soldiers. Her followers now numbered an amazing one hundred and ninety-three, including nineteen children—fourteen girls and five boys, ranging from ages one to eight. They lived—women only, except for the boys—on a hidden, mountainous island named Thrudr, or Strength, appropriately named because that's exactly what each and every one of them had gained with their independence. Their stronghold was accessible by a narrow landmass that connected a smaller, visible island to the hidden cave in Thrudr, but only when the tide was down once a day.

"I could scarce recognize you in that disguise, Medana," Agnis the Weaver said. "'Tis much better than the last visit when you pretended to be a leper."

They both laughed at the memory. It had taken Medana days to soak off the false pustules made of mud and sand and tree sap.

On this trip to Hedeby, Medana was dressed as a nun, complete with a simple brown homespun gown and veil over a tightly bound white wimple. The only thing showing that might identify her as the sister of three powerful, greedy Viking chieftains were her thick, dark blonde brows, violet eyes, and bruised-looking, overly lush mouth, a trait of men and women alike in the line of Bjorn, one of the legendary first kings of early Norseland. But it had been ten years since she was sixteen years old and had last seen her evil siblings; they would scarce recognize the woman she'd become, even without a disguise.

"Being a nun in July was not my best idea. It's hotter than the depths of Muspell, but I'll be back on the ship soon and change into my tunic and braies," Medana remarked as they sat at a table in Agnis's small house behind the permanent merchant stall they maintained in the market town. The walls were adorned with the products of Agnis's gift for colored patterns in the cloth she wove on the large loom in the back corner. The room was perfumed with the sweet scent of dried herbs hanging from the ceiling rafters—lavender, verbena, and such.

"We should make a good profit on all the goods you brought this time," Agnis remarked as she removed the wooden platters from the table. They'd just finished a simple meal of cold slices of roast venison, hard cheese, manchet bread, and weak wine. On the way to the low chest that held a wooden pail of dishwater, she patted the head of her nine-year-old son, Egil, who was carding wool in the corner.

Even though Agnis resided here in Hedeby and did in fact weave and sell fine wool cloth, she was also Thrudr's agent, offering all the products produced or harvested on the rough, mountainous island—furs, honey, leather shoes and belts, soapstone pots and candles, wooden bowls and spoons, bone combs, and such. A pregnant Agnis had been among the women with Medana when first she'd fled Stormgard all those years ago. They'd barely survived that first winter. And the next two years had not been very easy, either, as more and more women somehow found their way to their hidden sanctuary. Now they were inde-

pendent and self-sufficient, but there were things
they needed that they could not grow, catch, make,
or steal. Like grains, spices, metal weapons and
implements, rope, needles, a bull to serve their
milch cows, and vegetables they were unable to
grow in their northern region.

"Your visit is short this time," Agnis said, top-
ping off Medana's cup of wine.

"Yea, a necessity. Our old bull Magnus died,
and two of our cows are about to go into heat. We
needed to buy a young bull, which I did, and get
it back home to do . . . his duty."

Agnis laughed. "The things a woman must do!"

"As for the short visit, believe you me, my
women are full of complaints. This is their time
for"—she arched her brows meaningfully at
Agnis—"you know."

"Same as the cows," Agnis jested, laughing,
then glanced toward her son to make sure he
wasn't listening. Egil had put aside his carding
tools and was playing with a pet cat.

"Exactly!"

"Why are you not out there enjoying yourself?"
Agnis asked, waving her hand to indicate the town.

"That is not my idea of enjoyment," Medana
said, not after the experience that led to her departure from Stormgard. "But I do not begrudge
my women their bedsport, even if their time is
limited."

"Hopefully, some of the man seed will take
root," Agnis said.

"Pray Frigg it does." While they did not have
men at Thrudr since they were not willing to
trust their lives to the brutish actions of the male

species, they still yearned for one thing that only men could provide. And that one thing wasn't just sex. It was children. After any trip a-Viking, or a-trading, there were always a few women who found themselves breeding. Once, an amazing ten got with child on a trip to Kaupang, no doubt due to their extended stay when their longship took on water and had to be dry-docked for repairs. Of course, infant mortality and childbirth fever took a good number of babes and occasionally the mothers, as happened everywhere in the world.

Medana and her crew had gone a-pirating on their way to Hedeby, and their plunder had been exceptionally tradeable. That on top of the goods they'd produced at home and brought to market should mean a good year for the women back at Thrudr. No gnawing on roots and moldy bread as they had the first winter in exile when there had been no meat or stored vegetables for the cook fire.

Medana and Agnis talked long into the evening, dividing the profits of this latest endeavor, discussing plans for the future, and relating news of the people they both knew.

"Is Gregor still pursuing you?" Medana teased.

"Always. The man does not give up." Agnis grinned. 'Twas clear to one and all that Agnis had a fondness for the Russian goldsmith who visited the trading center several times a year.

"Mayhap you will give in one of these days?" Medana suggested.

Agnis shrugged. "Mayhap, but then I am enjoying the gifts he brings me." She lifted the neckline of her gown to show Medana a fine gold chain. "How is Olga doing?"

"She rules the kitchens like a hardened warrior." Olga was Agnis's aunt, who'd come to them two years past when her husband died.

Agnis shared some stories about her aunt that had them both laughing, but then she turned serious. "Your brother Sigurd was here two sennights ago." At the look of concern on Medana's face, Agnis immediately added, "I had Bessie take over the stall for me." Bessie was the shortened name for Beatrix, a Saxon holder of a nearby pottery shed. "I am certain he did not see me."

Medana let out a breath she hadn't realized she was holding in. She had reason to fear her brothers, even after all these years and what she had done to thwart their plans, but Agnis also had cause to be wary. Sigurd was Egil's father. If the child of his loins had been a daughter, Sigurd would not care, but a son, now that would be a different matter. Furthermore, he would be angered at Agnis, a thrall, leaving without his permission.

It was late when Medana returned to *Pirate Lady*, the longship anchored at the far end of the wharf. A guardswoman standing at the rail greeted her with a hearty "Who goes there?" It was Elida, Thrudr's mistress of threads, who was in charge of all sheep shearing, spinning, weaving, and clothes making. Everyone on the island had a title for the numerous jobs needed for them to subsist: Mistress of hunt, fish, and fowl. Mistress of farming. Mistress of animal care. Mistress of cooking. Mistress of laundry. In fact, there were so many titles these days, it had become a matter of jest, especially when someone had to be called mistress of the privy.

With a smile, Medana replied, "'Tis me. Chieftainess Medana." She smiled even wider at the title, which had been assigned to her as a sign of deference.

"Has everyone returned?" Medana asked.

Elida nodded, but she shifted her eyes hither and yon, never quite meeting Medana's gaze. She was nervous for some reason. Must be because this was the first time she'd been given such responsibility. Also a talented embroiderer, Elida had requested a chance to prove her worth as an archer in Medana's personal guard. Already Elida's small hands were calloused and scratched, and, even with practice, the slim woman couldn't hit a Saxon boar from three paces. It would take sennights for the ointments of her healer, Liv, to restore Elida's skin to the point where she could once again handle the fine silk threads. Medana doubted that Elida would be going a-Viking again.

Moving on toward her small quarters, Medana inquired politely of Bergdis, one of her rowers, "Did you find a man to mate with this eve?"

Bergdis, who was mistress of buildings and woodworking back home, rolled her wide shoulders—all the rowers were well-muscled on their upper bodies to handle the hard exercise required to pull oars—before replying, "Yea, I did. But only once. There was no time for more."

It must have been an energetic mating because Bergdis's tunic was lopsided, half on and half off one shoulder, and the two braids that she normally wore to keep her frizzy red hair off her face had come undone. Her thick eyebrows were more grizzly than usual. Pity the man she'd set her eyes on this night.

That was unkind, Medana immediately chastised herself. Bergdis was a good woman who'd overcome huge tragedy in her former life. She deserved every reward that came her way, especially if it was a child, please gods.

Medana shrugged. Her crew knew ahead of time that this visit to Hedeby was destined to be short. If they made good speed, they might go a-Viking on the way home, but they must be careful not to visit those places they'd plundered on the way here. Stealth was an important tactic for female pirates, not having the strength and manpower of their male counterparts.

She noticed that Bergdis seemed nervous, too, rubbing the palms of her hands together. "Is something amiss?" Medana asked.

"Nay. Why would you ask me that? I have done nothing wrong."

Bergdis's defensive response startled Medana. "It was only a question. I was not accusing you of anything."

Just then, there was a pounding noise coming from below in the hold of the longship. Bang, bang, bang! Like a booted foot kicking wood. "What is that?"

"Must be the bull," both women said.

"I hope it does no damage. Mayhap I should go down and make sure the creature is tied securely. I would not want him hurt. After all, his services are sorely needed. I swear Helga is in as much need of a man as many of you." Helga was one of their most fertile cows.

Neither of the women smiled at Medana's jest.

Her rudder master, Solveig, stepped up from behind her and said, "Not to worry. I will take care of the matter. You know I have a way with animals."

That was the first time Medana had ever heard Solveig had a way with animals, seeing as how she was mistress of shipwrighting, but Medana was not about to argue the point now.

Her chief *housecarl*, mistress of military, Gudron, a huge warrior of a woman who could heft a heavy broadsword with the best of men, handed her a wooden goblet. "Have a drink of ale to toast our voyage home." Medana noticed that Gudron had crystals twisted in the blonde war braids that framed her square face. No doubt she'd been man hunting this evening, like many of the others.

That was nice of Gudron, even if the ale did taste a bit sour. After taking a few sips, Medana handed the cup back to her. She yawned widely then. The two cups of wine, watered down at that, plus these new sips of ale, shouldn't be affecting her so. "I am off to bed for a few hours' sleep. We set sail at daybreak."

Whether it was the wine and ale or the sway of the ship or just exhaustion, Medana slept soundly and did not awaken until the ship was already under way. Which was odd. Her crew had always waited for her orders before setting sail in the past.

It was later, when they were already too far out to sea to turn around, that Medana learned what the noisesome cargo was that they carried below. And it was no bull.

CHAPTER TWO

That's bull . . .

Thork awakened from a deep, odd sleep and saw pitch blackness.

Where am I?

He could hear heavy breathing and felt the warmth of human bodies lying next to him. His comrades of the evening, he assumed. Bolthor and Alrek. Thork hadn't drunk that much ale, but what he had imbibed must have been mighty potent for him to take his rest in such close bodily contact with men.

Something else struck him then. The air reeked of an odorsome musk. Phew! When was the last time his men had bathed? He would have a talk with them in the morning, or else toss them in the nearest fjord for a good wash. Or mayhap it was ale breath or beer wind in the bowels. In any case, the air was gagsome.

Thork ached all over. His arms, his shoulders, his legs. Even his teeth hurt. He tried to open his mouth to flex his jaws, but his lips seemed to be stuck together.

He couldn't think clearly, especially since his brain started throbbing behind his eyeballs. With a sigh, he succumbed back to the mindless sleep, where he soon had the most delicious dreams as the bed furs undulated under him. Up, down, up down. He had so many peakings he lost count.

Alas, he had to awaken eventually, and it was daylight. Or as much daylight as he could see from the cracks in the wood ceiling above him. It took him several moments to realize that he was in the hold of a seagoing vessel.

"Mghiggt!" he heard from his left.

"Szofftrl!" he heard from the other side.

And behind him he heard a loud bellow that sounded like a moo, but was deeper, more manly. "Mrraaahew!"

Straining upward, peering right and then left, Thork saw with amazement that he and seven of his seamen were in the hold of a longship, trussed up like chickens, hands tied behind their backs and linked to their bound ankles. And it was seal rope, too, he noted, the strongest of all ropes, cut in one long spiral off a seal. Thin scarves across their open mouths were tied behind their heads.

If that wasn't bad enough, the bellower behind him turned out to be a big-horned bull, which was fortunately tethered by one front and one hind leg to spikes in the plank walls, using the same seal rope. Fortunate because the bull was not a happy fellow and was eyeing them like they were cows in heat. The bull began to paw the rush-covered floor with its free front paw and let loose with one long, angry snort, which resulted in a wad of snot flying in the air, just missing Thork's face. Then the animal lifted its tail and made one loud splat out of its backside.

Thus, the source of the loathsome odors.

Thork shuffled his body as best he could to put some additional distance between him and the beast.

Glancing from one of his men to the other with questioning eyes, he got nothing but shrugs and equal confusion.

What in bloody hell had happened to them?

He tried to recount the previous evening's events. He'd been drinking with Bolthor and Alrek in the alehouse. The other men had already gone back to his longships or were off wenching somewhere, including Jamie the Scots Viking over there, who appeared to be laughing behind his gag. Jamie ever was a lackwit.

He recalled walking back to the ship with Alrek and Bolthor, who, by the by, must have been some giant bundle to get down into the hold of a ship. Right now, his eye patch was askew, leaving the open socket visible. They'd put double rows of seal rope on him. And no wonder; Bolthor was strong as yon bull.

Still pondering the night before, Thork remembered that they had all felt rather nauseous and unsteady. Then they'd been attacked by the small people . . . the sodomites.

No! It all came back to him now. Not sodomites. Women! They'd been kidnapped by a group of barmy women. For what purpose, he was uncertain, but the idea of Viking men being overtaken by the weaker sex was beyond embarrassing. It was an outrage! They must have been given a sleeping draught in their ale.

Where were the rest of his crew, and what did

they think of his disappearance? Would they assume he'd taken off on some wild venture, as he very well might have in the past, before he'd turned a good leaf? Or would they be searching for him?

But women? Captured by women?

Someone was going to pay for this indignity. And inconvenience.

While the bull continued to growl and snort, blow slime, and strain against its bindings to come gore them, his men kept trying to talk behind their gags, resulting in garbled sounds. He shifted his body so that he was up against the side of the ship, where a nail stuck out. Working with painstaking slowness, being careful not to tear his scalp, he finally managed to rip off the scarf, freeing his mouth.

Then, shuffling on his side over to Alrek, he used his teeth to untie the knot in back of Alrek's head. Yeech! Alrek's hair tasted like fish oil. Had he been trying to tame down his cowlick again? Thork realized then that while it was nice to have the gags removed, there was no way they could cut or untie the seal ropes.

"Where are we?" Jamie and the others wanted to know as they one by one got their gags undone.

"We have been taken captive. That's all I know," Thork replied.

"For what purpose?" asked Brokk, a young orphan who'd seen no more than twelve winters, though he was tall and well-built for his age. Thork had been training him in swordplay with a goal of eventually adding him to his *hird* of soldiers.

"It's those sodomites we saw in the alehouse, I wager," Alrek contributed.

"Sodomites!" the rest of the men exclaimed with horror, envisioning no doubt the type of activities they might be subjected to.

"That is an offensive word," Thork said. "Man-lovers would be more sensitive."

"That is nah quite true," Jamie pointed out, "because 'man-lovers' could also refer to women."

"Man-to-man lovers would be better, I suppose," Alrek decided, and he was serious.

"Och! Since when do we Vikings care who we offend?" Jamie was enjoying the halfbrained discussion immensely.

Not joining in was Bolthor, who looked at Alrek and Jamie with his one good eye as if he'd like to whack them both aside their heads. "Idiots! Those were not sodomites. They were women."

"Women!" the rest of them exclaimed, even more confused.

Then Finn Vidarsson, best known as Finn Finehair, the vainest Viking to ride a longship, grinned through his neatly trimmed mustache and beard. "Are we going to be love slaves?"

"Good gods!" Thork muttered. That was ridiculous, of course.

Wasn't it?

"I think they are pirates," Alrek said.

Thork recalled thinking of pirates back in Hedeby when he'd first heard the name of the ship, *Pirate Lady*. But he'd never thought that the pirates were women.

Everyone turned to look at Alrek. "In fact, there were rumors in Hedeby of a female pirate called the Sea Scourge."

"Female pirates?" scoffed Jostein, who was

almost a graybeard at thirty-five or so. Jostein had joined Thork's band to escape females, or one female in particular—his wife, who intended to divorce him at the next Althing. For what reason, Jostein had been reluctant to disclose. Jostein had been a mere youthling when he'd traveled years ago with Jamie's father, Rurik, to Scotland, where he'd stayed and become like an older brother to Jamie . . . until his disastrous marriage. Or so Thork had been told by Jamie.

"The female pirates have been invading the usual spots where Norsemen go a-Viking," Alrek elaborated. "The leader known as Sea Scourge is said to be the ugliest witch of a woman, with purple hair, horsey teeth, and three breasts to nurse her black cats."

"Were you a wee bit *drukkinn* at the time you heard this blather?" Jamie inquired, not unkindly. Everyone was a bit gentle with Alrek, whose clumsiness was oddly endearing. Besides, they all admired Alrek for having raised his younger brothers and sisters from when he'd been only twelve years old and they'd all been orphaned.

"Nay, I was not *drukkinn*," Alrek replied with affront. " 'Tis true. There *are* female pirates and they *are* ruthless witches. Some say they dress as men and even walk and talk in a manly manner." He hesitated, then added, "In fact, 'tis said some have even grown cocks."

"Do they have breasts and cocks at the same time, I wonder?" a wide-eyed Brokk pondered. "And do all the pirate wimmen have three breasts?"

The rest of the men burst out in laughter, especially when Henry, a slant-eyed man of Asian blood, said, "If true, the women could swive and be swived at the same time." Henry's mother had been a thrall owned by a Saxon nobleman—thus his English name—then later he had been sold at a young age to a Norse chieftain. He'd been raised Viking.

Despite the ridiculous notion, they were men, and as men spent several moments trying to picture that possibility. Triple-breasted women! Ridiculous, of course. But intriguing.

"I knew a man one time who had breasts," Alrek said, still offended that his comrades had given no credit to his gossip.

"You speak of Dordin of Lade," Bolthor said. "He is just fat. Not womanly. If he would stop drinking so much ale and engage in a bit more swordplay, he would lose that chest flab forthwith."

The bull let out another unending mewl of unhappiness, or randiness, which caused them all to look at the huge animal. They couldn't help but notice its immense ballocks and a cock the size of a battering ram.

They glanced at one another.

Why would women pirates need a bull?

"Surely these lassies are not the kind who . . ." Jamie started to say.

"What?" Brokk asked.

"I have heard of such in the eastern lands. Bestiality, they call it."

Finn shuddered as he spoke.

"What?" Brokk repeated.

"I think it likes you," Alrek said to Jamie. "It keeps gazing at you, rather horny like."

"What?" Brokk again.

"I will tell you one thing," Bolthor said. "That bull gets anywhere near my arse, and it will be roast bull for dinner tonight."

"What?" Brokk growled with frustration.

"They are just jesting," Thork told Brokk. *I hope.* Then he looked at Bolthor and groaned. He knew what that dreamy expression on the older man's face meant. The verse mood was coming upon him.

"Methinks I should compose a saga about this," Bolthor said.

They all groaned.

But then Bolthor added, "I have not felt the urge to compose a saga since I last saw my Katherine. Mayhap my heart is finally healing."

How could they protest now? Bolthor had been married late in life to a Saxon lady who owned an estate that raised, of all things, chickens. Lots of chickens. And children. Lots of children. Katherine's four from a prior marriage and then one of their own. Apparently, Katherine had booted Bolthor's big arse out the door after he had composed one too many poems about her intimate body parts, the last being an ode to her gray-flecked woman's fleece. She'd issued an ultimatum to the giant skald. No more poems, ever, on any subject, or leave their marriage bed. She wanted him to settle down as a chicken farmer.

Being a Viking, and thus stubborn to the bone, he'd taken his wife's order literally and left not just their bed furs, but their home as well. He would show her! Leastways, that's what he had thought before thinking his actions through.

Bolthor had asked Thork if he could come with him on this trading trip to get away from his troubles and to bring some chickens to market. Apparently, he'd already saturated the Saxon market towns with the pestsome birds. Fortunately, Bolthor had finally sold the last of them in Hedeby and Thork had been able to clean the holds of his longships of the foul chicken shit.

But now they were stuck with a bull. And bull shit.

Is this where being good leads a Viking? Thork wondered.

But wait, Bolthor was clearing his throat.

"This is the saga of Thork the Great."

That was the way Bolthor started many his poems. Thork was no greater than the next man.

"A Viking man is born to be bad.
Plundering and pillaging, and might I add,
Wenching and drinking, sailing and a-Viking,
Wickedness untold does a Norseman bring.
But came a day one Viking man decided to reform,
To please his father and new morals form.
No more bad deeds would this sorry soul perform.
Alas and alack, the Norns of Fate stuck out their
*   big toes*
To trip up the man and add to his woes.
Mayhap the gods have another life map
To restore the man's spirit with one last mishap.
Or mayhap 'tis just the gods' way of saying:
Only a lackwit tries to sing
A hymn

So prim
And bitter
When wild is better."

"That was wonderful," Finn said. "Methinks you are improving with age."

Thork shot Finn a look of disbelief.

The others complimented Bolthor as well.

The bull bellowed. Thork wasn't sure if it liked the poem or not.

Enough was enough! Thork let loose with a loud bellow of his own. "Heeeyyyy! Open the bloody damn door, you witless wenches! Release us! At once! Lest you find yourselves at the bottom of the sea feeding the fishes."

"I'll lop off your barmy heads," Bolthor added in a voice loud enough to wake the dead, "even if you are demented women."

That's telling them!

"I have to piss," Brokk yelled. "You better let me out. If I wet my braies, you'll be real sorry."

Oh, that feeble complaint is sure to bring some action!

"I would not make a good love slave," Bolthor added. "My wife will come after you with a meat cleaver." To Thork, he confided, "Leastways, I think she would."

She would. Katherine might be irritated with her husband at the moment, but that did not mean she would stand by and let another woman, or women, have him. An angry Katherine was like a ferocious lion, despite the gray-flecked nether curls. It wasn't the first time she and Bolthor had argued and parted. She always took him back.

Thork thought of something else as the bull continued to bellow and snort. A bull of that age and size must have cost plenty of coin. A precious cargo.

"Your bull is sickening," Thork hollered. "Best you check to see if he is dying."

Immediately the hatch door above them swung open, and a dozen women in men's garments stared down at them. It took him several moments of blinking to adjust his vision to the bright sunlight.

Not a one of the women could be considered comely. One was missing a front tooth. Another was as wide as she was tall. Still another was long in the tooth . . . way long in the tooth.

Just then a female voice above deck some distance away asked, "What is going on here?"

The women peering down at him glanced at the as yet unseen woman raising the question in an authoritative voice and said as one, "Uh-oh!"

Was it the Sea Scourge? And did she really have purple hair, horsey teeth, and three breasts?

"Uh-oh!" he echoed the female pirates.

**There was going to be hell . . .
or Muspell . . . to pay . . .**

It was past noon when Medana awakened in her sleep furs, and by then the ship was well out to sea. She was still wearing her nun garments that she realized with a sniff of distaste had become odorsome from body sweat in the heat of this confined space.

How strange! Not just that she had gone to bed without removing her clothing or that she'd slept so long and deep, but that the women would set sail without waking her first.

Had she become *drukkinn* from just two cups of watered wine and a few sips of ale? She licked her dry lips and tasted something familiar. It was the sleeping herb her island healer often used to put a person to sleep while she sewed torn flesh or that one time she'd had to cut off two fingers of a women whose axe had slipped when cutting firewood. Medana herself had tasted it when one of her pounding head megrims had brought her nigh to her knees in pain.

But when . . . Ah, she realized suddenly. It must have been in the cup she'd been offered when she'd boarded last night.

But why?

There best be a really good reason.

Just then, she heard a loud bellowing noise. An unhappy bull.

But then she also heard other bellowing noises . . . ones that sounded like male voices. Unhappy male voices.

She frowned with confusion, then jumped up and rushed from her bed furs and out onto the deck. The dozen or so women who'd been gathered about the opening into the hold dropped the door and turned to stare at her with guilty innocence.

"What is going on here?" Medana demanded.

"Um," one of them said.

"The bull is a bit restless, that is all," another added.

Still another said, "There is naught for you to worry about. Mayhap you should go rest some more."

"I have rested more than enough. By the by, why did you not rouse me this morn before setting sail?"

Solveig stepped away from the rudder she'd been steering, handing it off to another woman, before she explained, "You seemed exhausted, and we wanted to show that we could do the work you have taught us."

Medana could not argue with that. Actually, Solveig was the one who'd taught all of them about shipbuilding and sailing, being the only child of a master shipwright who had been a hard and abusive taskmaster for his daughter.

"I should check on the bull. You know how much it is needed back at Thrudr. With good speed we will be there two days hence, just in time for our milch cows to be in heat. With the gods' blessing, there will be calves aplenty by autumn."

She was reaching for the latch on the hatch door when an angry male voice shouted from below, "Release us, you mangy excuses for women!"

Medana jerked back and turned to her crew, most of whom had suddenly become busy with other tasks. In fact, the rowers were rowing so fast their arm and shoulder muscles would be burning by nightfall.

"Is that a man down below?" Medana asked, narrowing her eyes with accusation at the women around her. Would they have dared to disobey the long-standing order to bring no men on board? Surely not!

Several male voices were shouting now. Not just one, as she'd first thought. *Oh. My. Gods! They did. This is bad. Very bad!* "Have you lost your bloody minds?" she shouted.

In the silence that suddenly overcame her crew, she could clearly hear the men speaking loudly from below.

"I'll lop their heads off, just wait and see."

"I'll lop off her breasts . . . all three of them."

"Do they know who we are? Simple split-tails! Are they so lackwitted they would capture Norsemen?"

"They have got themselves boars by the tails now," another added. "Mayhap you should write a saga about that, Bolthor. Feckless wenches and boars' tails."

"Are you saying my tail looks pig-like?" another male inquired with a laugh.

Still another man added, "Didst know that a pig's cock is shaped into a spiral, but when extended, it is as long as a boat."

"Finn, you are an idiot," someone else said.

Medana inhaled sharply and addressed her women, "Exactly how many boars' tails do we have below?"

"Three or four or so, methinks," Bergdis offered, a rosy blush rising on her already ruddy cheeks, which matched her bright red hair.

"*Exactly* how many?" Medana insisted on knowing.

"Eight," Gudron revealed, raising her square chin defiantly. "We would have taken more, but these men are so big they filled the hold. No room for more, especially with the bull."

Eight! "Why in the gods' name would you do such a thing?"

Elida, usually a docile creature who directed her weavers with a gentle touch, put now-roughened hands on her hips and raised her chin high, just like Gudron, except she was much shorter and the effect not so dramatic. "We did not have near enough time with the men on this visit. We are just borrowing them for a while until some of us are breeding. Then we will let them loose."

The others nodded, as if this was a logical explanation for their insanity.

"Bo-borrowed?" Medana sputtered. "What do you think these men—Vikings, at that—are going to think about a group of women *borrowing* them?"

"Surely they will not object once they get accustomed to the idea," Bergdis declared with a big smile that she immediately covered with the fingers of one hand. She was ever conscious of the gap in her mouth where one front tooth should have been, thanks to her husband who liked to batter all his wives when under the ale influence. Bergdis, her redhead temper tested one too many times, had reciprocated, taking out not one but two of her husband's rotten teeth. That's when she'd fled to Medana's sanctuary.

"Besides, didst ever know of a Viking man who would reject a good tupping when it's on offer?" Solveig asked. She should know, having been a paid harlot for a short period after running away from her father.

Much laughter greeted her words.

Medana leaned down and yanked hard on the latch, pulled the door up and over to land on the deck with a loud thud. It took her several moments in the bright sunshine to make out the figures below.

There were in fact the bull and eight rather large Vikings glaring up at her.

One of them, who appeared to be the leader, dropped his jaw and exclaimed, "Good gods! Captured by barmy bitches *and* a nun!"

Another one, a giant of a man with only one eye, said to the first one, "Dost think it a sin to lop off the head of a nun, Thork? Would it be so bad under the circumstances?"

"Who cares!" Thork replied. "I am damn tired of being good."

CHAPTER THREE

**Some women borrow a cup of
sugar; others borrow men . . .**

Thork was taken out of the hold, then retied to
the mast pole. The nun chieftain-ess of this
barmy band was assisted in the task by five of her
burly crew members. Thork had not seen so many
well-muscled women in one place in all his life.
The one who wore war braids on either side of her
scowling face looked as if she could heft an acorn-
stuffed, pregnant boar with little trouble, much
less a Viking man.

There were only females aboard this ship, doing
all the jobs traditionally reserved for men. And
judging by the cloth bags overflowing with gold
and silver objects over there, the swords that were
placed by each of the sea chests, and the scurvy
appearance of some of the women, who wore col-
orful cloths about their heads, tied at the nape, he
could only surmise that they'd been a-Viking.

Or pirating.

He was the only one who'd been brought out
thus far after his men gave him up as the *Sea Serpent*'s owner. The traitors! Bolthor was composing
sagas as fast as his thick brain could work. "When

Pirates Grow Breasts." "Three Teats in a Row."
"Row, Row, Row Your Cradle." "She Pumped
the Waves, Not a Butter Churn." "Have You Ever
Swived a Pirate?" "Ahoy, Sweet Mateys!" And his
men, instead of being outraged at their predica-
ment, were laughing like hyenas.

"You should be pleased," Bolthor had advised
when Thork had snarled at the women trying to
drag him upward. "Your boredom is surely gone
now."

Thork had advised Bolthor on what he could do
with his unruly tongue.

"Pirates!" he'd stormed at the nun leader when
he was secured. "Women are not made to do
men's work." He glanced pointedly at the oars-
women panting as they moved the heavy oars.
"Least of all pirating." He could not be too critical
of pirating itself since he'd engaged in the enterprise himself for a time . . . for a good purpose.
But women as pirates? Pfff! " 'Tis against nature."

She'd just arched her brows at him as if to say,
Oh really?

If there was anything Thork disliked, it was a
woman with a snide attitude. "Aren't you a little
long in the tooth for such nonsense?" he asked,
guessing she had to have seen more than twenty
winters, possibly more than twenty-five. "At your
advanced age, you should be home tending babes
and caring for a husband, not roaming the seas
like lunkhead sailors. Or praying your beads back
at the convent. Surely it is a mortal sin for a sister
of God to steal, is it not? Or, gods forbid, kidnap
men."

She gritted her teeth at his remarks. "Pretty

earring you are wearing. Are you not fearful that some might question your . . . um, manliness?"

As the heat on his cheeks rose, so did his anger. "The earring belonged to my father, and his father before him. Say what you want about me, but do not dare question the manliness of my sire and grandsire."

She shrugged. "How do you know we are pirates?"

Dumb as dirt! "If it looks like a snake, and slithers like a snake, must be it is a snake."

He could tell she did not like the comparison to snakes. "And a nun! What kind of nun does such devil's work?"

"I am not really a nun."

"Oh really?" He narrowed his eyes at her. "Are you the one known as the Sea Scourge?"

Noticing the blush coloring her cheeks, he observed, "No purple hair that I can see. Open your mouth so that I can see your teeth."

She pressed her lips firmly together.

He stared at her chest then. "Hard to tell if you have three breasts under that loose garment, but it appears rather flat. I suspect you have none."

Her brow furrowed with confusion. "Three breasts?" She waved a hand airily then. "Never mind. This is a pointless conversation."

He told her, anyhow. "The Sea Scourge needs three breasts to suckle her three black cats."

"Are you demented?"

"Mayhap a little bit." He grinned. Despite his circumstances—as in, tied to a mast pole in the hot sun—he was enjoying himself. *No, I am not. I am a captive. If anyone hears about this, I will be laughed out of every Norse port in the world.* He forced the grin down and scowled at her.

"Let us start over on a more civil note," she said, smiling tentatively at him.

No horse teeth, he noted, and returned her smile with a continuing scowl before replying with fake sweetness. "Yea, let us do that."

She ignored his sarcasm. "My name is . . ." She paused. " . . . Medana."

"I have ne'er heard of any Christian saint named Medana. Nay, that is a Norse name. Therefore, you bloody damn hell are not Sister Medana, lest you be one of Satan's mistresses."

"I already told you I'm not a nun. Your insistence otherwise is becoming tiresome."

So much for her polite approach!

"I must go change out of these stifling hot garments. Then we will have a little talk."

"Forget 'little talk,' you demented daughter of Loki," he told her. Loki, the jester god, was the closest the Norse religion got to demons. "You'd best talk quick and big if you value your life."

"Tsk, tsk, tsk!" Her amused clucking sound and pointed gaze at his bindings were meant to emphasize that he was in no position to make threats. "Blather, blather, blather," she observed, but he saw the fearful twitch beside her mouth. A mouth that was sinfully full and pouty. Demonic, if you asked him. Which nobody did, least of all Sister Pirate.

Glancing around after she left, he took stock of his surroundings.

The sleek dragonship with a swan neck was clinker built with overlapping planks of oak. The women sat not on rowing benches, but on their sea chests, as was the pattern on most longboats, their oars moving nimbly through the placid waves now that there was a breeze lifting the sails. Primitive battle shields hung over the side. With good winds, a well-built Viking vessel could make a hundred miles in one day. He figured that they'd traveled more than that already.

Seabirds flew overhead, looking for food. Their presence was a clear sign that the ship traveled close to land, though he could see none from his position.

He had to admire the way the female crew worked together. It was a small longship with only twenty oars on each side, but the women rowers managed to weave the light craft smoothly over the waves with the aid of a square black and red sail that unfurled to catch the wind. The helmsman—rather helmswoman—steered the side-mounted rudder fastened to the starboard. Others worked diligently at their chores, tasks they'd been well trained to perform. Heaving buckets of water up to swab the deck. Repairing sailcloth. Honing small swords and lances. Keeping an eye on the horizon . . . for pirates? Thork smiled at his own silent jest.

A tall, slim woman emerged from the doorway of a makeshift chieftain's quarters wearing a red brushed wool tunic belted at the waist over black braies and tall boots. Her sun-lightened blonde hair was pulled off her face and lay in one long braid down her back. Her violet eyes, under thick, dark blonde lashes, studied him as she stepped closer.

He studied her right back.

The nun?

"I know you!" he declared suddenly.

Fear flickered in her eyes but only momentarily. "Nay, you do not," she asserted.

He frowned with uncertainty. "Are you sure? As I recall, it was at King Haakon's court nigh on fourteen years ago. You were flirting with me, even though you were only a girling of twelve then, and I a virile fourteen."

"I ne'er did!" She did not smile, not even a little. No sense of mirth.

Well, his appreciation for mirth was running out, too. The humor in this captivity nonsense was wearing thin. "I strongly suspect who you are, and Medana was not the name you were given at birth. Nay, 'twas Geira, daughter of Jarl Edam of Stormgard."

"You have me confused with someone else," she insisted, suddenly engaged in pulling a loose thread from the hem of her tunic.

Was he wrong? Mayhap. But wait, unbidden, an old memory came to mind. "Lady Geira of Stormgard murdered a cousin of the king on the eve of her wedding, or so the story goes. Then she disappeared. Could that perchance be you?"

Rosy tints bloomed on the woman's sun-bronzed cheeks. "I have ne'er murdered anyone, and my name is Medana. I know who you are, though. Your reputation precedes you."

He arched his brows.

"Thork Tykirsson, the baddest Viking in the Norselands."

"Me?" He pretended affront. "I am no longer bad. I am on a quest to be good."

A small laugh escaped her lush lips before she caught herself. "How long have you been on this . . . quest?"

"Since last year."

"A whole year of being good? You must be suffering sorely."

"You have no idea." He rolled his eyes meaningfully. "You do know that I am going to have to kill you for this crime."

"What makes you think you will have the opportunity?" She stared at his restraints with an expression on her face that said clearly: *You are in no position to make threats, Viking.* "Do not mistake us for the weak females you have known in the past."

"No chance of that!" he scoffed, giving her an insulting head-to-toe survey, though, truth to tell, he did not find her body all that unappealing, even in men's braies. Especially in braies.

The rose in her cheeks deepened even more. "If you must know, your presence here is all a mistake."

"Oh?" *This ought to be good.*

"My women were disheartened over our shortened visit to the trading town, and so they decided to . . . to . . . to . . ."

"Have a stuttering problem, do you?"

She bared her teeth at him, then visibly made an effort to calm her temper. "They meant only to borrow you."

Surely she did not say what I think she said. "Borrow? Is that a new word for captivity?"

"Captivity? How silly! Ha, ha, ha!" She emitted a false, nervous laugh. "Truly, they only intended to keep you for a short time."

"How short?"

She waved a hand airily. "A few sennights."

His eyes widened and his jaw dropped before he managed to ask, "For what purpose?"

She looked away and appeared to be trying to find the right words. Finally, her gaze met his and he was struck by the violet beauty of her eyes, like a field of lavender he'd seen one time in the Highlands. "Um . . . harvesting."

"Um . . . harvesting what?"

He could tell she did not like his mimicking her, but she resisted the urge to make some snide remark. Instead, she revealed, "Man seed."

"I beg your pardon. You want us to plant seeds. We are not farmers."

"Not harvesting so much as breeding."

"Breeding what?"

"Babes."

"Aaarrgh!" If his hands were free, he would be pulling at his own hair. Getting a clear answer from her was like pulling a boar out of quicksand.

"If you must know, we live on an isla—on a mount—we live someplace where there are only women, and occasionally the women wish to bear children. Thus, they need men to plant the seeds. But they do not want them to be around after that."

There is an insult in that statement, I suspect. "Studs? You want men to do stud service? Like yon bull?" He glanced downward for emphasis.

The hatch door was open, and as if it heard him, the beast in the hold let out a loud bellow. One at a time, his men were being brought up on deck and tied to whatever stationary item the women could find. It took three women to bring up each man, five for Bolthor.

Jamie, the first one out, exclaimed, "Bloo-dy hell! That cow's breath stinks like old haggis. Or gammelost." Gammelost was the loathsome cheese many Viking warriors often took on long treks. So repulsive was it that some said it turned men into berserkers.

" 'Tis not a cow, you dumb Scot," Finn replied, the next one out of the hold. Even as he scanned his surroundings, his eyes going wide with astonishment at the all-female crew, he continued sniping at Jamie. "Do you not know the difference betwixt a bull and a cow?"

"Cow or bull matters not a whit," Alrek inserted. He fell on his face before being helped to his feet by the women. "If we stay down here much longer, we will smell just as bad. Whoa! I ne'er saw so many muscles on women in all my life."

"We already do smell like shit . . . shitty animals," Bolthor remarked with his usual honesty. If the men were free, someone would have probably boxed his ears, if they could, which they probably couldn't, he being as big as a grizzly bear and all that. The five women dragging him out of the hold appeared to appreciate his size, however, if their murmured compliments were any indication. Assuming that "I wonder if all his body parts are as big as his feet" was a compliment.

Meanwhile his men were fighting their restraints, to no avail. He wasn't the only one growing more and more frustrated with this ridiculous captivity. He stared at the witch who was the cause of their discomfort and, recalling her comment about wanting them for their seed only, Thork repeated, "Stud service? You women want to be swived?"

If her cheeks got any redder, she might burst aflame. "Not me, but, yea, some of my women do."

"Without the men's permission?"

"Come now, when have men ever been so discriminating as to care whether they spill their seed hither or yon?"

"I care." And that was the truth. As wild and careless as he might have been in the past, there was one lesson his father had taught him well. Do not breed bastards. Or, leastways, a real Viking man takes care of his own.

She shrugged. "Then you are the exception."

"And you sanction this halfbrained idea?"

"Of course not."

He crossed his eyes. "Then release us. At once."

She shook her head. "I cannot do that."

Crossing his eyes had accomplished nothing; so he tried glowering. "Why not?"

"You will kill us, or take us captive."

"There is that," he agreed. After a pause, he asked, "So what is your plan?"

"Plan?" She shifted uneasily from foot to foot.

"Pfff! You have no plan," he guessed. "Listen, unless you want us to die in captivity, you must give us food and water. And an immediate concern is the need to piss."

"You do not need to be so crude."

"'Tis a fact of life, M'Lady Pirate. What goes in must come out, and we men were drinking last night. Some more than others."

She pondered his words, tapping those lush lips thoughtfully. "Well, we could bring you, one at a time, to the rail to relieve yourselves."

"What . . . you plan to tug down our braies and

take our cocks in hand, aiming seaward?" He had to laugh at the look of horror on her face.

"What would you suggest?"

"I would suggest that you release us and let us take care of the matter ourselves."

She shook her head.

In the end, four women were assigned to each man, and they did in fact help the men take care of business, even down to the shaking of their staffs to remove any excess drops. It would have been undignified if it weren't so funny, especially when half of them got thickenings on being handled thus, causing the women to be more embarrassed than the men. And Brokk developed a shy bladder, requiring some coaxing, which mortified the boyling.

A short time later, after being fed chunks of manchet bread and dried lutefisk, the eight men were left alone while the women went about their chores.

It was then that Bolthor decided the occasion called for a saga. "The Lady Was a Pirate," he announced.

> "She was a lady,
> Or should I say matey?
> Arrr! Ahoy! Thar she blows!
> Shiver me timbers, and by jingos!
> No frail lass could she be,
> Once the lady took to sea.
>
> But the biggest mistake
> This pirate lady did make
> Was to tweak the tails

Of some Norse males
Because if there's aught
A Viking cannot bear
It is a dare
Especially when it comes from the fairer sex
Which challenges his self-respect.

So beware and await,
Yon female pi-rate.
Your fate is in the hands
Of fierce Viking bands.
Especially Thork the Great
Who will use you as bait.
Or even worse,
Take you on a different course.

Didst know our chieftain is looking for a bride?
And marriage to a pirate might just heal his pride.

On the other hand . . ."

Bolthor hesitated and frowned, unsure what could come next?

Thork could only imagine.

The female crew, who'd been listening while pretending to work industriously paying them never mind, laughed uproariously, while Medana looked as if she'd swallowed a whole lutefisk.

So Thork finished the poem for Bolthor:

"On the other hand, a pirate crew
Would make a tasty stew."

CHAPTER FOUR

Johnny Depp, they were not . . .

If Thork had been amazed before by the nerve of this crazy band of female would-be pirates, he was in for even more of a shock now.

They had been rowing steadily within viewing distance of the shoreline for most of the day, a not uncommon practice for longships, but then, after much mysterious conversation of female heads bent together glancing furtively at the men to make sure they weren't listening, the ship was turned around and circled back from whence they'd come. That evening, they dropped anchor.

Despite his constant questions, Thork remained ignorant of what was amiss. His men were equally puzzled. The consensus was the women, the weaker sex, needed a rest from all their rowing. Poor things!

"Now what?" he asked Medana as she approached him with a length of cloth in her hands. She wore men's braies and a belted tunic, and on her head a red linen scarf tied off to one side of her neck. The only thing missing was an earring. He hoped she didn't decide to "borrow" that as well. Other women, attired the same, also carrying strips of cloths, headed toward his men.

Uh-oh!

"I need to gag you."

"Why?" He strained his head to the side to avoid her hands.

"We are stopping for a bit of pirating, and we cannot risk your raising an alarm to the poor monks of St. Alban's."

"A bit of pirating? There is no such thing as a bit of pirating. You either pirate or you don't. And poor monks? Why not target a richer monastery? Barmy as beetles in a vat of mead, that's what you all are!" He was talking fast, trying to forestall that damn cloth she was wringing in her hands. It probably wasn't even clean.

"Barmy or not, we do what we have to do. And right now we want . . . nay, need what this poor monastery has to offer."

Taking a deep breath, he tried a different argument. "Your timing is not so great, if I may voice an opinion."

"Why stop now? Seems to me you have an opinion of everything."

He ignored her sarcasm. " 'Tis almost dark, in case you hadn't noticed. Unless you know the terrain, you will be at a disadvantage."

"We operate best in darkness when our victims cannot assess our weaknesses."

"You mean, they cannot tell that you are a band of lunatic women."

"Among other things." Her face was flushed prettily. Something she tended to do a lot, around him.

He rolled his eyes. Something he tended to do a lot, around her.

"I don't see why you can't wait until some other time, when we men are not tied up here on board. What if your victims fight back? What if they board the ship? What if they set the ship afire? We would be helpless to save our own lives, let alone help you women escape."

She pondered his words, then said, "Nay, we cannot take the risk. Besides, these are monks. Holy men take vows against violence. And these are cloistered monks. So they are bound to be even more peaceable."

"Pfff! I've known many priests who are as adept at swordplay as hardened warriors. In fact, once—" His words were cut off as she seized the opportunity and thrust the cloth into his open mouth, tying it tightly behind his head.

"If you must know," she said just before she sauntered off, "we noticed some goats when we passed by earlier today, and our cook, Olga, yearns for goat milk for one of her special recipes."

"Agfcsk!" he exclaimed. A goat? They were risking their lives for a goat!

Glancing around the deck, he noticed that his men were similarly gagged and bug-eyed with outrage. Except for Jamie, whose eyes were brimming with tears of mirth. The lackwit!

They watched helplessly as a dozen women climbed down a rope ladder that had been thrown over the rail. Some of them carried short swords, which they raised above their heads, floating on their backs toward more shallow waters. Others had knives held between their teeth as they swam toward shore. While some were adept at swimming, others could scarce keep their heads above water as they paddled like puppies who'd fallen into a fjord. There was also a small rowboat that had been lowered with two rowers inside. He wasn't sure if the boat would be used for all the booty they would steal, or for the goat. Please gods, not goats, as in more than one. The bull was bad enough.

Another thing the women hadn't taken into consideration. There was a full moon out tonight, and all their activity would be clear as day. Well, maybe they were aware of that fact, and that's why they hadn't anchored the longship closer to shore. Too visible.

The melee that followed would have been laughable, if it weren't so dangerous. Had the women not realized that the goats would not come willingly? Forget about the men setting up an alarm. The goats did the job very well.

Neah! Neah! Neah! Meeeyyyaa! Meeeyyyaa! Behh! Behh! Behh! The animals, huddled together in a group at the top of a small rise, bleated as one of the women attempted to pull a ram by a rope tied round its neck and another woman tried to shove its behind. The stubborn goat wasn't going anywhere until someone—it appeared to be Medana— got the bright idea to lead a female goat toward the shore. The randy goat then followed docilely behind, though both goats made an unholy noise of bleating protests. Even more hilarious . . . all the other goats were following, like sheep to the slaughter. There was no way the women could bring back a dozen goats. Was there?

And another female pirate had the bright idea to grab a duck, as well. A huge duck. Maybe it was a goose. Hard to tell from where he was. But the squawking that bird made was enough to wake even the most bone-weary monk from his sleep.

Quack! Quack! Quack! Behh! Behh! Behh! Somewhere in the distance some dog had been awakened, and added to the cacophony with its *Rfff! Rfff! Rfff!*

Meanwhile, several monks had their robes raised knee-high as they chased a woman clutching a huge silver crucifix that was almost as big as she was. Still other monks had torches in one hand and rakes and other garden implements in the other for weapons.

To their credit, he saw one of the women set fire to a hay mow, which diverted the attention of several monks, who tried to stop the blaze with buckets of water from a nearby well. And a few of the pirates stopped to engage the monks in "battle." No mortal wounds did they inflict, but they knocked two monks unconscious with blows to the head with the flat sides of their short swords. Another monk, shocked to see blood flowing from a slice to his arm, ran squealing back up the hill to the monastery.

The woman with the large crucifix almost drowned herself with the weight of her booty and finally tossed the object into the bottom of the rowboat and helped the others trying to get two goats into the boat and shoo the others back home. The goose escaped when it took a good nip of its captor's chin, drawing blood, and nigh flew over the water back to its goslings.

Finally, after what seemed like hours, but was more like a half hour, *Pirate Lady* was once more on its way to wherever they had been headed originally. They'd tried to put the goat and its mate down in the hold, but the bull was having none of that. The ruckus down below was alarming to Thork. If it went on much longer, the bull would kick a hole in the longship and they would all drown at sea.

Luckily, or unluckily, the women decided to tie the goats up on deck. Luckily, because the ship would not sink, and the whole bloody lot of them would not drown. Unluckily, because the goats did not take a liking to Thork and his men, who were still tied and gagged. The bearded billy goat, in particular, was giving Thork the evil eye, and Thork just knew, if the beast got loose, it was going to butt an important part of Thork's body.

The women, soggy wet and some of them battered and bleeding, were congratulating themselves on a pirate venture well done, as the longship skimmed over the waves in a fortuitous wind that had come up of a sudden. Eventually, they got around to ungagging the men.

When he was finally able to speak, he found himself speechless.

"See, all your worries were for naught." Medana beamed at him. Her head scarf had been lost somewhere, her blonde hair hung in unattractive clumps about her face, her tunic and braies clung to her slim body. No curves in sight. She was a mess. "We did not even have to kill anyone."

"Oh, that is a wonderful attribute for a pirate. No killing. Pfff!"

She raised her chin proudly. "We got our goat."

Tongues and feathers and
candles, oh my! . . .

Two days later, Medana huddled in her small sleeping quarters with Elida, Solveig, Gudron, and Bergdis. It was midday, and they were only hours away from Thrudr.

The stop at the monastery to steal the goats had taken longer than they'd expected. Not the pirating itself. But adjusting the goats into the ship life had created mayhem, especially amongst the men, who complained constantly about the smell, the bleating, even the "evil eye," of all things. More than once, she'd threatened to put the men back in the hold with the bull.

Even worse, her women were making fools of themselves in their attempts to make themselves tempting to the men. Yestermorn, Medana had even had to scold two young females who were trying to impress the men by dancing deftly above the sea waters on the shafts of the extended oars. To their credit, neither had fallen in.

But Medana had more important issues to settle.

"We cannot allow the men to see how we enter our hidden homeland," Medana proclaimed for about the fifth time. "It is essential that, after we release them, they cannot find us again."

"I still say that once we sate them in our bed furs, they will be so pleased, they will leave with smiles on their faces." This from Bergdis, who had taken a liking to the clumsy one named Alrek. The young man had nigh fallen over the rail when she'd handled his dangler in a particular way as she aided him in relieving himself this morn.

The leader, Thork, was not smiling, though. Not that she cared, but then, Medana hadn't been strolling back in forth in front of him with swaying hips and outthrust breasts. Not that he would smile at that type of attempt at seduction from her, anyway. He would probably laugh . . . with derision. In fact, he did sometimes as he muttered something foul about three breasts. The lout!

"Besides, you have made it abundantly clear that the men must be willing partners," Solveig added. "So why would there be a question of revenge?"

"Because you took them without their permission. Because you trussed them up like spring chickens about to be plucked. Because they spent a goodly amount of time in the hold breathing bull dung. Because they say the goats are as bad as the bull. Because they must take care of bodily functions with women watching . . . and touching. Because one of them has a shy bladder and has to be . . . coaxed."

The three pirate ladies ducked their heads sheepishly.

"We will just have to entice them to our bed furs then and hope they will be so pleased they will not want to lop off any body parts," Elida asserted, arching her shoulders back and her bosoms forward, for emphasis.

"Tempting and pleasing are all well and good, but that does not preclude thoughts of retaliation. I do not want the men to know where we are located. It's a chance we cannot take. A Viking man with vengeance on his mind would hunt down his prey with his dying breath. It is a game to them," Medana told the women. "Our safety is secure only because our location has been kept secret all these years."

"Blindfold them, then," Solveig suggested.

"It might work, but some men—especially sailing men—develop a knack for sailing directions by instinct. One of my brothers' seamen once said he could guide a ship home with his eyes closed. Another claimed to be able to sense directions by the changes in the wind, bird chatter, the sun and moon rays," Medana told them.

"There is only one solution then. Give them the sleeping draught again." This from Gudron, who wanted first dibs on the giant Bolthor. Apparently he had a large number of children back in the Saxon lands, thus proving his ability to produce babes. Not all his, some of them being stepchildren, but that didn't seem to matter.

Medana groaned her dismay. Thork had been outraged at having been dosed to helplessness. To do so again would raise his ire even more. But did they have any choice? "So be it!" she concluded. "Put it in their ale during the noon meal."

When she went out on deck, Thork summoned her in his usual obnoxious way, "Come! Here! Wench!"

She'd learned not to react to his baiting by voicing her annoyance, which was obviously his goal. "What now?" Walking over toward the mast pole, she tried not to notice that he was an especially handsome man, only a few years older than her twenty-six years. And he knew it, too. Even with days-old bristles on his face and his dark blond hair unkempt from the sea breeze, he was a fine specimen of Viking virility.

"Are we almost there?"

"Um . . . another day or two," she said. *More like another hour or two, but he does not need to know that.*

"Liar!"

"What?"

"Your eyelashes flutter when you tell an untruth."

She stared fixedly at the lout, trying her best not to blink. Then she couldn't stop herself and blinked repeatedly, narrowing her eyes at the scurvy cur.

He laughed. "How soon will you release us?"

They'd discussed this before, but he was no doubt trying to catch her in yet another lie. "As soon as we unload the bull and make sure he has not suffered from the voyage, we will restock the ship and take you back to Hedeby."

"And that will take how long?"

"A sennight at most."

"A sennight to mount a cow? Are you barmy? Have you looked at its cock lately? That beast is more than capable of swiving anything remotely resembling a cow's arse on a moment's notice."

I will not blush. I will not react to his crudeness. I will be calm and polite. "We have more than one cow," she informed him.

"And you expect us to wait while the randy fellow tups a herd of cows? Pfff! My longships will be gone by then. The instant you untie us, we are going back to Hedeby, that I assure you."

"Really? Eight men to row a longship?"

He narrowed his eyes at her.

"If you think you can force a woman to row when she does not want to, you have a lot to learn about women."

"I am going to enjoy torturing you before I lop off your silly head."

"You do not make it easy to be polite."

"Did I ask you for politeness? Politeness will be the last thing on my mind when I get my hands on you."

"Talk, talk, talk. I will not give you the opportunity." *There, I go. Reacting to his taunts again.* She bit her bottom lip to stop herself from saying more.

"Oh, I will have the opportunity. And, believe you me, all the time you have had me tied up here, I have been making lists in my mind. Lists of all the things I will do to you."

"Dost think I haven't felt the lash before?" she scoffed.

"By whom?" he scoffed back.

"My brothers, the evil trolls."

"Ah! I thought you meant real lashings."

"You do not think a leather whip against the bare back is real?"

His head jerked up with surprise.

"Broken skin, blood, and scars are not real?"

"What did you do to merit such ill treatment?"

She went lance stiff. How like a man to assume the woman must be at fault! "Breathe. Disagree with their profound wisdom. Hide the jewels my mother left me. Refuse to wed a vicious man." She could tell he didn't believe her. No matter!

"In any case, the lash is not the manner of torture I have in mind. I would much rather use a feather than a whip. My father taught me about the varied uses for feathers."

"Feathers?" She could not hide her curiosity.

He nodded. "First I will remove your clothing, tie your hands together, and attach them to a ceiling hook. After I examine your body . . . for blemishes and such . . . I'll use various feathers to stroke your skin, from your forehead to your toes and various spots in between."

"Why?"

"Why, why, why? You sound like that bothersome parrot my father gifted years ago to my aunt Eadyth. 'Tis said that such strokes are painful pleasure."

"Pfff! What nonsense!"

"After that I intend to lick you."

"Lick . . . *lick*?" she sputtered.

"Yea, but first you must be clean. I guess I will have to bathe you." He released an exaggerated sigh. "But the question is whether I should use soft scented soap in a brass tub to get you clean or whether I should just dangle you by your feet over the rail of my longship. I am leaning toward the latter." He smiled at her as if imparting some gift.

"You are wicked."

"Yea, it is one of my best traits."

"I thought you were trying to be good."

"Betimes a Viking must be bad to be good."

"That is the worst bit of male illogic I have ever heard." She started to walk away.

"Don't you want to know what happens next in my torture regimen?"

"Nay."

"I'm thinking about shaving your head. Nay, that is too gentle a punishment. Hmm. Yea, that is it! I will shave your nether hair."

She almost tripped over her own feet, but she

kept walking. "Loathsome lout!" she muttered under her breath.

He chuckled, then added, "And you do not want to know what kind of sweet torture I can inflict with a candle. A big candle."

Everyone within hearing was laughing. Even her women.

Home, sweet home, it was not . . .

The men were still drooping against their seal ropes by late afternoon when they arrived at Thrudr. The ship dropped anchor near the shoreline of a small, pretty island, known only as Small Island, one of thousands in the North Sea. This one drew seafarers who stopped on occasions, but only for short periods because it was mostly uninhabitable, with its wide, stony beaches, and it occasionally became submerged during heavy storms.

The only structure was a thatched hut and an attached lean-to under which were a small rowboat and fishing gear. Several large rain barrels sat outside the building.

Greeting them were the lone inhabitants, the mid-aged Salvana; her elderly mother, Sigrun; and a dog the size of a small bear. In fact, that was its name: Bear. Many a visitor with ill intent had been scared off by Bear, the lone survivor of a shipwreck off their shore some five years past.

During fair weather months, spring through fall, the two women preferred to dwell here, alone. Small Island was a stopping off place for distressed ships or traders, dropping off or picking up messages. Although it was not encouraged, the women of Thrudr sometimes wanted, or needed, to make contact with others back in Hordaland or Jutland or Norsemandy or even the Saxon lands. Traders were only too willing to provide the service for a small coin.

Any unwelcome visitors not put off by Bear were soon dissuaded by Salvana's bow; she was as tall as a man and as talented in archery. And by Sigrun, who was a scary image with her wild, flowing white hair, toothless smile, and the spiked club named Slow Death that she always carried with her.

Sailors ignored the much larger island, about thirty ship lengths away, because of its mountainous, impregnable terrain, with sharp cliffs and steep-faced forests leading right to the water's edge. This was Thrudr.

What most people did not know, and Medana and her women had discovered only by chance, was that Thrudr was a very large, bowl-shaped island with a flat, even valley in its middle. It was accessible only at low tide when a wide cave entrance became visible, connecting it via a narrow landmass to the smaller island. At high tide, the earthen strip was hidden again and the cave filled with water that rushed into the base of the mountain, coming through the other side into a waterfall that filled a pond—a pool, really, with upright sides, like walls.

At this time of the year, they had only a few hours to unload the ship onto the smaller island, including the men and the bull, both of which proved equally stubborn. The bull because it was a stubborn animal at the best of times, and the Vikings because they were heavy as deadweight and had to be carried by four women, one at each limb, sometimes lifting, sometimes dragging. There would be more than a few bruises on Norse arses come nightfall. Another reason for the men to enact revenge, Medana mused.

As soon as the landmass emerged from the falling tides and the cavern drained, close to midnight, the women, including the large number that had stayed behind, worked efficiently to carry the cargo, the men, even the lightweight ship itself onto log rollers into the cave and through to the other side. When they were done, huge bushes were pushed to the entrance, just as a precautionary measure, though a person had to be searching specifically for an opening to notice it among the trees. It was not yet dawn when they were able to breathe a sigh of relief.

The women were smiling profusely, Medana noticed, and not just because they'd returned from a profitable voyage. The sleeping men were tied to various trees about the central clearing.

Olga, the short, rotund cook, was the first to voice what all the other women who'd been left behind must be thinking. "Now that is what I call plunder! Medana, Medana, Medana! Methinks I will go a-pirating with you next time." She pinched the arm of the giant Bolthor, as if checking the flesh on a side of boar.

"Hey, he is mine," proclaimed Gudron. "We are more of a size, him being so big and tall."

"There are not enough men to go around," another woman complained. "We must share them."

"Well, I get the first few tups from the big one, then," Gudron conceded with ill grace.

Medana could feel her face heat with color. "No need for you to go a-pirating, Olga. We did not get these men whilst a-pirating. We got them at the trading town."

Siobhan, a voluptuous, red-haired, mid-aged woman from the Irish lands, who was circling the prettily mustached one, laughed. "What did you trade for them?"

"We did not trade anything for them. We . . . um, borrowed them," Medana tried to explain. She couldn't believe she was using the same lack-brained excuse that her women had.

There was a rush then for the bathing hut and the salt pond as one by one more than one hundred women attempted to cleanse themselves and don new garments, wanting to appear at their best once the men awakened. Medana could not imagine what the men's reaction would be once they finally opened their eyes to their new surroundings.

She did not have long to wait.

Sitting on a low stool, having bathed herself—but not because she wanted to impress some fool man, but because lice were always a problem when they returned from a voyage—Medana chewed at a fingernail, contemplating the village that had grown here in this harsh valley.

A series of ten longhouses with steep-pitched thatch roofs and gabled ends were centered around a clearing, like the spokes of a wheel. Beyond them were outbuildings; small pastures for cows and the new bull, which was already at its merry work; neat vegetable gardens; even a new enterprise, shipbuilding. Like much of the Norselands, Thrudr did not contain many hides of arable land, but the women, day by day, sennight by sennight, month by month, then year by year, had managed to create ploughlands to eke a living out of the harsh, hidden environment. What they could not grow or build themselves, they stole via their pirate ventures, or gained by barter in the trading towns of Hedeby, Birka, and Kaupang, even occasionally the Saxon market city of Jorvik.

Usually, she felt a fierce sense of pride and peace when she returned from a voyage. But not today. Her mind was too unsettled.

She sensed Thork's piercing glare in the dawning light before she raised her head and met his fury. He was finally awake, and struggling against his tight bonds.

"The other torture I have planned for you," he said, as if his earlier conversation with her had never been interrupted, "is that your naked body is going to be the figurehead on the prow of one of my longships. I intend to rename it *She Pirate*. Or *Fish Bait*. Far and wide, roving Norsemen will want to nab their very own live female pirate figureheads." He glanced around his surroundings, taking in all the women moving about their various chores. "And I will guide them here."

It was a ludicrous threat, of course. She tried to laugh, but she could not.

# chapter five

In the end, men will be men . . .

"We are going to release you now," Medana told Thork.

And about time, too! He was hungry and thirsty and angrier by the minute at the indignity of his capture, including a second time of being rendered unconscious by sleeping herbs. Besides that, his arse felt as if he'd slid down a hill of shale.

"Aren't you afraid I'll kill you once free?"

"What good would that do you?"

"It would feel damn good."

"Then what? You would have no way to get off the isl—no way to get back to Hedeby."

"You are certain about that?"

"Absolutely. My women and I have an understanding. If any of us get taken by you men, no one is to attempt a rescue. There is no way your killing one of us, or threatening to kill one of us, would get you home. And we are sworn not to reveal our secrets, even under threat of torture."

"Have you ever been tortured?"

She stood there, just staring at him, then ignored his question and went back to contemplating just how to go about untying the ropes that restrained him. A dimwit, for sure. "Are you waiting for a 'Please, M'Lady Pirate,' or gods forbid, 'Thank you for your hospitality'?"

"There is no need for sarcasm," she sniped, and began to undo the knots that bound his hands behind his back and around a slim tree. Other women were doing the same for his men, who were restrained at various spots about the central clearing of what appeared to be a village of sorts. Some of the structures were rather lopsided. An indication of inept building skills that got better over time? The runic writing above the lintel of the largest longhouse was expertly carved, though, with the message: "Men Stay Out!" Still others carried similar, if not more blunt messages in the vein of: "If You Have a Penis, You Are Not Welcome."

This has got to be the strangest adventure of my misbegotten life. Even stranger than that time in Byzantium when . . . "I beg to differ, M'Lady Lackbrain. Sarcasm is the least I can do to protest your dimwitted audacity. You dosed us with sleeping herbs again, did you not? I told you after the first time how I felt about that act. I told you that a Viking man cannot be left incapacitated and weaponless, an open target for his enemies. I told you that if you ever did it again, you would be very, very sorry." He favored her with his third fiercest scowl to emphasize his point. He had a wide range of facial expression meant to scare his enemies.

She paused in unknotting the sealskin rope that was apparently giving her some difficulty, but the expression on her face was not one of apology or fear, more like irritation. In fact, he could swear she murmured, "Loathsome lout!"

You have no idea how loathsome I can be, M'Lady Pirate.

Before he could voice that thought, she continued, "Mayhap the problem is that you are always telling me what to do. Mayhap you should proffer your concerns rationally."

"Proffer? What kind of word is that for a pirate?" He crossed his eyes with frustration. "Why does it feel as if the skin has been peeled off my backside?"

A slight amount of color bloomed on her cheeks. Very slight. Not quite a blush. "Um. We had to drag you part of the way here," she said, a mite apologetically, but then she ruined the effect by stating, "I have met pregnant boars smaller than you."

"If I had been standing on my own two feet and not a deadweight to be dragged like a dead bear . . . or boar, it would not have been a problem. Women have no sense!"

"Women have no sense," she repeated after him in a growly male voice. "Those are the words men employ when they are losing an argument."

"Huh?"

She sighed deeply and revealed, "Rending you unconscious was our only choice. We could not let you know the location of our home."

He glanced around, studying the terrain. They were in a valley, surrounded by steep mountains, much like a deep bowl. The flat bottomland was not large, and they must have worked hard to clear it enough to build a number of longhouses and outbuildings, a few garden plots, and a small pasture for cows and the new bull, who was already happily occupied at what it did best. Chickens ranged freely and sheep and the two new goats could be seen romping about in the rocky hill area, needing only forest pannage to subsist.

It was not unlike his father's estate at Dragonstead, except on a much smaller scale. Except there were only women here, except for the odd boy child here and there.

His ropes were finally free, and reacting with the swift instincts of a soldier, he grabbed her by the forearms, lifted her high, and slammed her against the tree. "Who is in charge now, M'Lady of the Ropes? How does it feel to be helpless? Shall I begin your torture now, or let you stew in the juices of fearful anticipation?"

She blinked at him with surprise, so fast had his moves on her been. As the haze of his anger began to clear, he saw up close how comely she was. Her skin, clear and sun-healthy, was mostly unlined, considering her age, except for a few lines bracketing her eyes when she frowned, as she was beginning to now. Her long blonde hair had loosened from its braid and was spilling about her shoulders. Breasts, fuller than he'd expected, pressed against the tautened fabric of her tunic. Only two of them, thank gods! And her eyes . . . Holy Thor! Surely only a goddess would have eyes of such a beautiful shade of lavender. He inhaled sharply and caught her woman scent. Clean skin, with no perfumed soap residue, but a scent of its own, honed his senses to an erotic sharpness.

Although he still pinned her upper arms to the tree, she was able to bend her one arm at the elbow and raise a hand to her mouth. He thought she was going to sigh into her fingertips, as some women did when close to him—a feminine gesture of helplessness—but what she did instead was place two fingertips in her mouth and let loose with a shrill, very unfeminine whistle.

Immediately, they were surrounded by a dozen or more women with weapons raised. Archers with bows raised. Swords that should have been too heavy for the weaker sex to carry. Crudely made wooden shovels and pitchforks. Even a long-handled soup ladle.

Beyond them, he saw his men begin to gather. They were weaponless but nonetheless able to fight, if he gave the order.

"Holy Thor!" he exclaimed, stepping back from her so quickly that her feet dropped to the ground and she fell onto her rump. "Are you trying to turn me deaf? I will be hearing an echo in my ears for hours to come."

She stood and began to dust off the backside of her braies, which caused him to notice for the first time that it was a very nice backside. Despite the seeming danger that surrounded them, he picked up the small leather thong that had been holding her braid in place, but instead of handing it to her, he tossed it to her other side. She bent over to pick it up, then glanced up over her shoulder as she noticed the direction of his gaze. Tsking her disapproval, she stood and said, "Lackbrain! You are surrounded by female warriors who would kill you without a second thought if I so ordered, and you stand there ogling my arse?"

He grinned. He couldn't help himself. If they hesitated to kill monks when a-pirating, he doubted they would kill him. Unless he really provoked them. So, of course, he said, "And a very nice arse it is, too."

His men laughed, and he could swear he heard a few giggles from her women. Bolthor would be composing a saga about it. "Female Pirates with Nice Arses," or some such.

Thork had no fears that she would order his death, considering the live and thriving monks. She'd already said that their capture was not her idea and that they would be returned safely to Hedeby in good time. Guilt . . . that was the difference between men and women. Women succumbed to it, and men knew how to ply a woman's guilt to their advantage.

She dismissed her women and told them to show the other men to their quarters.

"Should we lock them in?" one woman asked.

Medana shook her head. "They have nowhere to go."

We will see about that!

"Just stand guard." Turning to him, she said, "If you think to charm me with compliments on my private parts, you do not know as much about women as you think you do."

He knew plenty. And he could charm her if he wanted to, but he had more important things to do. Stifling the urge to grab her once again but this time shake some sense into her silly head, he inhaled sharply for patience and studied his surroundings. Something bothered him about what he saw. "I thought you said that Thrudr was an island."

"Um."

"I see no fjords." The only water he could see was a small pool against one hillside, and there were water barrels to catch rainwater outside a number of the dwellings. No well as far as he could see. "How do you access the seas?"

"Um. Did I say we lived on an island? Ha, ha, ha. You must have misheard me."

"Your eyes are blinking."

"'Tis dust on the wind."

He arched his brows. The morning sun beat down with not even a light breeze. Although he did get a faint whiff of salt water. Hmm. "When are you taking us back to Hedeby?"

"Soon." More eye blinking.

He noticed the longship was already up on trestles, and women in men's attire appeared to be working on its underside. How they'd gotten the boat inland without water access remained a puzzle. One he would solve soon. In addition, there was another half-completed longship on another trestle. Female shipbuilders? "What's wrong with your vessel?"

"Nothing of importance. The usual recaulking and small repairs."

"Do you have other longships, as well?"

She smiled, and her teeth were not horsey at all, by the by. White and even and scarce any receding gums. "Just the one that is seaworthy." No eye blinking this time. So presumably the truth.

"If there are no major problems with your longship, then we should be under way shortly," he said. When she didn't immediately agree, he grew suspicious. "If you are thinking about keeping us here until you have swived us silly, think again."

She bared her teeth at him but said nothing, a clear attempt on her part to restrain her temper.

Good to know that he could rile her so easily. "Any swiving to be done will be initiated by you or your men. My women have orders."

He almost laughed. Even in this short time since he'd regained his senses, he could see many of the women strutting about with the widened necklines of their *gunnas* half falling off their shoulders to expose the tops of their breasts, even those carrying weapons. Those wearing braies must have used crowbars to help pry their arses into the tight confines. Some even had berry-stained lips and cheeks, like painted harlots.

Not Medana, though. She wore a plain brown tunic and braies with her blonde hair hanging in a long braid down her back. If she only knew, her modest attire, compared to the others, only gave her more allure, even at her advanced age. A Viking man with experience, like him, would be wondering what she hid beneath. Not that he was considering her as a bedmate. Nay, his visions of her involved dungeons and whips and feathers. *Nay, nay, nay! I did not think feathers. I meant fetters.*

"Why are you smiling?"

"Oh, lady, you really do not want to know." He studied her and was amazed to see not a lick of fear in her incredible violet eyes. "Were you dropped on your head as a babe? Do you not have the sense to quiver with fright now that I am free to throttle you?"

She shrugged. "I have two hundred women here, give or take. You have already seen how quickly they come to my defense. You might succeed in killing me, but your fate would be the same within minutes. So save your brutish urges."

"Save your brutish urges," Thork mimicked under his breath as she led him to a longhouse where he and his men were soon assigned temporary quarters. Another woman showed them a place beneath the waterfall where they could bathe. Although not large, the timber building was not an uncomfortable dwelling, with one central hearth fire and sleeping pallets lining both of the long sides. After a serving maid set pottery jugs of ale before them and a cook roasted several rabbits over an open fire and put them on platters, along with flat circles of manchet bread, they were left alone, except for the guards outside.

"Pirates! We have been captured by female pirates!" Jamie grinned, as if announcing some wondrous event.

"They want us for one purpose only. Our man seed," Thork pointed out.

They all grinned then, except Thork.

And except for Bolthor, who constantly bemoaned the overlarge number of children he already had. Plus, "Katherine will kill me if I dare to lie with another woman. She'll say I planned this all so that I can fornicate and claim no responsibility."

And except for Jostein, who harbored sour feelings toward all women because of the dispute with his wife. Jostein's one and only wife, by the by, the man never having practiced the *more danico*, or multiple wives.

"Spare us your disapproval, Thork. Have you never fantasized about being a love slave?" This from Henry, who should have the least interest in slavery of any kind since his mother had been a thrall.

"Never." *But now that you bring it up, it does have a certain allure. Nay, nay, nay, it does not. I cannot fall into that trap.*

"Did you see the one named Lilli? Hair like wet sand, green eyes, bosoms out to here. She has been following me around like a besotted puppy." Henry sighed and cupped his hands out, far out, in front of his chest to demonstrate.

"Just because a wench wags her tail does not make her a docile pet. A dog is a dog. Beware of bitches. In the end, they all bite." This jaded view was expressed by Jostein, of course. What had his wife done to turn him so sour? Thork wondered, recalling a time, not so many years ago, before his marriage, when Jostein had been merry of heart.

"I canna think of aught better than taking a woman dog style," Jamie said.

By the runes! What has one to do with the other?

"What is dog style?" Brokk wanted to know.

Jamie proceeded to explain in detail, including an explanation of how that position allowed a man to strum a woman's "bud of paradise" whilst tupping away.

Jostein made a snorting sound and muttered something about never having heard of such strumming.

"No wonder your wee wife left you," Jamie concluded, ducking as Jostein attempted to punch him in his laughing mouth.

"I for one never noticed the one named Lilli. You can have her, but I get first dibs on Solveig, the rudder master," Finn said. "There is something about her that bespeaks experience in the bed furs." Thork couldn't help but notice that Finn had somehow managed to trim his beard and mustache already, probably after bathing in the pond. The rest of them were clean but decidedly scruffy-looking, while Finn managed to look like he'd just prepared for a royal feast.

"You do not want a virgin?" Brokk asked Finn. "Everyone says the best sex is like guiding a sleek longship down a narrow fjord, even if a dam must be breached first."

Everyone blinked with surprise at the obviously untried boyling.

"Brokk, Brokk, Brokk!" Finn patted his shoulders. "The best bedsport comes with a woman who knows what to do with a . . . a longship."

"I'm saving myself for Ianthe," Alrek said.

"Hah!" Finn snorted. "You have as much chance with her as I have with Isobel."

Alrek and Finn had fallen head over lackwit arses in love with the two women on a recent trip to Miklagard, the golden city known by the Greeks as Byzantium. Neither had been favored with reciprocated feelings from the two women, who now lived in the Saxon lands.

"I have not given up hope," Alrek said, raising his chin defiantly.

"Hope is the salvation of all men," Bolthor proclaimed, about to launch into a saga, no doubt.

Luckily, or not so luckily, Jamie continued with the previous conversation. "Personally, Siobhan, the bonnie Irish lass with the lush bottom, is more to my taste. I do like something to grab on to when taking the wild ride."

Thork had to smile. "Jamie! Forget about her buttocks. Siobhan is older than you by ten years at least. Plus she is in charge of all the outdoors, including the gardens and plough fields and animals, like pigs and cows and chickens. Do you see yourself as a farmer now?"

Jamie pretended to shiver at the prospect.

"There is naught wrong with a few gray hairs. In fact, I wrote an ode one time to my wife's nether hair, like pepper and salt it is."

"Thank you for reminding us about that," Thork said. He would have that image in his head every time he met up with Lady Katherine, especially if Bolthor kept repeating it.

"I do not know why Katherine was so upset," Bolthor went on. "My nether hairs are all white, and I would not mind if someone wrote an ode about mine."

"Thank you for sharing that," Thork said. Now, he would have that image, too.

"You know what I mean, Finn," Bolthor said.

"Me? Why me? I am a young man yet. Not yet thirty and two," Finn protested.

Bolthor gave Finn a meaningful stare with his one good eye.

"The time you saw me plucking it was only one gray hair. One. Only. One." Finn couldn't be more affronted if Bolthor had accused him of having a needle cock. Well, mayhap that would have been worse.

"Och! If not Siobhan, then Bergdis," Jamie compromised.

Thork had to laugh. "Bergdis is a rower on the longship. She is mistress of buildings and woodworking. I doubt you know how to even hammer a nail straight. And chopping firewood, now that's a job I'd like to see you do, day in and day out. By the by, did you notice her shoulders? She could pick you up and slam you down in a trice."

Jamie shrugged and winked at him. "Dinna fash yourself, laddie. A little pain ne'er hurt a Scotsman, especially when the gain is so sweet."

"What pain? What gain?" Brokk asked.

"Boyling, you need to learn a few facts of life," Jostein said to Brokk, but not unkindly, to Thork's surprise.

"Men in eastern lands often favor women with a little extra fat on the bone," Henry proclaimed with a slight slur to his words. He must have imbibed too much ale. Already? "A cushion for the ballocks, or some such thing. Plus their bellies make good cushions for sleeping."

Yea, definitely drukkinn.

"Besides, Jamie, did you not notice that Bergdis has a front tooth missing?" Thork asked.

"Weel," Jamie drawled out with a chuckle, "'tis nae so bad a thing if a woman is missing teeth," Jamie replied with a chuckle. "The better to blow a man's horn, mind ye."

"Hah! You have a very slim horn if it can fit in the space of one missing tooth," he countered.

"Pay no mind to Thork, Jamie. Everyone knows 'tis best for a man to find an ugly woman," Bolthor said before belching loudly. "They are more appreciative of any male attention they can garner that they will do anything."

Now, that would make a good saga. One Bolthor best not ever recite in front of his wife.

"Like ugly women being more likely to take a manroot down the throat?" Jamie inquired with a decided mischievous gleam in his Scottish eyes.

"That and other things," Bolthor said, surprising Thork. Usually, Bolthor was not so inclined to lewd talk, lest it be accidentally so. Like his not realizing it was lewd to talk about his woman's parts in front of one and all.

Brokk's jaw had dropped nigh to his navel.

Thork decided the conversation had gone way too far off track. "Take care, all of you. There are consequences to spilling your seed in any handy vessel. Do you want your sons . . . or daughters . . . raised by a *hird* of barmy women?"

"Barmy, for sure," Jostein interjected. "Do you know they've given themselves titles for everything? Each and every one of them is a mistress of something or other."

Jamie's eyes lit up. "I like the idea of that. Mistress of kissing. Mistress of fondling. Mistress of the tup. Mistress of the mouth swiving. Mistress of the best sex this side of the Highlands."

"Lackwit!" Jostein replied. "Not that kind of mistress. They are mistress of weapons. Mistress of the hunt. Mistress of gardening. Mistress of hog swilling. Mistress of the scullery. Dozens and dozens of titles. Every one of these women has a specific job and title, and they each claim to be equal. As if feeding chickens and swordplay require the same measure of talent!"

"Good gods!" Thork said.

"Now that you mention it, Lilli said something about being mistress of indoor stewardship, whatever that means."

"Just so I do not get seduced by mistress of the privy," Alrek said as he slapped a hand on his knee with glee at his rare venture into the land of mirth. He missed his knee and spilled ale all over the crotch and thighs of his braies.

Several of the men shivered with distaste at the idea of a privy mistress. Some even held their noses with distaste.

"I still say one of the titles might be mistress of sex, especially mistress of sexual perversions," Jamie insisted.

Jostein reached over and swatted him on the side of the head. "Dreamer!"

Jamie just grinned, taking no offense.

"Back to the subject of our being studs for their wicked ends." Thork tried to get back on track. "Will you risk never knowing if you have a child, let alone never seeing him or her?" Thork couldn't believe that he of the wild reputation was giving lectures on proper behavior.

Alrek, who had been responsible for his younger orphaned brothers and sisters from the time he was a mere twelve years old, clearly valued family. "They will not get my seed."

"What will you do when one of the wenches has your cock in her hands and her thighs spread wide?" Thork asked.

Alrek's face bloomed with color under his sun-bronzed skin. "I will think of a winter storm on the high seas with ice crusting the oars and wind whipping at the sails. That should cause any cock to wilt."

They all laughed.

"I realize that many men fornicate freely without regard for any children they might beget, but my father always taught me to take care that I do not spill my seed in fertile fields, lest I plan on caring for the harvest for many years thereafter." *Forget lectures. Now I am quoting my father . . . after all these years of trying to put distance betwixt us.*

"What makes you think we would be unable to return for any child of ours?" Finn asked Thork distractedly while cleaning under his fingernails with the point of his small knife.

"Do *you* know where we are?" Thork addressed his question first to Finn, then to the rest of the men.

They all shook their heads, as understanding came to them.

"There isn't a chance in Muspell that they won't do everything in their power to keep this location secret," Jostein concluded for them all.

"That is our first goal then. To discover exactly where we are," Thork directed. "We need a plan. As fighting men, we were taught from the time we got our first swords not to rush into battle. Study the enemy. Their strengths and weaknesses. What we can gain . . . or lose. What weapons we need to breach their fortifications. How to infiltrate their ranks." Thork knew that planning was not always a possibility, but it would seem they had more than enough time here to take care in how to proceed. "And what are our goals once we pinpoint where we are?"

"Escape, of course," Alrek said.

"Revenge," Finn added.

"Plunder," Henry further added.

"I think we should take them all captive and sell them in the slave marts," Jostein suggested.

"Wise words and worth considering," Thork said.

"Why not just lop off all their heads?" This from Bolthor, who had at one time been known as Bolthor the Berserker. The old man claimed to have long lost count of the number of enemy heads he'd lopped off with his far-famed battle-axe, Head Splitter.

"A bit messy," Finn remarked. As vain and prissy as Finn could be at times, he'd shed more than his share of sword dew in battle, but he preferred clean kills.

"That would be a lot of heads," Jamie also observed, though not with distaste.

"Eeew!" Brokk said, before catching himself. The youthling, whose skin had paled at the mention of beheading, was not blooded enough in warfare to become inured to the gross aspects of fighting.

"The eight of us might be able to overtake the women," Jamie said. "Make them the captives."

Not a bad idea, and they all pondered the possibilities.

"But would they then reveal all their secrets, once they are our thralls?" Thork asked.

"They will if we lop off a few heads," Bolthor said.

"Women!" Jostein exclaimed. "They are stubborn enough to resist, even with that threat. They appear excessively proud of this bond betwixt them. Besides, if a woman does not want to tell you something, she will not."

Once again, Thork wondered about the history between Jostein and his wife.

"We are not lopping off any heads," Thork declared then. *Unless we absolutely have to.*

"People in my homeland are adept at various

torture methods." This from Henry, who hadn't been in his Asian "homeland" ever, as far as Thork knew. "Tickling the bottom of the feet. Water dunking. Hanging face first over a cliff."

Everyone stared at Henry. Then Jamie laughed. "The only time I am tickling some lassie's feet is if I am flat on my back and she is bare-arsed naked on all fours facing *my* feet whilst tickling my balls with her tongue."

They all had to think a moment to see the picture in their fool heads.

"Did you ever really do *that*?" Finn asked Jamie.

"Yea, except for my tickling her feet part," Jamie replied with a grin. "When a wench is licking your balls, 'tis hard to think of anything, least of all whether she wants her toes diddled."

Thork shook his head at Jamie. 'Twas hard betimes to know when he spoke the truth or jested. As Vikings, they preferred to believe outrageous claims when it came to bedsport.

"Speaking of licking . . . have you ever heard of self-licking?" Alrek asked. "Boris the Braggart says he can lick his own cock."

The others hooted with laughter.

" 'Tis true." Alrek's face was high with color at being doubted. "I saw him demonstrate it once at a Yule feast in Holgaland."

"You must have been *drukkinn*," Bolthor said.

Alrek ducked his head sheepishly.

But then Henry told them, "I can do it."

They all turned to stare with incredulity at the Asian Viking.

"Must be because you are so short," Jostein observed, though there was disbelief in his voice.

"Or my staff is so long." Henry waggled his eyebrows at Jostein.

"Good gods!" Thork muttered. How had their conversation gone so far astray? Again! Time to get more organized in their planning. "Forget licking. We need the women to get us out of this place. Even if we discern our whereabouts, we cannot row a longship ourselves, and I doubt they would be willing to do the job for us, even under the lash. What we will do with them afterwards can be decided later. First of all, we must be careful and study our surroundings, discover any escape routes. Mayhap we can flag down a ship."

"But we must be sly in our explorations," Jostein advised.

"Pretend we are accepting of our capture," Jamie added.

Thork nodded. "And be careful what we drink or eat, lest we find ourselves in an herb sleep again whilst the women do what they will with our bodies."

That remark prompted silence as the men pondered what the women might do with their bodies whilst asleep.

"Can a man have sex with a woman whilst asleep?" Brokk wanted to know.

"Have you ne'er had sex dreams where you awakened with damp braies?" Bolthor asked Brokk.

The boy blushed his answer.

"Oh, this is just wonderful!" Jostein said with disgust. "Not only must we worry about what we do whilst awake, but now we must worry about what we do when asleep."

"Um, one thing . . ." Brokk hesitated, and his blush deepened. "Didst say there are ways to swive a wench and not plant your seed in her womb?"

Thork wondered if Brokk was an untried youthling, or had he breached a woman's portal already? Twelve was not an unheard of age for a first tup. He had been twelve himself when first the dairy maid—

"Yea, Thork, do tell," Finn urged with a wink.

Thork had to think a minute to recall what Finn referred to. Ah, the spilling of seed to prevent child begetting. He did in fact explain. Briefly. To his amazement, the other men listened as intently as Brokk. Did not all adult men know this? Did not even the Christian Bible mention Onan and the spilling of seed?

"I have heard of using pig's intestines," Jamie told them, "though my countrymen much prefer to use those for haggis."

"Halved lemons are said to work." This from Jostein, who'd probably never seen a lemon in his life.

"There are potions," suggested Henry.

After all Thork's talk, that's all the men could think about. Sex.

This was proven true when Bolthor announced a new saga: "When Vikings Plow Fallow Fields."

With a groan, Thork put his face on the table in front of him, and pounded his forehead three times. Then he pounded a fourth time, just for emphasis.

Bolthor cleared his throat and began, "This is the saga of Thork the Great . . ."

CHAPTER SIX

**The question was: Who could
be more devious? . . .**

Medana called for a council of the Thrudr leadership—eight in all, including herself—to discuss the course of action for releasing the "captives."

There was Gudron, of course, mistress of military, who had many women serving under her, such as mistress of swordplay, mistress of archery, mistress of weapon sharpening, and mistress of weapon storage.

And Elida, mistress of threads, who had workers in charge of shearing sheep, spinning yarn, weaving cloth, making clothing and blankets.

Solveig, mistress of shipwrighting, and her workers handled anything related to shipbuilding and repair. Somehow, with her rudimentary skills passed on by her father, they'd managed to maintain the small longship Medana and her friends had left Stormgard in, renamed *Pirate Lady*, and now they were trying to build one themselves. A very slow process.

Lilli, mistress of indoor stewardship, and her staff handled everything indoors, from cooking to laundry to cleaning of halls and sleeping chamber.

Bergdis, mistress of buildings and woodworking, had at least a dozen women helping her build and maintain the longhouses and animal shelter, not to mention making furniture and wood eating supplies, bowls and spoons and such. It was a learned craft that had some laughingly ludicrous results in the beginning, like lopsided roofs and spoons that gave splinters to the tongue. They were all learning.

Liv, mistress of healing, came from a long line of healers, some might say witches. She somehow kept track in her head of all the recipes for curing various illnesses and she'd trained others on gathering proper herbs and roots to constantly replenish their stores.

And finally, Freyja, who had been with Medana from the beginning, at one time her nursemaid, now mistress of hunt and fish. Tales of Freyja's early efforts to feed them would be the fodder of sagas told around winter hearths for years to come. If Medana ever had to eat hedgehog again in this lifetime it would be too soon. And fish. Always fish, before they'd learned to hunt and trap. Once a few years back, a whale had the misfortune to run aground on Small Island during a storm, and the women had food stores for a whole season.

Medana glanced around at her council members with fondness. The ties that bound them were long and sturdy.

She would have called an assembly for a full Thing, a governing assembly, but some of her guards needed to keep an eye on the sly men who, after two days here, were exploring too much of the island for her comfort and asking too many questions. The women had to work hard to distract the men's attention from the spill pond during the times of low tide when its change of depth would be obvious. Luckily, the tidal move most important to them fell late at night now, but that would not always be the case. It was a constant worry.

The devious knaves pretended to accept their "visit" here as "guests" with resigned patience until the women could return them to Hedeby, at the women's convenience. Hah! Medana had yet to meet a patient Norseman. They were up to something that boded ill for the women and their island.

Plus, the men were being nice. Something foul was definitely afoot.

If there was anything she'd learned, to her detriment, it was never to trust a Viking with a wicked smile.

And all eight of the Norsemen had wicked smiling down to an art. One, in particular.

"We need to let them go. It is only fair," Medana said right off as they sat about a table at one end of the "great hall," which was really not so great. Just the main room of their biggest longhouse.

The protests were unanimous:

"Nay!" Gudron growled at Medana. A growl from Gudron was naught to be dismissed easily, she being the size of a Viking warrior, with all the learned fighting skills.

"Not yet!" pleaded Lilli, a slight woman of more than thirty years who had told Medana on

more than one occasion that she feared her child-
bearing years were waning. "My eggs will soon
need a cane," Lilli moaned.

"What are you . . . a laying hen now?" Medana
asked with a laugh.

"Bok, bok!" Lilli responded, and she wasn't
smiling.

"Every hen needs a rooster once in a while,"
Solveig chimed in, lining herself up on Lilli's side.

"Lilli, you know better than most what irksome
creatures roosters can be," Medana said. "Strutting about as if they own the whole chicken coop.
Pecking and crowing."

"I can put up with a strut if it lands a babe in
my womb," Lilli asserted, her green-eyed stare
one of defiance, or was it pleading?

Just then, a loud bellowing could be heard.
Through the open double doors across the hall
from them they could see that the bull, aptly
named Swively, was preparing to swive one of
their five cows. *Again*. Helga, no doubt. Odin's
eyeballs! Within a month, all their cows would be
heavy with calves or walking bowlegged, or both.

But it wasn't Swively and Helga that held the
women's interest so much as it was the man
watching the bovine activity. It was Thork leaning
against the split rail fence, one boot propped on a
lower rung which caused his braies to tauten over
his buttocks. And a very fine pair of buttocks,
Medana had to admit.

Lilli summed up all the women's thoughts
when she said, "Cock-a-doodle-doo!"

Following a long bout of giggling and ribald remarks, Medana called the meeting back to order

by reminding the women, "We need to get rid of the men. The longer they remain here, the greater our problems."

"Another sennight at least, for Asgard's sake!" requested Elida, whose well-oiled hands were wrapped in strips of linen today to soften the calluses from her recent archery attempts. *So she can handle the fine wool in the weaving shed . . . or handle something else?* Medana wondered. If it was the latter, she'd best try a different hand treatment. She smelled like fish oil.

"I'm having my monthly flow. They cannot leave yet!" This from Liv the Healer, who was, no doubt, responsible for Elida's fishy smell.

"I need time to lose this belly flab. How will I attract a man with belly flab?" complained Bergdis, whose body was mostly hard-muscled from all that rowing, leastways on top. The bottom was a different matter altogether. Sitting on sea chests so long tended to give a woman's bottom and belly a bit of a spread.

"Watching that bull tup Helga, over and over and over, is turning my womanparts to mush," Solveig remarked.

"You jest!" Gudron exclaimed. "Didst see how fast Swively does his business. In, out, and he's done. Just like a man! All over in the blink of an eye. The poor cows barely have a chance to peak themselves." Gudron paused thoughtfully. "Cows do peak, do they not, Siobhan? You were raised on a farmstead. You should know."

"They seem to welcome the attention, or mayhap they endure the rut knowing it will lead to a baby cow." Lilli shrugged, as if it was of no matter. "Even so, my womanparts are throbbing, like a heartbeat."

"Mine tingle." Solveig pointed downward, as if they didn't know which womanparts she referred to.

"I tingle *and* throb," Elida said proudly, as if that were a circumstance to be desired. "So I need a man more than you do."

Solveig fisted her hands, as if she wanted to throttle Elida. "I tingle *and* throb *and* weep woman-dew."

"Hah!" Siobhan interjected. "I tingle *and* throb *and* weep woman-dew *and* have sex dreams that give me little sleep."

"It has been two sennights since the beginning of my last cycle, and everyone knows that is a woman's most fertile period, give or take a few days. Therefore, I should go first." When everyone turned to Solveig to learn where she had gained such information, she explained, "In the brothels, harlots need to know the best ways *not* to conceive."

Medana shook her head at the women's foolish competitiveness. "The men's presence here is creating disharmony amongst you women. We are friends, not rivals. This island has been a sanctuary of peace and safety for all of us, but it is fast becoming a beehive of bickering and unrequited yearnings."

None of her women looked at all guilty. In fact, they cast surly scowls her way.

"We have not coupled with them yet," Bergdis whined.

"Not at all?" That surprised Medana. The way

her women—leastways some of them—were parading their charms afore the men, you'd think at least one of the walking penises would have succumbed to the temptation.

"None!" Solveig exclaimed with disgust. "Although they do engage in a bit of sexplay."

"A bit?" Medana asked.

"Kissing, fondling, that kind of thing," Elida answered for Solveig with a wave of dismissal, as if that was nothing.

"And the leader . . . is he, too, doing his little 'bit'?" Medana could scarce believe she'd asked that question. She did not care what that loathsome lout Thork was doing. He was becoming a thorn in her backside with all his complaints. And constant harping on having known her before, or someone who closely resembled her. She feared he would leave the island and tell folks that Geira of Stormgard was alive and thriving. Her brothers, and the king's guardsmen, would be after her quicker than a fox on the scent of a hare. Not for one moment did she believe that ten years would have lessened their fury.

Even worse were Thork's rude surveys of her body followed by strange smiles. Like a bear licking its lips as it studied the hive of honey it was about to consume.

"Nay, and I really tried," said Siobhan. "I even showed him my bosoms, and everyone says I have magnificent bosoms."

They all stared at Siobhan's bosoms, which were indeed magnificent. Big and firm and without any sag, despite her having seen more than thirty-five winters.

Medana was only a few years from thirty herself, but she was not worrying about having a child. Mayhap not all women had the maternal yearning. As for bosoms . . . Medana had to restrain herself from glancing downward at her own breasts, which were small, but plenty big enough in her opinion; an asset, really, when having to be bound on those occasions when she pretended to be a man. But mayhap their size would be considered lacking when it came to men and their lustsome preferences.

"The issue for us to decide is how to let them go with the least repercussions on us," Medana said.

Forget repercussions. The women were still grumbling amongst themselves about how little attention they were getting.

"What is the sense of having captured the men if we cannot milk their seed from their bodies with our woman-channels?" asked Siobhan, who should know about milking, being in charge of the cows, among other things.

Still . . . milking? Now they see men as cows with udders? One-teated udders?

"The man with slanted eyes likes me, I think," Lilli went on. If anyone could attract a man it would be the voluptuous Lilli, whose waist was enticingly small compared to her generous hips and chest. "But Henry—that is his name—he is restraining himself for some reason."

"They are all restraining themselves," Bergdis complained, "and I do not understand why."

"Could it be because they do not favor being put to stud?" Medana asked with arched brows.

"Hah!" Olga the cook, mistress of the kitchen, a

short, plump woman who enjoyed her own foods overmuch, had just waddled in with a trencher of hard cheeses, oatcakes, and wild grapes to break the noonday fast. One of the few boylings on the island, Samuel, followed after Olga, carrying two pitchers of ale. "Men stud themselves out all the time," Olga continued. "My husband, may he rot in Muspell, certainly did it enough."

Samuel's eyes widened at the cook's words. Medana did not like the women speaking so freely in front of the child, who was only eight and would learn soon enough what the women thought of men. Well, some women, and some men. She raised a cautioning hand to halt speaking and asked Samuel if he would mind helping with the new shipbuilding this afternoon.

"You can help me sand the wood planks," offered Solveig.

Samuel's eyes lit up. It was a job he relished, unlike his usual chores around the kitchen, helping Olga.

Once Samuel was gone, Gudron asked, "Is it true that Malik begat twenty-two children?" Malik had been Olga's husband until his untimely death a few years back.

Olga nodded and showed her disdain by spitting into the rushes, a distasteful habit that Medana had tried to break her of, to no avail, thus far. "No sooner did the old goat die, in the process of swiving yet another maid, than his many worthless, illegitimate sons descended on our keep, pushing me out the door. Sad it was that none of my own sons lived past infancy."

"Worthless men may be, but they do serve their

purpose betimes," Gudron said. "I, for one, like the old one."

"Um, could we get back to the subject of—"

"The one with an eye patch? Gudron! His hair is threaded with white. Are you sure his staff can still rise?" Solveig inquired.

"You know what they say about snow on the roof but fire in the hearth," Gudron replied with a rare giggle.

Even Medana had to smile at that old saying, one that was no doubt perpetuated by men. "I thought you were interested in the leader," Medana said to Gudron. "You mentioned showing him your breasts."

Gudron waved a hand dismissively. "That one is too pretty by half. Nay, I want a man with more meat on the bone. And I mean one particular bone." She waggled her bushy blonde eyebrows for emphasis.

Oh good gods!

"When the Scots one drawls with that sexy burr, my inner parts nigh melt." This from Freyja, speaking for the first time in this meeting. In truth, Freyja rarely spoke, being more comfortable out of doors. The quiet Danish woman from Jutland had been sold by her father to a passing trader for a gold coin. Gods only knew what travails she'd suffered before finally being sold to Stormgard, where she cared for a young Medana, known as Geira then.

Medana cleared her throat. "As I was saying—"

"The clumsy one is adorable," Bergdis said, and sighed. "Have you noticed the bulge in his braies?"

"This is getting way off the subject at hand. Really."

But it was as if Medana was talking to air.

"I saw the pretty one plucking some loose hairs down below after bathing," Elida told them, "and what he worked around was nigh like a marble pole." She made a rude gesture over her lap.

"His man-hairs?" Olga asked incredulously.

Medana hadn't realized that Olga was still there.

"I ne'er heard of such a thing," Olga said. "Mayhap I should have him shave this wild hair on my chin. Ha, ha, ha!"

"He was not shaving," a red-faced Elida told them. "Just trimming and a little plucking. Must be why his thatch down there was oddly clipped and neat. Hmm."

Olga chuckled as she waddled off, carrying some empty trenchers. The news of man-hair trimming would be spread about the entire island by nightfall. The women of Thrudr, like women everywhere, did like a juicy bit of gossip.

"How about Jostein, the blond, brooding one?" Bergdis asked.

"That one is scary," Elida said with a shiver.

Gudron nodded. "When Gert tried to seduce him by bending over in her tightest braies, he told her to go bugger herself."

Medana choked on her ale. She couldn't imagine any woman wanting to display her backside before a man.

"Did you notice—" Solveig started to say.

But Medana thumped both fists on the table. "Enough! We have serious issues to discuss."

Now that there was silence, she said, "The men must leave. The question is how . . . and when."

They debated the various solutions.

"We are agreed then," Medana said after a while, "whether it happens tomorrow or a sennight from now, that whilst we could return them to Hedeby with no problem, providing the good weather holds, what we have no way of knowing is the outcome when we reach Hedeby. Will they want recompense or revenge, even though no great scathe has been done? Will they just let us return home?"

Seven mouths turned down. Not a single one of them believed that would be the case.

"Mayhap we could negotiate their release," Elida said.

Medana was surprised that Elida even knew the word *negotiate*.

"Before we ever put them back on a longship, they would have to agree not to punish us in any way once released in Hedeby," Elida explained.

The others nodded their heads and turned to her with anticipation of approval.

"That would be based on the assumption that men never lie." Medana hated that she was the one who always dampened their hopes.

"Can we trust their word, assuming they would agree to begin with?"

"Nay," each of them said.

"I have an idea," Gudron said. "The leader, Thork, is said to be the son of a powerful Norse jarl, Lord Tykir of Dragonstead. What if we sent a message asking him to come rescue his son?"

Medana sat up straighter. "I do not like demanding ransom for our . . . um, mistake."

She could tell that the women did not like her calling their actions a mistake.

"We are pirates, Medana. That is what we do," Gudron pointed out.

"We do not need to demand ransom, just ask that the father rescue the son," Elida added as a compromise to Medana's sensibilities.

"I still say there is naught wrong with pirates demanding ransom," Gudron persisted.

Medana sighed and agreed that ransom would not be such a terrible thing but insisted that care be taken to protect the whereabouts of their island.

"Once our mountaintop scouts spot dragon-ships approaching in the distance, we will give the men sleep herbs and place them on Small Island," Liv said.

The other women clapped their approval, but Medana groaned. Sleep herbs again? Thork had warned her and warned her what he would do if there was such a repeat. Still, she had to admit, "It could work, but only if the timing is just right. If his father, Tykir, responds in a positive manner. If his father's seamen are viewed when the tide is down but arrive when the tide is back up, hiding the land road to the caves. If Thork and his men have not discovered the secrets of Thrudr that would enable them to return. So many ifs!"

"Do we have a choice?" Solveig asked.

"'Tis worth a try, is it not, Medana?" This plea came from Lilli, whose green eyes were brimming with tears.

Tears? It was untenable to Medana that these men had created such havoc among her women.

"It will give us several sennights to seduce the men," Bergdis said, and the matter was settled.

Later that afternoon, Medana worked painstakingly with parchment, quill, and encaustum, the thick ink prepared from tree sap. By eventide, the scroll was in the hands of Salvana and Sigrun, who told her that the merchant ship that often stopped by for fresh water, which the women gathered in rain barrels, was expected any day now.

It was late when Medana returned to her longhouse, having had to pretend duties up on the mountains to hide her errand through the caves. Most everyone, except for her guards, was long abed.

She sensed a presence and put a hand to the knife sheathed at her side.

Thork stepped out of the darkness into the full moonlight. "M'Lady Pirate, you have been very busy."

"A chieftain's work is ne'er done. You should know that." How long had he been watching her? What secrets had he uncovered already?

He stepped closer, and she could smell evergreen . . . the clean scent of one of the hard soaps Lilli was renowned for. He must have recently bathed.

"It's late," she told him, backing up, her shoulders hitting the timber wall. "We can talk in the morning."

He shook his head and put a hand to her chin, lifting her face as he moved in, so close she could scarce breathe. "Foolish wench! 'Tis not talk I have in mind."

chapter seven

If his mother could see him now . . .

Thork was a master of sport, whether it be skillful moves in the board game *hnefatafl*, or the planning of battle strategy, but especially in the seduction arts. And he had Medana the Muleheaded Headmistress of Thrudr as his target now. She was too willful by half.

Dare to capture him, would she?

Dare to take him to some misbegotten island, would she?

Dare to give him a sleeping draught not once but twice, would she?

Dare to refuse his demand to return him to Hedeby at once, would she?

Dare to let her women do everything but stand on their fool heads to entice him and his men, would she?

Dare to act as if he were a guest and not a prisoner, would she?

Well, he fumed, *I have a surprise for you, M'Lady Pirate. I am a Viking, not a weak-sapped pet eager to do your bidding.* But slow and easy, that was his plan.

For a moment, he could swear he heard his mother's laughter in his head. Lady Alinor, who had endured one misadventure after another in his growing-up years, had warned him that someday a woman would turn the tables on him. He refused to believe that was the case now.

He'd well earned the reputation these ten years and more of being the wildest Viking this side of Miklagard, but he had not been careless or impulsive in his acts, regardless of what his father, or mother, might think. If he was bad, it was because he'd wanted to be bad and did so with a clear head and conscience.

He and his men had wasted two days now wandering about this bloody island the women called Thrudr, and what they'd learned had not been promising. The village was in the bottom of a deep bowl, the sides covered with heavy forests and rocky cliffs. On reaching the top, they'd discovered the North Sea surrounding the landmass on all sides, with no noticeable shoreline, just cliffs and woods up to the water's edge, and a tiny island a short distance away that seemed to be inhabited by two women. Hermits of a sort, he supposed. Thrudr boasted no wharves or even shores for docking a longship. There was no way the women could have portaged the longship, not to mention eight big men, up to the top of the mountain bowl lip and then down the inner side, leastways not overnight. And there was no path discerned by the men . . . so far.

Could they have been doused with the sleeping draught for longer than he'd thought? Mayhap even days?

Possible, but still, where was the path?

He and his men could overpower the women

easily, of course, or at the least overpower enough women strategically to take over Thrudr. And they could probably force the women to return them to Hedeby on their lone longship, though gods only knew how, lest he discover a sudden taste for flogging female flesh. They were a stubborn bunch.

In the end, it was important to Thork that they know Thrudr's location so that they could return someday, for retribution or to see their children. The latter, planting of male seed, was bound to happen soon if the women, some of whom cleaned up well into comely creatures, got their way. Even Jostein appeared to be tempted, although Bolthor kept muttering, "My wife will kill me, my wife will kill me . . ."

So the only answer was to work on Medana . . . or Geira . . . or whatever name she chose to go by these days. She would reveal her secrets, or he would die trying. His men would home in on other women. Someone was going to spill secrets, and, yea, they had bets going on who would succeed first . . . without spilling other things, like their seed.

Medana backed up against the wall and stared up at him as he moved in closer. He still had a hand on her chin, which quivered slightly, before she demanded, "What do you want, knave?" She started to raise a hand, no doubt to whistle for her women, but he grabbed her by the wrist, fighting the inclination to kiss the soft inner area where blue veins could be seen beneath the thin skin.

Remember, Thork, you are a Good Viking now. You do not need to swive every pretty maid who comes your way. Good Viking. Good Viking, he reminded himself.

He pressed her hand against the wall and his hips against hers. Despite two layers of clothing, his and hers, and despite his lack of attraction to the wench, his enthusiasm began to rise.

Damn enthusiasm! Remember, Good Viking, Good Viking . . . "Do not dare to whistle near my ear again, wench, or you will be sorry." *How, I am not sure, but I will think of something.*

"How would you stop me?"

You had to ask! He smiled, realizing he'd been given the kind of opening he relished with a woman. "I would tongue kiss you into silence. 'Tis hard to whistle when your mouth is full. Like a cork I will be." *That was good. Where do I get these ideas? Oops, Good Viking, Good Viking . . .*

"Must you be so crude?" Her upper lip curled with distaste. For a pirate, she had the sensibility of a noblewoman.

He used the knuckles of the hand holding her chin to trace a line along her jaw from one ear to the other.

She inhaled sharply, whether from outrage or arousal, he could not tell, but he was betting on the latter. Sometimes he was so good he surprised even himself.

Once again, he thought he heard his mother's voice in his head with her age-old refrain, referring to his conceit, *A peacock is just another name for a rooster.*

Enough with my mother! Why does she keep coming to mind tonight? It is my father with whom I need to redeem myself, and not much redeeming being done here on this bloody island. He moved his hand to cup the back of her neck. The fine hairs of the underside of her braid tickled his fingers, like silk threads.

"Tongue kissing is not crude. Well, betimes, it can be crude, but in a good way." *I wonder what her hair would look like if let loose. I wonder if it is as silken and golden as it appears in that braid. I wonder what she would do if I loosened it, and . . . Frigg's foot! Forget wondering, you fool! You are supposed to be seducing her, not the other way around. Aaarrgh! Good Viking, Good Viking . . .*

"Are you daft?"

You are making me daft. Or else being a Good Viking is. "Nay. 'Tis true. There are times when wet, sloppy, noisy kisses are the only ones that will do. Raises a man's sap quicker than anything else, except maybe a nude woman. Of course, a woman's sap rises, too."

"You *are* daft," she said.

"And your point is, Mistress of Pirate Daftness? Perhaps I should demonstrate." Before she could protest, and she surely would, he licked her lips, a moist swath against the closed seam, which caused her to gasp, giving him the perfect opportunity to dip his tongue inside, but only for a second. At this stage, with her not yet fully aroused, she would be more likely to bite his tongue. But, oh, he was tempted! And, really, he could still be a Good Viking whilst engaged in a little foresport, couldn't he?

She snarled her outrage.

Chuckling, he released her wrist and nape. Grabbing her hand, he urged, "Come. Let us go for a walk." *See, I can be a Good Viking.*

She balked. "A walk? 'Tis after midnight."

"The best time," he said, "or would you rather stay here and let me demonstrate some of my other kisses? Good idea! I have forty-three different kinds, at last count."

Muttering something about "daft men and daft kisses," she began walking, but he grabbed her hand, so she didn't get far. He began to lead her toward the salt pool on the far side of the bowl. There was a full moon tonight and he could see his way easily.

She balked again, and said, "Nay. Let us go the other way." The alarm on her face disconcerted Thork for a moment, but then she explained, "I want to . . . um, check on Swively."

"Swively?" He arched his brows.

"The bull."

"Ah!" he said with a grin. "Good name for the old boy. He has been busy, hasn't he?"

He could tell the subject embarrassed her. What an odd contradiction she was! Leader of a band of female pirates, therefore brave, to some foolish extent. Think goats! Brave, certainly, to have left her homeland to survive on her own on a remote, misbegotten island. Brave to be unafraid of him. It took some daring for a Viking man to go a-Viking or a-pirating, but for a Viking woman, it was beyond unbelievable. And yet, at the same time, she appeared guilt-ridden over the situation they found themselves in. And she blushed and trembled around him like an untried virgin.

As they continued walking, she tried to tug her hand away, but he laced their fingers tighter and drew her closer to his side. And he liked it. They passed guardswomen along the way, but at a nod from Medana, no weapons were raised.

"Tell me how you came to be here, Geira."

"Medana. My name is Medana."

"Ah, mayhap I was mistaken. Now that I think on it, Geira had a backside the size of a barge and no breasts to speak of."

Without thinking, she glanced downward. And realized her mistake immediately. Her lashes fluttered wildly.

"Tsk, tsk, tsk. Do not think to lie again. You do not do it well. I know that you are Geira, and truly, I care not why you killed Haakon's cousin, Jarl Ulfr. I'm sure you had good reason."

Her eyes widened and she tilted her head at him, as if trying to ascertain if he was telling the truth. "You would not alert the king, or my brothers, to my whereabouts? Or attempt to deliver me for punishment?"

Oh, I have punishment aplenty in mind for you, but not for past deeds. What you have done to me and my men merits its own reward. He shook his head slowly. "Nay. 'Tis no concern of mine, though I think you could go back and demand that your side of the story be heard. Why live in such a primitive setting when you could reside in more comfort befitting your high social standing?" At the stiffening of her body, he quickly added, "But that is for you to decide."

Her body relaxed as she accepted his words. "You ask how I come to be here. It all started with my three half brothers, who are the slimiest *nithings* to walk the earth. Sigurd, Osten, and Vermund. My father was a good man, despite practicing that despicable Norse custom of *more danico*. My mother, who was my father's second wife, died birthing me, her first and only child. My father grieved my mother's passing for years, and in so doing ignored what was happening around him, even on his own estate at Stormgard. As a result, his first wife, Valka, the meanest witch of a woman, took control. It was not so bad whilst my father was alive, but he died when I was ten. After that, Valka scarce hid her hatred for me, and she instilled that hatred in her three sons, as well. They made my life miserable, but I was able to get by until Valka died, may she rest in Muspell as we speak."

Blather, blather, blather. Women were always bemoaning their lot. Geira . . . or Medana . . . was not the first female to suffer a father with many wives and concubines. But not in his family. His mother, a Saxon lady and a Christian besides, would castrate his father with a dull blade if he dared bring another woman to their bed furs. As for irksome siblings or half siblings . . . that, too, was more common than not.

"Geira, Geira, Geira," he said in a patronizing manner that he could tell irritated her, "I saw you at the royal court at Vestfold on occasion. I already mentioned that time when I was fourteen and you eleven. You did not appear abused. In fact, you wore fine clothing and were seated just below the salt during feasts."

"Hah! They treated me like a beloved sister in public, but at home I was little more than a thrall."

He rolled his eyes.

She swatted him on the arm. "I have scars on

my back from thrashings that went too far. Especially when the greedy bastards got it into their evil heads to wed me to Jarl Ulfr. I was sixteen, a ripe age for the marriage bed, or so my brothers said."

" 'Tis true. The earlier a girl gets into the marriage bed the better," Thork said, just to irritate her more. "A woman needs to learn her place." *Beneath a man.*

She snarled at him.

And he found her snarling oddly endearing. Or at least satisfying.

"Beneath a man?" she sputtered.

Oops! He hadn't realized that he'd said that aloud.

"Greedy? You say your brothers were greedy. Did Ulfr offer them so much for your hand in marriage?"

"Yea, he did, but more important, I had a legacy of a dower estate passed on to me by my mother. A marriage contract was the only way my brothers could get their hands on that."

Thus far, Thork saw nothing unusual or alarming. "That is the way of the world, Medana," he said, choosing to use the name she went by now, even though she was, without a doubt, Geira. "A woman brings a dower to her marriage. It is a husband's right to those goods and estates."

His mother, who still maintained rights to her estates in the Saxon lands, would slap him up one side of his head and down the other for saying thus.

My mother, again!

Medana raised her chin with affront at his

dismissal of her complaint. "Did you know Jarl Ulfr?"

He shook his head slowly from side to side. "I do not think I ever met him, though I did hear stories from time to time. Hardly credible stories."

"Credit them! They were true. Freyja, my nursemaid at one time and later my companion, learned from servants in the jarl's household what an evil man he was.

By the runes! She heard from someone who heard from someone. How like a woman!

"Some men enjoy inflicting pain, did you know that?"

Yea, he did. But women tended to exaggerate. Men sometimes needed to wield the whip when laggard servants failed in their duties. Or wives, he supposed. It was not unheard of and not even frowned upon.

Before he could voice that opinion, he mind-whispered, *Yea, Mother, I know that is not true of men in our family. Yea, I know you or Aunt Eadyth would whip the man who did such to any underling of yours for small infractions.*

"Every girl or woman under the age of fifty on his estate had been raped at least once by Ulfr, if not his vicious men. He had a special chamber with chains and methods of torture that he employed on men and women alike, often for no more reason than a whim. It gave him pleasure to hear screaming. You do not believe me, I can tell."

I do not want to believe you, truth to tell. I do not want to believe there are men so evil. It makes me uncomfortable, especially when women judge all men by the same measure. "I ne'er heard such said of him, but then I have not lived in that part of the Norse-lands for many years."

"He raped me when I tried to back out of the be-trothal, but"—she raised a hand when he started to sympathize with her plight—"but that was not even the worst of it. He laughed at my weeping after the rape, and tried to force me to lick my maiden blood off his ugly manpart. It was too much. Without thinking, I raised a nearby poker and smashed him over the head."

He drew her into his arms, and though she struggled, he held fast. "Dost think anyone would blame you for such? You were only defending yourself." He kissed the top of her hair, an instinctive act, he told himself. It meant nothing. Bloody hell! He was supposed to be seducing her, not consoling her. Yea, she had a tragic past, but that did not excuse her present crime.

"You are a fool if you think I would be given fair hearing," she stormed, burrowing her face into his neck, where he was oddly touched to feel the wetness of her tears. He knew without being told that she did not often share her tears. "My brothers were depending on the huge bride price, which included my dower estate, Snow Pines, which is in the far north, too remote and cold for any purpose other than the harvesting of soap-stone, which is plentiful there. They would have been the first to cast stones my way. And, remember, the jarl was the king's cousin. I would not have stood a chance."

Without a strong man, or men, at her back to support her, she was probably right. Although men, whether husband or betrothed, could hardly be accused of rape. Could they? "You might be right, although my cousin John's wife, Princess Ingrith of Stoneheim, killed a man one time, without any consequence. Well, actually, it was Ingrith and her four sister princesses who did the killing, and their victim was a Saxon nobleman, not a Viking. Equally as vile as you say Ulfr was, though."

"You made that up!" she accused him, shaking her head at what she must consider a lackwitted attempt to make her feel better.

If she only knew! His family was every bit as outrageous as what he'd just related to her. In fact, Princess Tyra, Ingrith's sister, had once taken Adam, another of his cousins, captive—*Is there an irony there?*—but he did not think he would mention that to Medana. Nor the fact that the two ended up married.

Once Medana had her emotions under control, they resumed walking.

"I do not know why I'm telling you all this," she said after a period of companionable silence.

"Perchance you hope it will lessen your crime." When she scowled at him, he urged, "Finish, now that you have started."

"I fled Stormgard, where the assault took place, but I had no specific destination. In shock, I was. I found myself down at the wharves where the small longship was anchored, the one that would have been part of Ulfr's bride-gift to me, which would have no doubt been taken back once the ceremony was over. Little did I know that Freyja and some of the women followed after me, no more wanting to be part of Ulfr's household than

I had. And after that came some of Ulfr's much-abused servants. Before I knew it, there were more than a dozen women huddled on the ship, none of us knowing what to do next."

"Surely you would not have me believe that a dozen untrained women rowed a longboat through a fjord and out to sea."

"Of course not." She looked at him as if he was half brained.

He knew the look very well. His mother had perfected . . . aaarrgh!

"It was Solveig, whose father had been a ship-wright, who suggested we release the anchor and raise the sails to see where we would go."

That is the most ridiculous thing I have ever heard. Something a boyling would say. Like my brother Selik. "Let us jump off the cliff, Thork, and see if we can fly. Why can't we take a longboat down the fjord, Thork? Why, why? If fish can swim the length of the fjord, why can't we?" "Do you have any idea how dangerous an ill-manned longship can be? At best, you could have tipped over the light vessel and drowned," he noted. "At worst, you could have found yourself out to sea in the midst of a storm, and drowned."

"Which would have been a more favorable outcome than staying behind to face what I had done."

Death by stupidity. "A suicide pact then? You women were planning to die? You preferred that to the executioner's blade, assuming that would be the king's verdict."

She shook her head. "We had not thought that far."

Stupidity, for a certainty. "Did you bring coins to

bribe guardsmen, or weapons for defense, or food to maintain yourselves whilst in hiding, or extra cloaks to weather the cool night air?"

She stared at him dumbly.

The answer was, obviously not. Some of the old ones claimed that women had smaller brains than men. He was beginning to think they had the right of it.

Except women like my mother, he quickly amended.

"You are smiling. Do you find humor in my story?" Rather than be offended, she seemed rather annoyed with him.

He chucked her under the chin playfully. "I find humor in myself, not you, sweetling. As you have been talking, my mother's words of wisdom keep coming back to haunt me. A rascal of a boy I was."

"A rascal of a man, as well," she observed.

He smiled. She considered him a rascal. He was making progress.

"And stop with the endearments. You cannot sweeten me up with false expressions of fondness."

Maybe not so much progress.

"Finish your tale, Medana," he encouraged as they both sat down on a bench on the far edge of the village near the entrance to an orchard. The air was filled with the pleasant scent of fruit. Possibly plums. Or cherries. "I cannot wait to hear how a band of barmy seawomen landed on this island."

She swatted away his hand that was attempting to loosen the thong on her braid. "Must you sit so close?" She shifted her bottom along the bench. He shifted his bottom right after her. "If you do not behave, I am not finishing my story."

He pretended to wipe the smile off his face and sat up straighter. "I'm listening."

"The gods were with us that night, although it did not seem so at the time. A storm came up suddenly with strong winds and blinding rain . . . yea, I know, just as you mentioned, except we did not drown, though we no doubt looked like it. Soaked to the bone, we were. It was morning before it cleared, and we 'barmy seawomen,' who'd been clinging together in a huddle mid-ship, discovered that we were indeed asea, bobbing on waves with no land in sight."

His eyes widened more and more as she went on. This was the stuff Bolthor would love to embellish into a saga.

"We had no seafaring skills, of course, though Solveig did know how to manage the rudder. All day the ship took us where it willed with only a slight breeze to guide our sails. By evening, we saw land. The island. And that is the end of the story."

Even in the moonlight, he could see her eyelids fluttering. She lied, or leastways, she did not tell the whole truth.

He made a sweeping motion with one hand to indicate the village. "And was this all here, just waiting for you women to arrive?"

She made a snorting sound of disagreement. "Nothing was here. Everything you see was dug or built by our own endeavors. Suffice it to say, the first two years, there were many times when we might not have survived. And that is all I will say."

For now. "You are to be admired then, like our early settlers are. Or those Norsemen who settle in far-off lands beyond Iceland."

She slanted him a sideways glance, not sure if he was sincere or not.

"Truly. What is not to commend when people, women at that, take the poor lot that life hands them and make something of it." He chuckled, then added, "My mother would place you in high regard. In fact, she would say . . ." His words trailed off as he realized exactly what his mother would say. She would tell him to marry the lady, that she would be a perfect match for him and his wild ways.

Horrified, he stood suddenly. "We will talk more in the morning. I am suddenly in need of my sleep."

But the nagging idea stayed with him. Wouldn't this solve all his problems with his father . . . and mother? Forget about the merchant's daughter in Hedeby. He could marry Lady Medana of Stormgard and leave her here after the wedding. He would have all the benefits of marriage, including his father's goodwill, and none of the disadvantages.

It was definitely his mother's voice in his head now. Laughing hysterically.

chapter eight

**A mother's heart is the same,
even back then . . .**

Lady Alinor read aloud the missive that had just been delivered by Mustaf the Arab. The traveling trader, who sat across the table in Dragonstead's great hall from her and her husband, Tykir, was quaffing down ale like a sailor too long at sea.

> *We have your son Thork. Send one hundred mancuses of gold to Small Island for his release. Otherwise, we will lop off the loathsome lout's head. Or slice off his too slick tongue and set the loathsome lout out to sea in a leaky boat. Once the ransom is paid, do not stay on the island, but return in one sennight. At that time, you will find the loathsome lout and his seven comrades, safe and unharmed.*
>
> *The Sea Scourge*

Alinor was thoroughly confused, as were others listening to her read the letter. But then, her eldest son ofttimes baffled her and enraged his father with his wild and disappointing ways. More so, of late.

First, they'd gotten word from Thork sennights ago that he was on his way home. She'd been ecstatic, making preparations to welcome the prodigal son home. In fact, she'd invited her other sons to come home for the welcome celebration. Well, Selik was already here, being only sixteen and not yet having his own estates, but Starri and Guthrom had come from afar at her urging. Meanwhile, her husband had done naught but scowl at the prospect of Thork finally deigning to honor them with his presence. In Tykir's defense, Alinor had to concede that Thork had done much to hurt his father.

But then ten days ago, some of Thork's comrades had arrived telling an unbelievable tale about Thork having disappeared from the market town of Hedeby, leaving his longships and seamen behind. "I told you, I told you," Tykir had said to her, "it is another of his foolhardy jests." Alinor wasn't so sure; it would be cruel of Thork, if true. Nay! She was worried.

And now this!

Alinor picked up the parchment and read through the words again.

We have your son Thork. Send one hundred mancuses of gold to Small Island for his release. Otherwise, we will lop off the loathsome lout's head. Or slice off his too slick tongue and set the loathsome lout out to sea in a leaky boat. Once

*the ransom is paid, do not stay on the island, but
return in one sennight. At that time, you will
find the loathsome lout and his seven comrades,
safe and unharmed.*

The Sea Scourge

"Where did you get this?" Tykir demanded of
Mustaf, grabbing the parchment out of Alinor's
hands and crumbling it into a wad that he tossed
into the rushes.

Mustaf, alarmed at the harshness of Tykir's
tone, wiped his mouth and thick mustache with
the back of one shaking hand. It would not be
the first time in Norse history that the messenger
was killed. "On Small Island. A stopping-off place
north of Hedeby. A well-known spot for getting
fresh water and passing of messages," Mustaf
rushed to say.

"And my son is being held there?" Alinor
pressed a hand to her wildly beating heart. How
much worry could one mother withstand? "I do
not understand. Who is the Sea Scourge?" she
asked.

"I know! I know!" said Starri, their second
eldest of four sons, Thork being two years older.
He was the only one of her sons who'd inherited
her red hair and freckles, although on him they
were attractive, his hair a darker red and just a
smattering of dots on his sun-darkened skin.
With a grin, he sat down next to Mustaf, poured
himself a cup of ale from the pottery pitcher, and
informed them, "She is the leader of a band of pirates."

"*She?*" Alinor and Tykir exclaimed at the same time.

"Yea!" Starri waggled his eyebrows at them. "The Sea Scourge is the leader of a band of female pirates."

Tykir slammed a fist down on the table, causing them all to jump and ale to slosh over the rims of cups. "That does it! Now the rascal has gone too far! Captured by females! What kind of man is he? What kind of Viking? He has done some wild and barmy things in his time, but this tops them all."

Alinor punched her husband in the arm. "You would blame the boy for being captured?"

"Captured by *women*!" he emphasized. "Yea, I blame him for that. He no doubt planned it all as some grand jest. And he is a man, not a boy, though you would ne'er know it by his actions in recent years."

"You are being ridiculous. He is in danger whilst you blame him for this and that. Actually, though . . ." Alinor tapped her lips with a forefinger. "Did you notice that she referred to him as a 'loathsome lout'? Must be she is fond of our son."

"Are you daft? What kind of female illogic brings you to that conclusion?"

" 'Tis what I called you when you were trying to woo me to your bed furs. 'Tis what Eadyth called your brother Eirik when he was behaving as all lustsome Viking men do. 'Tis just another form of talking foresport."

"Oh gods! My parents are going to talk about sex again! Can I gag now?" Starri grinned as he spoke. All their children were accustomed to the open affection between their parents. Not that she was feeling anything near affection for her mule-headed husband at the moment.

"Send for the scribe. I have a message for Mustaf to take back to that bloody island," Tykir shouted.

"Must you bellow?" Alinor complained, putting her hands to her ears. "There is a ringing in my head."

"I do not bellow."

"Like a bear." She smiled at her husband.

"I'm gagging over here," Starri said. "Next you'll be kissing and licking each other's tongues."

"Starri!" Alinor chastised.

Starri shrugged. "Heed me well, I have been living with you two for nigh on twenty-six years. It starts by you insulting each other, then you are staring at each other with cow eyes, then before you know it, the bed furs are shaking so much above stairs that the floor nigh falls through."

"Starri!" It was his father speaking now.

Truth to tell, Tykir was still a virile man, despite his mostly gray hair, despite his fifty and more years, despite the limp from an old battle wound that had become more pronounced over the years. And Alinor was a woman who appreciated her husband's virility, despite being close to fifty herself, her flaming red hair now muted with silver threads.

Father Peter, the resident monk, had just arrived with parchment, quill, and a pot of ink. "You wanted to send a message?" he inquired of Tykir.

"Yea, I do. Very simple."

To the Sea Scourge:

Keep him!

Tykir Thorksson,
father of the loathsome lout

"Do. Not. Dare," Alinor seethed.

"Do not interfere in men's work, wife. I am the head of this family, and—"

Alinor stood and dumped the contents of the pitcher over her husband's head.

Everyone including her loathsome lout of a husband was laughing as she swanned out of the great hall, chin held high. She was not laughing, though, as tears leaked from her eyes. She was worried about Thork.

Her mother's heart ached for the love child she and Tykir had created all those years ago, before they were even wed. He would always be special to her. And now he was in danger, and her husband didn't care.

We will see about that! Lady Alinor sent her own message.

War of the Roses, Norse style . . .

Tykir slept in his bed furs alone for the next two nights, and he did not like it. Not one bit. Alinor was being foolish and would not listen to his very logical reasons for rejecting the ransom demand.

Some Viking men would not put up with such willfulness from their spouses. True Norsemen would pick up their stubborn women, toss them over their shoulders, smack them on their ample rumps (though Alinor's was not so ample but just right), and force them to the bed furs. Or else they would just take another woman to bed.

His marriage to Alinor had never been like that. Not only did he not practice the *more danico* (she would cut off his manpart if he dared try), but he was happy with her alone. They had been outstanding bed partners from the beginning . . . well, not the very beginning when he'd loathed her precious Saxon sheep and she'd loathed his Viking ways. In any case, he missed her sorely.

"Mother is very angry with you," his youngest son, Selik, told him when they broke fast that morning.

As if he didn't already know that! He looked at his sixteen-year-old like the lackbrain boyling he still was betimes, though he was of an age to be a full-grown man off a-Viking and married at least once. Some birds needed a good shove out of the nest, though Alinor had told him to leave the bloody nest himself when he'd made that suggestion to her recently. She coddled her sons, if you asked him, which no one did. And it was certainly not a subject he intended to bring up now, not when she was already angry at him.

"I mean, she is even more angry with you than she has ever been before," Selik went on.

Yea, a good shove, that's what he needs.

"Even the time you accidentally shot her prized ram in the arse with a stray arrow." Selik was grinning at him.

Hah! That arrow had not been so stray, truth be

known. The smelly beast had butted him one too many times. *And do not think I cannot do the same to you, son of mine, if you keep smirking at me.*

"What are you going to do about it?" Selik persisted, meanwhile starting on his fourth bowl of porridge topped with honey and raisins. Where the lean young man put all that food was beyond Tykir. Had he ever had such an appetite? Probably.

"What do you think I should do about it? Best you know now, afore you ever wed, never coddle a woman, or she will have you under her thumb for life." He turned quickly to make sure Alinor had not overheard him. Luckily, she was nowhere about.

"You could try saying you are sorry," Selik suggested.

"But I am not sorry."

Selik shrugged.

"I have a better idea," said Guthrom from Tykir's other side. Guthrom—who'd been silent so far as he stared into his morning ale, suffering from a *drukkinn* bout yestereve—was four years older than Selik and considered himself far superior in all ways. "You should buy Mother a new amber necklace."

"Your mother has more amber necklaces than she could ever wear."

Starri came up then and added his two pence. "In my experience with women . . ."

Oh gods! Now I am going to get a lecture on women from my son!

" . . . a man does not have to have done anything wrong to apologize. In fact, an all-encompassing apology sometimes serves best. In other words, say you are sorry but do not specify for what." Starri beamed at him as if he'd imparted some great wisdom.

"Go away!" Tykir said to his sons.

None of them did, of course. Instead, his sons tossed about several other suggestions, none of which resounded with Tykir. There was only one solution, and he'd known it from the start. Getting up from the table, he went off to set his plan in motion.

It was several hours later when Tykir saw Alinor walking toward the fjord and rushed to catch up with her. "We need to talk, wife," he said, taking her by the arm.

She shrugged out of his grip and continued walking, him beside her. "You talked. I disagreed. There is naught more to say, except you are a loathsome lout."

That was surely a good sign, her using that term. It had become a form of endearment for them. Leastways, that's what he told himself. He limped along beside her, his leg hurting more than usual on this damp day, following a night of rain.

Noticing his limp, she slowed down.

That, too, had to be a good sign.

She stopped suddenly and stared ahead. Three of his longships had been moved off their trestles on the field and into the water. They were being prepared for voyage.

"You are going a-Viking? Now?" she inquired with equal anger and hurt.

"Not a-Viking, oh you of little faith!"

She arched a brow at him and put her hands on her hips. He loved when she took that battle stance with him. Once he made her strike the pose naked. What a night that had been!

"A-rescuing, that is where I am going."

At first she did not understand, but when she did, she launched herself at him, knocking him to the ground, her atop him. "Thank you, thank you, thank you, oh, I knew you were not such a loathsome lout. I knew deep down that you cared about Thork." She kept kissing his cheeks and chin and mouth and even his nose between words.

He would have told her that he always cared about his son, that had never been the issue, but it was her stubbornness that changed his mind. More specifically, her absence from his bed furs. Mayhap he would save that explanation for later.

Starri came up then from one of the longships, stared down at the two of them, and made a snorting sound of disgust. "Oh gods! They are at it again!"

CHAPTER NINE

Now she was in BIG trouble . . .

Medana was nervous. Very nervous. And she hated it.

She felt as if she were walking a narrow precipice, always checking right and left and over her shoulder to make sure she did not slip. Just like the old days back at Stormgard when she had to be constantly on guard lest she cross the path of her half brothers. Danger had lurked around every corner.

Same was true now, though it was danger of a different sort. Captive Vikings. They lurked everywhere. Asked too many questions. Pretended to be compliant visitors whilst waiting for an opening to pounce.

Her biggest fear wasn't physical violence, though that was always a possibility, she supposed, especially when Thork had taken to grinding his teeth every time she told him it would be one more day before they could return them to Hedeby. First, she'd told him, "The bull needs to be acclimated to his new home."

"If that randy beast gets any more acclimated, he'll wear his cock down to a nubbin."

Each day, she'd had to come up with another reason for delay. "The fall oats need to be planted from the seeds we purchased in Hedeby."

"Give me the damn seeds. My men and I will plant them in one bloody day and be done with the job."

"'Tis is a new field we are clearing. Before we can plow, we must clear all the rocks. And we have no mule to pull a plow. So . . ."

"Muleheaded women abound here. They could easily pull a plow, especially if you hitch them together and give them a good kick in their donkey arses." He'd stared pointedly at her backside.

Foul man! "The sheep need shearing."

"I can think of something else that needs shearing."

Is he looking at the joining of my thighs? Frey's bones, he is! Foul, foul, foul! "Five of my best rowers have developed stomach ailments."

"I know of a purge that will cure them in no time. From both ends."

Foulness must come naturally to some men. "Many of my women are having their monthly flow. Terrible cramps. Bloody rags. Bad moods. Whew! Your men would not want to be around them now."

Usually men fled when a discussion about women's cycles came up, but not Thork.

"They have all begun at the same time? Remarkable! And how is it that this happenstance is not affecting their efforts to lure us men to their beds? A little blood ne'er repels most warriors, you know, but women are usually more squeamish about engaging in—"

"Aaarrgh!" she'd said to cut off the brute's crude talk and stomped off, his laughter following in her wake.

She was running out of excuses.

And always, like a wolf baying at her door, was the fear of disclosure. Once the men found the cave entrance and left Thrudr, only one of them needed to engage in a bout of ale blather, and the safety and security of the island hideaway would be lost forever.

Oh, how she yearned for the peace of mind she'd come to cherish as chieftain of this island sanctuary!

And there was another thing. She and her crew should have been off a-Viking, or rather a-pirating, again by now. With almost two hundred inhabitants, there was a constant need for goods that they could not provide for themselves and the treasure to purchase them.

In fact, there was a particular nunnery off the coast of Ireland, a small but rich one that they had been aiming to hit sometime soon in the usual hit-and-run type invasions the women of Thrudr had perfected. Not being as strong as male pirates, they had to rely on creative methods of attack . . . in other words, slyness. Besides goods and produce, that nunnery had a nice peach orchard. Medana yearned for fresh peaches, and decided that they would somehow dig up some of the fruit tree saplings there to bring back and plant on Thrudr.

Medana did not feel guilty going after holy places because, really, hadn't the Christian One-God preached humbleness in his Holy Book?

What need was there for nuns devoted to a simple life to hoard gold chalices or mules or fine samite silks or silver crosses? Or peach trees?

It was the waiting that made Medana twitchy.

When would they hear from Thork's father? Two sennights had passed already. What if they got no reply? Mayhap they needed a second plan for getting the men off the island.

Worry, worry, worry.

Going into the kitchen, she grabbed a piece of manchet bread and a thin slice of hard cheese, having missed the morning meal. Olga didn't pay her presence any mind as the big woman towered over Henry, the slant-eyed Viking, who was arguing with her about the correct spice to use with lamb.

Medana munched as she walked across the grounds, noticing the activity here and there. The young Viking, Brokk, sat on the ground under the shade of an evergreen tree playing the board game *hnefatafl* with some of the children. Supposedly, the youthling had been taken under the wing of Thork when he'd been discovered on the streets of Jorvik, half starved and homeless after the death of his parents.

The giant, one-eyed Viking, Bolthor, was teaching some of the women a better way to heft a broadsword that would put less strain on their shoulders, the whole time composing a saga titled, "Why Women Should Not Try to Be Men." Talk about foul! Bolthor had a tongue that was earthy to say the least. The beginning of his poem went something like:

If women could grow cocks,
They would, not to mention stones
. . . male stones, or rocks.
And decorate the balls and staff
With lace and trim of golden chaff.
'Til the package would be so heavy
'Twould more resemble a Yule tree . . .

That was as far at the poet warrior got before Medana left. Truly, he must be the world's worst skald.

Then there was Alrek, the clumsy one, on the roof of one of the longhouses helping to replace a rotted section of thatch. Every time he moved, Medana feared he would slip and break his leg. Then they'd never be rid of these men.

Finn, the vain Viking, stood behind Liv, who sat on a stool outside the weaving shed. He was demonstrating to a half dozen watching women how to make an intricate braid in her long hair, the kind that was worn by men and women alike in some far-off country.

Two other men were dragging an enormous dead log down from the forest to be chopped into their never-ending supply of firewood. The hearth fires required vast amounts of fuel for meals and for heat during the long winter months.

The air of cooperation was misleading, but not to Medana. It was the lull before the storm that was sure to come.

She finished eating her small repast as she approached the area where Solveig was building a new longship. Well, attempting to build it.

This was a project they worked on only in spare

time. They were learning as they went. No one wanted to go out in a boat that might very well leak due to poor construction.

Solveig came up and sat next to her on a pile of sanded boards.

"What is he doing there?" Medana asked, pointing to the center of some new activity. "And what is that thing? The animals do not come over here."

Thork was working with some women who carried wooden buckets of water to fill a long trough that must have been recently built. A dozen cows could have stood withers to withers to drink there with room left over.

"Even though he is not a shipwright, that Viking knows more about building sea vessels than we do. All those planks we had prepared for the stern and bow must needs be kept wet for a period of time so that they can be easily bent to the curves we need. I should have known. Now that Thork called it to my attention, I remember my father doing such." She shook her head with disgust.

Medana made a tsking sound. "Solveig! You do the best you can, and look how well you maintain *Pirate Lady*. Without you we would never be able to leave the island."

Solveig was clearly not convinced. "All that sanded wood wasted!" She looked pointedly at the stack they were sitting on.

Well, at least it could be used as firewood, or possibly some other building purpose, like fencing, or outbuildings.

Today Solveig wore a belted, knee-length tunic

with no leggings, and sleeves that had been torn off at the shoulders to accommodate her hard labor in the midday heat. She used a forearm to wipe the sweat from her forehead.

In fact, Thork was attired the same way. Somehow, he looked a lot more tantalizing with the muscles of his arms and legs exposed as he worked. His dark blond hair was pulled back off his face and tied with a leather thong at his nape. The hair on his arms and legs was so fine it appeared almost nonexistent. Truly, he was a fine specimen of a man. Healthy, sun-bronzed, well-muscled.

She glanced away quickly before he could catch her ogling him. Her lascivious interest would amuse him, no doubt. Actually, the man had been avoiding her since the night he'd accosted her and invited her on a "walk." She wondered if all the men were so easily resistant to the women. Just then, her question was answered, without words.

As Solveig turned her head this way and that to ease a muscle cramp, a bruise mark stood out on the flesh where her neck met her shoulders, the kind men were wont to make when engaged in bedsport. A suck kiss, some called it. Boylings did it apurpose with young maids to show their prowess. Grown men did it because . . . because they were boylings at heart.

"Solveig!" Medana teased. "Dare I guess how you have been spending your nights?"

Solveig put a hand to the spot where Medana was staring and rubbed it with a prideful grin on her face. "You should see Lilli. She has suck marks up one side and down the other on her body from that Henry. Even one here." She pointed to an area low on the belly. Very low.

Medana gawked and could not stop staring at that spot, even though she could, of course, not see through the cloth. "Your capturing the men has been successful then? I cannot countenance your methods, but if the end result is more babes next spring, well"—Medana shrugged—"it was worth it, I suppose."

"Hah! First of all, not all the men are having sex. Some still resist. And those that do succumb are following some practice suggested by yon oaf." She motioned with a jerk of her head toward Thork, who was carrying some long, narrow planks over his shoulder and laying them in the bottom of the trough, which was still being filled bucket by bucket.

"Practice?" Medana frowned with confusion.

"Yea. A method for preventing male seed from sprouting inside a woman's womb."

Medana was still confused.

"Spilling the seed outside the body at the last moment," Solveig explained.

"Really? And the men still get their grunting relief that way?"

"Must be, though most men would not inconvenience themselves thus. These men, though . . . especially that one"—Solveig gave Thork a glower of disgust—"are determined not to leave any children behind. Have you ever heard of such?"

"I cannot say that I have," Medana answered, though she was unsure if Solveig referred to the method or the reasons behind it.

Thork noticed their regard and gave them a

little wave, seeming to be amused by Solveig's disdain. He must know why Solveig was irritated with him.

"Of course there are other methods to prevent a seed from taking root," Solveig went on.

Medana shouldn't be surprised at Solveig's claim. With her background in a brothel, Solveig was often a font of information for the women.

"Other methods?" Medana couldn't help asking.

"Yea. In fact, that smaller Viking, Henry, wanted to put a pig intestine on his cock and have sex with Lilli, but she was having none of that."

"Like sausage casings," Medana deduced.

"Exactly. In any case, Lilli refused. So they did it the spilling way."

There were mind pictures here that Medana really did not want to have.

"But we women are not giving up," Solveig said with determination, standing to return to work. "Freyja is teaching us how to belly dance."

"Freyja? You cannot be serious. Freyja is more than forty and she has no belly to speak of."

"You would be surprised. Freyja learned the dance many years ago when she was in a sultan's harem, afore being sold as a slave to your father. Didst know that belly dancers have better peakings?"

Peakings? What is that? "Why did she never tell me about belly dancing? She was my nursemaid, you know."

"The subject never came up, I suppose. In any case, I am having trouble jiggling my breasts and undulating my stomach folds at the same time. But I will learn!"

Medana sat, dumbfounded for a moment, then shook her head like a wet dog to rid her mind of those images. Just then, the young boy, Samuel, came rushing up, a rolled parchment held tightly in his little hands.

"Mistress, mistress! I have a message for you." He came to a sliding stop in front of her, panting for breath.

"Where did you get this?" she asked, taking the scroll in hand.

"It was left in the message slot by the pond last night."

"Thank you, Samuel. You may go back to the kitchen and tell Olga that I said you could have an oatcake."

Samuel looked conflicted, gaping at the huge trough being filled with water, no doubt envisioning himself taking a leap inside, and salivating at the prospect of a sweet treat dripping with honey. His growling stomach won over. He skipped, then ran off, back to Olga's domain.

Medana looked down at the scroll with a dragon seal on it, then tore it open, and read the brief message inside.

To the Sea Scourge:

Keep him!

Tykir Thorksson,
father of the loathsome lout

Dismay must have shown on her face because Solveig, still standing before her, inquired, "What is amiss, m'lady?" Despite them all being mistress of this or that, the women could not seem to forget her higher social status in regular society.

Medana read the message to her.

Solveig gasped. "How sad for Thork! But what does it mean?"

"Clearly, the father will not be coming to the rescue."

"I do not understand why."

"Perchance Thork's father has no high regard for him."

"Or he might think it is a jest," Solveig suggested.

Medana shrugged. "Perchance."

"Actually, now that I think on it . . ." Solveig let her words trail off, and her face turned red.

"What?"

"Just a tiny memory I recall. Naught of importance. Time for me to go sweat some more," Solveig said, having a sudden need to go back to work.

"What?" Medana insisted.

"The young boy traveling with the Vikings said that Thork was headed back to Dragonstead to make peace with his father after a life misspent. Before we captured him, of course."

"He's not that old to have a misspent life."

"Apparently, he crammed a lot of misspending in those few years," Solveig commented with a jiggle of her eyebrows.

"Oh my gods!" Medana realized in that instant that, if what Solveig said was true, Thork was going to be furious with her for having caused further problems with his father.

Just her luck that Thork approached them then.

"Mistress of Shipwrighting," Thork said with a nod of greeting to Solveig, and "Mistress of Every Other Thing," to Medana. The oaf got an inordinate amount of pleasure over the titles the women had assigned themselves here. Personally, she did not think it was so funny.

Solveig, the traitor, smiled at Thork and scurried off, giving Medana a moue of apology over her shoulder.

Before Medana had a chance to scurry off herself, Thork dipped a ladle into a bucket of water he was carrying and took a long drink. Then he dumped the whole bucket over his head and shivered, whether from the cold or the delight, she wasn't sure. In truth, she sat frozen in place watching with fascination as droplets traced interesting paths down his neck, over the exposed section of his chest, before blazing a trail down, down, down.

He chuckled, then winked at her.

Mortified, Medana realized that she'd been practically drooling.

"Do you mind?" he asked, but sat down beside her on the stack of boards without waiting for her permission.

Regaining her senses, she quickly laid the parchment on her other side. "Thank you for assisting Solveig. You were of great help to her."

"I really do not know much, just what I have observed in passing. How long have they been working on this boat, anyway?"

"Three years."

"What?" He started to laugh.

"You may find mirth in our struggle, but believe me, it is the way we have accomplished everything here. If we do not know how to do something, we try, and try again, until we get it right."

He shook his head at her, as if she and her women were hopeless. They weren't.

"What was that you were reading?"

"Nothing."

"It could not have been nothing by the expression on your face and the guilty manner in which Solveig hurried away."

"Um . . . naught of importance," she said.

He tilted his head to the side. "You are blushing and your eyelids are fluttering. What is it?" He reached across her lap for the missive.

She did the only thing she could think of. She lifted her rump and slid the parchment under her.

He arched his brows with amusement and before she had a chance to rethink her position, saw his hand pressing against her chest, tipping her backward. While she found herself on her back on the ground behind the pile of planks, he grinned and picked up the parchment.

She scrambled to her feet and tried to grab the damning letter. "Give that to me. It's private."

He held it high over his head. "What is it? A love missive?" Suddenly, furrows of confusion deepened on his brow as he stared at something on the back of the parchment. "*What?*" He yelled out his question, the ice in his voice ominous.

She dusted off the backside of her braies, trying to give herself time to come up with an explanation. None came.

"This is my father's seal." He tapped the red wax and cut her with a sharp glance. Then he turned it over and read the short message.

For a brief flicker of a moment, she saw hurt in his green eyes, but it was immediately replaced with an anger that turned his skin livid from the neck upward to his forehead. "What . . . have . . . you . . . done?"

She started to back away.

"Answer me," he shouted, coming forward menacingly.

"I sent a letter. Naught to be in such a temper about." She stood her ground, deciding it was useless to keep backing up.

He came up to her, almost nose to nose. "Tell me."

"I . . . we . . . the women of Thrudr . . . asked for a little reward for taking such good care of you. Rather, putting up with your annoying ways."

"Reward?" He arched a brow.

"One hundred mancuses of gold for your release."

"Is that all? My father is a wealthy man. Why not ask for a thousand? Bloody hell! You could have asked for a longship, seeing as how it's taking you so long to build one yourself."

She wavered uncertainly for a moment. Was he jesting, or being sarcastic, or serious? "Should I have asked for more?"

"Aaarggh!"

That was dumb of me. Why would I ask for more if his father wouldn't even give a hundred for him?

"You lackbrained, lying witch. All this time you claimed regret for your women taking us captive. All this time you played the innocent. All this time

you promised to return us to Hedeby, no harm
done. Now I find out there was a reason behind
your madness the whole time." He grabbed her
by the upper arms, lifting her off the ground, and
shook her so hard her teeth clattered.

"I ne'er lied," she cried out. *Not precisely. Not at
first.* "We are pirates, Thork. 'Tis what we do to
sustain ourselves. In the end, asking for ransom
seemed the most reasonable thing to do, *for pirates.*"

He set her back on her feet and shoved her away
with disgust, wiping his palms on the thighs of
his braies, as if just touching her was repulsive.

Righting herself by leaning against the water
trough, she tried to calm her racing heart. But
when Thork glanced at her, then at the trough,
she moved away a short distance, not wanting to
tempt him into tossing her into the water, an idea
he clearly contemplated.

Meanwhile, her women were watching closely,
some of them gathering weapons. Thork's men
were approaching, too, weaponless, but formida-
ble and threatening just the same.

Despite their disparate numbers and weapons, she knew her women would lose any actual
battle. She needed to calm the stormy waters. "I
can explain," she said.

"I doubt that mightily."

"We can come up with a compromise that
works for both of us."

"I doubt that mightily," he repeated as he paced
back and forth, a short distance one way, then the
other. Sparks of displeasure shot out at her from
his fiery green eyes.

She wondered with what was probably hysterical irrelevance if he got those beautiful green eyes from his mother or his father. Most blond Vikings had blue eyes, and his mother was Saxon. But that was neither here nor there. "Let us sit down with a cup of ale. I am certain we can come to an understanding."

"The only understanding I want from you is the news that we are being taken off this island. Today!" He tilted his head in question, waiting for her compliance.

Not yet. "We need to come to terms first."

His face, which had already been flushed with anger, grew redder, and a vein in his forehead rose with prominence. "Terms? What makes you think you are in any position to dictate terms?" He inhaled deeply and exhaled, as if for patience. "Name one term."

Ooh, he is not going to like this. She ducked her head into her shoulders, bracing. "You must let us give you men the sleeping draught one more time so that—"

Thork never let her finish, but instead spun on his heels and began to stomp away, his men following close behind him.

"Hoist your sails, M'Lady Pirate," Thork called over his shoulder. "This Viking is declaring war."

CHAPTER TEN

**And then the other shoe . . . uh,
missive . . . dropped . . .**

All the rest of that day, up until dusk, Thork
and his men worked industriously, carrying wood, rush-filled mattresses, foodstuffs,
and other supplies up a path into the mountains
almost to the top of the valley's rim. They were
building on to and reinforcing a small longhouse
that was used by hunters.

Not only did the women hunters catch their
prey—boar, rabbits, deer, even the occasional
bear—but there was evidence in racks and a smoke-
house that they skinned and dried the animal
skins here, then preserved the meat in the smoke-
house. The primitive, thatch-roofed longhouse was
vacant now, probably until the fall when preparations would begin for the coming winter.

As the men came and went, the women watched
their movements with interest, but none stopped
them, or asked what they were about. Word must
have spread about Thork's fury over Medana's
letter and her suggestion that the men allow themselves to be put to sleep. Medana herself had the
good sense to make herself scarce. Otherwise, he

might very well have shifted his load of planks—
those ruined by the mistress of shipwrighting, which he was using to expand the hunters'
lodge—to her shoulders and steer her like a slave.

Thork worked like a demented person, not
wanting to give himself the chance to dwell on
what that fool woman had done to him . . . or
wanted to do. By her deeds, she'd put the final
torch to the funeral pyre of any relationship he
might have been able to salvage with his father.
How dare she? How bloody hell dare she?

Keep him! Every time Thork heard his father's
words in his head, his anger grew to the point
where he might very well explode, like overfer-
mented ale in a too-tight jug. Medana would pay,
and she would pay plenty for her misdeeds, and
not just by getting them off this island.

"Has Brokk had any luck yet?" Thork asked
Bolthor, who was chopping firewood for their
cook fire.

Bolthor straightened and pressed both hands
into the small of his back. "By the runes! I am getting too old for this. My back feels as if it's breaking, from naught but a little axe work."

Thork looked pointedly at the pile of kindling
and logs that was higher than the giant's head.
"Not such a little amount of axe work, my friend.
And ne'er let it be said that the man of the far-
famed battle-axe Head Splitter is getting too old."

"Your kind words are appreciated." Bolthor's one good eye gleamed with pride. "As for
Brokk . . . he has not yet returned, but I wager he
will succeed. The clever bugger! Before nightfall,
we will know how to get off this damn island."

Thork agreed.

"Katherine is going to kill me for leaving home in the first place. As if she gave me any choice! But several sennights on an island with two hundred women . . . that will be hard to explain, even though I am more than innocent."

"Me too," Thork admitted with some surprise. Three sennights was a long time for him to go without sex, and it made no difference if it was of the Onan variety or not. Some of the others had already succumbed, and more would join their ranks if they stayed here much longer. Even him.

"Mayhap we should have used the bratlings on this island from the beginning," Bolthor suggested, wiping the perspiration off his forehead with the back of a hairy forearm.

"Nay. Fierce as you might be in warfare, I know that you would not countenance harming children to gain your ends. None of us would."

"Some Viking men—Saxon and Frankish men, too, for that matter—wouldn't hesitate to chop off body parts of young hostages . . . fingers, toes, ears, and such until they gained their ends. They did it to your uncle Eirik when he was a lad. A finger, as I recall. Nigh drove mad your grandsire Thork, for whom you are named."

He and Bolthor looked at each other and their upper lips curled with distaste. Nay, that was not the way for Thork and his comrades-in-arms, and that did not make them weak, either, in his opinion. Instead, they'd commissioned Brokk, who'd made friends with the little ones here on the island, to use his game and storytelling talents to gain the information they needed.

Once they knew how to get off the island, they would leave, even if they had to tie the women to the rowing benches. And Thork would put their leader on the prow to lead the way.

In the meantime, Thork and his men would stay apart from the village in order to guarantee that any food or drink that passed their lips would not be tainted with the sleeping draught. Just to make sure, they would have their very own taster to ensure their safety. That would be Medana.

"I know, I know!" Brokk shouted gleefully as he ran into the clearing, coming to a skidding stop before Thork. Once all the men had gathered around the boy, and he managed to catch his breath, Brokk told them, "'Tis the pond. That is the means of getting off this island."

"Huh?" the men said as one.

"The pond on that slope above the village is actually a tide pool. When the tide is up, the pond fills. When the tide goes down, it empties to reveal a tunnel through the mountain. Once through the tunnel, there is a narrow strip of land connecting Thrudr to Small Island. Remember that day we climbed to the top of the mountain and we saw a tiny island in the distance. That is how they get the longship from here, out to the sea, and back again. It must all be done with the tides, at exactly the right time."

For a moment, there was silence as they all pondered this news.

"Now that I think on it, the pool water does have a salty flavor," Finn said. "I noticed when I bathed there a few days past."

A few days past? Hah! Finn bathed practically

every day . . . more than any man Thork knew.
And Vikings tended to bathe more than the average man, so that was saying a lot. In fact, some
said it was the reason why women from many
countries welcomed Viking men to their bed furs.
They stank less than their own countrymen. That
and their innate beauty and manliness, of course.
His lips twitched with humor.

But that was neither here nor there. Finn should
have realized that something was amiss there.
They all should have.

"And have you noticed that the women keep
steering us away from the pond?" Jostein pointed
out. "Especially toward nightfall."

"Here I thought it was because they could not
resist my virility." Jamie appeared genuinely annoyed, but then he saw them gaping at him with
disdain. "What? 'Twas a reasonable conclusion
for a braw laddie like me. How was I to know the
women were begging to take me in their beds,
rather than on the grass beside the pond, for such
a reason? Good thing I did not yield . . . what? I
did not totally yield. Just a wee bit of foresport."

"Lackwit!" Thork muttered.

"Methinks that would make a good saga. 'Braw
Lads Who Are Not So Braw,'" Bolthor said to Jamie.

"Methinks you would look good with two eye
patches," Jamie replied.

"I feel such a fool," Henry interjected. "I engaged in more than a wee bit of foresport with
Lilli on the grassy plot near the pond, three bloody
nights in a row, and I ne'er saw any evidence of a
tunnel."

"Now, Henry, men will be men when their enthusiasm is rising," Finn assured the Asian man. "When the carnal haze covers a man's eyes, all he can see are teats and arse. 'Tis a fact of life. The gods made us that way."

"Wise words, Finn!" Jamie was grinning like an idiot.

"That's so the mead haze that blinds a man's eyes when he is in the midst of *drukkinn* madness keeps him from seeing how unlovely are some teats and arses he brings to his bed furs." This from Jostein, who usually didn't have much of a sense of humor, let alone a droll one.

"That would be good fodder for a poem, too." Bolthor stared dreamily up into the sky as the verse mood came upon him. "Maids Get Prettier at Alehead Time."

"There are maids that are comely,
And those that are homely.
They have the same female bits,
Drawing men to them like nitwits.
Still, a pretty face and shapely form
Make it easier for a man to perform.
Except when in the midst of drukkinn *madness,*
Who can blame a man for being remiss?
Yea, betimes ale causes a man to go blind,
And in the morn, he does find
The beauty he bedded and did actually cajole
Is in fact a wart-nosed, ugly troll.

The moral of this saga; men should always pick
Their bedmates with a clear head."

"Aaarrgh!" Bolthor's sagas were getting worse and worse.

And, to his chagrin, Thork was beginning to understand so many previously confusing details about the women on the island, while his men sat about spouting nonsense and Bolthor found excuses to wax poetic. "Must be that the low tide occurs during the night at this time of the year," he mused with an abrupt change of subject.

Brokk nodded vigorously. "Yea, that is what the children say. After midnight when most of them are long abed."

Thork recalled immediately the night he had taken Medana for a walk and she had balked at going in the direction of the pond. She must have been laughing afterward with her women friends at the fool she had made of him.

"It really is a clever idea for a hiding place," Henry conceded. "I never would have imagined such, especially from women. Methinks I will have to reevaluate the craftiness of the female species."

"Hah! You are just now learning that women are born slyboots?" This from Jostein again. Thork once again wondered what had happened to him over the years to turn him bitter.

"Well, not so much clever, as fortunate," Thork commented. "No one could have dreamed up or built such a hidden tunnel. Lucky they were to stumble onto it. Yea, luck landed in their path and they pounced on the opportunity, I give them credit for that." Something occurred to him then. "That is why they want to use the sleeping draught again. If they are going to take us back to

Hedeby, they want us to be unaware of how they get in and out of Thrudr."

"So that we will not come back to lop off their heads?" Bolthor asked.

"That, or worse." Thork would take great pleasure in enacting his own revenge when the time was right. Mayhap he would take the Sea Scourge—better named Thork's Scourge, if you asked him—as his captive once he left the island. He could keep her chained in the hold of his longship when he went a-Viking or on a trading mission, or chained to his bedpost at night. Naked, of course. Or he could put her in a wooden cage and charge folks to come view a female pirate. Naked, of course. Or he could sell her in the slave marts. Naked, of course. A Viking female pirate in a sultan's harem would appeal to some Arab men. Or he could just kill her, and be done with it, naked or not. In any case, she would be sorry for crossing wills with him when he was done with her.

In fact, it was time to begin taking back control of his life. Time to get their "food taster."

An hour later, he and his men approached the village. They were all fully armed with makeshift lances made from tree limbs, slings with small rocks, and small knives and swords they'd pilfered here and there, not to mention the axe Bolthor had been using. Thork led the point of an arrow position, three men spread out on either side of him, and one behind.

Medana stood in the open double doorway of a large shed, taking a break from the shearing of a dozen sheep. The place smelled of damp wool, sheep dung, and human sweat, the air filled with the sound of bleating lambs and swearing women who struggled to hold on to the squirming beasts. Without forewarning, he walked up to the mistress of everything and announced, "Lady Medana, you are cordially invited to be our guest up on the mountain."

She jerked around with surprise, not having heard his approach for the baa-ing and cursing. Then she arched her brows at him. "Guest?"

"Yea. You know what a guest is. 'Tis what you called us men when you brought us to your island home. Now, you will come to *our* island home. As a guest."

"The hunters' hut? That is what you call home? Not so grand an estate for a fine jarl as yourself."

Did she dare show amusement at his expense? Oooh, he could scarce hold on to his temper. "The very same hunters' dwelling, which we have made ready for you."

"For me?" No longer amused, she had the good sense to grow fearful.

"Well, you and us." He waved a hand to encompass all his men.

She noticed the weapons they carried. "What do you want?"

"You. Well, to be precise, you as our guest."

She narrowed her luscious lavender eyes at him. "Thank you, but nay, I have too much work to do."

"Uh, mayhap I was not clear. You have no choice." He extended a hand to her—the free hand, his other having moved to the hilt of his pilfered sword. "Come peaceably, or come unpeaceably. Either way, you will come."

"Is that a threat?" she asked, extending two fingers up to her lips.

The shrill whistle—a call to arms—pierced the air, causing her women to pick up any weapon to hand, even long-bladed shears. But his men closed ranks, as planned, and he was able to grab the wily witch by the waist and toss her over his shoulder, arse upward, and begin to stomp away.

"Give the order for your women to stay back, or I swear, I will tell my men to kill them."

"You are outnumbered, you loathsome lout."

"Outnumbered we may be, but there will be a dozen female bodies on the ground afore you can whistle again."

"Stay!" She braced her hands on either side of his waist and raised her head to yell to the women. "No need for violence. I am just going to visit with Thork for a short time."

As short as I decide!

The women backed up, reluctantly, some of them calling out rude remarks to his men as they did so. His men rather liked the rude remarks, if their chuckles and grins were any indication.

"You can put me down now," she said to his back, having lowered her arms. Her lips were nigh about level with the crack of his behind. Not that he would mention it at the moment. He took inordinate pleasure knowing her breath brushed his arse.

"I'll put you down when I am ready, though you do weigh as much as a horse."

"You overbearing oaf!"

"I am exaggerating, of course. You are no more heavy than a big pony. Or yon cow."

"Very funny! Your shoulders are very bony, you know. I will no doubt have bruises on my stomach."

"Not to fear! I will smear ointment on your belly. Seems to me there was some fish oil in that bundle of household goods we brought up this afternoon."

"You are not putting smelly fish oil on me."

"Hah! You are already malodorous, m'lady. You smell like a sheep that has been wallowing in mud."

"You smell like a stinksome Viking."

"Ah, well, we will save water then by bathing together this night."

That caused her to go silent. He was silent, too, as the strain of carrying her up the inclined path began to take a toll. When he finally got to the clearing before the hunters' hut, he was panting for breath and at first didn't recognize the rustling sound as he lowered Medana to the ground. But then he did.

"What is that?" he asked.

"What?"

"That rustling sound when the placket of your braies rubbed against me as I lowered you."

"Oh. Naught of importance." She slapped a hand over the side flap while her eyelids went afluttering and color bloomed on her cheeks, even more than had been caused by blood rushing to her head when upside down.

He reached out a hand. "Show me."

"It's not my fault."

He arched his brows. Now that sounded like guilt, pure and simple.

She pulled a folded parchment out of her placket.

And he saw red stars dancing in front of his blazing eyes when he noticed the wax seal. "You wrote another letter!" he accused her.

"Nay, nay, nay!" she said, backing away from him. "'Tis just that there were apparently two responses to my one missive. The other was ... um, misplaced for a short time."

"Two responses from my father?" Thork couldn't help himself. A hope came unbidden in his sorry self that his father had changed his mind and was coming to rescue him. Not that Thork needed rescuing, not any longer—well, not ever—but it would be nice to know that his father cared, that he trusted him to have changed.

"Nay, not from your father. From"—she hesitated—"your mother."

At first he couldn't believe what he'd heard. In fact, he hit the side of his head with the heel of his hand to clear his ears. "My mother?"

She nodded.

He let out a growl that startled even himself, and Medana backed up more.

"Do not be alarmed, Thork. It is actually a very nice letter," Medana said, placing it on a wood stump that stood between them.

A nice letter? This ought to be good. He unfolded the parchment and began to read.

Dear Sea Scourge:

Pay no mind to my husband. The loathsome lout is too proud by half. Much as he loves his

*son, Tykir has been hurt by Thork's actions of
late. He will regret his hasty reply, in time.*

*I notice that you refer to Thork as a "loath-
some lout." How interesting! That has become
an endearment of sorts in my family. 'Tis what I
call my lackwit husband when he behaves badly,
as all Norsemen are wont to do without the
greater wisdom of their women to guide them.
Is it possible that . . . well, pay no heed to this
mother who wants only the best for her son.*

*I look forward to meeting you. Please send
me news of my son. Does he still grind his teeth
when upset? Is he sleeping well? Make sure he
changes his smallclothes regularly. Some men
need prodding in that regard. Well, Thork's problem is not changing smallclothes but not wearing any to begin with. Can you imagine? His
favorite sweetmeat is figs dipped in honey.*

*Give Thork my love and tell him that I miss
him sorely.*

Yours till we meet,
Lady Alinor of Dragonstead

Thork ground his teeth before he caught himself and would have been amused if he weren't
so outraged. His life had been on the slippery
slope to Muspell even since he had come into the
clutches of "the Sea Scourge."

His men came up then and noticed the parchment in his hands and the new anger flooding his
face.

"Uh-oh!" Alrek said.

"Someone is in big trouble," Jamie added, and looked pointedly at Medana.

"Take the wench and tie her to the bedpost," Thork ordered.

"You are a bullheaded, lackbrained dolt," Medana said. "Threats will gain you naught."

"Naked?" Jamie asked Thork hopefully.

Thork shrugged. "Why not?"

The struggling Medana fought the men's arms that attempted to restrain her, protesting to one and all that she was innocent. Mostly.

When her gaze locked with his, pleading, he was unmoved. "You will make a very nice prow head on my longship . . . the one previously called *Pirate Lady*, which I have decided to rename *Viking's Revenge*."

"You cannot take our longship. Without *Pirate Lady*, we could not survive," she protested.

"You should have thought of that afore taking us captive," he said. "I intend to put her out to sea on the morrow."

Her shrieks could no doubt be heard all the way to the village, or out to Small Island.

He did not care. Not even when she threatened, foolishly, "Wait 'til I tell your mother."

There was an ancient saying that revenge was a bitter brew not worth its aftertaste, but the old one who coined that phrase had clearly not been a Viking.

CHAPTER ELEVEN

Hunger games can be effective . . .

Medana was not naked, but she wished she were. By late that evening, tethered by ankle and bound hands to the bed frame in the tiny, dark, stuffy, windowless room, she was sickened by the smell of her own sweating body, and she'd been well on her way to needing a bath before this monstrous event had commenced.

Finally, after what must have been six or more hours of having been locked inside the addition to the hunters' longhouse, the door opened and Thork sauntered in, big as he bloody well pleased, carrying a torch that he stuck into a wall bracket.

"Good eventide, Mistress of Pirates."

"Go to Muspell, Master of Toads!"

"Tsk, tsk! Someone is not happy."

"You would not be happy, either, if you were bound and kept in a close space with no water or way to relieve yourself."

"Oh? You mean like the hold of a ship? Except you are spared the company of an angry bull."

She hadn't thought about that. Still . . .

The lout grinned as he approached her.

She eyed him warily. 'Twas always best for a

woman to be on her guard when a man grinned like that.

"Frigg's foot! It smells like a sheep pen in here," he exclaimed when he got closer.

"Well, Frigg's foot! You do not smell like a flower, either. Not that I care!" She noticed the stains on his tunic, and continued, "Your blood could gush out 'til you are bone dry inside and I would not lift a finger to help you. You could have blood seeping from your eyeballs, and nose, and ears, and I would just call others to come observe the wondrous sight."

"You are a heartless wench," he declared with amusement. "Fortunately, it is not my blood. I was skinning a boar that Jostein killed for our dinner." He pinched the fabric of his leather tunic to hold it away from his chest and examined the various stains with distaste.

"That is another thing. I have not eaten since breaking fast this morning. Do you intend to starve me, too?"

"There's an idea." He went down on one knee and began undoing the ties about her ankles. "Come," he said, taking hold of the rope about her wrists and tugging her off the bed.

"Where are we going?"

"To the pond. To bathe."

Uh-oh!

Noticing the expression of dismay on her face, he informed her, gleefully, "Your secrets are uncovered. We know all about the pond and the tunnel."

"Oh." She stared at him for a moment, trying to figure if this was an attempt to trick her. Eventually, she shrugged. He had been bound to find out sometime. "Then you know that the pond will be draining soon. Do you relish a mud bath?"

He chucked her under the chin. "Nay, though I would not mind seeing you swathed in slimy mud. I might even pelt you with a few mud balls."

She made a decidedly unfeminine snort of disgust.

And brute that he was, he just laughed.

"Do not be surprised if I pelt you right back."

"I would be surprised if you did not. Not to worry, though. I intend to be at the pond early enough to witness the draining. Whilst it's still deep enough for us to bathe."

She made another snorting sound of disgust, but inside she quailed at his reference to "us" in bathing.

He took the torch from the wall holder, tugging her along behind him by the tether. Almost tripping as she tried to keep up, she muttered under her breath.

"Did you just call me a loathsome lout? According to my mother, it must mean you are smitten with me." He batted his ridiculously long lashes at her. No doubt, he thought she was enthralled by his pretty green eyes.

"I'll never call you a loathsome lout again. Odious oaf better suits you, anyway."

He laughed.

She was getting tired of being a source of mirth for the loath— odious oaf.

Two of the men were sleeping on pallets about the main room of the hunters' hut. Outside in the clearing, a fire smoldered in the middle of a stone ring, over which a half-eaten suckling boar still spit and sputtered on its makeshift roasting spear.

Her stomach growled at the sight of several slices of blackened pork sitting on a wooden platter, along with chunks of manchet sopping up the juices.

"Wait," she said, digging in her heels. Leaning down, with her wrists still bound, she grabbed a piece of bread and wrapped it around a slice of blackened pork. Taking pity on her, he undid the rope binding her wrists and shoved her down to sit on a log that served as a bench before the fire. "Stay here until I return, wench," he said, and started back toward the longhouse.

"Do not call me wench. It's disrespectful."

"Stay here until I return, M'Lady Wench," he amended.

She made a scowly face to his back, but he paid her no never mind, just went off on some chore or other that was apparently more important than she was. How Medana had gone from captor to captive in such a short time was a puzzle to her. Actually, she did not consider herself a captive exactly since she had agreed to offer herself up in exchange for the longship, but everyone else seemed to.

In fact, his men, some standing guard and two of them sitting before the fire, watched her with interest.

Immediately, she gulped the food down, ravenously. The meat was undercooked inside and tough, but she did not care, so great was her hunger.

"You should not rile him so," advised Bolthor,

the giant who claimed to be a skald as well as a warrior.

"Who?"

"Thork." The answer came from Finn, the vain Viking, who was cleaning the dirt from under his fingernails with the tip of a short blade. If reports were true, Finn had been having incomplete sex with one of the women every night this sennight. Incomplete as in no seed entering the field where it needed to be planted. Thork's idea, she had heard.

"And why should I not rile him?" she asked, the question directed at both men.

"Your contacting his family was cruel, especially since the boy was on his way home to make peace with his father." Bolthor's craggy face was stern with admonition.

"Boy? Thork is hardly a boy."

"I have seen more than fifty winters. I fought aside his father at Ripon. Carried him from the battlefield, even. To me, Thork will always seem a boy."

Duly chastised, Medana kept her silence.

"Thork is a good boy who may have been wild in the past, and who may have made an irresponsible mistake or two," Bolthor continued.

"Wild is an understatement for what I have heard of his reputation."

Frowning at her interruption, Bolthor went on, "But the boy reached a bend in his life path. He took a vow to be good. And now it is all for naught. He may never reconcile with his father, and it is all your fault."

"That is unfair. You cannot—"

"Furthermore, you have probably lost him his bride," Finn interjected.

"Huh?"

"Thork had just picked out a bride in Hedeby afore you captured him," Finn explained. "Another effort on his part to please his father. Which was going too far, if you ask me. I would have bought the old man a longboat or several barrels of fine Frisian wine, for gods' sake. Not anchored myself to a wench to make amends."

"Dost forget Isobel?" Bolthor reminded Finn. "You would have wed the Saxon lady in a trice if she'd been willing."

"That was different," a disgruntled Finn replied. "And do not dare compose another saga about it, either."

"You do not like my poems?" Bolthor asked.

"That is beside the point," Finn evaded. "Mayhap I will be like you. Marry late in life and breed a horde of bratlings."

"I did not breed a horde. I was married as a young man and lost both my wife and two daughters. Katherine already had four children when we wed, and we had only one babe betwixt us."

"Five children? Five? Shouldn't you be home caring for your large family?" Medana asked.

"Yea, I should," Bolthor replied, slicing her a glare with his one good eye, "except someone waylaid us. Someone prevented Thork from going home and getting himself a bride. Someone delayed me from returning to my home and a wife who will have my head on a silver trencher."

So the brute is betrothed. Why that seemingly irrelevant fact should matter to her was a puzzle, but somehow it did. "'Twas not I who captured you men," she said defensively. Her excuse sounded weak even to her own ears, and both men arched their brows at her mincing words.

"'Twas you who demanded ransom for him," Finn pointed out.

To hide her discomfort and to feed her continuing hunger, she made quick work of eating another piece of bread and meat.

When she'd finished her short meal, Bolthor handed her a ladle of water. That, too, she gulped down. When he inquired, "More?" she nodded, and he refilled the ladle from a nearby rain barrel that they must have dragged up the mountain.

Bolthor and Finn watched her intently.

"What?" she asked.

"Are you tired, m'lady?" Finn asked.

What an odd question! "Nay. Why should I be tired? I have done naught but lie about for half a day." Something occurred to her. "You are worried that I might have tainted the drinking water with sleep herbs, aren't you?" She yawned widely and loudly. "Perchance I *am* ready for bed, after all. Suddenly, I feel like I could melt down to the ground in a puddle and sleep like a hibernating bear."

"Why are your eyes blinking?" Bolthor asked.

"Because she is lying," Thork said in passing. He'd already amassed a pile of clothing and linen cloths. To Finn, he asked, "Did you bring any soap?"

Finn nodded. "In the sack under the sleeping bench on the far side of the hearthstone."

Thork began to leave again, never once asking

if she needed anything. Like more food, or an opportunity to relieve herself. He did stop to address Bolthor, though. "Keep an eye on the sly witch lest she slip away afore I can torture her secrets out of her."

He'd already said he knew about the pond. What else did he think she was hiding? "You already know all my secrets," she griped.

"I doubt that mightily. Besides, I need to practice one of my best torture methods. Pulling out toenails with my teeth."

Bolthor and Finn barely stifled their chuckles.

She shivered inwardly but raised her chin. "Put your mouth anywhere near my feet and you will get a knee in your most precious body part. And I do not mean your winsome face."

Thork let out a hoot of laughter and tipped his head at her as if giving her credit for a good response. But what he said was "You like my face? And that is not even my best feature."

How he could make jest in the midst of such dire circumstances—dire for her, leastways—was indicative of his still wild character, in her opinion. Not that she would voice it, or that anyone would care. The grin on his too-pretty face boded ill for her. And, yea, the lout *was* pretty with that silky blond hair, sun-bronzed face, finely sculpted nose and chin, high cheekbones, and the best feature of all, his green eyes. Not that she took notice of such things. Usually.

Once he was gone, she remarked to no one in particular, "He really is a loathsome lout." And she did not mean that in a nice way.

chapter twelve

Rub-a-dub-dub, baby . . .

The level of the pond had already dropped the length of a big man's foot by the time Thork arrived there with Medana. Bolthor and Finn stood guard a short distance away, keeping an eye on the women warriors who attempted to approach.

"Tell your women to go back. Tell them you are safe," he demanded.

"Am I safe?"

He shrugged. "As safe as you can be, as long as you obey orders."

"You seem to be under the mistaken notion that you are in charge. This is our island."

"Believe me, M'Lady Pirate, I *am* in charge. And you would do best not to rile me further."

"Blather, blather, blather," she muttered.

"What did you say?"

"Nothing." She turned to address the dozen or so worried women who hovered a short distance away. "Go back to the village. Take them back, Gudron. All will be aright by morning."

"An optimist, are you?" Thork inquired once they were alone again.

"A realist. I cannot see how keeping me for an extended time would be to your advantage."

"Do you not?"

They'd arrived at the pond, and Thork dropped his pile to the ground. While he began to remove his belt, he asked, "How long does it take for the pond to drain?"

"About two hours. At its full depth, it is the height of four men, standing atop each other, feet to shoulders. About four fathoms. And about thirty paces across, if one could walk on water, as you can see."

Thork studied the steep-sided pond as he began to disrobe. Because the pool was not slanted along the sides, the depth was the same throughout. Thork figured that he would have more than an hour of a good depth for swimming . . . or bathing.

"What are you doing?" She gaped at him.

"Taking off my braies." He'd already toed off his boots and pulled his tunic over his head. "It defeats the purpose of bathing if one does so fully clothed. Besides, I need a clean tunic and braies if I want to survive my own stink. Same goes for you, by the by."

She was staring at a particular part of his body and therefore didn't respond, at first.

"That . . . that . . ." she sputtered, pointing to his cock, bared now that he'd shimmied out of his braies; it was already halfway enthusiastic. Much more staring by her, and he would be into a full-blown cockstand.

"Do not take it personally. My fifth limb salutes at the least thing. Once, I got aroused watching a bowl of leavened dough rise. Resembled a woman's buttock, it did."

He could see her by the full moon, but not too clearly. He would bet his best sword she was blushing, though.

Abruptly, she spun on her heels, away from him, gazing at nothing in particular.

"Take off your garments, Medana, whilst the water level is still high."

"Um, methinks I will bathe later."

"Um, methinks you will bathe now. Fully clothed or naked, I care not, but you will be in that pond forthwith."

"Can you not leave me my dignity?"

"Like you left me mine? I seem to recall male body parts being held over a ship's rail to piss."

She waved a hand airily. "Men are not so squeamish about such things."

"Mayhap so, but a man's male part has difficulty distinguishing between sex and pissing when a female hand is holding it. Lots of cock-stands were visible during the ship's sailing, you must admit."

She looked at him as if he'd said something particularly vulgar. Hah! If she thought that was vulgar . . . Enough! Picking her up from behind, by the waist, he tossed her into the pond and jumped in after her.

The water was cool and refreshing, and, yea, slightly salty. When he rose to the surface and shook his hair off his face, he observed Medana struggling, her arms flailing as she tried to swim toward the edge.

"Can you not swim? A pirate who cannot

swim?" He pulled her up, and her arms instinctively wrapped around his neck. Her hair was wet and stringing about her face, her garments a sodden mess.

"Yea, I can swim, you loathsome lout, but not with the weight of wet clothing and boots to pull me down."

"You called me a loathsome lout," he pointed out, meanwhile liking the feel of the slim woman in his arms. A particular body part liked her particular body part as well, as evidenced by a continual rising of enthusiasm that pressed against her thighs. Thus far, she hadn't taken note of that fact; when she did, she would probably have a screaming fit. "Must be you like me, as my mother inferred."

"Like? Like? At this moment, my sentiments are just the opposite, you . . . you . . ."

"Odious oaf?" he offered, and pushed her back against the far side of the pond and extended her arms to each side to hold her up. He didn't hear her response because he'd ducked under water and yanked off one of her half boots, then the other, not an easy feat when she was attempting to kick him. He rose to the surface, gave her a quick kiss—why, he had no idea; because he could, he supposed, or mayhap just to halt her harangue—and went under again where he commenced to tug down her braies, baring her lower body, which he could unfortunately not see. He would later, though, he promised himself. Just because he knew it would annoy her. Or so he told himself.

"You took off my braies and smallclothes, both

of them at once," she charged, as if he didn't know what he had done.

"Yea, a talented fellow I am at removing female clothes, though I cannot say I have taken breeches off a woman afore."

"That's not what I meant."

"I know what you meant," and before she could fathom his next step, he grabbed the hem of her tunic and raised it up and over her head and off her arms. Arms that immediately returned by necessity to the pond's edge to maintain her balance or risk sinking under water again.

Which left her breasts and upper body exposed to his scrutiny.

And scrutinize her, he did.

Her breasts were not too big, and not too small. Just right. Round like plump peaches, with tiny berry nipples. He fancied small nipples, truth to tell, no doubt due to the time he got a rash from being with a woman who had nipples the size of candle stubs. Not that the two things were related, but still, men tended to make associations like that. And there was not a bit of sag in Medana's breasts, considering her age, though that might be because of her position, arms stretched out, causing her back to arch.

She was beautiful. And it wasn't just her breasts.

How could he have not noticed afore? Oh, he'd not considered her witch ugly, but on the other hand, he would not have considered her more than passable in appearance, especially for a female so long in the tooth, prone to wearing men's garments. Even with her hair plastered about her face and the frowning expression she cast his way, even with the sheep smell that still lingered on her body, she was the most tempting morsel of femininity he'd viewed in a long time. If ever.

And that was alarming.

"Lecherous lout!" she said, noticing his regard, and turned, trying to lever her arms and crawl up the side.

Which gave him a view of her arse. Two rounded globes of white ivory, like an inverted heart, the point being her narrow waist.

A sharp jab of lust shot through his body.

She glanced back at him over her shoulder and couldn't help but see what he was admiring. Which caused her to scramble even more to get away from him.

"Nay, nay, nay!" he said with a joyous laugh. "You are not getting away from me so easily." She was out of the water up to her knees and attempting to crawl forward, but he grabbed her legs and pulled sharply, causing them both to fall backward and into the pond. He heard Bolthor and Finn laughing in the distance.

He still had a hold on her, by the waist now, when they both came up in the center of the pond.

She was sputtering and spitting out water. So it took a moment for her to realize that they were treading water, front to front. Her breasts pressed against his shoulders. His cock was a lance between her knees. For a moment, he feared that he might shoot his enthusiasm out like an untried youthling, unable to control his passions.

He motioned to Bolthor and Finn to make themselves scarce. Medana would not enjoy an audience to her nudity, or what he was contemplating. The two men laughed as they moved away.

He knew the instant she realized how close he was, and how aroused, because her eyes widened, her wantonly full lips parted, and her entire body stiffened. Quickly, he cupped her buttocks with his big hands and drew her flush against his body, giving her no means of escape.

She gasped.

He gasped.

Then he smiled and nipped at her lower lip, pulling back quickly before she did more than nip him back with her own teeth.

"It feels good, doesn't it?" he suggested against her ear as he moved his shoulders back and forth so his collarbone would brush against her nipples.

"It does not feel good," she protested, and tried to wriggle out of his grasp, which only caused her nipples to get more abraded.

To his immense satisfaction, he noticed her eyelashes fluttering. She lied. It did feel good to her.

Giving her no time to contemplate his next move, he brought his mouth to hers, slanting his lips this way and that, creating a moist, warm path of carnal pleasure. At first his kiss was soft and coaxing, but when he deepened the kiss, demanding more, she moaned softly, giving him the opportunity to slip his tongue inside her mouth and, pray gods she would not bite off the tip.

She didn't. Instead, she moaned again and opened wider.

Not one to waste an opportunity, Thork thrust deeply, in and out. Wet sounds of arousal were created by both of them. At first, Medana was tentative in the deep kissing, as if unfamiliar with that carnal exercise, but soon she was participating fully, giving as good as she got.

His manpart was getting equal exercise, between the tight space between her lower thighs. It wanted desperately to be somewhere else, up higher, and tighter.

He drew away slightly to look at Medana. She stared back at him, as if stunned. "What are you doing to me?"

"You know what I am doing, sweetling. You are no virgin."

He realized his mistake immediately, even before she flinched as if he'd struck her, and said, "That was crass, even for an ass such as you."

She'd claimed to have been raped. Perchance that had been her only sexual experience. Under those circumstances, his remark *had* been crass. Cruel, even.

"I apologize, Medana," he said as quickly as he could get the words out.

She turned away when he attempted to kiss her again. Opportunity lost! For the moment. He hadn't even touched her breasts. Yet. Or other intriguing body parts. But he would. A seasoned warrior knew when to retreat and when to advance. This was retreating time.

He reached a long arm over to grab a square of hard soap sitting on the pile of garments and sundry items he'd brought with them. It was not the harsh soap made of lye and wood ashes suitable for laundry, but a unique scented soap perfected by women of Thrudr for sale in the markets of Hedeby, Birka, Kaupang, and Jorvik. This particular one smelled like honey. Others were flower, fruit, pine, oats, even butter scented.

"Come," he said, taking her hand and beginning to swim away from the edge. It was then he noticed that, rising in the middle from the already receding waters of the pond, was a large, flat boulder. "You could have told me of the hazard, Medana," he admonished. "'Tis fortunate that I did not dive in and crack my head open."

"Yea, 'tis fortunate," she replied.

"That was a poor jest."

"What makes you think I am jesting?"

"Sarcasm, then. Not a trait best suited to women."

"Blather, blather, blather," she said, and swam away from him, thus proving that she could, in fact, swim. And swim well.

He placed the soap on the boulder and followed her lead. Swimming under water as long as his leather lungs would hold, he burst up several times like a sea dolphin, spurting water. He saw her smile one of those times, and found himself pleased that she was no longer offended by his ill-chosen words. Not that she had not engaged his wrath aplenty in many regards, but stabbing her in such a vulnerable spot was unconscionable. What would his mother think? *My mother! I am nude with a woman who is nude, and I am thinking about my mother. Truly, Mother is becoming a thorn in my conscience.* He was the one smiling now.

The water was a cool contrast to the warm night air. Enjoyable.

Floating on his back, he stared up at the clear, starry skies. "Have you ever studied the stars, Medana?"

"Not really," she answered, treading water some distance away.

"There was an old seaman that worked my father's trading ships for years, and he told me and my brothers how sailors used the stars to navigate their ships. But mostly, my brothers and I would lie in the fields at night and pick out various figures in the sky. A bear. A fox. A fish. What seemed to be a milky pathway. A woman's arse."

"Oh, you!" she said, and swatted water at him. "Little boylings do not think of such things."

"You would be surprised. Young males, with no access to the real thing, can conjure up plenty. Like randy dogs ready to hump the nearest leg, or tree, or any standing object. When I was twelve, young Brokk's age, I was already rearing at the bridle to try my charms on whichever maid was willing."

"And I'll bet there were plenty." She leaned back to float as well, but when she realized how visible her breasts and nether hair would be to a lecherous fool such as himself, she swam over to the boulder instead, and holding on, she craned her neck upward.

"Now see what you have done! All I can see is a male body part. You put that wicked idea in my head." She was smiling as she spoke, and he rather liked her teasing him.

"Is it big? The male part in the skies? If so, it must be mine."

"Tsk, tsk, tsk!" she said, still with a smile in her voice. "You mentioned your brothers. How many do you have? And are there sisters, as well?"

"I am the oldest of four brothers. No sisters."

"I have only brothers, too, but brutes they are, always had been. We were never close. Are you close to your brothers? Do you see them often?"

He swam over to lean against the boulder beside her. But then he picked up the soap, lathered his head and face and shoulder, and went down deep to rinse off his upper body and soap the lower regions, front and back. It would be nice if Medana did it for him, but he knew enough about women to recognize that it was too soon. He came spurting up beside her and began to soap her hair before she had a chance to protest, which she did.

"I can do it myself. Stop that."

Not only had he soaped her long tresses but he was working the soap into her shoulders and neck, massaging the tight muscles. She reeked of honey, in a good way. "I know you can," he replied huskily, "but I can do it better."

"Be that as it may . . ." She grabbed the soap out of his hands and went off a short distance to take care of her own cleansing habits. Unfortunately, he was unable to see clearly, despite the full moon. Mostly, she did her soaping under the water.

When she returned with her hair finger combed behind her ears, she set the soap on the boulder and said, "I asked about your family. The fact that you have been gone so long . . . Were there problems before you left home all those years ago?"

He shook his head. "We were a close family. Not just my brothers and me, but my father and mother, too. I had a good home, growing up. Now that I am older, I realize that I took for granted what many children do not have." He shrugged. "I have not seen my mother and father for five years, and because of the estrangement from my father, there has been little contact with my brothers, as well."

"What went wrong?"

"Nothing went wrong, precisely. My reputation for being wild was earned long before I left home, if you must know. My mother, Lady Alinor, claims I came stomping out of the womb ready to raise trouble. Mischief was my motto. And, truth to tell, my father was said to be a bit wild himself afore he married, so he has no right to condemn my wicked ways. Still, I had decided to reform and was going back to Dragonstead when . . ." He let his words trail off.

"When you were captured by female pirates," she finished for him.

"As you say." He was deep in thought for a long moment as memories assailed him. "Starri and I were the closest, him being only two years younger. Starri most resembles my mother with his red hair and freckles. Guthrom came six years after Starri and is eight years younger than me; and then Selik was not born for another four years; so there is a twelve-year difference in our ages. Selik was always trying to keep up with the rest of us, even as a toddler scarce out of his swaddling clothes. He is still at home, I believe."

"And the others . . . where are they?"

"Last I heard, Starri was handling my father's merchant vessels with a base in Jorvik, whilst Guthrom was soldiering in the king's service. Starri married young, to the daughter of a neighboring jarl. Dagne was her name, and Starri was smitten from the first time he saw her. She died two years past of a wasting disease. Supposedly, he still grieves mightily and vows ne'er to wed again." He glanced over at Medana, wondering why he was talking so much of personal things he usually kept hidden. Well, not hidden. Just not brought out to examine like a running sore.

She stared back at him. "Thork, you need to go home. You need to make amends with your father. Methinks your brother Starri needs you. And mayhap you need him, too."

Way too perceptive the wench was! "That is precisely what I intended to do," he reminded her.

"Oh! Do not place all the blame on me. You have had five years to return."

"Well, too late now."

"It is ne'er too late."

He shrugged. "For now, we must get out of this water before we are shriveled up into an old codger and an old crone. Unless . . ." He let his words trail off.

"Unless *what*?" she asked suspiciously.

"Unless you would let me lick your skin to see if it is as honey sweet as it smells."

"Lick yourself. You used the same soap."

"You are cruel, wench. Cruel."

She smiled again, and he was coming to love her smile. Nay, not love. Appreciate.

"Before we go, Thork"—she swallowed visibly as if to gain courage—"you mentioned taking our longship. You cannot do that. Without *Pirate Lady*, we cannot survive here."

"Then return to your various homelands."

She shook her head. "I would face trial by Alth-ing and death, for a certainty. But I am not con-

cerned about just myself. There are thralls here
who have fled from cruel masters. Wives who
could no longer bear their husbands' vicious
second and third wives, not to mention concubines. Orphans and the disgraced. Women who
no longer fit in regular society . . . if they ever did."

"You should have thought of that . . ."

She put up a halting hand. "I need no more re-
minders of what I have done or not, as the case
may be. Please, Thork, is there naught I can do to
change your mind?"

Oooh, she should not have said that. Not when
he was nude, and she nude, and she had those
pretty little nipples, and his staff was the size of
a lance, and she had seen a male part in the skies,
and he had been celibate for three whole sennights. It would be conniving, not chivalrous, his
mother would say. But his mother was not here.
And chivalry be damned! Thork was tired of
trying to be good.

"If you shared my bed, as a woman, I might be
willing to negotiate."

Medana surprised the spit out of him by not
even hesitating to answer, "Agreed!"

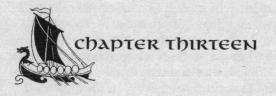

CHAPTER THIRTEEN

**It wasn't the tunnel of love, but
it might lead there . . .**

Thork sat on the grassy area beside the pond for several hours with Bolthor, Jamie, Jostein, Alrek, and Finn, passing a skin of mead betwixt them.

Thork had taken a charmingly embarrassed Medana back to the hunters' hut wearing naught but a thin chemise, and left her there after awakening Brokk and telling him to guard her locked door. She'd gazed at him with confusion before he left, and no wonder. After she'd agreed to spread her thighs for him, he'd put her to bed, alone. He would have joined her there, gladly, but he feared what he might start and be unable to complete to his satisfaction, or hers, when he had so much to do yet tonight.

"Later," he had promised her with a quick kiss.

"Mayhap," she'd responded grumpily, but she'd licked her full lips as if to get his taste. He took that for a good sign.

"It really is an amazing feat of nature, is it not?" Jostein commented, calling Thork back to the present.

"I have ne'er seen such in all my travels," Jamie added. "Leastways, none that were not manmade like those of the ancient Romans."

"Should we go through tonight and examine it further?" Jostein suggested.

"Yea!" they all agreed enthusiastically.

'Twould be an adventure of sorts, Thork thought. "Can you go get two more torches, Alrek?"

Alrek nodded and was off.

"How do they get the longship down to the base of the pond and through the tunnel, out to sea?" This from Bolthor, who was casting his head one way and another, trying to figure out how it could be done.

"Henry says that they use a sledge to get the longship over to the pond. Then they tip the boat downward a bit until one end is sitting atop the boulder, facing the tunnel, with the back end still on the ground. With fifteen women on each side, they carry it through the tunnel. Longships are not all that heavy, as we know."

They all gaped at Jamie after he gave this lengthy explanation.

"How in bloody hell did Henry learn all this when we only found out about the pond and the tunnel this afternoon?"

"Pfff! Where do you think?" Jamie grinned. "That's where he is right now. The lucky sod! Off tupping the Lilli pad again!"

"You are just jealous," said Alrek, who'd returned with two lit torches.

Thork could not help but notice the scorch marks on Alrek's tunic. The clumsy halfwit! Had he not realized that he could have brought the torches here to be lit with the one already blazing from its post stuck in the ground?

"Henry best be careful or there will be slant-eyed babes aplenty on this island come spring," Thork said, taking another long draw on the wine bag.

"Just one babe," Alrek said. "Lilli is the only one who's gained his fancy."

"That is even worse. The lackwit will be wanting to stay. That is how women trap men all the time. Make them think they are the one and only virile man in the world. Boost their conceits 'til they start thinking their shit is gold. Then they . . ." Jostein's words trailed off when he saw that they were all staring at him. "I am just saying," he grumbled.

"We'll wait a little while longer, until the water is all out and through the tunnel, but it will be muddy."

"I just cleaned my boots," Finn whined.

"I'd rather keep mine on," Bolthor said. "There are no doubt rocks and mayhap even snakes."

"I guess I could clean my boots again on the morrow," Finn said.

"Do we need to worry about the women blocking the tunnel after us, or stealing their leader back?" Alrek wondered.

"Are you thinking they could move yon boulder?" Jamie scoffed.

"Women are wily creatures. You ne'er know what they can do when they set their minds to it," said Jostein, the cynic.

"Besides, some of them are witches and could no doubt move it with magic," Jamie added with a mischievous glint. He was teasing Alrek, who tended to believe everything he was told.

"The boulder will not be moved," Thork said with finality, "but there is still the question of whether the women warriors will storm the hunters' hut to rescue their leader whilst we are gone, and mayhap harm Brokk in the process." Thork pondered the question a moment. "Nay, I think they realize by now that their fate is in our hands, whether it be today or in the future. Their only recourse now is to work with us."

"Besides, Brokk is twelve years old, almost a man," Bolthor interjected. "We do not give him enough credit for defending himself."

That was probably true. Many a Viking youthling was considered an adult by that age and was allowed to go a-Viking. But not fight alone against a horde of enraged women.

"There is a more important issue to the women than rescuing their leader. They will not want to give up their longship," Jamie pointed out.

"They will have to," Thork said. Even though he'd inferred to Medana that they would negotiate that point, there was no way Thork and his comrades could get back to Hedeby without the vessel. Whether they would return it to the women . . . that was the question.

A short time later, they were through the tunnel, which was really not that long—about ten ship lengths—and on to the narrow strip of land that connected Thrudr to Small Island. The tide was down and the waves were breaking far out to sea.

They stood in a huddle, staring back at the way they'd come, up, up, up to the top of the steep mountainside. There was naught but trees right down to the shore that was a scree of rocks. He could see how uninviting this island would seem to any passing seafarers, and why they might stop at Small Island for water without daring an exploration of the larger island.

"I am going up to the top of Thrudr again to study the surroundings, now that I am better informed," Thork said. "And if the gods are with us, we will be taking the longship out to sea tomorrow night."

"Not tomorrow night," Bolthor proclaimed. "Big storm coming tomorrow night."

"Bolthor! How can you say that? Look at those stars. Clear skies at night, sun on the morrow."

Bolthor shrugged. "Storm tomorrow night. You will see."

"Do you feel it in your bones?" Jostein asked snidely.

"Nay, I feel it in my missing eyeball."

Thork did not know if Bolthor was jesting or not. No one liked to question him about his missing eyeball.

"Well, should we go back now or go on to Small Island to explore more?"

They turned as one to look at the two women standing at the end of the narrow connecting lane. They'd been aware of them all along. An old crone with hair like a gray haystack, with a dog the size of a small bear barking at her side. And a somewhat younger crone who was brandishing a large wooden pitchfork.

"Not tonight," Thork decided. He was not in the mood for killing women, and those two looked like they were geared up to fight to the end.

When they returned to the pond and then used the water trough he'd built for the new shipbuilding project to wash off their mud, Thork said, "We will take turns guarding the hunters' longhut, two at a time. Alrek and Jamie, you two go first. In a few hours, Jostein and Finn can take over. Bolthor, you can rest after all the woodcutting you did today. We will make plans in the morning for how to proceed."

"And where are you off to now?" Jamie asked Thork.

"To bed."

There wasn't one single person who thought he had sleep in mind.

Where's a prince when Sleeping Beauty needs a wake-up call? . . .

Medana knew she'd shocked Thork when she'd agreed so quickly to his proposal that she share his bed furs in return for saving their longship. What he didn't realize was that she'd had time to ponder their dilemma the whole time the men had been on her island, knowing that eventually the men would take back the reins of power and with it the women's only means of survival, their only connection to the outside world. A longship.

And, really, it was no great sacrifice to Medana. She'd been tupped before. There would probably be pain, but only for a short time, if her experience with Ulfr was any indication. She'd suffered worse when she cut her thumb nigh to the bone with an axe the first winter they were in exile.

An invasion of her body. A sharp, piercing pinch. A grunt. And it would be over.

More difficult to endure would be the indignity of the act. But then she'd swum in the nude with Thork a short time ago, and that was not so bad. In fact, she'd rather enjoyed herself. The rogue could be charming when he set his mind to it. Not that she was taken in by that false seduction. She was no feckless maid easily swayed by false wooing.

But where was he now? She lay stiff as a board on the rush-filled mattress, waiting for him to come. But he did not. What if he'd changed his mind? Would she care? Of course she would care. It would mean that he was backing out of their arrangement. And the longship would be lost.

Medana yawned and rolled over, then back again, the straw rustling under her. She tossed off the linen blanket and stared up at the crude ceiling. Now that the men had added on to the hunters' hut, mayhap she could find a better use for this region of Thrudr. She could set up one of the women as a goatherder here. Goats liked mountainous terrain and needed little care. They could subsist on forest pannage, like acorns and wild fruits. Plus their milk made wonderful cheese, as Olga had already demonstrated.

Or the boys, as they grew older, might make a place apart from the women, but that was another problem altogether . . . what to do with the boylings as they grew into youthlings and then adult men. Would they stay on the island or want to move away? She could send them to Agnis, she supposed, to be trained as merchants.

Or mayhap she could use the longhut as her

own private retreat. Nay, that would be selfish of her. Why should she have the luxury of her own home, apart from the others?

How about making the place into a romantic spot where the women could bring men to couple. Oh, good gods! A breeding hut? That would be encouraging the women to capture more men. Soon the island would be overrun with children . . . and men. Goats would be better.

Then, too, Bolthor had noticed a problem with some of the laying hens. Apparently, aside from being a warrior and a skald, he was also a chicken farmer. Before he'd married his wife, Katherine, she had an estate, Wickshire Manor in Northumbria, that was noted for its poultry. Chickens still flourished there today. Hard to picture a big, brawny Viking tending chickens, but then Norsemen were known to adapt to all circumstances. Even being stranded on an island by female pirates. In Bolthor's opinion, they should kill all the existing poultry for food and start anew with a new flock come autumn. Which would mean going a-Viking sometime soon, or going to market to purchase the stock.

So many decisions to be made!

Eventually, Medana fell asleep under the weight of her roiling thoughts. And her dreams were troubled, too. They took her back to a time long ago before fear and caution became her everyday bywords. She was a girling, sitting in a field of wildflowers, watching the dancing of various butterflies when a tall figure approached. Instead of being afraid, she rose to her feet and then ran as fast as her little legs would carry her, jumping up into a pair of warm arms that held her close. It wasn't her father, surely, or one of her older brothers. Nay, must be a stranger.

It was no wonder then that she awakened slowly to realize that she was pressed willingly up against a warm body that held her close, her face nuzzling the crook of his neck. One of her hands rested on the fine hairs of his chest, under which his heart beat strongly.

She should have been intimidated, but she was not. How odd! Mayhap this was still a dream.

"Wake up, my beautiful slugabed," he murmured, and kissed the top of her head.

Not a dream!

"Is it time to get up?" She barely restrained herself from pressing her lips against his neck. Or worse yet, to lick his skin. To see if it carried the salt flavor of the pond, she told herself. "Is it morning already?" With no windows, the room was very dark. Still, through the rough chinking in the walls, a grayish light appeared.

"Almost dawn. In about an hour. But, nay, 'tis not time to get up yet. 'Tis time for . . . something else."

Ah, the coupling I agreed to. She rolled over on her back. "Shall I lift my chemise so you can do it?"

"Do what?" He was leaning over her. She could feel his breath against her face, coated with the not-unpleasant scent of mead.

"The swiving."

He leaned forward and buried his face on the pillow beside her head. She could feel his chest heaving.

"Are you laughing at me?"

" 'Tis hard not to. Have you resigned yourself to being the mistress of martyrdom tonight?"

"What if I have?" she asked, not liking to be the subject of his mirth. When she attempted to shove him away, he just levered his elbows to either side of her shoulders and settled his heavy body atop hers.

Oddly, he did not feel too heavy. And, despite the night air that was cool, he was warm. Even hot. Like an erotic blanket, she thought, and almost giggled at her fancifulness.

"Are you smiling, Medana?"

Surely, he could not see in the darkness. She immediately forced her lips into a tight line. "Of course not. What have I to smile about, you big oaf? You are crushing me."

"Am I?" he asked, but did not move.

It was then that she realized he was nude. Completely. Not that she wore much clothing. Just the thin chemise he'd handed her down at the pond. She wouldn't move then if he paid her a king's treasure, not wanting to call attention to any particular body parts, especially the one jabbing at her thigh.

"Just so you know, Medana, no martyrdom will I allow you. You will enjoy the bedsport as much as I will."

She rolled her eyes. How like a man! "Get on with it then. Much work awaits me in the morn."

"I have news for you, sweetling. The only thing you will be doing in the morning is what I allow you to do."

Sweetling? He calls me sweetling? Is this another ploy on his part? "But I thought . . . you clodpole! We had a bargain."

"And it is time you fulfill your part of that bargain."

Must I? Mayhap if I scrunch my eyes closed tight and think of fresh honey on warm oatcakes, or the smell of new-mown hay, or a warm longhouse on a cold winter's night, it will not be so bad. "What should I do?"

"Stop talking, for one thing." When she stiffened with affront, he added, "For now. I have other plans for your mouth."

She was about to speak, despite his admonition not to, when he laid his lips over her, turning this way and that until they were perfectly aligned. The most disconcerting thing was that his mouth was open. And wet. And he spread that wetness to her lips, especially when he dipped his tongue inside her mouth, then used her moistness combined with his to lick a path over her lips.

Lick, press, thrust, suck, lick, press, thrust, suck . . .

Suck? When did I open her mouth so wide that he could engage my tongue?

She tried to focus on any one enticing thing he did, but he kept changing tactics. Hard to concentrate when so much was happening at once. "Wait, wait, wait," she tried to say.

But he was thrusting his tongue deep into her mouth. Then drawing back. In again. Then back. Over and over. It should have been revolting to her. She should be gagging. Instead, her arms crept about his bare, broad shoulders, attempting to draw him closer. She sensed his muscles flexing at her touch. Was that good or bad? Her breasts felt fuller and needful of touch . . . not an itch exactly, more like a yearning, which she attempted to assuage by arching her body. It was not enough. Nor did it satisfy the private place between her legs that seemed to throb.

But wait. He was doing something else now. The slyboots! His mouth was at her ear, where he was blowing, for Asgard's sake! Blowing, and sticking the tip of his wet tongue inside. Every fine hair on her body stood up and waved. 'Twas as if there was a direct line between her ear, her nipples, and the nether throbbing.

She moaned, she could not help herself.

He chuckled and said against her sensitized ear, "Like that, do you, Medana?" She would have been irritated at his question, except his voice was huskier than usual, as if he, too, were aroused.

Before she knew what he was about, he rolled over onto his back with her atop him. She struggled to maintain her balance and found herself arched on extended arms with her breasts nestled against his chest and she was half kneeling, half reclining over him, her woman place spread wide against his belly. This position gave him freedom to let his hands roam, and roam they did while he tried to distract her with more deep kisses. Actually, she might have been the one deep kissing him. Hard to tell when she was trying to keep track of where his hands strayed.

His palms caressed her back from shoulders to thighs, long sweeping forays, followed by deep massages of muscles. Despite the darkness, he was learning her body by touch alone. A carnal exploration, that's what it was.

But then his hands were between them, lifting her breasts from underneath, his thumbs strumming the nipples into hard points. Where they had been aching before, they were now throbbing with the same rhythm going on down below in her woman place. The whole time he was kissing her mindless. And she could swear he was smiling as he kissed her. Smile kisses.

She drew back slightly, and although she could not see his face clearly, she asked, "Are you smiling whilst you stick your tongue down my throat?"

"Yes. Because I am happy? Because I am enjoying myself? You should be smiling, too, or else I am not doing my part well enough."

"That is the most ridiculous thing I have ever heard." But inside she was beginning to wonder. Her women yearned for bedsport, mostly for the getting of children. Leastways, that's what she'd always thought. Except for the few with wanton tendencies, sex was a duty, not a sport to be enjoyed. But now . . .

"You were smiling before. I know you were." He was back to the long caresses of her back and shoulders and breasts.

"That's because I was likening you to a warm blanket when you plopped your body over me like a big horse."

He chuckled. "Most men would not mind being likened to a horse, especially certain parts."

"Oh, you! That is not what I meant." She tugged at his wrists then because his fingers were playing a new game with her breasts. Tugging on the nipples, even pinching them, and twirling them between a thumb and forefinger. "Stop that!"

"Why?" His big palms were squeezing her breasts now, almost like Cook when she kneaded bread.

Do not smile, Medana. Whatever you do, do not smile. "Because it makes me feel tingly, all over," she said before she could bite her fool tongue.

"Tingly is good." He chuckled.

"See. You are laughing again. Laughter and sex do not go together. Must be this is a perversion."

"If it is, it is a good perversion. You are thinking too much, Medana."

But then she could not think anymore because he cupped her buttocks with his big hands and moved her body upward so that her breasts dangled above his face. She had not even known her breasts could dangle, small as they were. Before she could question what he was about, he took one breast into his mouth, cloth and all, and began to suckle her. Deep, hard, rhythmic.

To her mortification, if she'd been capable of such coherent thought, her lower body began to buck against his belly, and she let out a long, keening moan. Blood drained from her head and shot to all her extremities and various intriguing spots in between. Was it pleasure or was it pain? She was not sure. Pleasure-pain, she decided.

When it was over, whatever it was, she found herself splatted out over his body—a body whose manpart was still hard and pressed against her . . . whilst dawn light had emerged, giving the room a hazy, gray light. She raised her head to look down at Thork.

The loathsome lout was smiling.

CHAPTER FOURTEEN

**He'd like to needle her . . .
pine needle, that is . . .**

If Medana could see herself the way he did right now, she would have a screaming fit.

Her blonde hair had come loosened from its braid during the night and was mussed and tossed into wanton waves that would do the king's harlot proud. Her lips, especially full to begin with, were swollen and rose-tinted from his kisses. Her chemise had slipped off one shoulder, half exposing all of one breast with its small, taut nipple. And her woman's nest had deposited a swath of wetness on his belly as clear evidence of her peaking.

She was a pleasure to look at and a pleasure he intended to enjoy in every wicked, carnal way imaginable, but not right now. Especially since Brokk had been knocking at the door intermittently for some time now. He figured that if it had been an urgent matter, the boy would have stormed in. The door could not be locked from inside.

"Medana, sweetling," he said, leaning up to kiss her startled lips, "you will have to wait to have your way with me. Brokk is at the door."

She blinked several times in confusion and then groaned when she realized her position, straddling his body with her chemise hiked up to her hips, her arse no doubt a sight that would delight Brokk, even if he was just a boyling, especially because he was a boyling.

"My way? My way? If I had my way—" Before she could berate him, as she was sure to do, he rolled her over on her back toward the wall and pulled the linen up over them both. "Come in, Brokk."

"Sorry I am, Master . . . I mean . . . Jarl . . . I mean . . . oh, bloody hell! Jostein said to ask if he should go deer hunting today or not."

Jostein was clearly wondering if it would be a wasted effort considering that they would be leaving tonight. Actually, since Thork had had time to ponder things, he realized that even if they got the longboat through the tunnel tonight, they might not be able to leave immediately. Supplies would have to be gathered and a crew, even a reluctant one, would have to be put together.

"Yea, tell him to hunt today, as planned." Even if they were able to leave right away, the women left behind could use the excess meat.

After Brokk left, Thork turned to Medana, who was backed up against the wall, putting as much distance between them as was possible, which wasn't much. "Do not say one word," she ordered. "Do not smile. Do not do one single thing to make me feel worse than I already do."

He tilted his head to one side. "Why would you feel bad? I would think you would be feeling mighty good about now. Relaxed and all squishy inside. 'Tis the way of love play."

She put both hands over her ears and squealed. "I told you not to talk about it."

He laughed and stood, stretching to get the kinks out of his body. It was a small bed, not made for a man his size.

At first, she gaped at his cockstand—impressive, if he did say so himself—but then she squeezed her eyes shut tight. "I wish there was a crack in the floor that I could fall through."

"Why? I am the one who should be embarrassed. Not you."

She opened one eye a slit and watched as he drew on a pair of braies, carefully, considering the size of his enthusiasm. "Your mother would be upset that you are wearing braies with no small-clothes," she observed.

He chuckled that she would bring up his mother at a time like this. "I suggest you do not tell her. If you should ever have the pleasure of meeting her."

"Gods! I hope not!"

He chuckled and drew a clean tunic over his head and belted it, inserting a knife into a side sheath. "I have work to do for the next few hours. After you are garbed, I trust that you will stay here and not run off."

He waited for her nod of agreement.

"You will find water for your morning ablutions and cold fare to eat, if you are hungry." He sat on the edge of the bed and drew on one boot, then the other. When he stood again, he told her, "Later this morning, I want you to accompany me to the top of the mountain so that I can get a better look at the sea on the Small Island side."

"You went through the tunnel last night, didn't you?"

He nodded. "We can discuss that and other things later. Oh, and Medana, there are two things I would like to say to you."

"What?" She eyed him suspiciously.

"You were a joy in the bedsport. Your pleasure was my pleasure."

"For the love of Frigg!" she muttered, her face flaming at his discussing their intimacy.

"Furthermore, what we did last night was just a foretaste of the meal to come. Mayhap whilst we are atop the mountain today. Make sure to bring a blanket. On the other hand, sex on the pine needles has a certain attraction."

Her beautiful violet eyes went wide. "In the daytime? You would not dare."

"I would dare, for a certainty." *And now that you raise the question, I must needs consider it a challenge. Is there a Viking alive who can ignore a challenge?*

"Another perversion!"

"I am a man, Medana. A man likes to see what he is doing."

He thought she called him a loathsome lout as he was leaving. For some reason, that "endearment," coming from her, gave him pleasure.

Wine: a rogue's best friend . . .

Medana was panting for breath, lagging far behind Thork, by the time they reached the top of the mountain late that morning.

Could be because he'd forced her to wear a

plain russet *gunna* that dragged on the ground—
"more womanly," he claimed—and hauled a
blanket over her shoulder like a sack containing
various food stuffs—*how long does he expect us to
linger?*—or could be because she'd had so little
sleep the night before—*and doesn't that conjure
images I do not want to ponder?*

He, on the other hand, wore the tunic and braies
he'd arrived in, which had been laundered by the
women. A leather tunic, the fabric of which had
been tanned and dyed to a supple brown smooth-
ness molding his wide shoulders and narrowing
to a wide leather belt that emphasized his waist
and hips. The same fabric had been used for his
slim braies, but dyed black. His boots, cross-tied
up his calves, must have cost a fortune. His dark
blond hair was clean from the previous night's
bath; its healthy sheen gave off golden hues in
the sunlight. And, of course, there were those remarkably green eyes that seemed to sparkle with
mischief, and other things, when he chanced to
look her way.

He was Viking male at his virile prime.

Best she beware lest he lure her in with all his
roguish talents.

When they got to a small clearing amid the
trees that was used by the Thrudr guardswomen
to watch the sea, they saw Effa, an older woman,
armed with a short sword, who stood waiting for
them, her weapon aready.

"Go back to the village, Effa, and do not return
until you get orders to do so," Thork told the guard.

Effa raised her chin in defiance and looked to
Medana for confirmation.

Medana nodded and said in a gentler fashion, "Do as you are told, Effa. We will stand watch for a while. Tell Gudron you have my permission to return."

"Are you sure, mistress?" Effa asked. "He looks like a scoundrel who might do you harm."

Thork arched a brow. "Me? A scoundrel?" he asked with a pure scoundrelish purr.

Before he could say, or do, something more, Medana interjected, "I will be fine," although she was not altogether certain of that fact.

Reluctantly, Effa stomped off.

Medana dropped her bundle close to the fire ring though there would be no need of a fire today. Thork dropped his own bundle as well and told her, "Rest here for a while. I want to explore the area." The sun was shining brightly overhead and while she would have relished a short respite, Medana was curious to see what he was looking at. So she followed after him.

Some days, when the skies were overcast, a mist hung over the mountaintop and visibility was nonexistent. But today, skies were clear, and Small Island was a big dot down below.

"Hedeby is in that direction, is it not?" he remarked, pointing south. "And my father's estates in the Norselands are to the north, the other way, correct?"

She nodded both times.

"It must be brutal cold here in the winter."

"It can be. The first winter, I thought I would die of frostbite. We could never keep a fire going. And the wood we gathered was green, not seasoned enough to burn steadily. We learned, though. And now we start gathering firewood in the spring. By the time of first frost, we have enough stacked up to last two winters." She knew her voice was prideful, but then she and her women had suffered enough to deserve a little pride.

"And the two old hags down there with their bear protector?"

Medana smiled. "Hags" was probably an accurate description, and their dog Bear did resemble a small bear. "That is Sigrun and her daughter Salvana. They lived on Small Island long before we arrived, subsisting on the barter of fresh water in rain barrels to passing seafarers. They also provided a message service. In return, they were given all the products they needed to survive . . . food, clothing, and whatnot. After we came, they partnered with us, but chose to remain on their own island, except when fierce storms flood their home, which they do on occasion. Then they come through the tunnel to stay with us."

"Why don't they just stay here? Less of a chance of passersby discovering your existence."

"I do not know their history, but I suspect it was horrid. They choose to be by themselves. And believe me, Bear is more of a protection than you might think."

"I can imagine. I had a dog one time. Foolheart, I called him, because he had no fear at all. Foxes, wild boar, even bears. A beast with more bravery than good sense. When he was a puppy, he nigh knocked himself unconscious trying to butt heads with one of my mother's favorite rams. As he got older, he had more nicks and bruises, including half an ear and a bent tail."

Sounds like some Vikings I know. She heard the affection in his voice, despite his deprecating words. "Where is your dog now?"

"I have no idea. He stayed behind when I left Dragonstead. He would be old now, for a dog. No doubt, dead."

Her heart ached for Thork. Over a dog? She should guard herself if she was softening toward him so easily.

Luckily, he changed the subject. "You keep guards up here to watch for coming ships, don't you?"

She nodded. "And on other sides of the mountain, as well. Usually, we have at least a half day's notice on a clear day, such as today. Or if sea vessels are spotted on the opposite side of Thrudr, it can be almost a full day before they make the bend and approach Small Island."

They turned back on the path atop the dense woods and made their way back to the clearing.

"I hear you are betrothed," she remarked.

He was as surprised by her comment as she was that she'd blurted it out. Instead of answering he asked, "Where did you hear that?"

"Here and there."

"Well, your informant was only half right. I *intended* to become betrothed after visiting my father and gaining his approval. No final betrothal agreements were made."

"But the woman was picked out and everything."

"Not everything," he said with a smile. "There was no consummation of the betrothal."

Hmm. 'Twas the practice for many a couple

especially anxious to be wed, and not frowned upon at all. Merely a sealing of the vows of promise. That was one of the reasons she feared the reaction she would get to claims of being raped by her betrothed. "Were you tempted?"

Thork glanced at her with surprise.

She'd surprised herself by asking such a lack-brained question.

"Why all these question about a betrothal that has naught to do with us?"

"Does it not?" She shrugged. "Just curious."

He was not convinced of that, she could tell. "But, if you must know, nay, I was not tempted. Berla is comely enough, but very young. I am certain in time I would be tempted, though."

"Would you have set up a home in Hedeby?"

"Good gods, nay! My father years ago set aside land adjacent to Dragonstead for me. I could settle my bride there."

"Settle your bride? You mean, settle you *and* your bride, don't you?"

"Well, I would go a-Viking, or harvesting amber, or become a merchant Viking. Betimes, I would return home to my estate—"

"In other words, you would continue on as you always were. Free to do as you will, whilst your wife keeps the home fires going?"

"And breeds babies," he said with a twinkle in his rascal eyes. "You make much ado over what is the usual marriage practice."

"An arrangement, then?"

"I suppose you could say that."

"Just like mine with Jarl Ulfr."

He cast her a disapproving scowl. "Not the

same at all. It would be a clear choice on both our parts."

"How do you know it was a choice on her part? How do you know if her father was forcing her to his will, for his own purposes? How do you know—"

"What does any of that matter now? There will be no wedding, thanks to your interference."

"One more question. Did your mother and father have such an arrangement when they married?"

"Nay, they did not. Crazy in love, they claimed to be, and still are. Really, you would be embarrassed to be around them, Medana. Even at their advanced ages, they are always touching and kissing and saying the most outrageous intimate things to each other, in front of one and all."

"I think that's rather nice."

"Pfff!"

They had arrived back at the small clearing and she stood staring at him. She'd lost him his bride. She did not like feeling guilty over yet another thing because of her actions, or those of her women. "Mayhap I could go to her father in Hedeby and explain the circumstances, or I could write another letter to your father, this time explaining that none of this was your fault."

"Don't you dare!" He swatted her on her bottom with an open palm. "Enough of your meddling, wench! Help me stretch out this blanket so that we can break our fast. I have not eaten at all since last night, and I am very hungry." The look he gave her then was one of hunger, all right, but not necessarily for food.

After they spread out the blanket, having to kick aside some stones that would be lumpy or even sharp underneath, she unloaded the vast amount of food he'd brought . . . slices of ham and bread; some hard-cooked eggs; skyrr, the soft cheese favored by Vikings; a bunch of grapes; and two peaches.

Thork undid the bung on a large skin of some beverage that he held to his mouth and drank deeply. Surely not "Adam's ale" or water. More likely real ale or mead. "Mmmm. Good!" He handed it to her then and said, "Drink. You may need this."

She didn't like the gleam in his eyes as he extended the bag to her. Still, she was thirsty after that long trek up the mountain. She took a drink, then exclaimed, "Wine! This is the prized Frisian wine I was saving for a special occasion, and you were chugging it down like water. 'Tis meant to be sipped."

"I consider this a special occasion." He motioned with his hand for her to drink more as he folded himself down onto the blanket and began to open the packets of cheese and bread.

She took another sip. It was delicious, of course, but it should be, considering its cost. Actually, it hadn't cost them anything, other than the effort in pirating a wealthy merchant's estate in the Irish lands last year.

"More," he insisted, taking a big bite out of a slice of ham. "I mean it, Medana, drink or I will pour it down your throat."

Swearing silently, she took several big swallows before wiping her mouth with the back of her hand, then setting the leather bag carefully onto the edge of the blanket. After sitting down herself and tucking her legs sideways with the *gunna* covering her completely, she nibbled on a piece of manchet smeared with skyrr. "Why is it so important to you that I get *drukkinn*?"

"Not *drukkinn*. Nay, that would not be good. But relaxed, that is what you need."

She declined to ask him why, fearing what he would answer.

But he told her, anyway. "Wine is a thigh spreader for many women."

She gasped. "What an obnoxious thing to say!"

He shrugged. "A man uses all the tools at his disposal. If I had the case of feathers my father gifted me, I would employ those."

She definitely was not going to ask about that.

But all this nonsense was beside the point. Medana was never one to avoid unpleasantness, and it was past time she got the rogue to discuss his plans for Thrudr. "We should probably settle several matters afore we do this . . . uh, thing."

He extended the wine bag. She drank again and handed it back to him. She noticed he was taking only one drink for every two of hers. And while he'd initially taken a long draw on the bag, he was only sipping now.

"This . . . uh, thing . . . will happen regardless. Why spoil the day with useless chatter?"

Rude oaf! "I do not consider the fate of our longship useless chatter."

"Are you done eating?" he asked.

Definitely rude! "I suppose."

He yanked the remaining bread and ham from

her hand and began to tuck everything away in the cloth bag. Gulping, she took a long swig from the wine bag, without being ordered to do so. Best she be careful or she would be too weak to even stand, let alone do whatever he intended for her.

He did not even glance her way when he said, "Stand and take off your *gunna*."

"*What?*" Her eyes darted here and there. The sun was so bright. He could not really expect . . .

"Or mayhap you need more wine," he suggested.

"I have had more than enough wine. My brain feels fuzzy as it is."

"Fuzzy is good." He leaned back on his elbows. "Come now, Medana. Show me what I have bartered for in this negotiation."

"Can't we wait until it's dark?" *Or never?*

"Would you rather I undress you?"

"Nay!" He would probably touch her in inappropriate places in the process. She stood, shakily at first, and fiddled with the twisted rope belt at her waist. "Shouldn't you undress, too?"

"You first."

"I do not see why we have to undress at all," she grumbled.

"Oh, Medana, you have so much to learn. And here is some good news. I am an excellent teacher."

Dropping the belt to the ground, she toed off each of her leather slip shoes and with a sigh of resignation, lifted the *gunna* by the hem up and over her head. She would not look at him as she stood in her chemise, nigh transparent from so many washings.

When he was silent for too long, she glanced his way and saw that he was sitting now, alert as a dog on scent. His eyelids were half mast, his cheeks flushed, and his lips parted. She might not be experienced in the sex arts, but she recognized the expression on his face. It was pure lust. "Undo your braid and finger comb your hair out, over your shoulders," he said in a voice raw with male lust.

She did as he'd asked and noted the way his nostrils flared and his hands fisted as he tried to contain his passions. But the one-sidedness of her standing almost nude with him lying there totally clothed struck her as an act of humiliation, and, although she did naught to shield her intimate body parts, tears welled in her eyes.

He was on his feet immediately. Standing before her, he tipped her chin up and asked, "What is amiss?"

Is he dense? "Everything, you big nasty troll! You seek to prolong my agony by mortifying me."

"I do not!"

"Why am I naked and you are not? To take away all my pride, that is why. There is inequality in our positions."

"If that is the problem, I can resolve it faster than you can blink." He unclothed himself with such speed she knew he'd done it many times before. But now, because of her complaint, she was faced with a nude—and very aroused—Thork. "Now we are unequal but in the opposite way. You are clothed and I am not."

"Hah! I do not call this being clothed." She glanced at him and saw that he'd been teasing.

"Another problem easily solved," he said, and drew the chemise up and over her head.

Medana looked at his face. She dared not look lower, not at his body or her own.

"Why did you feel humiliated to stand before me almost nude? Did you not know that I was admiring your body? Sex engages all the senses: touch, taste, smell, hearing, *and* sight."

Medana couldn't begin to imagine what he meant by that. Really, from her own limited experience, and from what she'd heard her women say, sex was not a long, drawn-out affair. Yea, some men bothered with a little kissing or fondling, and some women did appear to enjoy the coupling, but in the end it was just a bodily function.

She drew herself up straight on a deep inhale and asked him, "What do you want from me, Thork?"

He gazed at her, let his eyes drift over her body, from her mouth to her curling toes, then held eye contact with her before saying, "Everything."

And, gods help her, in that moment, Medana wanted that, too.

CHAPTER FIFTEEN

She was a scream . . .

Medana, the female pirate, was, in fact, a goddess.

To Thork, leastways.

Tall, slim, with a narrow waist flaring out to womanly hips. Above and below, light blonde curls sparkled in the sun. Her breasts were perfect half globes of polished ivory with pale rose centers. Her incredible violet eyes fringed with thick, darker blonde lashes only added to her allure. And, damn his twisted soul, but he admired her stubborn hands-on-hips, legs-spread battle stance, too.

"Can I look at you?" he asked.

"You are already looking."

"More. I want to examine all of you."

"And if I say you nay?"

"I will just sneak peeks when you are not looking."

"Odious oaf!"

"Willful wench!"

"Randy rogue!"

"Delicious delight!"

Her eyes shot up to catch his gaze, and her lips

trembled slightly with uncertainty. She had no conception of her own comeliness, he knew that. By the time he was done with her, though, she would know. That, he promised himself.

"Cunning charmer!" she tossed out belatedly.

He laughed. "Aren't you going to call me a loathsome lout?"

"Not if I have to bite my tongue bloody!"

He moved around her body, studying her, head to toe, then a return journey. He didn't touch her at all. Just gazed with appreciation at all her "delights." To his amazement, she did in fact have scars across her back. From her brothers' lashes? He couldn't dwell on that now, but, for a certainty, there were three Viking cowards who would sample the flavor of his wrath when he caught up with them.

For now, he moved his scrutiny of Medana lower, and, blessed Valkyries, even the backs of her knees were pretty. And the dimples on each side of her buttocks? Oh, he intended to kiss each of them. As soon as possible.

"What are you doing back there?" she asked over her shoulder.

"Admiring your arse."

"You never were!" She swiveled around and was about to pummel his chest at what she thought was mockery.

"I was, I was," he said, grabbing her by the waist, then lifting her higher by putting his hands under both buttocks.

Instinctively, she raised her knees and wrapped her legs about his hips.

Gods bless instincts! He swung her around in

a circle several times, joyfully. Then he lowered himself down to the blanket, resting on his knees, taking her with him, under him. Thanks be for strong knees! When she lay back, glaring up at him, her legs were splayed on either side of his knees, which he widened even more.

"Ah, Medana, I am going to enjoy playing with your body."

"My goal in life: to be a man's play toy."

He chucked her lightly under the chin for her sarcasm. "And my goal today will be to bring you joy in the love play, too."

"Why would you care one way or the other?"

"You are so green in many ways. Do you not know that a woman's joy is a man's pleasure?"

"You made that up just now," she accused him.

He shook his head. "Nay, 'tis a well-known fact."

"Well, 'tis one many men have not yet learned if what my women relate is true."

"That I concede. But you are not to fear. I am an expert in these matters."

"Praise be to Asgard!"

"Be careful, m'lady, or I may have to punish you for your continuing sarcasm."

She opened her mouth to speak, then closed it firmly, deciding for once that silence might be the better path to follow. Wise woman!

He sat back on his knees and studied what he could see of her body. "I did not give your breasts near enough attention last night. Methinks that would be a good place to start."

"To st-start?" she sputtered.

"Some men have a preference for big breasts, but—"

"Mine are certainly not udders."

He smiled. "Is it not fortunate that I am not an udder man?"

Whatever she was about to reply to that got frozen on her tongue as he began to fondle her breasts. Lifting them. Massaging them with wide circles of his palms. Tweaking the nipples 'til their hue changed from dusky rose to pale red. "Do you like this kind of love play?" he asked her.

She refused to answer.

So he leaned down and began to suckle one nipple, while flicking the other with a middle finger.

A little yelp of surprise escaped her lips, and she stiffened as if bracing against the passions he was clearly igniting in her. When he changed breasts and had both nipples equally stiff and her back was arched up for more, he asked again, "Do you like this kind of love play?"

"Yea, I do, damn your hide. If you stop, I might have to scratch out your pretty eyes."

"You like my eyes?" he murmured just before taking almost all of one breast into his mouth, then drawing back slowly until he released the nipple with a wet pop.

"Of course I like your eyes. Every woman who sees you does, and you know it, too."

He did know that women liked his eyes, but for some reason her liking his eyes pleased him immensely. "What other body parts of mine do you like?"

"As if I would tell you! Your conceit needs no more puffing up. Yikes! Now what are you doing?"

"Licking your belly."

"Why?"

"Why, why, why? Have I mentioned my Aunt Eadyth's irksome parrot? Reminds me of you. Does there have to be a reason for everything? Just lie back and enjoy."

"I hardly think that I would enjoy—"

"Shhh! Oh, look what I found here. A thatch of spun gold. I wonder what secrets I will find underneath." He inserted a finger between her folds and stroked until she dewed against him. "Just as I thought. Honey."

She whimpered. "Would it do any good to tell you what a perverted man you are?"

"Only if you mean it in a good way." He continued stroking her and told her, "You are wet for me, sweetling."

"It's probably all the wine you forced on me, leaking out."

He choked back a laugh. "Nay, 'tis not wine, though I warrant your woman-dew is just as sweet."

Her eyes, which she'd had scrunched tightly closed, shot open. "You would not dare to taste me *there*."

"Actually, I would dare, but not just yet. I do not want to shock you too much too soon. But if you keep on questioning every little thing I do, I might need to do something drastic to still your flapping tongue."

She muttered something about his being the flapping tongue, but then she closed her mouth and eyes. You'd think she was going to the gallows.

Using his knees, he spread her wider and gazed down at that mysterious place women held so private. Lovely, it was, in an earthy sort of way. Like the petals of a flower carrying the glisten of raindrops. When he studied her enough with his eyes, he studied her with his fingertips. Stroking. Flicking. Inserting. Always avoiding the one spot that would surely bring her to the brink of peaking. As the bud unfurled, her thighs tightened and several times she bucked up reflexively before she caught herself. She was biting her bottom lip to keep from crying out.

"If you could see yourself here the way I do, Medana," he said in a voice raw with his own arousal, "you would know what power women hold over men."

She made a gurgling sound of protest.

"I wonder, Medana, if I could turn that little whimper you just made into a scream. Of sex joy." He used his elongated cock then to touch the nubbin of pleasure at the top of her cleft.

She flinched and tried to escape him by shuffling her bottom upward on the blanket.

But he would have none of that. Placing one hand firmly on her belly, he gripped his cock with the other and used it to strum the unfurling bud like a musician plucking a stringed instrument.

Involuntary tremors shook her body, and disjointed words pleaded for relief. She did scream then, a long wail of intense pleasure, as her hips rose, wanting more and more of what he was giving her.

Her peaking died down, and his senses became heightened as desire licked through his body to the point of pain. He could not hold himself off anymore. Caught in the throes of a driving need, he thrust himself inside her tight sheath. Then, bracing himself on his straightened arms, he waited for her to realize what he had done. And tried to curtail his own fast-approaching peak, especially when her molten folds shifted to accommodate his size.

When she came back to her senses, he asked, "Are you all right? Am I hurting you?" *Remarkable that I can put two words together!*

She only then appeared to realize that he had impaled her and was seated inside her body almost to her womb. "Oh. Oh!" She wriggled a little from side to side, then told him, "Nay, it does not hurt. Precisely. But . . ."

"But what?"

"There is a lot of you."

"Thank you." *Now, wiggle your arse again, sweetling. Yea, juuust like that.*

"I did not mean it as a compliment," she gasped out.

"Believe me, that was a compliment."

"Whew! How did you squeeze it all in without me noticing?"

Holy Thor! I've got a talker here. Some women moan excessively during sex, some even scream. Medana is clearly a nervous talker. Ah well, she is new to bedsport. I should be patient. "The slickness of your excitement eased the way. Woman-dew, it is called."

"You mean, the honey business."

He laughed. *Chatter, chatter, chatter.*

"Do that again."

"What?"

"Laugh. When you laugh, your dangly part shakes inside me."

On the other hand, there is much to be said about a talkative woman. "Uh, just so you know, my dangly part is no longer dangly."

"I know. Dost consider me a total lackbrain?"

Is that a serious question? "Can I move now?"

"What? I thought we were done."

Did someone mention lackbrain? "My dear naïve pirate miss. We have just begun." He withdrew almost totally, then slammed back in to the hilt so that his nether hairs blended with her nether hairs. Looking down, he fancied it resembled woven threads of two shades of gold. In fact, he moved slightly from side to side to blend the threads more.

She jerked. Apparently, that movement must have brushed her sweet bud. And then she screamed.

And it was a good scream, too.

There was no time to ponder any more as he began the serious business of swiving, and, yea, he took his swiving seriously. What Viking man worth his reputation did not?

He rocked her gently at first with long slow strokes 'til she made small mewling sounds of pleasure, but then not so gently and not so slow. Her mewls became cries. Sometimes when he was buried in her hot depths, he gripped the cheeks of her arse and rotated his hips so that the bone above his cock ground against the pearl of her arousal. That trick caused her inner muscles to ripple around his staff.

The sound of wetness, moist flesh smacking against moist flesh, was carnal music to his ears. Thork's blood thickened with enthusiasm, and his heart hammered against his rib cage. He was catapulting fast toward his own peaking, but he wanted her to come to a second bliss, if possible.

By the time her stretched inner muscles began to clutch and unclutch his now massive cock, his nerves were inflamed with the need to let loose his self-control. He glanced down at her and saw her eyes dilated to a full dark violet color. Something intense flared between them then, especially when she reached up and fingered the edges of his jaw and parted lips. How could she be gentle when he felt so fierce?

"I. Cannot. Wait," he roared out as he withdrew and spilled his seed upon the blanket between her thighs.

Afterward, he lay atop her, trying to calm his panting breaths.

To his surprise, Medana was caressing his back and shoulders and upper arms. When he raised himself on levered arms to stare down at her, he saw the glow of wonder on her face. "That was amazing. Can all men do that?"

He wasn't exactly sure what she meant. Probably the bringing of a woman to peak in the bedplay. He did not like her inferring that she might test his skills by bedding other men. With a surge of possessiveness he would no doubt regret later, he replied. "Only me."

Standing, he took her hand and yanked her to her feet. "I need to flip this blanket lest we end up lying on the damp spot."

Color heightened her cheeks when she realized what he referred to. Still, she managed to overcome her shyness enough to ask, "Do you get . . . uh, satisfied by doing it that way?"

"Satisfied, yea, I do, but would it be better if I stayed the course, inside? Of course it would."

"Well, I appreciate your not planting your seed in me."

She was pulling the chemise over her neck and shoulder. He could have told her that he would be removing it again shortly but decided that some words were best unspoken.

"Don't you want children, ever, Medana?"

"I gave up those kinds of dreams a long time ago. Yea, I know that I could do it like some of the other women have, alone, but I would prefer, if I ever bear babies, to have them in a home with a husband."

"A rather traditional view from a nontraditional female pirate," he remarked.

"Can I not be both?"

"Apparently you are."

"You were a pirate at one time, too. 'Tis hardly fair of you to criticize me for doing the same."

"There is a difference. You are a woman and I am a man." He paused to let her know he was well aware of the difference after their recent activity.

"Men have been using that excuse for centuries. And women have been proving them wrong for centuries."

He wasn't precisely sure what ways women had outdone men, but she was probably correct. All the women in his family were independent and capable of caring for themselves . . . his mother, his aunt Eadyth, his cousins. "I was a pirate for a good cause. To undermine that evil King Edred."

"And we are pirates to survive."

"Must you always be at cross-wills with me?" When she just shrugged, he added, "Besides, I never criticized you for being a pirate. Just for being a pirate who captured *me*."

She shrugged again. He was coming to mislike her shrugs, not that his view would stop her.

"If you were pirating for a good cause, why is your father so upset with you?"

He could feel his face heat with color. "That was not the only bad thing I have ever done."

She made a muffled sound of suppressed laughter.

"Beware, M'Lady Pirate. Now that I no longer have to be good to please my father, I may try my bad on you."

"I thought you already had."

"Not even a bit."

Enough of this line of conversation afore he tossed her to the ground and tried her charms, again. He walked away from her and glanced around their surroundings and out to sea. All was calm. The two dots that were Sigrun and Salvana moved about Small Island, working industriously on some chore that involved dragging a long piece of driftwood, probably intended for firewood. The big dog was tugging one way while they tugged the other. "Too bad the pond is so far away. I could use a good wash after all that exercise." Medana had come up to stand beside him. He waggled his eyebrows to indicate what exercise he meant. When he was a younger, less experienced male, he used to practice waggling his eyebrows in front of his mother's polished brass. In time, he'd perfected the art. There were so many types of waggles for so many occasions, most of them sexual in tone.

She ignored the waggle and said, "There is no pond up here, of course, but there are headwaters for the mountain stream. A small waterfall and an equally small pool."

"Lead on, my winsome leader," he said.

She mumbled something about "winsome indeed!" but she didn't protest when he laced his fingers with hers while they walked a distance from the clearing along a well-trod path that she explained without his asking. "The guardswomen up here use the headwaters for drinking water. And bathing."

It was indeed a small waterfall and the spillover pool no more than thigh-high and two arm's lengths across. It was not a true headwater, either, since it merely led to a tiny stream trickling down into the valley. An unreliable source of water for the women.

But the water here was cool and clean. After sluicing himself with handfuls of water, he gave in and just lay down under the water. When he came back up, Medana had removed her chemise and was sitting in the deepest part, her breasts demurely covered. Not that he couldn't see through the clear water, but he decided not to inform her of that fact.

It always amazed Thork how women could perform the most wanton acts during the night and then turn blushing virgin on the morn. Not that they'd coupled in the dark or that Medana had been all that wanton. But it was early hours yet. He could only hope.

Thork's stomach growled then, and he realized he was ravenously hungry. "Is there any food left?" he asked Medana.

"I was thinking the same thing. Yea, there's plenty."

On the way back to the clearing, Thork glanced at Medana and winked. "Have you ever heard of the Viking S-spot?"

CHAPTER SIXTEEN

*Alas, paradise can last only so
long. Thus, Paradise Lost . . .*

Medana soon came to the conclusion that Thork was insatiable. And to her shame, she was proving insatiable, too.

What if she developed a craving for sex? What if she had a dormant harlot inside her that Thork had managed to tap to life? What if she liked it so much that she became like some of her more wanton women, those who could not wait 'til they went to market towns so they could be tupped by men? And not just for babies, either. Would she be encouraging the pirate women to capture more men in the future, just so they had sex partners for a time before discarding them like used goods? Like men did to women?

When they'd returned to the clearing, Thork's hunger had dissipated, or rather was replaced with a different kind of hunger, and he'd coaxed her into removing her chemise so he could examine her for ticks. He'd sworn he saw some in the woods. And, damn her foolish heart, but she'd let herself be coaxed. And checked him for ticks, too.

Then he'd proceeded to show her the Viking

S-spot. With his tongue! On her body! Or in her body, to be more precise. Praise be Valkyries! She blushed even recalling what he had done. What she had allowed him to do.

Afterward, they'd devoured the rest of the food and wine, and now the insatiable rogue was giving her that look again.

"What?" she asked, a dimwitted thing to say in the circumstances.

"Do you not think it is time for you to reciprocate?"

"Reciprocate what?" Another dimwitted question.

"Making love."

"I would not know where to start." Which was the wrong thing to say because he lay himself down on the blanket. Still naked. Folded his hands behind his head and looked up at her with the innocence of a shark.

"Just do whatever you want. You could start by touching me."

She just barely stopped herself from asking where. He would probably point to his staff that was already beginning to rise. Again.

Unfortunately, he seemed to be reading her mind. "Not there! Leastways, not yet."

"Turn over," she said. "I get too distracted by . . ." She waved a hand at *it*. "I will have more nerve to touch you if you are not giving me those lascivious looks."

"Lascivious!" he hooted, but turned over onto his folded arms after taking care to adjust his cockstand.

She began by brushing his braid to the side and

charting the strong tendons in his neck with her fingertips. Next she gave attention to the wide breadth of his shoulders. She gained inordinate pleasure watching his muscles bunch at those mere touches.

He had scars all over, as any Viking warrior did, including a wide slash from one shoulder to the opposite waist. She traced it with one fingertip and asked, "Where did you get this?"

"The Battle of Essex. I joined King Harald Bluetooth for a period in fighting King Edred's ranks. The Saxon foeman got much worse than a mere scar, believe you me. Attacking a man from behind! But then, that is the Saxon way."

"It is our way, too," Medana confessed. "When we women of Thrudr are forced to fight, we must use any means possible, being weaker than men in physical strength. Cunning is a necessity for female pirates."

She thought he would laugh or make some derogatory remark about cunning coming natural to women, but he remained silent.

So she continued touching him. The ropes of muscles in his arms. The striated planes of his back, which tapered to his waist and narrow hips. His buttocks she saved for later. If she dared! Instead, she walked her fingers down his thighs and legs.

He shivered and spread his legs slightly.

"Am I doing it wrong?" she asked.

"Oh, Medana! You are doing it just right."

Encouraged, she examined the backs of his knees and his ankles and his long, narrow feet. He was a well-formed male, there was no doubt about that. Only then did she allow herself to touch his backside. His buttocks were hard, high globes of sheer muscle, unlike hers that seemed to be soft and squishy, something she'd noted when bathing. Through the parting of his thighs she could see his ballocks covered with a light furring of fine blond hairs.

She said something then that she never thought she'd say to a man, "You have a very nice arse."

"I know. 'Tis one of my best features."

His face was hidden, but he was probably smiling. "Unlike humility, which has to be far down the list."

"How did you know I have a list of my assets?" he teased.

She leaned forward and kissed the enticing curve at the small of his back. A vulnerable-looking spot.

He rolled over, and she was kneeling at his side. His best side, truth to tell. Even if she only referred to his face.

Stark cheekbones highlighted a bronzed face. Then there were those incredible emerald-fire eyes. He had a strong nose and full lips, which were parted now with arousal.

She loved that she could arouse such a rascal of a man.

He folded his arms under his head again, as if giving her freedom to do what she willed. That position called attention to his underarms, where straight blond hairs protected the soft skin. She rather liked that part of him, too. In fact, she touched the hair in one hollow to see if it felt as silky as it looked. It did.

His flat male nipples drew her. Fondling them in the same manner as he had treated hers, she was pleased to hear his indrawn breath. When she leaned forward and put her mouth to one of them, he stiffened. When she suckled, he groaned and muttered an expletive.

"You do not like that?"

"I like it too much, and you know it, too."

She smiled. "Shall I do it some more?"

"If you don't, I might have to kill you."

She took that for a yes. When she had played his nipples for a long time, he growled, "Enough! Move on!"

Glancing downward, she saw that his shaft reared up from a thick thatch of blond curls. He was so engorged that a bud of man seed seeped out on its tip. Blue veins stood out on its long length, and the mushroom head was ruddy in color. "Can I touch?"

"Please." He took her hands and showed her how he liked to be caressed with fists that did not meet around his breadth, one above the other. Pumping lightly, then not so lightly. With a roar of pure male satisfaction, he growled, "Take off that bloody chemise afore I tear it in shreds and toss it out to sea."

She did as he asked, without question. How had she gotten so aroused just trying to arouse him? Was it the reverse of what Thork had told her earlier, that a man's pleasure was a woman's joy?

"Now climb on top of me," he ordered gruffly when she'd lifted the chemise up and off her body.

"Huh?"

He leaned over and picked her up by the waist, settling her on his thighs. She could feel the dampness in her nether parts. By the gleam in his eyes as he stared at her there, he was aware of that dampness, too.

"Take my cock in your hands and guide me to paradise," he ordered.

She did not need him to explain what he meant. She lifted her bottom slightly up and forward. Then, taking his staff in hand once more, guided him to her woman's channel, and little by agonizing little, she sank down onto him.

For a brief moment, she thought she might faint, so intense was the ecstasy of being filled by this man. Her inner muscles were clenching him in welcome, and he looked as if he might also faint.

"How does that feel, Medana?" he husked out.

She did not want to discuss it. She just wanted to feel it. Still she told him, "Like I am being impaled by living, breathing, warm marble."

He nodded. Again, humility was not one of his great traits.

"And you?" she asked. "How do you feel?"

"Like I am being coated in warm honey. And hugged. Your moist folds are hugging me in welcome."

Just as she'd thought.

"Lift yourself up and then down, slowly. Like riding a horse."

"I have not ridden a horse since I was a girling. And that was bareback in a farmstead field."

" 'Tis said a person never forgets. And bareback is appropriate, don't you think?"

I do not want to think. I just want to feel. "Stop talking and show me what to do."

With a chuckle at her ordering him about, he showed her with his hands on her hips the way to undulate to a certain rhythm. She was a good pupil, apparently, because at one point, he told her to stop and rest, and with him still filling her, he tunneled his fingers in her hair and pulled her face down to his.

"Kiss me, Medana," he urged. "Kiss me like I am your man just home from a-Viking and you have missed me sorely."

To her amazement, she was able to do so, probably because a lackwitted part of her liked the image of him being her man. And while she settled her lips over his and gave him kisses full of all the nuances she could come up with, he played with her breasts. When she drew on his tongue, he responded by plunging deep into her mouth. And her lower regions did their own counter rhythm. Every time she tried to move on him, he held her still and said, "Not yet. I am not ready yet."

If possible, he seemed to have grown even more inside her. And she seemed to unfurl even more to assist his enlargement.

Finally, she tore her mouth off of his and sat back firmly on her buttocks, which sat firmly on his ballocks. Panting for breath, she said, "If you do not move soon, I am going to throttle you."

He grinned. "Now I am ready." With those words, he flipped her over on her back, managing to keep himself inside her, probably because he was lodged so deep. With a laugh of sheer joy, he lifted her knees up and over his shoulders and began to pummel her with hard, lengthy strokes that caused stars to explode behind her eyelids. All the skin on her oversensitized body sparked with carnal fire. Everything centered on what he was doing to her down below. When he placed a thumb between their bodies over that bud she'd come to know as the source of woman pleasure, she could not contain her excitement anymore. Keening out her ecstasy, she shattered around him with wildly convulsing spasms.

And he, with chest heaving, catapulted right after her with a triumphant shout. She wasn't sure, but she suspected that he'd forgotten, or been unable, to pull out at the last minute. For now, satiety overwhelmed her, and she felt her body relaxing into the most peaceful sleep. Only half awake, she sensed Thork rising off her and pulling her into his arms. He, too, fell asleep.

It could have been minutes, or even hours, when she heard, "Bloody hell! I canna ken this scene afore us. Is it the Christian Garden of Eden, or Odin's Garden of Delight?"

"Must be Eden. There's Adam the Viking. And Eve," another voice said.

"I dinna see any snake," the first voice remarked.

"Right there. Betwixt Adam's thighs."

"Ah! The only thing missing is the apple."

"I see two apples. With berries on top."

Medana's eyes shot open, and standing there gazing down at them were Jamie and Bolthor.

Bolthor stared through his one good eye at her body, still in Thork's embrace, and said, "This would make a good saga. 'When Adam Was a Viking.' Or 'The Pirate and the Viking.'"

She shoved a laughing Thork off the blanket and used it to cover her nakedness as she scrambled to her feet. Thork, on the other hand, suffered no such modesty. He stood with an arrogance that was maddening.

"What are you two doing here?" Thork asked, hands on naked hips.

"We thought we should come get you if we are going to get the longship through the tunnel tonight," Jamie explained. "I mean . . ." Jamie realized his mistake immediately and glanced to Thork for help.

Thork just shook his head and scowled at the witless scamp.

At first, Medana had trouble weighing the significance of the Scotsman's words. Was he saying . . . ?

"I keep telling the dumb Highlander that a storm is coming tonight, but he would not listen. So I came along to check out the view." Instead of looking out toward the sea, Bolthor was gazing at her with the oddest tilt to his head, as if trying to figure out something. Probably how a seemingly sane woman would be demented enough to let a rascal like Thork swive her silly.

Medana had other thoughts on her mind, though, as understanding began to seep into her befuddled brain. She turned to Thork, "You plan on taking my longship through the tunnel? Tonight? All day you have been seducing me with lies and deceits whilst planning to put the knife of betrayal in my back."

"Isn't that a bit of an exaggeration?" He smiled at her.

She did not smile back.

"It is not what you think, dearling," he said, and stepped toward her.

She put up a halting hand while the other held the blanket closed. Fighting to control the hurt that caused her heart to ache, she spat out, "Do not 'dearling' me, you troll." On those words, she turned and began to stomp away and down the path to the hunters' longhut. Tears filled her eyes and she let them run freely.

When would she ever learn? Men were loathsome louts.

"Did you call me a loathsome lout?" he called after her.

She made a universally known, coarse gesture of disdain over her shoulder, the one particularly favored by seamen and Vikings.

Of course, she heard Thork's laughter behind her. The loathsome lout!

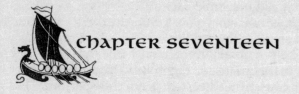

chapter seventeen

Tiger by the tail . . .

Medana took off down the path like a scalded cat. But after tripping on the edge of the blanket she'd wrapped around herself like a shroud and stubbing her bare toe, yelping, "Ow, ow, ow," she stormed back, dropped the blanket in front of him and Bolthor and Jamie, nose pointed north, and slipped on her *gunna* and half boots.

It was only a brief glimpse she'd given them of her naked body, but they were all bug-eyed with appreciation. Even Thork, who'd seen plenty of that naked body for the past five hours or more.

Turning to Bolthor, she glowered. "If you voice a poem about this, I will cut off your tongue when you sleep and roast it for the pigs to eat."

"Me? What did I do?"

"You looked at me."

Bolthor blinked his one eye. "I am a man. Men look. I may have only one eye, but I am not blind." Now it was Bolthor whose nose pointed north.

"What are you laughing about?" She turned on Jamie.

"Dinna turn your rage on me, lass."

"Lass my ass!" Thork muttered.

Medana graced Thork with a killing glance for daring to speak.

"I am laughing at Thork," Jamie explained.

Huh?

"He tried to trap a tiger with honey, he did."

Thork had no idea what that meant, and neither did Medana, apparently, because she gawked at the lackbrain laird as if he spoke some strange gibberish. In truth, the Scottish manner of speaking betimes resembled a foreign language. A burr, they called it. More like a slur, if you asked him, which no one did.

Thork began to approach her. "Medana, give me a chance—"

She didn't even glance his way. Instead, she began to exit the clearing again, swanning off like the bloody queen of all the world.

Clothing himself quickly, Thork told Bolthor and Jamie to gather up the blanket and remaining foodstuff. Then he rushed after Medana. He had some explaining to do. Not that he had to justify himself. All rules of courtesy were nullified when he became a captive. He tried to ignore the voice in his head that said, *But the rules changed when you made love.*

Just then a clap of thunder broke overhead, and he saw dark clouds moving in from the east. Bolthor had been right. There would be storms soon. Which meant there would be no longship through the tunnel tonight.

He smiled. That would give him plenty of time to make amends with Medana.

He couldn't wait.

Jamie had mentioned a tiger. He had other

ideas. "Here, kitty, kitty. Someone wants to lick the milk off your mustache," he sang under his breath as he strutted at a leisurely pace after one tempting feline.

Life was good.

Spill that, you lout! . . .

Medana's life was becoming a disaster.

Thork intended to take Thrudr's longship, and life on this island would never be the same. In truth, it would never be the same even if they left *Pirate Lady* behind. The men were making too much of an impression on the women, and one man in particular would leave his mark on her. The beast!

While she was hurt and angry over Thork's perfidy, the bigger issue was how to prevent that catastrophe from happening. There was little she could do while trapped up here at the hunters' longhouse. And apparently her dubious charms weren't enough to sway him. Oh, she could walk right off this mountain and down to the village, where her women would do their best to protect her, but she knew without a doubt that Thork would come right after her, and she did not want to risk even one of her women being hurt.

To make matters worse, a fierce storm was rising, foretold by fiercesome claps of thunder and lightning bolts from an almost black sky, and it not yet time for nightfall. Winds were starting to rise, and it was so humid you could nigh cut the moisture in the air with a knife. She prayed that Sigrun and Salvana would be able to make it through the tunnel to Thrudr before all Muspell broke loose. Summer storms on the North Sea were naught to dismiss casually. If only the rains would hold off for another five hours or so.

"Medana! You are to stop haranguing my men," Thork said, coming up to her where she was stirring a huge cauldron of rabbit stew thick with vegetables someone had managed to pilfer from the gardens below—carrots, onions, turnips, and such. "You are not permitted to go down to the village. So stop making excuses for why they should allow what I precisely disallowed."

She crossed her eyes and mumbled something about tiresome tyrants. Thus far, she'd managed to avoid talking to the scoundrel directly, and she ignored his commands to do this or that, or to not do this or that. Like bothersome gnats they were, not worth reacting to.

"Do you hear me, you stubborn wench?"

"All of Thrudr hears you. I need to go down and assist my women in preparing for the storm."

"They are doing fine without you. Henry and Alrek are helping them to batten down any loose planks on the buildings and to bring the animals under cover."

"Pfff! Henry is probably off tupping Lilli somewhere, and Alrek might very well hurt himself if a loose plank flies his way."

Thork barely suppressed a smile. "My men know their duty. Your only responsibility is here, with . . . us." She could tell he meant to say "with me." She might have smacked him with the long-handled ladle she was using if he had.

"What are you so afraid of that you will not let me out of your sight?"

"The sleeping draught," he answered without hesitation.

She couldn't deny that she had considered using it again. Her silence was an affirmation to him.

"Once the stew is done, we'll bring the cauldron inside. The stew, along with a supply of bread Brokk is bringing up and a tun of ale, should hold us through the worst of the storm. You will first taste anything we bring up from the village."

"Oh gods! I am going to be trapped in a confined space with eight men. Will I be expected to serve all of you?"

He didn't bother to suppress the smile this time at her ill-chosen words. "Only me," he said, and reached out to brush some loose strands of damp hair off her forehead.

She swatted his hand away.

"I know you are angry with me, Medana, but try to understand my side of things. We need the longship and some of your women to get us back to Hedeby. You never gave me a chance to say that the longship will be yours to return to Thrudr."

"Are you really so dimwitted that you do not understand the problem? You men now know the location of Thrudr. If we take you back to the market town, others are bound to see us and ask questions. It takes only one person to mention our secret hiding place. How soon do you think it will be afore my brothers come storming our sanctuary? Or the king's men?"

Thork recalled the scars on Medana's back and vowed to find time to confront her brothers about their wicked ways. But she needed reassurance now. "We will take a vow of secrecy," Thork said. "We will take care not to let others see you."

She shook her head. "It might not be intentional, but it will happen. Mayhap just a chance word when *drukkinn*. Or loose lips during bedsport. Mayhap even greed if a reward is offered. You cannot guarantee what others will do, even close comrades."

He inhaled and exhaled with exasperation.

She had more to say, though. "I must needs consider Agnis, as well."

"Who in bloody hell is Agnis?"

"Our agent in Hedeby."

He was the one crossing his eyes now, and he looked adorable doing it. Like a little boyling who was not getting his own way.

"If my brother Sigurd discovers Agnis's whereabouts, a war will ensue. That, I guarantee."

"Why would your brother care about Agnis? Was she one of his wives?"

"She was a thrall that he took to his bed furs."

"Unwillingly?"

"Hah! Do thralls have any choice?"

He shrugged. Thralldom was a fact of life, and not just in Viking lands.

"He will be especially angry if he discovers that Agnis harbors his son Egil."

"Hell and Valhalla! You women really are barmy. I cannot deal with this now. We will discuss everything later. And try not to pop any more surprises on me."

Here's a surprise, lackwit. "What if I am with child?"

He released an exhale of relief. "That is a problem you need not worry over. I told you that spilling man seed outside the body is an almost foolproof method of preventing childbirth."

"But you didn't."

He cocked his head to the side. "Didn't what?"

"Pull out. That last time."

"That's impossible. I always . . ." The horror on his face would have been mirthsome if she wasn't so horrified herself.

It was a dark and stormy night . . .

The rains finally came, and came, and came on the tail of driving winds that would leave damaged crops, fences, and trees. More deadfall for the women to cut for firewood. Hopefully, Thork would be long gone by then.

Or would he?

Everyone was asleep by now, except him and Bolthor, who sat by the hearth fire in the hunters' hut, a necessity on this chill night. After all the hard work preparing for the storm, the men had been exhausted. Their snores and sleep snuffles were background noise to the crackling fire.

He'd just told Bolthor what he had done, or not done, to Medana, seeking the old man's advice. The skald did have five children betwixt him and his wife, four of them from her previous husbands, now long gone to the Christian Heaven, or wherever their life deeds had sent him.

"Could you in good conscience leave Medana knowing she might be carrying your seed?" the skald asked.

"That is what keeps me awake this dark night."

"I can tell you this, I married at a young age, but I lost my wife and two little daughters." Thork started to ask him a question, but Bolthor raised a halting hand. "Nay, I do not discuss that dark time in my life, but that is why I never planned to wed again, or have more children. I love Katherine's children and the one of my loins. I love them all, and that is a fact. I miss them sorely." Tears filled his one eye.

Thork pressed a hand to Bolthor's shoulder. "Soon, my friend. Soon, you will be home again."

Bolthor nodded, then grinned. "The reason I am telling you is this, my boy. Having a child is a blessing. Do not miss it. Besides, your mother would kill you if she learned you had a child somewhere not under your own roof."

"I have no roof." Well, land, but no buildings. Yet.

"Dost think that matters? Believe me, I have witnessed your mother's wrath." Bolthor, being closer in age to Thork's father, had been friends to his parents for a long time. In fact, Bolthor had served with Tykir in the Battle of Ripon, where he lost an eye and his father had sustained a thigh wound that caused him to still limp on occasion. "I recall the time your mother got infuriated by Rurik's constant harping on her being a witch, which she was not, as you know." Rurik was Jamie's father. "She nigh scared the spit out of him by inserting an eel skin under her *gunna* trailing on the ground, because witches are said to grow tails on occasion. Then there was the time she took sword in hand and . . ." On and on, Bolthor related tales of his mother's fiery temper. He had heard them all before.

"What concerns me more than my mother's re-action is Father's."

Bolthor nodded. "He will have further disdain for his wild son."

More important, Thork realized, *Can I, a man of honor, abandon my child, or the mother of my child, living hand to mouth on this godsforsaken island?* He put his face in his hands and groaned. "How did this happen?"

Bolthor laughed.

"I know *how* it happened, but why now did I slip after all these years of practicing controlled lust?"

"Medana," Bolthor replied.

"Nay, I cannot blame her."

"I meant that 'tis Medana herself," Bolthor ex-plained. "She made the difference."

Just then, a wet splat of rain hit Thork's head and he shifted slightly on the bench. One thing they'd discovered right off when the rains had started was that the roof leaked. In lots of places. Those men sleeping about the room had to con-tinually move their sleep furs to evade new leaks. One more thing to fix on the morn.

Thork stood and yawned widely. "Time to get some sleep. You too, old man. There will be much to do come daylight."

Bolthor agreed, standing, and then laying a fur along the bench they'd been sitting on. Would it be wide enough and long enough to hold the giant? Not Thork's concern.

When he entered the added room, the air was cold as a troll's arse on an iceberg, not having a fire in there. He shivered and removed only his boots before sliding between the two furs that warmed Medana on the bed, one under and one over.

He thought she was asleep until she said, "Touch me and I will cut off your balls with the knife I have under my pillow."

Chuckling, he moved closer, his one foot touching her leg.

"By the runes, you are cold," she said.

"And you are warm." He snuggled closer, despite her warning. He'd been threatened with worse weapons and survived. Soon her warmth heated him and he yawned again with the need for rest. Just before he fell asleep, he murmured, "As for the baby, Medana, you are not to worry. I will not abandon you."

"You idiot!" she replied. "I *want* you to abandon me."

"You are under my shield now, sweetling."

She told him what he could do with his shield and it was not a pleasant picture. Still, he was smiling as he fell asleep, his big body wrapped around her smaller one. At first, she lay stiff as a pike, but in time she relaxed.

During the night, his hand somehow strayed and lay across her flat belly. And stayed.

If it's not one thing, it's another . . .

The storm damage was not so bad. Mostly cleanup of debris, repairing thatch roofs, and chopping deadfall into firewood. Medana conceded, with ill grace, that the men had been a gods' send in terms of all their help. It would have taken the women alone a sennight to accomplish what they'd done in one day with the men helping.

Fortunately, Sigrun and Salvana and their dog Bear had managed to get through the tunnel in the midst of the storm. The men would help repair the damage on Small Island after the tunnel opened tonight.

The question was: Would the men be taking *Pirate Lady* with them?

The women vastly outnumbered the men, and they could hold them off for a while, but the men were far superior fighters. In the end, the men would do what they wanted to do. Craftiness went only so far. Besides, in the end, it was the right thing to do . . . to release them willingly. *Some pirate I am!*

Their fate was in the men's hands now.

Truth to tell, some of the women were becoming way too accustomed to the men's hands. Medana had awakened during the night to find Thork's hand on her belly, and she'd done naught to remove it. There was much to be said about the calloused hand of a Viking man and the wicked pleasure its friction could give a woman. There was also much to be said about the gentle hand of a Viking man placed over a woman's belly, as if in protection. Was this related to that silly shield business?

Thork was gone from the bed by daylight when Medana had awakened to find the bed furs tucked around her, like a cozy cocoon. She'd tried to avoid him today because, frankly, she was still blistering furious with him for luring her into sex with the promise of them keeping their longship . . . or the inferred promise.

But now he was approaching her at the side of the hunters' longhouse where she'd been hanging clean clothing on the various bushes. Brokk had helped her for the past few hours to boil them in an enormous laundry kettle over an open fire. There were plenty of limbs and leaves to keep the water hot for another hour or so.

It was tedious work that she normally delegated to the mistress of laundry when down in the village. But she did not set herself so far above others that she would not do menial chores. Besides, her other choice had been to gut an enormous amount of fish that had been caught in nets at the pond entrance to the tunnels. During a storm, fish were often thrust inland, out of their usual sea environment.

Thork caught her still doing laundry around noon, and the first thing out of his fool mouth was "Are you or are you not?"

"What? Angry?"

"Nay, not angry. I already know you are angry. I meant, with child."

Her face heated with color. "How would I know?"

His face bloomed with color, too. By the looks of him—damp tendrils escaping his hair clubbed off his face, perspiration beading his forehead, damp stains on the underarms of his tunic—he had been working hard, too. "The usual way," he offered hesitantly.

"Thork! It has been only one day."

He shifted from foot to foot, obviously uncomfortable with the subject.

She was uncomfortable, too.

"Women sense these things, don't they?"

"I hardly think they do any sensing after one day."

"Well . . ." More foot shifting. "When will you get your next monthly flow?"

For the love of Frigg! "I do not know. A sennight or so, I suppose."

He nodded. "I will have to wait until then."

"And then what?"

She could tell he wasn't expecting that question. His brow furrowed with concentration.

"If I am breeding, what will you do?"

He stared at her for a long moment. "I have no idea. Marry you, I guess."

"Oh really? And would I have any say in that decision?"

"Of course. I mean, would you not want to make your . . . our child legitimate?"

"That depends."

"On what?"

"Would you expect me to be a docile bride like that young girl in Hedeby? Stay home while you gallivant all over the world, free as a bird whilst I stayed here, or at your estate, just waiting with bated breath for you to return and grace me with your wonderful presence. Wouldst you expect me to give up pirating to become a docile bride?"

Gallivant? What the bloody hell is gallivanting? And docile? She wouldn't recognize docility if it bit her on the nose. That's what he thought, but he told her, "Sarcasm ill suits you, m'lady."

"I'll tell you what ill suits me, you bloody idiot. I would not marry you if I were carrying ten of your children."

Further conversation was forestalled by Alrek rushing forward, and almost landing in the laundry kettle.

"A strange ship has arrived," he announced as he panted for breath. "The folks aboard have alighted and they are walking about Small Island."

Thank the gods that Sigrun and Salvana were safe here on Thrudr. Usually the ships that normally stopped for water or to deliver or pick up messages sent only one or two men to shore.

"Is there a flag on the ship?" Thork asked.

Alrek nodded vigorously, still trying to catch his breath.

"The Dragonstead flag," Alrek finally told them.

"My father has arrived," Thork concluded.

Medana did not look happy at all about this latest happenstance.

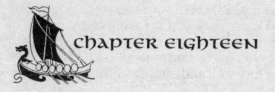

chapter eighteen

Fantasy Island, it was not . . . or was it? . . .

They had arrived on Small Island following a storm that had kept them landlocked in the market town of Kaupang. And now there was no one to be found on the island.

"This is probably another of Thork's warped attempts at humor. My instincts were correct at the start. We have come on this wild chase for naught." Tykir had been griping ever since his longship had left the wharves at Dragonstead. More so when they'd had to stay another day in Kaupang to avoid the storm.

"Blather, blather, blather," was Alinor's response, although she was disappointed, as well. Of course she was. But, unlike her husband, she didn't immediately lay the blame on Thork's shoulders.

She had insisted on coming ashore with Tykir and some of his seamen, along with Starri, Guthrom, and Selik. All they'd discovered was a ramshackle hut that had been damaged by the storm, remnants of a vegetable garden, and evidence that someone had been living on the small island until recently. Obviously, the inhabitants had sought refuge somewhere else until the rain abated. But where? And when would they return?

Further troubling Alinor was the question of how Thork and seven other Viking men could have been living on this small space, along with a bunch of female pirates. They would have been "elbows to arses," as her husband was wont to say. It was a puzzle, and Alinor did love a good puzzle.

While the seamen who'd come ashore with them were piling fallen limbs and other debris to make a fire, her husband was bent over at the waist, examining some animal scat with a stick. "I think there must be a bear living on this island."

"It's probably bird droppings."

"'Twould be one hell of a big bird. Come here, Starri, look at this shit and see what you think," Tykir called out.

Men! They focus on the oddest things. "Bears would not be living on an island this small, lackbrains."

Tykir and Starri shrugged, not convinced.

"I wonder if they might be on that other island," she remarked to no one in particular. When Tykir glanced her way, she pointed to the steeply pitched, mountainous island some distance away.

"I do not see how. There is no shore to speak of. Climbing to the top would require the skills of a mountain goat."

"See. You should have let me bring some of my sheep. I told you it would make a good gift."

"Alinor," he said on a sigh, as if she were too dense to understand manly things, "you do not give gifts to pirates." Adding under his breath, "Especially not stinksome walking blankets."

She rolled her eyes. Tykir was not fond of her sheep, even the far-famed curly-horned ones.

Again, in that condescending voice she hated, he went on, "The Sea Scourge asked for gold, not woolly beasts."

She bared her teeth at him, and he realized, too late, that he'd gone too far. He pretended to cringe in fright.

"No one mocks my precious lambs and gets away with it." She wagged a forefinger at him in warning.

He pinched her bottom. "I was just teasing."

She shook her head as if he was a hopeless case, but then she asked, "What shall we do?"

"Go home."

"I swear, husband, if you say one more time that we never should have come to begin with, you'll be swimming the whole way back to Dragonstead."

He grinned at her. Her husband loved when she got "feisty" with him. "I'm here, aren't I?"

"We will just have to wait until the inhabitants of this island return," she said.

Tykir raised his eyebrows at her. "Are we going to be staying on the ship or in that broken-down hut?"

"Neither. You are going to set up a campsite for me. You did bring tents, didn't you?"

"I always have tents on board," he replied, grumbling again. But then he brightened.

"I know what you are thinking, you scoundrel."

Her husband of almost thirty years was practically a graybeard, but inside, and down low, he still had the desires of a young man. In fact, he looked particularly handsome today in his black leather braies and rust-colored wool tunic with the amber pendant on a gold chain hanging to the middle of his still wide chest. He'd woven amber beads in the gray-threaded war braids framing his face. His golden eyes crinkled with mischief. He might be more than fifty, but there was still a spark in the old man.

He winked at her. "Remember the time we pitched a tent on that Baltic Island where I was harvesting amber. I swear, Starri was started in your belly that night."

"I can hear you," Starri reminded them of his presence nearby.

"Did we make love three or four times?"

"I think I'll go hurl the contents of my stomach," Starri said, and walked away.

She smiled. "Four, if you count that thing you do . . . you know."

They exchanged a knowing glance.

"The Viking S-spot," they said at the same time.

Immediately, Tykir gave orders to the men, "Go back to the ship and bring the tents. Guthrom and Selik, take care of food supplies and the trunk with our clothing. Starri, check out the inside of the hut and see if it's habitable."

"It smells like old woman," Starri complained.

Alinor turned slowly on her heels to glare at him.

Realizing his mistake, Starri said, "You are not old, Mother." He had the good sense then to do as he'd been told.

Turning back to Alinor, Tykir said with mock sternness, "You will owe me for this favor, Alinor."

She put a fingertip to her chin, as if pondering. "There is this thing I heard about involving bed-sport. An unusual . . . um, position."

"What?" he asked, immediately interested.

She whispered in his ear, then stepped back. "Are you shocked?"

"Alinor, Alinor, Alinor, when will you learn? You cannot shock a Viking, especially when it comes to sex." Then he yelled loud enough to wake the dead, "Where is that bloody tent?"

Time to face the (Viking) music . . .

It was past midnight and the tide was getting low. Thork was preparing to go through the tunnel to meet with his parents for the first time in five years. Nervousness had him pacing back and forth. He didn't know what to expect.

The fact that they came must mean they planned to rescue him. Not that he needed rescuing, but they didn't know that. So, yea, he was pleased. Still, he was unsure exactly what reaction there would be.

From their lookout atop the mountain earlier that day, they watched as tents were erected on Small Island, and a campfire built. Good thing Sigrun and Salvana weren't out there. From all the trunks and barrels brought ashore, you'd think they were planning a long stay. *Medana will have a screaming fit.* In fact, there was an air of festivity below. *Hope they brought some of Aunt Eadyth's famous mead.* Truly, he should not be surprised. That was his parents. They never did anything in a small way.

It was hard to tell from the distance between the mountaintop and the island exactly who had accompanied his parents, but Thork was fairly certain that he could pick out Starri, Guthrom, and Selik. *Oh joy! A family reunion!*

Thork had argued with Medana throughout the day and early evening. They must go out and greet his parents. He knew his mother and father. They would not just retreat. His mother, especially, loved a puzzle, and she would consider Medana's ransom letter and an empty Small Island a personal challenge to solve.

In the end, Medana, with a woeful resignation, gave her consent. In her mind, all was lost, now that others would know about Thrudr. While Thork would do his best to maintain her secrets, she was correct in saying he could not guarantee what others might do.

To her credit, Medana was going with him through the tunnel. Reluctantly. Along with his seven men (*Bolthor was composing sagas faster than his thick brain could retain them*), unarmed (*yea, Medana was apparently aware that the men had been pilfering weapons one at a time; how else would Bolthor have been able to chop wood?*), and seven of Medana's women (*fair is fair, she'd contended, a warped pirate logic, Thork supposed*), with weapons (*pirate ladies must keep up their image*). She'd insisted on those equal numbers, and, Thor's hammer, they really were dressed for war, each one carrying a short sword, battle-axe, and shield. Some, like Gudron, even wore a leather helmet. One of them, Elida, carried a bow and quiver of arrows. Demented, that's what they were. One sweep of his father's arm and they would be on their way to Valhalla or Asgard or wherever fallen female warriors went.

Medana, too, was attired like the pirate she was with leather tunic and braies, high boots cross-gartered up to the knees, and a red scarf wrapped around her head and tied in a knot to one side of her neck. Even in the male attire, she appeared beautiful to Thork with those amazing violet eyes and sensuously full lips. And other body parts.

His mother would love her on sight. His father would fall over laughing.

"Why are you smirking?" she asked as movable stairs were being carried over to the almost empty pond for ease of descent and ascent. They would have only two hours before the steep-sided pond started filling again, so no time could be wasted.

"I am not smirking. I was smiling."

"You are happy to be seeing your parents, then?"

"Of course." *Actually, I was picturing you lying on a blanket, minus all those garments, with your blonde hair billowing out like skeins of silk, your thighs spread, your breasts arched up—*

"But nervous also," she remarked.

"Huh?"

"Nervous about your parents." At the questioning tilt of his head, she explained, "You are wearing a path around the pond with your pacing, and you have developed a twitch in your jaw."

He clenched his jaw tightly. "And you . . . are you nervous, Medana?"

"As a cat on hot coals."

"My father and his men would not hurt you,

unless they were attacked first. Even then, they would avoid physical violence with women. Even pirate women." He waggled his eyebrows at that last part of his comment.

"Do not make mock of me."

"I was not. You are the one who named yourself Sea Scourge."

"I did not! Some miscreant monk who did not want to give up his sack of gold coins is the one who did that. All I did was kick him in the shin and knock him to the ground afore making off with the unholy hoard of treasure."

He shook his head with amazement. The possible mother of his child off a-pirating and attacking priests! Lady Alinor would probably not be too happy about the priest business, being a Christian and having been raised in a Saxon household. Thork never told people that he was half Saxon because he considered himself all Viking.

But on to other matters. "Do you know if—"

"Do not ask me again," she warned. "I already told you, at least a dozen times, that I will not know for a sennight or more."

"I just thought . . . well, do these things not come early betimes?"

She crossed her eyes with frustration, and looked damn adorable when she did. " 'These things' do not come early for me. Now, stop asking."

He glanced down to her stomach.

"And stop looking at me there."

He went down the ladder first and waited for Medana at the bottom. And enjoyed watching her descent as the fabric of her braies tautened over her buttocks. Which reminded him that he hadn't taken her from behind yet, dog style, one of his favorite sexual positions. He wondered if he'd get the chance now.

"You better not be ogling my arse," she warned.

"Of course not," he replied, and continued to ogle. Mayhap he would still get an opportunity to try other positions. There must be dozens. Mayhap even hundreds. Nay, he could not think of that. Not now. Not when he was about to face his mother. She would know what he was thinking. Mothers, leastways his mother, could practically read the minds of their naughty sons. *Gods! You would think I am eight years old and not twenty and eight.*

He took her hand, but she pulled it away. "We are not greeting your parents hand in hand."

"Why not?"

"Because it would imply we are lovers, which we are not."

"Right," he agreed. *Although, you must admit, we were lovers already, and we might be again, please gods. It is in the hands of the Norns of Fate now. Or my mother's, if she finds out what I have been up to.*

Torches were being carried by some of his men, and a full moon had just emerged from behind a cloud cover. So there was reasonable nighttime visibility, more so when they emerged on the other side where the moon and stars reflected off the water.

As they walked across the narrow landmass connecting the two islands, he could see that everyone was abed for the night in the three tents and on the ground. Torches on tall poles set at intervals gave some additional light. Two guardsmen were up and on duty but they studied the seas, not expecting to see anyone coming from this direction.

"Hail! We come as friends!" Thork shouted out.

Startled, the two guards jerked around and noticed them for the first time. "Foemen! Foemen!" one of the guards yelled, not recognizing him.

Oops, Thork had forgotten to mention his name. Too late!

His father's other men were rising, too. Out on the longship, torches were being lit. His brothers, naked as the day they were born, emerged quickly from one of the tents. All of them drawing weapons.

Which caused Medana to cut him with a killing glance, as if he'd led them into a trap. She let loose with one of her two-fingers-to-the-mouth whistles. A call to arms.

"Are you demented?" he barked at her.

Guthrom raised a battle cry. "Weapons! Weapons!"

Others were clamoring about in a rush to arm themselves.

"Death to the pirates! Hew them down!"

"An ambush . . . we are being ambushed!"

Guthrom was closest, so Thork roared at him, "Lower your sword, Guthrom! It is me, Thork."

Guthrom didn't hear him apparently because he not only failed to lower his sword but he grabbed a pike as well.

Selik was trying to pull on a pair of braies one-handed while he held a broadaxe in his other hand. And he was yelling, "They came from the sea. Must be underwater warriors. Water gods . . . and, bloody hell! Goddesses, too. Must be they are Valkyries."

He heard Jostein mutter something about, "If these are Valkyries, I do not want to go to Valhalla."

"Is it possible the Water Valkyries are the pirates who took Thork?" Guthrom asked no one in particular.

My family! Thork thought in the midst of the chaos. *I should have expected that things would not go smoothly.* How anyone could mistake the women of Thrudr for Valkyries was beyond Thork.

In the confusion, one of the women shot out an arrow, and hit a member of his family high on one thigh. Guthrom! No wonder! He'd been standing there making a fool of himself with those ridiculous speculations about the women. But whoa! A little higher and his brother's manhood would have been in peril.

Guthrom dropped his sword and gaped at the arrow sticking out from his thigh. The stunned expression on his face was one Thork would relish telling him about. Later.

The whole time Thork was shouting, "It's me. Thork! You bloody idiots!"

Starri picked up several of his throwing knives. Thork recognized him immediately by his red hair and freckles, noticeable even in the half light. If Starri released even one of those knives, someone was going to be dead, so expert was his brother at this particular skill. Thork was about to rush forward and tackle him to the ground, but just then, a loud, booming voice bellowed, "Halt!

Lower your weapons, you bloody lackbrains. It's your lackbrain brother Thork!" Emerging from the tent was his father, who was tying the cords on his braies. Peeping out from behind him was his mother in a night rail, covered with a shawl over her shoulders.

Everyone froze in place, even the women. His father was an imposing figure. And, gods be praised, Thork could see by the torchlight that his father was remarkably the same since last he'd seen him, except for a little more white in his long, sleep-mussed hair. If he'd expected to see a graybeard bent over at the shoulders as some aged folks tended to be, or if he'd thought that old war wound would have deemed his father a cripple by now, Thork was sorely mistaken. And pleasantly so.

The frozen tableau seemed to go on for an hour, but it was probably only a moment before a feminine voice said, "Thork?"

It was his mother.

She took one step forward.

He took one step forward.

Like a whirling dervish, his mother then nigh flew through the air and launched herself at him. Lifting her off her feet into his embrace, he felt her tears against his neck "My son. My son," she kept crooning as her hands patted his back, as if he were a babe and not a full-grown man. When she drew away from him to study his face, she chastised, "How could you have stayed away so long? Do not ever do so again."

It was time to face his father, who'd come up behind Lady Alinor. He'd managed to don a belted tunic, and around his neck was the familiar chain with the hanging star-shaped amber pendant. From a young age, Thork and his brothers had been fascinated by the bloodred drop caught in the yellow stone centuries ago.

Nothing had changed and everything had changed.

"I should knock you to your sorry arse," his father growled.

There was silence all around. Even the women pirates waited with bated breath to hear what the high jarl would say.

"You should," Thork agreed.

"Are you well?"

"As well as can be expected having been captured by a *hird* of dangerous female pirates." Thork was trying for a tone of levity.

His father did not smile, but instead scanned the crowd behind him, giving a nod to his friend Bolthor, then Finn, Jostein, Alrek, and Jamie, whom he also knew well. Henry and Brokk had never met Thork's father.

"Wait here a moment," Thork said to Medana. "Whatever you do, don't kill anyone."

She curled her upper lip with disdain at his lame attempt at humor in such a dire situation.

He went over to check on Guthrom's wound, which turned out to be nothing more than a scrape. The arrow was already removed, and his mother wrapped a linen strip around the wound, while Guthrom winced and complained. "Stop being such a whineling," his mother cautioned. She'd tended much worse injuries when they were boys.

Thork couldn't wait then. He turned to Starri, the brother he'd been closest to, and said, "Sorry I was to hear of Dagne's death."

Starri did not acknowledge his sympathetic gesture. At first. Then he said, "You did not come for her funeral. Where were you when I was grieving?"

"In a Saxon prison," Thork replied.

Starri laughed. "A likely story," but then the two brothers hugged, and all was forgiven.

Thork took his mother by the arm and led her back to where his father still stood talking to Bolthor and Thork's other men. Medana and the women still had their weapons in hand, but fortunately they'd heeded Thork's order not to move. Thork went to stand beside Medana, as a show of support. His mother went to his father's side and was chatting softly with Bolthor.

"Can I assume you have composed a saga to tell me about this happenstance?" his mother asked Bolthor.

Bolthor beamed. "Several, in fact, m'lady."

Tykir turned his attention back to Thork. "I am curious to learn how a presumably fierce Viking warrior could allow himself to be captured by females, and how you all seemed to rise out of the sea just now. Are they witches, as well?"

Thork felt Medana stiffen beside him. He squeezed her arm in reassurance.

His father's eyes latched on to his hand on his captor's arm. His father didn't miss a thing.

"At low tide, a narrow strip of land emerges, connecting Small Island with that larger island behind us. See the tunnel that allows entrance, but only for an hour or two each day, depending on the tides."

His father glowered at Thork . . . and sighed. Before Thork could respond, his father pulled him into a big hug that nigh broke his ribs and had him standing on the tips of his toes. His father was only slightly taller than his sons, but he was massive in the breadth of his chest and the size of his arm muscles. He would not let go for a long time and then only when he said against Thork's ear, "I am much grieved with you, son, and you will pay for your sins, believe you me. For now, though . . ." He seemed to gulp. "I missed you."

When finally released, Thork saw tears in his father's eyes, and that, if nothing else, caused shame to envelop him. "I will never stay away again."

His father's fierce expression softened. "Now, introduce us to these captors of yours."

"This is Medana, the leader of the Thrudr sanctuary." He winked at Medana to give her a nudge of assurance.

She scowled at his wink.

"She is queen, so to speak, of Thrudr, that mountainous island over there," Thork continued, knowing that Medana would hate him giving her that title. " 'Tis where I have been living nigh on three sennights now."

His father studied the island and the tunnel opening, understanding coming gradually to him.

"I still think they came up from the water," Selik said from behind them.

"Spare us your youthling wisdom," his father snapped.

Selik just grinned.

His father gave his full attention to Medana now. With a sweeping glance of condescension, he said, "The Sea Scourge, I presume."

"Precisely." Thork motioned her forward.

Her chin was raised high as she stepped up beside him and in an icy voice of equal disdain said, "Welcome to Thrudr, Jarl Thorksson." In the Norse culture, men took their father's first name as a surname. Thork had been named after his grandfather Thork, Tykir's father. "I have heard much about you, as well as your good wife," Medana continued, nodding at his mother, whose jaw had dropped long ago and continued to gape open.

Catching herself, Lady Alinor spoke up, "I look forward to knowing you better, Medana. Is that permissible for a captor and the captive's mother?"

His father snorted his opinion as to what would be permissible or not permissible when he was around. "They are pirates, not bloody Valkyries."

"But I thought—" Selik started to say.

"Hush!" Guthrom said, nudging Selik with an elbow.

"Permissible? Since when, wife, must we extend courtesy to outlaw Norsewomen?" his father grumbled.

Lady Alinor gave her husband a sweet smile, at the same time warning, "Watch your fool tongue, husband."

Thork also introduced Medana to his three brothers, who by now were much more interested in the women. They were all fully clothed now, but not before the ladies of Thrudr had gotten an eyeful. Plus, most of Guthrom's one leg was visible through the long slit in his braies.

"And these are some of the women of Thrudr," Thork went on. "First off, this is Gudron, mistress of military." That should be obvious to one and all, with the large woman dressed in full battle gear, including a leather helmet, chain mail, and both a short sword and a pike.

"That is a nice sword," Selik commented. "Is it pattern welded?"

Tykir reached over and swatted his youngest son aside the head before Gudron could reply.

"What? All I said was—"

"And this is Bergdis, mistress of buildings and woodworking," Thork interjected before his father and Selik got into a wrestling match. Not an uncommon occurrence. The short woman with frizzy red hair carried an axe, possibly the one Bolthor had been using for firewood. She smiled, showing a space where a front tooth was missing. "Bergdis is an impressive rower when the women of Thrudr go a-pirating."

"With those shoulders, she could no doubt pull a longship herself," his father muttered under his breath.

"Delightful to meet you, Bergdis," his mother spoke up before his father said any louder what he was thinking.

"Solveig is the mistress of shipwrighting, having been trained by her father, who was an expert shipwright."

Solveig beamed at Thork for the compliment, and for not having mentioned how long it was taking to build their own longship.

"Impressive," Tykir admitted grudgingly.

"Liv is the mistress of healing. Freyja, mistress of hunt and fish. Lilli, mistress of indoor steward-ship . . . cooking, laundry, and the like. Do not be scowling so, Henry. Everyone knows you have first dibs on the fair Lilli."

"Good gods! The pirate women have been se-ducing you men," his father remarked with dis-gust.

"Not all of us!" Jostein and Bolthor said as one.

"They want our man seed and that is all," Alrek revealed, then ducked his shoulders when he saw the attention he had garnered.

His mother arched a brow at Thork, wondering exactly what he had done, probably assuming he had spread his man seed far and wide. Nay, just in one womb. Possibly.

"By the by, Bolthor," his mother said. "Your wife is looking for you. Lady Katherine sent a longship to Hedeby to see if you might be there."

"I am dead. Dead, dead, dead," Bolthor moaned, putting two hands to his heart. "If she finds out where I am, on an island of women, I might as well just lie down and die."

Thork grinned at Bolthor's dramatics. "Finally, this is Elida, mistress of threads and an archer-in-training. She is the one who managed to shoot you in the thigh, Guthrom."

Guthrom cut a scowl at Elida, promising retri-bution later.

Elida just gave him an embarrassed wave and confessed, "I was aiming for your belly."

Guthrom exhaled with a loud whoosh of dis-gust.

And his father chuckled, "Good thing she did not hit those manparts you are always bragging on, Guthrom."

"Then I would ne'er have any grandchildren from you," his mother added, also with a chuckle.

"Not to fear! You could have hired yourself out as a eunuch in one of those eastern harems," Starri offered.

"You always said you wanted to check out some harems, Guth." This from Selik, who had grown into a man since Thork had been gone.

Guthrom was not amused by any of it.

That was the way with his family. A conversation started on one subject and always veered off in five other directions.

The women, Medana included, were astonished by this interplay among his family members. Little did they know that it was the norm, nothing unusual.

"What is all this 'mistress this' and 'mistress that' about?" his mother wanted to know.

Medana explained, "When I first came here ten years ago, there were only a dozen of us. Now, we are almost two hundred women."

His father, Guthrom, Starri, and Selik exclaimed as one, "Two hundred women!" Then they turned as one to Thork as if he'd personally amassed such a large gathering of females.

"Go on," his mother encouraged Medana while scowling at her three sons and husband for the interruption.

"We established the village on Thrudr, through the tunnel there. Over the years, more and more women joined our refuge. From the beginning, we decided that everyone would be equal on this island and everyone must work. Thus, we gave each job, no matter how small, a title. Mistress of this or that."

Thork was amazed that Medana would be revealing so much about Thrudr, but then she was resigned to their life there never being the same. How could it be?

"That is fascinating. I cannot wait to see the island," Lady Alinor said to Medana, then realized when her remark was met with silence that she hadn't been invited to visit. Not that his father couldn't insist on entrance, and he would, but it was best to go in an amicable manner.

When the silence continued for an embarrassing amount of time, Thork decided he would have to intervene. Taking Medana by the arm, he pulled her aside. "Medana, you have to invite my family inside. You cannot expect them to just turn around and go home."

"But . . . I thought . . ."

"You thought what?"

"That you would meet your parents and that you and the men would stay here on Small Island overnight, then go back to Hedeby on the morn."

You think so little of me, do you, Medana? "And where would you and your women be?"

"Back on Thrudr. It would not be the most satisfactory solution since now some outsiders know of our hideaway, but the best under these conditions. Yea, I know they are your family, but still they are outsiders, you must admit. That is the consequence of our having brought outsiders to the island to begin with, meaning you men."

Me? An outsider? After all we shared? He stared at her for a long moment. "Are you daft? My parents travel all the way here and that is the hospitality you offer them?"

"We are pirates. We do not offer hospitality."

Stubborn wench! "Pfff! And besides, you are not schluffing me off so easily."

"Schluffing? That is a new word," she remarked irrelevantly.

"I just made it up." He glanced down at her belly. "Do I need to remind you why I will not be leaving right away?"

She flung her arms out with an air of resignation and walked back to the group. "Lady Alinor, it would be my pleasure to welcome you to Thrudr. Our accommodations are simple, not what you are accustomed to, but please accept our hospitality."

"Thank you so much, Medana," his mother said.

"Only Mother and Father and my brothers," Thork said in an effort to appease Medana. "The others will have to stay here on Small Island."

His father was not happy about that fact but he agreed, "Tell those women to put away their sorry weapons. I could hew them all down single-handed."

Gudron did not like that observation, not one bit, if the flexing of her fingers on the hilt of her sword was any indication, but she remained silent when Medana gave her a silent message with a motion of her head.

After gathering some belongings, they prepared to walk over the land strip. The tide was already rising. There would be only a half hour's time at most.

Still, Bolthor stopped them all and said, "This occasion demands a saga."

"Nay!" Thork, his father, and three brothers said, but his mother gave Bolthor a quick hug and said, "What a wonderful suggestion!"

"This is the saga of Thork the Great," Bolthor began.

"I thought *I* was known as 'The Great' in your sagas," his father snickered.

"Ah, I meant no offense, Tykir. Let me start over."

> "This is the saga of Thork the Great, son of Tykir
>   the Greater."

Thork and his father both rolled their eyes, which didn't slow Bolthor down at all.

> "Viking men are sometimes wild
> Causing mischief since a child.
> Thork was the worst of all,
> Never walking away from a brawl.
> Wenching, pirating, guzzling ale,
> Thork did all with a lusty hail.
> Never mind his mother's tears.
> Never mind his father's sneers.
> But then a pirate lady did come
> Plucked the rascal away like a juicy plum.
> But the plum was tart,
> And capturing him proved not very smart.
> Because now the Viking had the pirate's heart.
> Or mayhap that is wrong.

Mayhap we should sing another song.
What if the Viking is now lost
In the love skeins by a pirate tossed?"

Silence met Bolthor's saga. Then one by one everyone turned to look at Thork and Medana.

Thork turned on his heels before anyone could ask questions or make mock of him. He did hear his brothers' laughter following him, and his father said, "What can you expect from a wild child?"

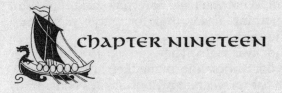

CHAPTER NINETEEN

**A man can't control where
his eyes wander . . .**

Two days Thork's family had been on the
island of Thrudr, and they showed no signs
of leaving anytime soon.

Medana chastised herself for meanspirited-
ness. Truly, they were a nice family, even the
blustering Tykir, and the three handsome brothers had dozens of her feckless women all atwitter,
but Medana had to think beyond the imminent
departure of these most unusual visitors and the
men they'd captured. Most of all, she had to make
plans for Thrudr . . . how to protect it from invaders, assuming the women would be vulnerable
now that their secret was out, or might leak out
any day now.

She was walking with Alinor now—that's how
the lady asked to be called—showing her the various industries carried on by the women. They had
just left the weaving shed.

"I am going to send you one of my prize curly-
haired rams and several good ewes. I mean no
insult, but you need to breed a better quality
sheep, Medana, if you want to make better qual-

ity wool. What you have now may suffice for your own clothing needs, but for trade, merchants demand the best."

Alinor was right. They did get low prices for their wool fabrics. Improving their stock had been on her list for years now, but always something more important took precedence.

"You have already promised to send some of the far-famed mead and timekeeping candles made by your sister-by-marriage Lady Eadyth. I cannot continue to accept so many gifts when I . . . when I . . ."

"Captured my son?" Alinor finished for her with a grin.

"Yea."

"But it was my understanding you were not personally to blame for the, um, crime."

"'Tis true, but a leader is responsible for those under her."

Alinor nodded her head in agreement. "I must tell you that I am very impressed with the community here at Thrudr, and I want to do everything in my power to make it continue to thrive. Women must help each other." She put up a halting hand when Medana was about to speak. "I know you are worried about your secret location being made known to one and all, but, really, you just need to rethink how you operate. Arm yourselves better . . . from the outside. Establish better security on Small Island and at the tunnel entrance."

"And how would we do that?" Alinor had been told the history of Thrudr. Surely, she understood the problems.

"Men," Alinor answered. "You need men on the island."

Medana rolled her eyes. "That is where our problems began. The women captured your son and his comrades."

"Ah, but that was different. They were looking for men to give them children and naught else. Not men to populate your island permanently."

Medana felt her face color at Alinor's bluntness.

"We will address that later. Speaking as a mother, I would not be happy if I knew that I had grandchildren that I would ne'er get to know. While many men have no qualms about where they spill their seed, in a good family, a good man takes responsibility for his actions."

Medana had to commend Alinor for raising her sons with such principles. Alinor's appearance was unremarkable. She was not a beautiful woman in the traditional sense, not with her wildly curly, bright red hair, dusted with silver threads denoting her age of close to fifty years, and big, rust-colored freckles that covered almost every surface of her body. Tykir, on the other hand, was a very handsome man, even at his age, with mostly gray, dark blond hair. He was the type of man that women would have salivated over when he was young, even if he'd had no social status or wealth.

"How did you meet your husband?" Medana asked. "Oh, I am sorry. I did not mean to ask such a personal question."

Alinor laughed. "Believe me, I get asked that question a lot. And the story is worth relating, over and over. When the Norse king's manpart took a right turn, halfway down, he was convinced that I, a witch, had put a spell on it. So he sent Tykir to my home in Northumbria to bring me back to the Norselands to correct his crooked cock. I did not go willingly."

Medana blinked with incredulity at the astonishing woman. "And did you? Straighten it out?"

"Good heavens, nay! Tykir did capture me, and we did go back to the Norse court, but I am not a witch. In the end, the overused manpart corrected itself."

Medana shook her head to clear it of all the additional questions Alinor's vague answer had raised. Like, had Alinor been Tykir's captive, and yet fallen in love with her captor? Nay, that was a question best left unspoken . . . and too similar to her own situation. They had come to the side garth of one of the longhouses where soap was being made today . . . the special scented soaps that Elida was noted for. The air was filled with the pleasant aroma of roses, lavender, honey, and evergreen. Alinor picked up several of the drying squares and sniffed. Smiling, she asked if she could take a sample of each back with her to Dragonstead. "Eadyth would be interested in your honey soaps. Where do you get your honey, by the by?"

"In the markets, or"—Medana felt herself blushing again—"on pirate ventures. We manage to harvest some wild honey on Thrudr, but not enough for all our purposes."

Alinor smiled, seemingly not shocked by female pirating.

What an unusual lady!

"When I send you the ram and sheep, I will have Eadyth send some beehives and crates of bees to start you off on your own enterprise. In fact, I can guarantee that Eadyth will want to come herself . . . to offer her assistance, but out of curiosity as well."

They were walking now back toward the larger of the longhouses where the evening meal would soon be served. The men, Tykir included, slept up at the hunters' hut, but they all assembled down here when breaking fast. Tonight they would be serving a special feast since an exceptionally large wild boar had been killed and had been roasting all day in a fire pit.

"Even if what you say is true about men here on Thrudr," Medana said, resuming their earlier conversation, "that would not solve all our problems. As you know, I killed the man my brothers betrothed me to. I took the longship that would have been my bride-gift. My brothers cannot gain ownership of the small estate left me by my mother unless I am dead, or married to a spouse of their choice who would give it to them."

"First things first, dearling." Alinor patted her on the sleeve of her tunic. "You had just cause to strike out at that evil Ulfr. His reputation was well-known in some parts. Even after ten years, you could probably find women or servants who suffered his perversions."

"Hmpfh! There are several here on the island."

"You need to go back to King Harald's court and ask for a hearing to be held at the next Althing. In fact, one is scheduled for next month in Vestfold, I think."

"Nay, nay, nay! My brothers and Ulfr's family and friends at court would testify against me."

"Medana, Haakon was king back then. He is dead now."

"Still the same royal family."

"You have powerful people at your back now, Medana. Not just my son Thork, but my husband, other high jarls in the Norselands who would do Tykir's bidding in a trice, even Tykir's brother Eirik, who is a Saxon ealdorman."

"That is all well and good, but—"

"And here's a fact you might not know. King Harald and my husband are cousins. Tykir's father, Thork, and Eric Bloodaxe, once king of Northumbria, were half brothers. Oh, Thork was illegitimate, but that is of no matter, the blood tie is still there. Harald Greycloak is one of Eric Bloodaxe's many sons."

Medana was shocked. Thork was of royal blood, even if from the wrong side of the blanket.

But Alinor was still talking. "My husband was a noted warrior at one time and he has told me numerous times that the best strategy is to be the aggressor, not to wait for your enemy to attack."

Tears welled in Medana's eyes, not because she believed anything could be done for her, but because so many would be willing to try.

Just then, they came upon Thork and his father and three brothers, who were helping Solveig with the new longship, which was already framed out. In just one day, they'd accomplished more than the women had in the past few years. Of course, there were many women standing about who had duties elsewhere. They were trying to get the attention of the bare-chested men, none of them having given up on the man seed business yet.

Tykir walked over and kissed his wife on the cheek. Thork tried to do the same to Medana, but she turned her head away, hissing, "Behave, you oaf!"

"You forgot odious."

"What are you blathering about?"

"Odious oaf. Remember?" He winked at her.

She tried her best not to look at him, to notice the vast amount of exposed skin, every bit of which she had touched with pleasure. Not that she was recalling that.

"Alinor, dost know that Thork does not intend to leave with us?" Tykir said to his wife.

Alinor raised a brow at Thork.

"Father mentioned possibly leaving Thrudr tonight and setting sail from Small Island on the morrow. I am not ready to leave yet, nor is Henry. The others will go with you to Hedeby and you can send my longship back here, assuming that my men are still there."

His longship? More men? Nay, nay, nay!

"I know why Henry wants to stay, but why you?" Alinor asked.

"I would think you would be anxious to return to your wild ways," his father added, his eyes twinkling with some mischief.

"I already told you that I have reformed and that I was on my way back to Dragonstead when I was captured by Medana."

"Not by me. By my women," she corrected.

Thork waved a hand airily at the distinction.

"If you were on your way to Dragonstead, why not return there with us?" His mother's brow furrowed with confusion.

"Because I have matters yet unsettled here."

"What matters?" his father asked with exasperation. "Your mother is already planning a return trip to Thrudr with her bloody damn sheep."

Alinor cut her husband with a glare.

"With her pretty damn sheep," Tykir amended.

"You cannot stay here," Medana told Thork.

"Why not?"

"Because you . . ." She realized that he was just waiting for her to give him an opening about the possible pregnancy. "Because you must go to Hedeby and complete your betrothal to the fair Berla, daughter of Jarl Ingolf Bersson."

"You are promised?" His mother clapped her hands with joy.

"To Bersson's daughter?" his father exclaimed at the same time.

"Promised to be promised," Thork told them, "but I have changed my mind." He smiled at Medana.

"Oh gods, now I will have Bersson coming to Dragonstead demanding you honor your agreement," Tykir said.

"Nay, you will not. I did not agree to a formal betrothal. I was waiting for your approval."

"I approve," his father said quickly.

"I do not," his mother added. "Do you love Berla?"

"Of course not."

His mother rolled her eyes. "Dumb as dirt my sons are."

"Hey, what did I do?" his three brothers asked.

"Why does he say 'of course not'?" Tykir asked Alinor, as if Thork were not just standing there like a grinning stump.

Alinor shrugged. "I want a love match for my firstborn," she said.

Thork groaned.

Thork should not be groaning. He was the one who had started this conversation. Well, not about Berla, but about his staying on Thrudr.

"We had a love match, husband," Alinor was chattering on. "Would you not want the same for Thork?"

"Not if I have to wait 'til he is a graybeard for it to happen."

Thork grinned as if he'd won some argument.

But it was just a postponement. Medana knew that neither Tykir nor Alinor would let the matter rest until they discovered what Thork was up to.

They found out soon enough.

During the feast that night, when the great hall of the biggest longhouse was loud with conversation and laughter, Brokk asked Thork a question. Unfortunately, Brokk's question came at just that moment when there was a lull in the noise.

"Why are you always staring at Medana's belly?"

Everyone turned to stare at Thork, and then at Medana's belly.

Medana stood and stormed out the door, leaving Thork to answer all the questions that were sure to come. Served him right!

Oops! He did it again! . . .

"It's not what you think," Thork told his parents.

"Pfff!" his father said.

"You were staring at the lady pirate's belly?" Starri asked from his other side. "Well, I do not blame you, but, with the men's braies these women wear, it is their arses that draw a man's attention more, in my opinion."

"Shut your teeth, lackbrain," Thork said.

"I thought it was a woman's breasts that men admired most." This from Selik, who had seen sixteen winters but sounded like an untried youthling. Mayhap their mother had tied him to her apron strings overlong, though he could not imagine his father condoning that. When Thork had been sixteen, his father had shown him his collection of feathers, *and* explained their carnal purposes. By then, Thork could have explained a thing or two to his father about sex.

Guthrom, who was still brooding over being shot by an arrow from a woman's quiver, had his barely wounded leg propped on a barrel. He advised Thork, " 'Tis past time for you to leave this barmy place, lest you find yourself trapped by the women's wiles."

Several women seated nearby gasped with outrage. One of them, probably Elida, who had been subjected to Guthrom's constant scorn, looked at his brother and said, "Do not fear, Lord Full-of-Himself Viking. No wiles will be directed your way."

Lady Alinor pounded her fist on the table and stood suddenly. Addressing Thork with narrowed eyes, she asked, "Is Medana with child or is she not?" She had on her do-not-fool-with-me-son! expression.

"I do not know."

"Pfff!" his father said again.

"*Could* Medana be with child?" his mother persisted.

"Mayhap."

"Wiles, I tell you. Beware of the wily traps," Guthrom warned.

Tykir, standing to his full impressive height, glared down at Guthrom. "Go walk off your miserable, mead-sodden state."

"I cannot walk with this gimpy leg," Guthrom complained.

"Then limp it off," his father said in a roar that brooked no argument.

His mother gave his father a little smile of thanks for his intervention. Then they all turned back again to Thork, who had the good sense to stand as well, preparing to go after Medana and make amends, if he could.

"Mayhap?" His mother tilted her head at him. If possible, the freckles stood out even more on her pale face, a sure sign that she was not happy with him. "Explain yourself, son."

Thork shook his head. "This is a matter for Medana and myself to resolve. You will get an explanation only if, and when, Medana deems it wise."

On those unexpected words and five gaping mouths, he stormed off to find the pirate maid who might or might not be carrying his child. He found her leaning against the back wall of the cow byre, chomping away on a carrot.

A carrot?

Uh-oh!

Women had odd cravings for food when they were pregnant, didn't they? He seemed to recall his mother saying that she ate so many blueberries when she was carrying Selik, it was a wonder he wasn't born blue.

Should he remark on that fact to Medana?

Not if he valued his skin!

She put the carrot in her mouth and glanced sideways at him through half-lidded eyes.

He almost swallowed his tongue. Thus, it was in a choked voice that he said, "Please accept my apology, Medana." *And would you mind if I replace that carrot with something else?*

She took a huge bite off the end of the carrot and crunched away.

Ouch!

"Go away."

Instead, he walked up and leaned against the byre wall beside her. "I really am sorry."

"For what? Ruining my life?"

I would not go that far. "For embarrassing you."

"I told you to stop staring at my belly."

"I cannot help myself." *Eat some more carrot, sweetling.*

"Because you are suddenly anxious to be a father?"

How many times do I have to tell her that sarcasm ill suits a lady?

Mayhap now is not the time to remind her of that fact.

"Nay, I am not anxious to be a father. Not at this time, leastways."

"At least you are honest. About that."

The implication being that he was dishonest in other regards. He would overlook that insult for now. "You did not let me finish. I would not choose to have planted my seed in you—"

"Me? That is what riles you most, is it not? That your first child might be born of a lowly female pirate?"

There is naught lowly about you, Medana. If you only knew!

"Your mother told me about your blood ties to the Norse royal family."

He laughed. "Medana! Those ties are so long and twisted and broken. I do not consider myself of that status and, truth to tell, I would not want to be. What a family of vipers! Now, if you would stop interrupting me, wench," he growled with mock ferocity, "I could finish what I started to say."

"Go on."

"While this is not the best of times to be contemplating fatherhood, or motherhood, I find myself more and more fascinated by the prospect. That is why my eyes are drawn to your stomach so often. Is it possible that a tiny son, or daughter, is already growing in there?"

"Well, drawing attention to my belly is not going to make it true, or untrue," she sniped, then put a hand to her face before commenting, "Your mother must consider me a harlot."

"Are you serious? Rumor is that my mother and father rutted like rabbits before they were married, and I know for a fact that I was already a growing seed afore the wedding."

That seemed to make her feel better. So he took a chance and linked his hand with hers, the one not still clutching a carrot. Raising the double fist to his mouth, he kissed the back of her hand and said, "I know you are worried about being with child. Nay, let me finish. And I know you are worried about your island and how your secret location is now vulnerable to attacks. But I want to assure you that I will not abandon you."

"You mean, if I am increasing?"

He shook his head. "Either way, I will find a way to protect you."

She remained dubious.

He unlinked their hands and moved in front of her. Bending his knees so he was on eye level with her, he tipped her chin and entreated, "Trust me, Medana. Can you do that?"

"I have trusted only myself for a long time. I do not think I could place my fate in another's hands."

"My family then. My parents. They are outrageous and betimes a bit barmy, but they treasure honor above all else. Do you think they would leave you here without protection?"

"Well, I could probably trust your mother," she said, "but only because she now thinks I might be carrying her grandchild."

"You do not know my mother. Yea, she yearns for grandchildren and fears none of her four witless sons will ever produce any for her afore she is feeble and unable to lift a tiny squalling body. But she cares very much about the abuse of women. Ask her sometime about the three husbands she was forced to take, and buried, afore she wed my father. Ask her about her brothers, if you think you are the only one with greedy, grab-land, vicious siblings."

"Really?" She tried to smile.

He took that for a good sign. Putting his fingertips to the pulse beating in her neck, he gave her a soft kiss to seal his pledge of protection. Then he kissed her a little harder, to show he was sincere. Finally, he gripped her head, tunneling his fingers in her hair, and kissed her deeply, because he could. And because she was not shoving him away.

Her skin carried the aroma of roses, from the soap she'd used to bathe, no doubt. He had used the pine-scented one. Together they would complement each other. *Evergreen roses*, he thought with an inward smile. He would have to tell Medana, later, to try that combination in soap making. It could be their signature soap.

Good gods! My brain must be melting if I am fantasizing about soaps when my cock is having altogether different fantasies.

He took the carrot that still dangled from one hand and tossed it over his shoulder. Then he hitched her body up so that her feet were off the ground, and her legs must needs wrap around his hips for balance. Placing her arms around his shoulders, he settled his open mouth over hers and kissed her for a totally different reason. Because he was hungry for her.

"You are a troll," she murmured at one point, and nipped at his bottom lip.

"Kiss me hard enough, my dear pirate, and I will turn into a glorious god."

She tried to laugh but his tongue got in the way.

A madness of sorts overtook him then as his mouth seduced hers with wicked intentions he hadn't even known he harbored. Leastways, sex had not been his intention when he'd come after Medana. Well, there were different kinds of apologies, he supposed.

His hands roamed everywhere, reacquainting him with all her parts . . . her breasts, her back and shoulders, her hips and buttocks.

When she moaned into his mouth, he moaned back into hers. They anticipated each other's needs and wants in ways he had not imagined were possible. Sometimes she mirrored his actions, sometimes she initiated delicious ones of her own.

Somehow, and he would swear later that he didn't know how it happened, he found his braies at his ankles, and her braies at her ankles. He put his fingers to her cleft and she anointed him with her woman-dew. That was all the encouragement he needed to place himself at her slick entrance.

With eyes half blinded with the glaze of arousal, he begged in a voice so husky he scarce recognized himself, "Let me, Medana."

Her eyes, too, seemed unfocused. But she must have heard him because she nodded, and took his phallus in hand guiding him inside her, bit by agonizing bit. The whole time her inner folds were clenching and rippling around him in welcome.

It was short and incredibly satisfying. One, two, three thrusts and it was over. But in the process she bit his shoulder to hold back her cries, and he murmured incoherent sex words against her neck.

Once they had reached their mutual peaks and were sated, he slipped out of her body, and they both drew their breeches back up. As they were trying to relace themselves, Medana said, "Now you have really done it."

"*We* did it," he corrected.

"It matters not who did the doing. You did not pull out. Again."

That shocked Thork. He was meticulous about spilling his seed outside his partner's body. Fifteen long years he'd practiced that kind of control. Now he'd failed to do so. Not once, but twice. "Well, I guess it does not matter if you are already pregnant."

"You idiot! What if I wasn't pregnant? What if you made me pregnant this time?"

Oops! he said to himself, but would not dare to say aloud.

" 'Tis obvious that I am unable to resist your charms. Your kisses obviously bestir my passions. One touch of your calloused fingertips, and it is like spark to tinder," she admitted. "So, in future, you must stay away from me."

A wash of inordinately intense pleasure swept over him at her words. "Sweetling! You should not tell me that. Now I will be unable to stay away." Not that he could, anyway.

There was no time to say more because his mother was looking for them. "Thork, where are you? Medana, we must talk."

He put a forefinger to his lips to warn Medana to remain silent. Into her ear, he whispered, "Stay here while I distract my mother."

She nodded.

He kissed her quickly then and murmured, "Remember. Trust."

Sauntering around the corner of the byre, he called out, "Mother, have you found Medana? I cannot imagine where she might be hiding."

"Tsk, tsk, tsk!" She sniffed the air, and Thork winced. His mother could pick out the musky scent of sex at twenty paces when her sons had been boys. Why would it be any different now? "What have you done, Thork?"

He was not going to discuss *that* with his mother. "Trust me, Mother. I will make everything aright."

"I am not the one you need to convince."

He knew that.

"Do you love her?"

Thork flinched. It was a question he hadn't expected and truthfully hadn't even considered. Tentatively, he replied, "I do not know."

"You should come back to Dragonstead with us, or go to Hedeby. Just leave the poor woman alone."

"I cannot."

"Well, that is your answer then."

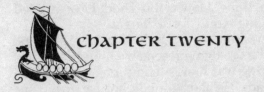

CHAPTER TWENTY

**Did the Brady Bunch have family
meetings like this? . . .**

Medana thought she couldn't be any more
embarrassed, but sitting in a meeting with
Tykir, Alinor, and Thork to discuss her intimate
condition was beyond humiliating. Medana had
agreed to sit down with them in the rush of ex-
hilaration on learning that Thork's parents would
be leaving Thrudr that evening . . . and hopefully
Thork would accompany them.

They were sitting on benches at the far end of
the hall of one of the smaller longhouses, sipping
at wooden cups of Lady Eadyth's delicious mead.
Thork sat beside her, and his mother and father
faced them from the other side of the table. His
father wore war braids intertwined with crystals in his dark blond and gray hair. A beautiful
star-shaped amber pendant on a gold chain hung
down over his leather tunic. Alinor looked equally
impressive in a deep green *gunna*. Her bright red
hair with a small smattering of silver threads was
held off her face with a twisted silver fillet in the
shape of writhing dragons. They made a handsome couple and their affection for each other was

a palpable thing. How could Thork have avoided such a loving family for so long?

And speaking of . . . well, thinking of Thork, he looked more than presentable himself. He, too, was wearing war braids today, interspersed with amber beads. He had a thunderbolt earring in one ear only, giving him a rascally look. He was close-shaven and smelled of pine soap. Nigh irresistible, she had to admit.

"These cups are remarkable," Alinor said, examining the fine carving on the one in her hands. This particular set had animals on them with a forest background. Deer, squirrels, birds, and such.

"Tofa, our mistress of woodcarving, makes those. Aren't they incredible? You should see the work she does on chair backs. We can sell as many as she makes in Hedeby."

"I think I met her yesterday. The woman with long black hair worn in a coronet about her head?"

Medana nodded.

"She had the most adorable little girl with her."

"That would be Rikva. She is four years old. Mistress of turnips, we call her. 'Tis her job to pull out neeps in the garden."

Everyone smiled at that.

"There is not one single person here who does not have a job and a title," Thork bragged, as if he had a proprietary interest in the island.

Medana looked at Thork with surprise.

"Now, let us be forthright here, Medana," Tykir said. "Are you or are you not with child?"

Medana looked to Thork for help. He just shrugged.

"As I have told Thork repeatedly, I will not know for days yet, mayhap as much as a sennight. I ne'er had reason to keep exact track of such things in the past." Medana didn't think her face could get any hotter.

She was wrong.

"There are early signs betimes," Alinor mused. "Do your breasts feel overly full and overly sensitive?"

"How would I know, with all the handling by calloused fingers they have been subjected to of late?" Immediately, Medana regretted her impulsive outburst. But it was too late, of course.

Thork was grinning like a preening peacock as he turned his hands over to expose his calloused palms and fingers. His father was chuckling with pride. His mother was eyeing the two of them speculatively.

"Well, there are other signs, as well. Like moodiness," Alinor continued.

"She snaps my head off every time I get near her," Thork told them.

"I did that from the first time I met your irksome self," Medana said.

Again, Thork grinned with ill-placed pride.

"And piss. My lady wife had to piss all the time when she was carrying," Tykir disclosed.

Medana had been visiting the privy a lot, but she'd attributed it to nervousness with all the people about.

"Of course, a sure as certain sign is that the nipples and aureolae, those rings around the nipples, get darker in color." This intimate detail from Tykir again.

"Father!" Thork chided with a laugh.

"Lackwit!" Alinor slapped Tykir on the arm.

"What? 'Tis the truth."

"You do not discuss female parts in public," Alinor explained.

"This is not public. This is family," Tykir grumbled.

Me? Family?

Alinor turned her attention to Medana with a questioning expression on her face.

"I have not looked there lately," Medana said, with an even hotter face. Any more blushing, and the skin on her cheeks would catch fire.

"I could check for you," Thork offered.

She was the one slapping *Thork's* arm now.

"How about food cravings?"

She exchanged a glance with Thork, whom she knew was recalling the carrot last night. Which brought other images to mind. She could tell they had like minds when he winked at her. The rogue!

"None that I can think of," Medana lied.

"Remember the time you caught me eating gammelost and honey, heartling," Alinor said to her husband. "That is how you knew I was carrying Thork."

Thork made a gagging sound, and Medana wasn't sure if it was at the idea of stinky cheese and honey, or the prospect of his parents getting nostalgic.

"Well, whether you are increasing or not is not really the issue, Medana. You are a highborn lady compromised by a highborn man, and that requires a marriage," Tykir declared.

"Nay!" she and Thork said at the same time.

"Let us not rush things," Thork said.

The insensitive rat!

His mother gave Thork a look that would melt a rock.

"I did not mean—" Thork tried to hedge.

"I would not marry the loathsome lout if he knelt on burning coals and begged me," Medana proclaimed.

Alinor smiled, and Medana realized that she'd slipped by calling Thork a "loathsome lout."

"We have decided that you should come back to Dragonstead with us," Tykir said in a voice that brooked no argument. "We will leave some men behind for protection of Thrudr. That way your concerns over the vulnerability of the island will be taken care of. You will be out of reach of your brothers or the king's men, if it comes to that, since you will be under my shield. And you and Thork will have an opportunity to make decisions about your future together. Know this, my dear Medana, if you are carrying my grandchild, it will be born in marriage. I know from personal experience the scorn that illegitimacy carries."

This was a long speech for Tykir to make, and they all remained silent taking in his words.

"I do not want to leave Thrudr," Medana insisted.

There was no time for further discussion because Brokk, the young Viking comrade of Thork's, came stumbling in. "Ships . . . there are ships headed toward Small Island."

"Well, we often have ships stop by for fresh water, or to deliver and pick up messages left by other passing vessels."

Brokk shook his head vigorously. "Bolthor said they carry flags that are identifiable, even from the mountaintop. Lady Katherine's . . . she is Bolthor's wife, and he is moaning and flailing his arms like a scared chicken. The two others have white thunderbolts against black fields."

"My brothers," Medana gasped.

Tykir stood and rubbed his hands together. "Nothing like a good fight to whet an old man's juices!"

"You are not fighting," Alinor told her husband.

Tykir picked his wife up off the bench and kissed her deeply on the mouth. "Try and stop me," he said. "Come, Thork, we must gather the men and plan strategy."

Thork looked at Medana as if considering the same.

"Do not dare," she warned.

He grinned and rushed out with his father, Brokk following after them.

"Wait!" Medana said, but they were already gone.

Alinor sat back down across the table from Medana, then glanced around at the empty cups and empty benches before saying, "That went well, didn't it?"

The worst possible thing happened . . .

Thork stood on the mountaintop with his father and Starri, staring down at Small Island. It looked as if the three new ships were staying. That meant that one of his father's men must have told them about the tunnel.

Of course, Medana, Gudron, and several of the pirate warrior women were there, too. Medana insisted it was their island, their problem, and they must be involved in the solution.

Bolthor was there also. Guthrom, Selik, and Thork's other men were down in the village assembling every weapon on the island to get an idea of total inventory. They would also be helping to train the women warriors in fighting techniques they might not have yet mastered and refreshing their own skills. There were plenty of swords and lances and bows and arrows aboard his father's longships, but they didn't want to rush out at first low tide and alert Medana's brothers that the island was now under the shield of the Thorksson family.

"I will go through the tunnel first to forestall Katherine coming through," Bolthor decided. "I fear for her safety when Medana's brothers are here for their own devious purposes."

"That is a good idea," Tykir said, "although my seamen know enough to offer her protection. Plus, Katherine did not come here without her own guardsmen. If you go through alone, they will not feel threatened."

"Medana, I think you need to stay out of sight. At first, leastways," Thork said.

She immediately stiffened, willful wench that she was. "I will not cower like a timid bird."

" 'Tis not bravery that is needed here. Strategy is more important. Outwitting the enemy," Tykir told her, putting an arm around her shoulders and squeezing. If Thork had tried that, she would have clobbered him on the spot.

"I understand. We women have had to resort to strategy as well, to compensate for our weak points. When a-pirating, we rarely confront our victims head-on," Medana said.

"Well said!" This from Starri, who showed his admiration with a full-body survey of Medana in her usual tunic and braies.

Thork did not want Starri admiring Medana. "Then you will appreciate why you must stay out of sight," Thork told her. "We do not want an immediate confrontation. Best we get a feel for your brothers' reasons for being here before engaging in any fighting."

"Oh, I know why they are here. They want my land, meager as it is compared to their estates. They would take Thrudr, too, just to be mean. They gain their ends by having me tried for murder, then petition to the king to release my inheritance, especially since I have no daughter. Or they will force me to wed a man of their choosing who will be the puppet holder of the land. Of course, my life would soon be forfeit, either way. In the latter case, they would not want to risk my bearing a girl child who would be next in line."

"But you might *already* be carrying a girl child," Tykir said.

Medana put her face in both hands and groaned.

"What?" Tykir asked.

"Medana hasn't mentioned anything to her women," Thork told his father with disgust.

"Why not?" His father was sincerely confused. To him, naught was sacred.

"You are breeding?" Gudron asked Medana in a voice filled with hurt that Medana would not have told her, presumably one of her closest friends.

"Nay, I am not breeding," Medana replied.

"But she could be," Thork interjected.

Medana sliced him with a glance so icy he might just have icicles growing on his eyebrows.

"I have an idea," Starri said. "I could marry you, Medana."

Thork, stunned into momentary silence, turned slowly, very slowly, to gaze at his traitorous brother. His father was tapping his chin thoughtfully, as if actually giving it consideration.

"Why would you make such a ridiculous offer?" Medana asked Starri.

"It would give you further protection. And I have been wed afore. I like married life." Starri shrugged and ran a fingertip up the sleeve of Medana's tunic in a playful manner.

"Medana will wed you over my dead body, Starri. Forget that idea."

"Thork! That is not your decision to make," Medana said.

"You want to marry my brother?" he inquired, and felt pitiful in the asking.

"Nay, I do not want to marry your brother, or you, or anyone else. For the love of all the gods, stick to battle strategy."

Tykir looked from Medana to Thork and back again. Then he smiled. The sly old codger!

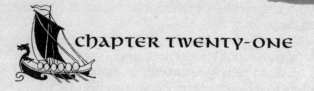

chapter twenty-one

Never try to trick a trickster . . .

Bolthor went out through the tunnel later that night.

He would greet Medana's brothers and assure them of a cordial reception awaiting them on the island of Thrudr. Once her brothers, depending on how many had come, left his sight, Bolthor would reunite with his wife—assuming she was in the mood for a reunion—then order some of the seamen aboard Tykir's longship to gather as many weapons as possible and take them to the waiting men and women.

The worst part was the waiting, in Thork's opinion.

Medana was up at the hunters' longhut with Brokk, where she would stay until given the word that it was safe for her to come down. Thork had promised to send her periodic messages about who had come and what they wanted.

Finally, torchlights appeared to be approaching through the tunnel. Several well-garbed men were at the head, leading a dozen guardsmen carrying broadswords and battle-axes.

Thork stood at the forefront with his father and

mother, his three brothers behind them, waiting for the visitors to come up the moveable stairs. All over the village, men and women carrying weapons stood at attention, a show of strength to their visitors.

Once on the grassy area, his father said, "Welcome to Thrudr. I am Jarl Tykir Thorksson of Dragonstead, and this is my wife, Lady Alinor, and my son Thork. Behind us are my other three sons, Guthrom, Starri, and Selik. And over there are Mistresses Gudron, Berdis, and Solveig, representing the community of Thrudr." The women wore helmets, chain mail, and gauntlets; they carried shields and deadly short swords.

Tykir then arched his head for a reciprocal introduction.

The first man wore a fine blue wool tunic over black braies, belted with a gem-studded belt, and carried a sword whose silver hilt must be worth a fortune. He said, "I am Jarl Sigurd Torsson. I believe my sister, Geira, may be residing here. I have come to take her home."

"Ah, I knew your father well. And these other men?" Tykir asked, ignoring Sigurd's remark about Geira.

"Two of my *hersirs*, Alfrim and Serk," he said, indicating the men on either side of him, "and those behind me are *housecarls* assigned to Stormgard."

"And your brothers?" Tykir asked. "I understood there were three of you."

"I come alone," Sigurd said, clearly impatient with the questions. "Where is Geira?"

"There is no one here named Geira, is there?" Thork said, inclining his head toward Gudron and the women. They all shook their heads.

"She probably goes by another name," Sigurd said. "The Sea Scourge, some call her." That last information Sigurd imparted with a sneer.

"Ah, yea, the Sea Scourge," Tykir responded.

"She is indisposed at the moment," his mother interjected, "but come join us for a cup of ale 'til she is available." It was their intention to put the sleeping draught in their drinks, but only after they gained certain information.

At some point, Thork intended to enact his own vengeance on Sigurd, as well. Just payment for the scars on Medana's back. But that would come later.

Sigurd was not happy at being forestalled.

"You must know that there is only a two-hour time period for the tunnel to be open," Thork said as they began to follow the group warily to one of the longhouses.

"Time enough!" Sigurd commented, exchanging meaningful glances with his men. They were up to no good, that was certain.

In the wake of Sigurd's coming onto the island, Bolthor and Katherine managed to slip through the tunnel and bring a few weapons with them. Not many, not wanting to call attention to themselves. They had no news to report. Katherine said the men on the two boats that had arrived the same time she had were very closemouthed and had little to say when she asked questions. Once they knew she was no threat to their plans, they ignored her.

An hour later, the Torsson group was growing increasingly impatient in the hall of the largest longhouse. Thork didn't plan on giving them the tainted drink until they got more information out of them.

Alinor asked Bolthor to say one of his sagas as a means of forestalling the men.

"This is the saga of all Viking men," a flustered Bolthor began.

> *"Viking men are kind at heart.*
> *Some are even very smart.*
> *The best of them are strong in battle,*
> *But home hearth they can also straddle.*
> *Love their wives and concubines . . ."*

Katherine elbowed her husband in the ribs for that mention of concubines, but still Bolthor went on trying to distract the villainous visitors.

> *"Tend their children with no whines.*
> *Balance is the key for many a Norseman*
> *When he is head of his clan.*
> *Virile but gentle*
> *Strong in battle, strong in the bedsport . . ."*

It was obvious that Bolthor was struggling to finish his poem under such pressure, and Sigurd and his men were becoming restless.

"Where is my sister? I demand to see her now!" Sigurd said, standing and glaring at his surroundings. "What kind of demented place is this, anyhow, with naught but women?"

"A pirate hiding place," Thork responded, figuring that the secret was out by now, anyhow. "So tell me, why are you looking for Med— for Geira, after all these years?"

"I ne'er stopped looking for her, but it was believed that she had died long ago until—"

"Until—" Thork prodded.

"Until I found my thrall Agnis at Hedeby hiding my son from me."

Oh, that was not good news. Medana would be very, very upset. That must be how Sigurd had learned of the island's whereabouts and about the tunnel, not from his father's seamen. "Where are they now?"

"On my longship." Sigurd indicated with a jerk of his head the direction of Small Island. "I am taking her and my son back to Stormgard with Geira." By the brutish expression on his face, Thork knew without a doubt that his plans for all three back there would not be pleasant. Scars, at the least.

"I thought Geira was guilty of some crime or other," Alinor said with a wave of her hand, as if she couldn't recall exactly what crime.

"She is, but that is a matter for my family to handle. Geira should have come to us to begin with."

Hah! You were the ones to put her in that dire situation.

"Women! They are willful creatures, are they not? Not capable of thinking on their own," Tykir said.

His mother appeared to be gritting her teeth, knowing her husband had good reasons for such insulting words.

"My thoughts exactly," Sigurd said.

"Do you intend to send her to King Harald to account for her crime?" Tykir inquired with apparent casualness as he took another long draw on his horn of ale.

"We shall see. It depends on how agreeable she is to a marriage we have arranged. A man of superior breeding. A little older, of course, and some say hard as stone, but then women need the guidance of a man with discipline."

For a moment, Thork feared his mother might leap over the table.

A marriage arranged for Medana with an elderly man? "Over my dead body," Thork murmured, which was becoming a familiar refrain by now.

"That is not one of Medana's brothers," Freyja said, coming up to whisper in Thork's ear.

"What? Are you sure?"

"Positive." Thork recalled then that Freyja had been Geira's nursemaid at one time. Another thought came to him then. He should have known. The Sigurd imposter did not have the violet eyes and full lips of the Torsson clan.

He frowned with confusion, about to tell his father of this twist in their plans when there was a commotion outside. It was Brokk being helped by the young boy who'd been sent to give Medana their latest message. Brokk had a deep gash on his forehead, and he was dragging one leg, which might be broken.

"Lock the doors!" his father yelled as Sigurd or whoever he was began to scramble into possible flight with his men.

A bloody fight ensued, and to their credit, the women of Thrudr proved just as valuable as the men in fighting these miscreants. In the end, there were injuries on both sides, and the Sigurd poser was dead of a sword through the heart . . . Thork's.

Only then did the implications of Brokk's injuries filter into Thork's thinking. "Where is Medana?" he asked Brokk, whose wounds were already being treated by his mother.

"Gone! Three of her brothers came, after you all left the tunnel area. They took her away."

A roaring in Thork's head caused him to shake his head to clear it. He was trembling so hard he could scarce stand aright. "Where did they take her?"

"I do not know. Out to their ship. They may be gone by now," Brokk said, tears in his young eyes. "They hit her, Thork. In the face. And back. And belly."

A full-blown rage overtook Thork, turning him berserk.

"But that is not why she went with them," Brokk continued, gasping for breath.

His mother gave him a drink of water.

Brokk went on, "Medana went because of some woman and child being held captive on the ship. They threatened to kill the woman and dismember the boy slowly, unless Medana came willingly."

Agnis and Sigurd's son, Thork concluded.

His father handed Thork a sword, and Starri gave him his favorite knife.

"One more thing," Brokk choked out. "Medana said: 'Tell the loathsome lout not to follow me.'"

"Oh, Thork!" his mother said behind him. She knew as well as he did what the hidden message meant. "Loathsome lout" was intended as an endearment.

Thork ran as fast as he could, jumped into the pond where water was already starting to pool, and sloshed as fast as he could out to Small Island.

The longship had already pulled anchor and was sailing away. No care for the men they'd left behind. They'd got what they came for.

The terrible trouble just kept getting more terrible . . .

Medana was living her worst nightmare. She was back in the hands of her brothers, vulnerable to whatever dire fate they planned for her. Agnis and Egil had been taken, too.

The only thing she was unsure of was Thrudr. A dozen or so of her brothers' men had gone through the tunnel, and surely the great Tykir Thorksson, his four sons, Thork's men, and the Thrudr women would have been able to withstand their attack, if attack had been her brothers' plan and not just a distraction. At least for the moment, Thrudr was safe, but its future was uncertain now that men knew about the sanctuary for women.

There was a groan on the floor beside her, and Medana rolled over and onto her knees, stifling a groan at her own pains. "Do not fret so, Agnis. I am here now."

Agnis opened the slits of her swollen eyes. "Medana? Oh gods! They've taken you, too. And your face. And arms. What have they done to you?" Immediately, Agnis tried to sit up in panic. "Egil? Where is my son?"

"Shhh!" Medana said, helping Agnis to lie back down. "He is asleep over there. Unharmed. Settle please, Agnis. We do not want to call attention to ourselves. Shhh!"

"Where are we?"

"In the shelter of Sigurd's longship. My brothers are on the other ship. We have been asea for hours now." Agnis's eyes darted about the small room in the center of the longship, created by drapes of sailcloth. Dawn light showed through some of the parted folds.

"Where are they taking us?"

"I'm not sure. Probably Stormgard, but mayhap to King Harald's court in Vestfold."

"Oh, the things Sigurd said to me! And did! He punched with a closed fist. And kicked me. And took a belt to my back. In front of his very own son! I know he is your brother, but he is an evil man, Medana. Evil to the core."

Medana had not realized that Agnis might have injuries on her back, too, when she'd tended her face and arms and legs. She would check later. "I do not consider Sigurd a brother. He is naught to me. Nor are the other two villainous brothers of mine, Osten and Vermund, who follow every word of Sigurd's as if he were a god. God of evil, that is what he is. *Nithings*, all of them!"

For now, she needed to rest, to maintain her strength for the fight that was sure to come. What nature that fight would take she did not know, but it was coming, sure as dawn followed night.

"Do you know what the worst part was, Medana?" Agnis said, turning her head to look at her through those pitiful eye slits.

"What, sweetling?" She tried to brush some blood matted hair off her face.

"Gregor was there. I thought he cared for me, he said he did. But when Sigurd told Gregor that I belonged to him and that he should leave, Gregor just gave me a disappointed look and left me to Sigurd's evil devices."

"Men! They are all alike," Medana said. But as she drifted into a pain-riddled sleep, she realized that she no longer really felt that way. Thork's men were not like that, nor were Tykir and his followers. She did not think any one of them would leave a woman in distress or beat her bloody.

And Thork . . . She closed her eyes and felt hot tears sting her bruised cheeks. He was so much more than she had thought on first meeting him. He was everything she'd dreamed of in a man. Would he understand her silent message to Brokk when she'd referred to a "loathsome lout"? Would he know she loved him?

After all, there was no longer any reason for him to stay with her. Whether it was due to Sigurd's kick to her belly or her regular monthly flux, she no longer carried Thork's baby. If she ever had.

And wasn't that the saddest thing of all?

First, you need to just breathe . . .

Thork's rage could not be contained.

He wanted to swim through the tunnel, under water, until he got to the outside, then swim the considerable distance out to Small Island.

"Impossible! Have you lost your mind, Thork?" his father yelled, as he and his brothers held him back.

Then he wanted to attempt to climb up and over the mountain.

"It cannot be done, Thork. Believe me, many of us have tried over the years. There are no footholds," Gudron said in a softer voice than he'd ever heard come out of her thin lips.

His father led them—his mother, his brothers, his men, and the warrior women of Thrudr—into the biggest longhouse, and they all sat down.

"Well, here is one thing I guarantee," Thork stormed, and plopped down hard on his bench. "There will be steps built up and down that mountain in the future, if I have any say."

"And why would you have any say in the future doings of Thrudr, my son?" his mother asked.

"You know bloody hell why. Because I love the bloody damn willful woman and I will no doubt have to live on this bloody damn awful island for the rest of my bloody fool life. That is why."

His mother smiled and patted his arm, as if that was the answer she'd been seeking.

His father, on the other hand, swatted him aside the head and said, "Do not swear at your mother."

Thork blinked, unaware that he had been swearing.

"Leave be, husband. He is not himself," his mother said to his father.

"Hah! I will tell you this. If the boy does not calm down, I am going to douse him with that sleeping draught the women here are famous for."

"You would not!" Thork stood and cast accusing eyes at his father.

"Listen, Thork, just breathe. Inhale deeply and exhale slowly. Calm yourself down," his father said, shoving him down onto a bench and sitting down beside him. "You are no good to yourself or anyone else in your present condition. You cannot think when you are so distraught."

"How would you feel if it was Mother?" he snapped.

"I know exactly how it feels. Your mother's lackwit brothers captured her one time."

Really? That was one story he had not heard. Thork rubbed a hand over his forehead. "It is just that I am worried. What is happening to her, at this moment? Brokk said they hit and kicked her while still on the island. What might they be doing now she is on their territory?"

"You cannot dwell on that, Thork," his mother said. "Medana is a strong woman. Let her take care of the day to day. You need to think longer term."

"Here is what we are going to do," his father said, motioning for the others to come closer, the men as well as the women. "Thork, you will be taking the Thrudr longship to Hedeby, where you will take possession of your three longships, which are hopefully still there. Then you will send one longship to Northumbria under your brother Guthrom, to ask for your uncle Eirik's assistance. Starri, you will take another longship to Dragonstead, where you will gather not only our men and longships, but go to our neighbors for their assistance. Thork, you will take the third longship to Stormgard, although I have my doubts about whether Sigurd and his brothers would go there. Your mother and I will go to King Harald's court, where they will have to bring Medana eventually. They could not marry her off, if that is indeed the brothers' plan, without the king's consent."

"What about us?" Gudron asked.

"You and your women will of course go with Thork to Hedeby, but then you should return to Thrudr in your own ship. Selik will come with you, then return to the island with you. It is important not to leave the island vulnerable in the midst of all this chaos. Bolthor, can you and Katherine stay here to hold things together?"

Bolthor agreed, reluctantly.

"We can fight, too," Gudron asserted, raising her chin in defiance.

"And you will probably have to," Tykir said. "Word will be out. Every miscreant in the world will be hastening here for the treasures they think you hoard on the island."

Several women made harrumphing sounds at the idea of treasure on Thrudr, where day-to-day subsistence was a chore.

"Are we in agreement?" Tykir asked then. At their nods and vocal assents, he added, "We have all day to prepare our weapons and ready the longships. Have I covered everything?"

"One more thing," his mother said. "Let us pray. Whether to my Christian One-God, or your Norse gods, we must seek guidance and protection from above."

They all bowed their heads, in silence.

Thork took a deep breath and in his head said, *Help me, God of my mother, gods of my people. Help me find Medana and keep her with me thereafter. Help her to withstand whate'er her brothers throw her way until we arrive. Help me be the man she wants and needs. Help me!*

He could swear a voice in his head replied, *She called you a loathsome lout. You are halfway there.*

chApTER TWENTY-TWO

**Nightmares are just dreams
turned upside down . . .**

For two days Medana was awaiting, or rather
dreading, the return of her brothers to Snow
Pines, her dower estate in the far north of the
Norselands. Actually, it would be the return
of Sigurd and Osten. They'd left her youngest
brother, Vermund, to watch over them with a
small group of *housecarl*s.

Nor that they'd seen much of Vermund. He
seemed to be in a perpetual state of ale stupor
since their arrival, as were his *housecarl*s.

Medana and Agnis and Egil probably could
have walked out the door, but where would they
go? It was some distance by land to the nearest
fjord, and even then she did not know if there
would be any longboats there. Although it was
summertime, the weather was chilly and there
was daylight most of the day. Land of the Midnight Sun.

"What will become of us?" Agnis asked, not for
the first time.

They were in the summer kitchen, detached
by a roofed, open-sided walkway from the keep's

main scullery, which was filthy and ruled with
an iron hand by an often *drukkinn*, equally filthy
cook. Here they worked with the meager proven-
der available—barley flour to make unleavened
bread, dried fish and venison, and a little honey
crystallized in pottery jars that would suffice for
oatcakes.

She could ask Vermund to hunt some game for
their table, but she didn't want to call attention to
them down in the lower level where the kitchens
and their bedchambers were located.

"I will marry Jarl Leistr Adilsson and go off to
his estate, which is said to be run-down, but that
is probably because there has been no woman in
charge for many years."

"Oh, Medana! How can you?"

"How can I not? I do not care about Snow Pines.
I would sign it over to my brothers in a trice, but
apparently the Odal laws are strict about such in-
heritances as mine, and the only way a male can
gain ownership is through marriage." *Or death.*

"But he is said to be a hard man."

"I have lived in a household of hard men for
years. I know how to evade their evil clutches. I
will survive."

Agnis was at the cook fire, stirring the honey to
make it regain its more liquid nature. Every once
in a while, she would stretch and press her hand
to her lower back. As the whip marks healed and
tightened, she was in pain, though the woman
never complained. Agnis was just so glad that
Egil was safe. He was outside now, foraging for
nuts and fruit.

Agnis's face was still puffy and black and blue

and yellow in spots. As was Medana's, though not as bad as Agnis's. That was one of the reasons Sigurd and Osten had brought them to Snow Pines . . . to heal. Oh, not out of any great sympathy for the pain the brothers had inflicted—they were, after all, only women—but Medana must be presentable when they took her to court to get the king's forgiveness for her "crime" and permission for her to wed Jarl Adilsson. Or else a death sentence from the Althing court, which amounted to the same thing.

In Agnis's case, Medana's cruel, miscreant brothers wanted her healthy because they intended to sell her in the slave marts of Hedeby, the very town where she had been living freely for almost ten years. Agnis didn't know that yet. Egil would be taken back to Stormgard, where he would be a thrall in his own father's household.

"It will not be so bad. Leistr is old. If I can outlive him, mayhap I can make my way back to Thrudr," Medana said.

Agnis looked at her, frightened for her future. "Dost think I would be able to go with you? Egil and I?"

"I do not know," Medana lied. She still hoped . . . for what, she wasn't sure. Oh, she knew Thork and his family would have searched for her, but by now they would have probably given up the search. Still, she was hoping for a miracle.

One of her biggest concerns was Thrudr. Once her brothers satisfied their greedy hunger with Snow Pines, they would look for other easy ways to fill their coffers. They might go back to Thrudr, thinking to find treasure, or if naught else, they would take the women as slaves, a tradeable commodity. Female pirates would garner a high price as a novelty.

Gudron would fight to the death, as would many of the others, but could they withstand the type of attacks her brothers would launch?

On the other hand, mayhap Thork and his father would make good on their promises to protect the island. She could only hope so.

Egil came rushing in then, his basket half full of nuts and berries. "Men are coming. Many men."

Medana's heart lifted for a moment. *Thork. Thork has come.*

"I think it is my father," Egil whispered in a fear-riddled voice.

Medana's shoulders slumped.

Egil had the good sense to rush off and hide, but she and Agnis sat frozen in their chairs, awaiting whatever would come. They had almost an hour to wait.

Sigrun and Osten stomped in eventually, without a greeting. Not that she noticed their rudeness, so stunned was she by their appearance. Despite their fine garments, the two men looked as if they'd been in an alehouse brawl. Sigurd had a blackened eye and a scab growing over a cut in his bottom lip, and she wasn't sure, but she didn't think he'd had that bump in his nose before. Osten was limping and had one arm in a sling. Both had bruised knuckles.

"What happened to you two?" she blurted out.

"You happened to us," Osten snarled.

"Me?" She was taken aback. "What have I to do with your injuries?"

"Thork Tykirsson came to Stormgard looking for you, and when he could not find you, he went berserk."

At first she frowned with confusion. *Thork? He came for me?* She smiled, widely.

"You find humor in our pain?" Sigurd asked incredulously. His face flooded with color and he approached her with fisted hands.

She moved quickly, putting the table between them. "I was just surprised by your sudden appearance. What you see is happiness . . . happy to have company." *My eyes are probably blinking madly, if Thork's test for lying is true.* "We have been lonely here at Snow Pines, haven't we, Agnis?"

Agnis, who still sat at the table, frozen with fright, nodded her head briskly.

"How is it, my dear sister," Sigurd said, "that you cried rape when Ulfr bedded you, but you spread your thighs with ease for Tykirsson, who is known to be wild and dangerous, an outcast from his own family?"

"I . . . I have no idea what you mean." *I will not blink. I will not blink.*

"Liar! Once he realized that you weren't at Stormgard, Tykirsson championed your cause for vengeance. The brute dared to attack us, in our very home. Believe you me, King Harald will hear of this outrage once the Althing commences."

"I ne'er asked Thork—"

"Thork, is it? How is it that the man knows of the scars on your back, girl, lest you were his harlot? Lest you set him on a path of retribution?"

"Of course she is a harlot. There is naught new in that," Osten contributed.

"Everyone knew about the beatings I suffered at your hands, anyone who lived at Stormgard," she tried to say, but her brothers had already moved on to another complaint.

"We have more immediate problems." Sigurd took Medana by the arm and hauled her to her feet. Glaring, he spat out, "You have been here at Snow Pines for nigh on two sennights, and this keep is a pigsty."

You are just now noticing? Where have you been the past ten years when this estate has been moldering away?

"I wouldn't sleep on the bed linens here! They are no doubt loaded with lice." Sigurd's eyes, which matched hers in color, were bulging with outrage.

You would be right about the bed linens. Except for those Agnis and I boiled and rinsed, boiled and rinsed in the laundry tubs.

Sigurd was going on about the greasy tables in the great hall, the moldy, stinksome rushes, the salon, the corridors, even the stables. "Why haven't you cleaned the place?"

"Me? You expected me to clean the entire keep?" Medana asked with consternation. She was accustomed to hard labor, but while Snow Pines wasn't a large building, it would still require more than her and Agnis, to maintain it. "There is no staff here to speak off," she sputtered out. "The steward and house servants left long ago when none of them were paid, and no women are safe here with . . ." She let her words trail off when she'd meant to mention Vermund and his *drukkinn* comrades.

But her unfinished explanation didn't matter.

"If I had my way, I would beat you bloody and send you to a nunnery." He shoved her away, causing her to stumble and have to catch her balance with the edge of the table.

Osten picked up where his brother left off. "And the food! The roast boar is rancid, and I saw dead weevils in the bread." He glanced around the small, meticulously clean summer kitchen and picked up an oatcake, popping it into his mouth. " 'Twould seem you know how to care for yourself well enough, though."

Now they are going to blame me for their filthy cook? What next? The garderobes?

Sigurd's attention turned to Agnis then. "Go prepare a chamber for me and my brother, thrall. And wait for me in my bed."

Agnis, who a short time ago had been an independent, happy merchant in Hedeby, cowered and scurried off to do Sigurd's bidding. And Medana felt helpless to do anything about Agnis's position. She would grab a knife and stab her brother in a trice if that would save Agnis, or herself. But that would only cause more problems for them. Nay, she needed to act docile and accepting until she could come up with a plan.

Gathering all her courage, she motioned for Sigurd to sit down at the table. "We must talk, brother."

"Must we?" Sigurd arched a brow with scorn, but he sat down.

Meanwhile, Osten was already seated on the same bench and stuffing bread and honey and oatcakes into his mouth.

"What do you want of me?" she asked, sitting across from the two brothers.

"Not what I want of you, but what you *will* do. We leave in the morning for Vestfold. The Althing will start in five days, where we will present a case for pardon of your crime against Ulfr and permission to wed Leistr. Throughout this whole process, you will act repentant and humble. And you will do everything in your power to make yourself agreeable to your betrothed. In fact, if he chooses to test your wares afore the wedding, there will be no talk of rape this time."

Inside, she cringed, but she would not show her brother how repulsed and frightened she was. "Is that all?"

Her sarcasm fueled his anger even more. "Dare you take an attitude with me, you demented bitch?" He half stood and reached across the table with an open palm raised high, about to slap her, hard.

Osten pulled him back just in time and cautioned, "No marks. Remember. Leistr must believe she comes willingly."

With a sigh of resignation, she looked directly at first one brother, then the other. "You cannot sell Agnis. She and Egil must come with me after I wed. I will not cooperate, otherwise."

"You have no choice," Sigurd snapped, and she could tell he was barely restraining himself from doing her some bodily harm.

"Wait, Sigurd," Osten said. "If giving up Agnis will ensure Geira's compliance, then let it be so. As for the boy . . . you have sons aplenty. A thrall son will make no difference."

Idiots! My brothers are callous idiots.

Sigurd hesitated and then nodded. Gods only knew if he would keep his word, but his concession would give them time. For what, she wasn't sure.

"Why? Why do you go to all this trouble?" she asked then. "Take Snow Pines. I'll go away, and this time you can have me declared dead."

Sigurd laughed and it was not a nice laugh. "You lackbrain split-tail! Snow Pines is of little importance to us. Leistr will die soon after your marriage, and we will get our hands on his vast wealth. After that, we will find you another husband. A graybeard again, of course. And from there, at your age, we figure you may manage at least three more marriages afore you lose your comeliness."

"Comeliness?" she choked out, the least important of all the filth her brother spouted.

"Yea. Men seem to find you attractive," Osten explained. "I cannot see it myself."

"Me neither," Sigurd said with a shiver of distaste.

Medana sat there, stunned, in the face of her brothers' leering looks. Their plan for her was so much more evil than she ever could have imagined. She suspected they weren't talking about natural deaths for her husbands.

And she knew in that moment that her nightmare was about to get much worse.

It was like a giant festival, except he wasn't feeling very festive . . .

Thork had run into so many dead ends he no longer knew where to search for Medana anymore. He was beyond worried about her condition, with the vicious nature of her brothers.

One of the first places he had gone after regaining his men and longships at Hedeby was Stormgard, where he was told on arriving that Medana's brothers Sigurd and Osten were in residence. After ascertaining from some guards they'd captured that Medana was not there and hadn't been for more than ten years, he had stormed into the great hall, uninvited.

"Which of you is lord of this keep?" Thork had bellowed.

"I am," said one of the men sitting at the high table on a dais with another man and two women, probably their wives. Both men stood and proceeded to come down the steps toward him. People throughout the hall stopped eating and drinking to see what was happening.

"I am Sigurd Torsson, and this is my brother Osten."

"Where is Vermund?"

"How would I know? I am not my brother's keeper. Ha, ha, ha. Who the hell are you, and how did you get in here?" Belatedly, Sigurd had glanced toward the back of the hall and saw a dozen of Thork's men, along with Guthrom, in full battle gear, lining up to block the door, in the event someone might make a foolish attempt to escape. If they failed to find Medana here, Guthrom would be off to Northumbria for assistance.

"I am Thork Tykirsson of Dragonstead. You may have met my father Tykir Thorksson . . . or his cousin King Harald."

Sigurd had cocked his head to the side. "Why

did you not say so? Welcome to Stormgard. Wouldst care to share a cup of ale?"

Was he serious? The lackbrain! "I would not share a cup of anything with you. Where is Medana?"

"There is no one here by that name." Sigurd had turned to his brother. "Is there, Osten?" Osten shook his head.

"You know very well who I mean. Geira. Your sister."

"Ah," Sigurd had said, about to give a signal to some of his *housecarls* to come to his assistance.

"I would not do that if I were you." Thork had put a hand on the hilt of his broadsword. "You and your brother would be headless afore they could reach me."

Sigurd had gasped, and Osten blanched, putting a hand to his neck.

"Geira is not here, as you well know if you managed to get by my guardsmen outside," Sigurd had said. "What do you want with our sister, anyhow?" Osten had asked.

"She is my betrothed." *Well, almost. If I ever catch up with her, she will be. Mayhap. Nay, she definitely will be. After all, she called me a loathsome lout that last day.*

"She never is!" Sigurd's already florid face had filled with color. "She is betrothed to Jarl Leistr Adilsson."

Ah, so that was the latest puppet they'd lined up. "Is that so? Has the king given his permission? The king who is my father's cousin?"

He had thought about telling the men that Medana carried his child, but he did not know if that was the case now, or if it had ever been the

case. Or if they might mistreat her even more if
they suspected her of having shared his bed.

"Where. Is. She?" he had gritted out.

Sigurd had shrugged. "Probably off pirating or
whoring, from what I hear of her recent activities."

Sigurd's ill-chosen comment had caused Thork's
fist to fly to Sigurd's lackwit mouth. "That was for
the scars on your sister's back." When he broke a
stool over Sigurd's head, he had proclaimed, "And
that is because you are a *nithing* of a man who feels
big only when overpowering women."

A melee had broken out then with Thork
taking on Sigurd, Guthrom going after Osten,
and the rest of Thork's *hird* fighting the Stormgard
warriors who had been seated. It had not been
a fight to the death. Thork needed the foul Torsson brothers alive if they were to find Medana's
whereabouts. There had been numerous injuries
on both sides, though.

After that, Thork had gone to King Harald's
court, then to Hedeby and Kaupang and Birka,
trying to get news of Vermund's whereabouts,
figuring his absence to be telling. He'd even approached Leistr's holdings in the Danish lands,
but the old man was absent. Lacking success in
those places, he'd gone to Dragonstead, where
his father had reported equal failure, though he
was gathering support from his neighbors for the
upcoming Althing. Then Thork had gone back to
Stormgard, where he had posted guards to watch
for the Torssons' doings and any travels they
might be making. Eventually they gave up.

It was as if Medana had disappeared from the
face of the earth.

So now Thork was about to arrive at Vestfold, where he would meet up with his father and all their supporters to await the Althing. He and his father had tried submitting petitions to the king for an audience, but the king was overburdened with preparations for the Althing and kept putting them off.

Bolthor and Katherine had gone back to their home in Northumbria. The skald had promised to come back, if he was needed.

Guthrom and Starri were with Thork, plaguing him at every turn over what he should do when next he met Medana.

Believe me, I know exactly what to do when next I meet Medana. I am going to grab on to her and never let go.

There were already a hundred or more longships of various sizes lined up along the wharves of Vestfold and anchored a short distance out in open waters. The Althing was to begin tomorrow. His parents, who'd been there for days—bless their kind hearts—had saved a spot for him, and he and his seamen were able to maneuver the longship into a tight space.

Once he alighted and hugged both of them, his father said, "Medana's case will be heard before the law court at the Althing two days hence. You will have a chance to speak after her brothers."

He brightened at that. "Do you think Medana will be here?"

"I haven't seen any sign of her or her brothers yet, but she is sure to be here for the court. Otherwise, I doubt the king will allow her case to be heard. He was not too fond of my requests that

he absolve her in her absence, despite my continu-
ally reminding him of our blood ties," his father
related with a chuckle as they all began walking
toward the king's castle and beyond.

"'Cousin? What cousin?' King Harald kept
saying. 'This is the first I have e'er heard you brag
of any kinship with me, Tykir,'" his father related
with a loud guffaw.

The royal castle was a large one, but not large
enough to accommodate all the people who were
arriving. So a tent city was rising in the grounds
beyond the castle for many hectares in the distance. That's where they would be staying.

An Althing was a gathering of all noble Norsemen and freemen to discuss issues involving the
country, usually their bloody Saxon enemies; to
settle arguments; to arrange marriages; and to
have a generally fine time with all kinds of en-
tertainment. Thork did not feel one bit like being
entertained.

As they walked through the pathways that had
been made among the tents, he saw many wondrous sights. Vendors of all kinds sold everything
from silver combs to silk fabrics, animals to longships, exotic fruits to homegrown honey. Crafts-
men plied their skills on precious metals and rare
woods. Music came from some of the tents, sing-
ing and instruments. Games were played. Horse
races arranged. Wrestling matches. Gambling.

Starri stopped at one of them to speak with a
very attractive woman with straight, pitch-black
hair and a pearly complexion. A widow who had
been a friend to Starri's dearly departed wife, his
mother told Thork with a twinkle in her green eyes.

His father was buying a flagon of wine from a drinks merchant to take back to their tent.

While they were waiting, his mother said, squeezing his arm, "I have a feeling that all will be over in a few days."

"Yea, but will it be to my liking or not?" he grumbled.

" 'Tis in the Lord's hand now," his mother prophesied.

He rolled his eyes. "I cannot stand by and wait for some celestial being to handle my problems."

"And who said that you should? Pray to God, but sharpen your sword. That is my philosophy." Even after all the years of living in the Norselands, his mother had never given up her Saxon Christianity.

"My sword is always sharp," he grumbled some more.

"Ah, but there are swords, and then there are *swords*," his mother said.

On that mysterious message, Thork decided to join his father at the drinks tent. He could use a beer . . . or twenty.

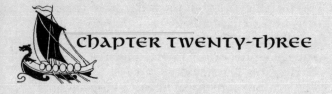

CHAPTER TWENTY-THREE

**Breaking up is hard to do, even
back in Viking times . . .**

Medana was in Vestfold. By the end of the day tomorrow, when she would appear before the law court, all would be settled.

Thork was here somewhere. She knew he was, but she could not think on that now. She girded herself with resolve. She would be strong. She would do what she must, even if it meant an end to any happiness she might have had with "the wildest Viking to ride a longship."

She was walking now between her brother Sigurd and her betrothed Jarl Leistr Adilsson. Both handsome, albeit older, hardened men with a slash of cruelty about their square jaws.

But Medana was not the weak woman she'd been ten years ago. She'd demanded a private meeting with Leistr in which she'd promised to come to him willingly if he would "buy" Agnis and Egil from her brother.

"Why should I do that?" Leistr had snarled after grabbing for her and pressing hard kisses to her closed mouth.

"Because I can be a pleasing bedmate. Because,

gods willing, I can give you sons, which you never got from your previous wives. Because I can make your home a pleasant, welcoming place for you to return to after going a-Viking or a-fighting."

Adilsson had considered her words and apparently found some appeal because Agnis and Egil were now at Leistr's estate under Osten's watch, awaiting her wedding, after which they would become Medana's thralls. As if she would ever keep slaves!

Medana was dressed today in fine raiment befitting her station, her brother having generously allowed her access to a trunk with her old garments. A violet *gunna* covered by an ankle-length, open-sided apron of dark purple samite silk in the Viking style. The *gunna* was pleated and trailed slightly in the back. The apron had matching gold pennanular brooches attached to the loops of both shoulders. On her feet were gold-embroidered purple slippers. Her blonde hair hung in a thick braid down her back, intertwined with pearls and amethysts.

She saw Thork before he saw her.

He, too, was dressed in the best finery. A deep green wool tunic brought out the green in his eyes. The tunic was belted at the waist over black braies and boots. His blond hair was clubbed back at the neck, calling attention to the thunderbolt earring in his one ear. He looked more the pirate than she had ever been. And, oh, she loved him so in that moment, so much that her heart clenched with pain.

Sigurd's fingers pinched her upper arm, noticing the direction of her stare. "Remember Agnis," he hissed at her. "You seal Agnis's fate and that of her whelp. Some men at the slave marts have a preference for pretty boylings."

She got the foul message and nodded.

It was Thork's brother Starri who called his attention to her. Starri, the opposite of Thork in appearance, with his dark red hair and freckles, was nonetheless a handsome man. They'd been talking to a dark-haired woman with creamy, English rose type skin.

When Thork first saw her, his face brightened, but then he turned thunderous when he saw the two men at either side of her. Sigurd's injuries had not yet healed, and his chin showed a decided dark bruise.

"Medana!" Thork exclaimed, coming up to her. "I have been so worried about you." He went to reach for her, but her brother pulled her back.

"As you can see, my sister is fine. No need to worry. Have you met her betrothed, Jarl Leistr Adilsson? They expect to be wed next sennight."

"Medana?" Thork asked. When she didn't respond, he said, "You don't have to do this."

Yea, I do. "It is my wish," she lied, and made sure her eyelashes weren't fluttering.

Thork gasped, and it almost seemed as if he had tears in his eyes. "We need to talk," Thork insisted.

She knew he would not give up, so she turned to Sigurd and said, "I will speak to Thork for a moment. No need for concern." And to her stony-faced betrothed, she said, "He needs to be told of our plans."

They allowed her to step away with Thork, but she knew it would be for only a few moments.

"Thork, I am fine, as you can see. I appreciate all you have done for me, but I must go on now and do what is best for me and . . . for me and those I care for." She gazed pleadingly at him, wanting him to accept her decision without being told details.

"What about me?" he asked.

"You?" She pretended not to understand. "Oh, I forgot to tell you. There is no baby."

He flinched. "Did that miserable brother of yours cause you to lose the baby?"

"I do not think there ever was a baby," she told him, which was partly true. There might not have been.

"I am so sorry," he said, putting his hand on her arm.

He is sorry. Does that mean he wanted our baby? Oh, I cannot think about that now. She shrugged away. She could not allow him to touch her, or she would be lost.

"Why are you doing this?"

"Doing what?"

"Acting as if you do not care. I know you do, you called me a loathsome lout in your message to Brokk that last day." He smiled, trying to cajole an answering smile from her.

She girded herself not to react to his charm. "Why would you care?"

"Because I love you, you foolish wench?" he said in a voice low and husky with meaning.

She moaned softly, then straightened. "Nay, you do not. That is guilt speaking. And I do not love you, either. It is over, Thork."

He stared at her, struck dumb by her assertion.

"There is one thing, Thork . . ."

He didn't even respond. Just stared at her, coldly.

"I would appreciate all you could do for Thrudr."

He cocked his head to the side. "You do not intend to go back? Ever?"

She shook her head. "The Norns of Destiny are leading me in a new direction."

The expression on his face was one of both anger and confusion.

As she walked away, tears streaming down her face, which Thork could not see, she felt him staring at her back.

"It is done," she told Sigurd and Leistr when she returned to them. "Please do not ever mention his name to me again."

Later that night, Lady Alinor slipped into her tent. She put fingertips to her lips to warn Medana to speak softly.

"What is wrong?" Alinor asked right off. "Why have you rebuffed my son? He is in a *drukkinn* rage, at the moment."

Medana shook her head sadly. "I cannot help him."

"Can you help yourself, my dear?"

"That is exactly what I am doing."

Alinor pondered her words, then glanced around the small tent. "Are you here alone? No maid?"

"Just me. My brother is in the next tent."

"Not even the young woman and boy that were taken the same day as you?"

"Nay, they are not here. They are back at Leistr's estate." Medana averted her eyes when telling this. The old lady saw too much.

"Safe?"

She nodded.

"Just one question, Medana. Do you love my son?"

Medana could not answer.

But Alinor had gotten what she came for. She patted Medana's arm and left, but not before advising, "Pray." She was smiling.

It was a medieval version of
Law and Order . . .

The elderly, white-haired law speaker, Steinvor of Lade, stepped up to the dais of the massive, open-sided tent where the Althing court would be held. If she were not so scared, Medana would have been fascinated by the Althing procedure.

The king sat in the center of a long table on the raised platform, surrounded by more than a dozen jarls and minor kings who would help settle the disputes of the day. Among them was Thork's father, Tykir, who looked down at Medana and winked. Tykir's jewel-adorned raiment would have done any king proud. The wink jarred her, but only for a moment. She sat stoically between Sigurd and Leistr, both of whom had firm hands on her forearms as if she might jump up and run away. Not at this late date.

Steinvor rapped his staff on the wooden floor of the dais, a call to attention, not just to the hundred or so men assembled in the tent but to the many hundreds sitting out on the grassy slopes on either side. They all had weapons and shields to be used in the *vapnatak*, the weapon clatter, the way voting took place at an Althing. There were no women present, except for those accused and witnesses who might be testifying. Medana did not want to turn around and see if Alinor might be there, for fear she would see Thork and lose all her nerve.

"Hear ye, one and all. The law court of King Harald is about to begin. I will recite the laws of old so they will be remembered." He commenced outlining the laws of the Norselands, the crimes and punishments. There were no written documents, so he would list one third of them today, from memory, and the other two thirds tomorrow and the next day in the subsequent law courts. Such things as the penalty for thievery, which was chopping off of a hand, or a fine so large that the person was unable to pay it. A witch could be stoned. Certain *wergilds* were assessed for various crimes, depending on the severity of the crime and the social status of the victim.

Finally, it was time for various cases to be heard. First up was a charge of adultery for which a man wanted recompense from his wife's lover's family. Not only was a public flogging of the woman levied, but her family would have to take her back home in disgrace. Her lover would have to pay an oxen and five mancuses of gold to the aggrieved husband, but no flogging for him. Male justice!

Next came two farmers who had a boundary dispute, which was settled by one having to pay the other for having pastured his cows on the other's land. The evidence was cow piles the aggrieved man brought to the court, much to the amusement of the crowd.

A man who murdered a friend by pushing him off a cliff was let go with a stern warning. Apparently, both men had been *drukkinn* for days and equally to blame.

Finally, it was Medana's turn.

The law speaker read out her accused crime. Murder.

To her surprise, Tykir stood and addressed the king. He was dressed in such fine attire, he could have been one of the minor kings. "I respectfully submit that this case be dismissed. The family of the dead man, Jarl Ulfr, has agreed to my family paying a *wergild* of five hundred mancuses of gold. In return, we will *not* ask for a *wergild* on Lady Geira of Stormgard for rape and bodily assault."

For a moment, Medana forgot that she was Geira.

"*What?*" Sigurd shouted as he stood and shook a fist in the air. "What right has this family to interfere in my family's business? Geira is my sister."

King Harald, already bored with the morning's events and anxious to be off to something more entertaining, like enjoying his new third wife, asked, "Does that mean, Sigurd, that you would prefer to pay the *wergild* on your sister's behalf?"

"Well, nay, but . . ." Sigurd's face was red with humiliation. Everyone knew how tight-fisted Sigurd was with a coin, and now they also knew how little he valued his sister.

"Let us take a vote," the law speaker said.

The air was filled with the loud weapon clatter.

"The matter is now settled," the law speaker proclaimed.

"Next?" the king prodded the law speaker.

"Wait," Sigurd yelled. "I need the king's permission to arrange a marriage between my sister and Jarl Leistr Adilsson."

"Why would you need my permission?"

"Because we wish to grant Jarl Adilsson my sister's dower lands at Snow Pines as part of the marriage settlement."

"You wish to break the Odal rights?" the king homed right in to the heart of the matter. "Are there any objections?"

Thork stood and glared their way. "You are bloody damn right there are objections."

"And who are you?" the king asked as Thork stepped forward.

"Your . . . um, cousin," Thork said, addressing the king. "Twice or thrice removed. I think."

"Another close relative I ne'er knew about?" the king said to Tykir.

"Exactly. He is my son," Tykir proclaimed proudly from the other end of the dais table.

"And what have you to do with this case?" the king asked Thork.

"Medana . . . I mean Geira . . . is my betrothed."

"Wh-what?" Leistr sputtered, standing in outrage. "She is *my* betrothed."

The king rolled his eyes. "Things are becoming clearer and more confusing." He sighed and motioned to Thork. "Go on, explain this situation to me. And make it quick. My stomach is growling."

"This man," Thork said, pointing to Sigurd,

"sorely abused his sister over the years and then offered her in a marriage to a man known for his perversions. I will not go into details here, to spare the deceased's family, but they were well-known at the time."

"That is not true. I did what was best for my willful sister," Sigurd contended.

"Does anyone want to know what I have to say?" Medana said, standing between her brother and Leistr.

"Nay!" the king and most of the men shouted.

"Women do not speak at Althings," the king declared. "Sit down."

Well, that is not fair, but why should I be surprised?

Into the silence could be heard a clearing of the throat. An exaggerated clearing of the throat. Everyone turned to see the king's third wife, a woman one third the king's age, with bosoms that drew every male eye in the vicinity. She said nothing, but she had her ring-covered fingers gripping her hips and an eyebrow arched in disbelief. Clearly, she was not happy with her husband's remark about women.

"Mayhap we could make an exception and let Lady Geira speak," the king conceded.

There was some grumbling in the crowd while Sigurd and Leistr protested vehemently. But Thork was smiling. Little did he know that there would be little to smile over shortly.

The king propped an elbow on the table and braced his chin on the open palm. "So, Lady Geira, or should I call you the Sea Scourge?"

Uh-oh. Not a good start. "Um. Lady Geira will do."

"You do know that the only reason you are not

being called before this court for crimes of piracy is that no men will admit to being bested by females?"

"We stole from women, too," she said before she could bite her fool tongue.

The crowd loved her response, and they cheered and whooped with laughter.

"Good to know," the king said drolly.

She felt herself blushing.

"My king, I protest this farce. Letting a woman speak . . ." Sigurd blustered.

"Shut up!" the king said bluntly. Then, turning to Medana, "You were saying?"

"I appreciate the Althing court's decision regarding my . . . uh, crime. And I appreciate all the Tykirsson family did to gain the *wergild*. However, I must accede to my brother's wishes now."

"Which means?" The king was clearly ready for her case to be ended.

"I will marry Jarl Leister if the court approves."

"Vote called?" the law speaker called out.

"Wait!" Thork yelled. "I would beg the court to dismiss the Torsson men's guardianship of Lady Geira and transfer it to . . . to . . . my father."

Tykir looked surprised at this turn of events but immediately spoke up. "Yea, I would be a better guardian."

"And why is that?" the king wanted to know.

"Because I would not beat her bloody."

The crowd roared and Sigurd looked as if he would explode from all the blood rushing to his face. "I protest. I did only what any man would do to discipline his charge. We all know how willful women can be."

Everyone turned to the king's young wife to see her reaction. She was not happy.

"Be that as it may, and, yea, a husband, or a father, or a guardian has the clear right to use the rod when necessary, but what has that to do with the message Lady Geira just imparted to this court?" the king asked.

"She is being coerced," Thork charged.

Medana could not look at him when she declared, loud enough for all to hear, "I am not being coerced. I go to Lord Leistr willingly." She put a hand through Leistr's arm for emphasis.

"For approval of the marriage of Lady Geira to Lord Leistr, do we hear aye or nay?" The weapon clatter clearly favored the marriage.

The king said, "Now, how about that case where the man claims to have two cocks, which he was exposing in the marketplace? I can't wait to hear that one."

She glanced over to see Thork being held back by his brothers. Quickly Sigurd and Leistr whisked Medana out of the tent and toward the wharf, where Sigurd's ship was ready to set sail. She had no chance to talk with anyone, and what could she say, anyhow? The die was cast. In order to save Agnis and Egil, she would wed a man old enough to be her grandfather. But then, other women faced such a fate all the time. She would have to learn, after ten years of independence, how to be a submissive wife.

By nightfall, she was halfway to Stormgard. Sigurd had anchored his longship near the shoreline, giving the rowers a chance to rest. She was in the tiny quarters in the center of the vessel, wait-

ing with dread for Leistr to come insist on his pre-
conjugal rights. In the meantime, he and Sigurd
were on deck celebrating their victory with a tun
of ale.

She'd cried 'til there were no more tears and
had fallen into a half sleep when she was awakened by a loud noise. It sounded like the longship
had hit something hard, but how could that be?
It was anchored some distance from land. *Bang!
Thud!* Then sounds of shouting.

Peeking out through the sailcloth curtain,
Medana was amazed to see huge iron hooks
being tossed over their ship's rails by another ship
that had come up beside it. The men on the other
longship were tugging on the ropes until the two
longships were rail to rail and men could jump
from one boat to the other.

"Pirates! Pirates! We're being attacked by pirates!" she heard one of Sigurd's men shout.

*Oh my gods! Please do not let it be the women of
Thrudr. They will get themselves killed in an out-and-
out battle.*

"Ahoy there! Prepare to be boarded," a loud
male voice hollered. She'd recognize that voice
anywhere. Thork! Peering out, she saw dozens of
men clamoring over the rails, swords and lances
raised high. And not just Thork, who was bare-
footed and dressed in pirate attire, right down to
knee-length, cut-off breeches and a red kerchief
wrapped around his head in a rascally fashion.
His father and brothers Guthrom and Starri were
similarly attired. While Thork's thunderbolt earring in one ear glittered in the moonlight, Tykir
and his other two sons wore gold hoops.

She ducked back inside when she saw there was actual fighting taking place. In fact, Thork's sword cut a bloody swath across Sigurd's chest, causing her brother to drop to his knees with a shriek of pain. All around was the clamor of metal hitting metal, bodies falling, battle cries, and screams of pain.

When the noise died down somewhat, she peeked outside again, and saw Sigurd, Leistr, and the crew gathered together near a plank that had been erected on one rail, extending out over the water. Tykir came up and stood directly in front of her, arms folded over his chest, barring her from coming out on deck.

"What are they doing?" she asked.

"The scurvy bastards are being given a choice, the blade or the plank."

" 'Tis death either way," she decided. "You have to stop Thork."

Tykir shook his head. "The men can swim to shore and eventually find a way home."

"But some of them . . . Sigurd . . . are wounded."

Tykir shrugged.

"I have to stop him." Medana tried to step around Tykir's big body.

"Nay, wench, you are Thork's pirate booty. He wants you to stay here until he can deal with you."

"Pirate booty? Me? Deal?" she sputtered.

"Here, have a drink," Tykir offered, handing her a wooden cup, filled with what turned out to be wine. She didn't want wine, but before she could tell Tykir, the drape had been dropped with a warning that she would be tied to the mast pole if she came out again. In fact, a huge crate was pushed in front of where the opening would be so that she couldn't get out even if the big man was no longer guarding her.

All she knew of what was going on was shouting, laughter, screams, splashing, splashing, splashing, cursing aplenty, and threats. Then she felt the movement of the ship. She could hear male voices, occasionally Thork's, and it appeared they were drinking to celebrate their pirate venture. At one point, Tykir exclaimed to someone, "If I'd known pirating was so much fun, I would have done it long ago."

Finally, the longship dropped anchor. She heard the same loud sound again of wood against wood. The two longships bumping each other. Much talking and laughing. And movement. Then silence.

Were they leaving her here alone on a ship to die of thirst or starvation? Nay, that was too ludicrous to imagine. But what were they about? What was Thork about?

Eventually, she drank the wine and lay down on a rough pallet, never intending to sleep. Just rest. But sleep she did, and soundly.

It was mid-morning by the time she awakened with a dry mouth that tasted like—she licked her lips—oh nay! The sleeping draught!

But that wasn't all. She felt a warmth on her skin. Her bare skin. Slowly, she opened her eyes to find the sun beating down on her. And she was tied to the mast pole. Naked.

Blinking, she was finally able to focus. Thork stood a short distance away, sipping at a drink.

Not a sleeping draught, she would wager. There appeared to be no one else on deck, and no other longship nearby. And thank the gods for that because the scoundrel was naked, too.

"Well, well, well, wench," Thork drawled out. "Finally, you awaken."

"Have you lost your mind?"

He shrugged. "Probably."

"Where is everyone?"

"Gone?"

"And the men you forced overboard. Are they dead?"

He shrugged. "Are you worried about your betrothed?"

"Nay, I am worried about you, and about . . ." She could not mention Agnis and Egil. There might still be a way to save them. "Go back. Get Sigurd and Leistr. Mayhap it is not too late."

"It is too late," he said, and picked up a leather case, carrying it over to set on the deck near her feet.

What was it? Ah! She soon found out.

He undid the ties and opened it to reveal a specially designed velvet lining to showcase dozens of different kinds of feathers.

"What are you going to do?" she squeaked out.

" 'Tis not what I am going to do. 'Tis what *we* are going to do."

He picked up one long-quilled feather with hundreds of silky tendrils, which he ran sensuously through his fingers. "You have heard of going a-Viking and a-pirating," he drawled out in a sex-husky voice. "But we, my fine wench, are going a-feathering."

Feathering his nest, Viking style . . .

Thork was relieved to have Medana back with him, but he was also blistering mad that she'd chosen Leistr as a husband. In front of the entire Althing. A clear rejection of him. Humiliating.

She would pay, but in his own particular way.

He walked around, studying her nude body from all angles. "Well, well, well, who is a captive now, wench?"

She groaned inwardly, realizing his intent. He was reversing the tables on her.

"I cannot decide which side and which part of your body I like best."

"Hmpfh! I can guess. You are a man. Men home in on one thing only."

He flicked the silky feather over her mouth in reprimand. "I am not every man. I do have favorites, though. Those full, kiss-some lips of yours, for example."

She licked her lips, probably trying to make them less kiss-some. He had news for her. She had done just the opposite.

"Your violet eyes are unusual and attractive."

She lowered her lashes in an attempt to hide their beauty. He fluttered the feathers over her breasts, causing her lids to shoot open. And she gasped. A good sign, he believed.

"I like your breasts, but then you already know that from past experience." Her breasts were arched out nicely with her arms tied at the wrists behind the pole, but he fancied that she arched even more.

He walked behind her. "And, praise the gods

for your lovely arse." The twin globes with their matching dimples could be seen from behind on either side of the pole. With mischievous intent, he ran the quill end of the feather along her crack, and she led out a yelp of protest. "Stop that!"

He knelt down in front of her. "Truth to tell, I even like your feet."

Her toes curled in reaction, especially when he fluttered them with the feather.

She whimpered.

"Ticklish, are you, sweetling?"

He glanced up and realized he was facing her nether hair. His cock, which had been standing out for what seemed like hours, jerked in appreciation of her beauty there. He brushed the feathery fan back and forth over the blond curls, noticing how she stiffened in a futile attempt to halt what he was hoping was her rising arousal.

"I do not suppose you would spread your legs so I can feather your female folds."

She made a choking sound that he took to mean, *Not bloody likely!* before she pressed her legs tightly together.

"Ah, well. Later." For now, he decided to move on to a different feather. As he surveyed the collection, he remarked, "So you wanted to marry the old man?"

"Wanted? Nay? Decided to, yea."

He practiced painting her lips with a stiffer-bristled feather. Back and forth until she parted her lips and stared up at him helplessly. He leaned in and kissed her briefly. That was all the bodily contact he could allow himself lest this game of torture be over before he had gained what he wanted.

"Why?" he asked. "Why did you do it, Medana?"

"Betimes a woman has no choice. Betimes she makes adult decisions to protect . . . well, just suffice it to say, it was time for me to grow up and accept what women throughout time have done. Accept the marriage that is best for their family."

He was "painting" a thick line up the inside of one leg, from ankle to groin, then down the other leg from groin to ankle. He performed this exercise several times, and was rewarded with a soft groan. "Are you saying that you needed to protect your brothers?"

"Huh?" She stared at him through passion-glazed eyes.

"You mentioned protecting your family. Your brothers are your family."

"You are confusing me. Oh, please do not do that."

"What? This?" He was "painting" increasingly smaller circles around her breast until he got to the nipple, which he gave an extra splash of "paint," back and forth, back and forth. Mayhap later he would try the same with wine, or honey. Then he did the same thing to the other breast.

She was keening now. Her violet eyes had dilated and turned almost purple. She was panting. And her chest was heaving.

Bloody hell, he was probably panting, too.

He picked up an even stiffer feather now, almost like a turkey feather. But before he used it on her, he undid the ties that restrained her to the pole. To his immense satisfaction, she did not move.

"The worst thing about what you did at the Althing," he told her then as he used the stiff bristles over all the most erotic parts of her body—breasts, neck, shoulders, backs of knees, arches of feet, her buttocks, and, yea, her nether folds, "is that you showed so little trust in me."

She blinked at him in confusion. He might have gone too far in his torture play.

"You made me feel less than a man when you thought only you could solve your problems. Why did you question my ability to protect you and your . . . family?"

She brought her hands around to the front of her, and seemed surprised that she was free. "You do not understand."

"Nay, *you* do not understand. Agnis and her son safe at Thrudr. My men rescued her whilst we were at the Althing."

At first she didn't understand. "Agnis is safe?"

He nodded.

Then she choked out, "You knew why I did it?"

"Not at first. My mother is the one who alerted me."

She sank down to her knees and began to weep. At the same time, she drew her long hair, which had come undone from its braid, over in front to cover her breasts. Her hands folded over her private place.

Thork felt shame then that he had brought her to this point.

He dropped the feather and went over to pick up his braies.

She raised tear-filled eyes and asked, "Why have you done this?"

She waved a hand at her nudity and the mast pole.

"To punish you a little, I suppose. A bit of tit for tat, I suppose," he said, "and because I love you, I suppose."

"That makes no sense."

He shrugged, his heart aching with the intensity of his thwarted emotions.

"What are you doing?" she asked as he stepped away.

He was about to shimmy up the mast pole to raise the flag that would alert his father's ship anchored in the distance that it was time for them to leave. It was way sooner than his father would have expected. His father and brothers would have a grand time jesting about his lack of charm in the love arts. Not that he had attempted any charming or love play. "I'm going to raise the flag to summon my father's ship." He turned and was about to drag on his braies, deciding bare shimmying might result in some splinters in parts where a man didn't want a splinter.

To his shock, he was tackled from behind, landing flat on his face. And Medana was sitting on his back, pummeling his shoulders. When he was able to breathe, he turned over, and she was still atop him, refusing to budge.

"What in bloody hell was that?" he asked.

"You do not tell a woman you love her and then shimmy off up into the air."

"I do not?"

"Nay, you do not, you loathsome lout." She was glowering at him in the most appealing fashion.

Loathsome lout? In that moment, he began to hope. Did she mean those words as an endearment? He rolled again, and now she was on the bottom, his lips within breathing distance of hers. "Does that mean what I think it does?"

She nodded. "Can you forgive me for not trusting you?"

He leaned down and kissed her lips, for a long time, before replying, "Can you forgive me for . . ." He waved a hand toward the mast pole and the leather case of feathers. "I will burn the whole lot."

"Are you barmy?" she said. "You are going to finish what you started with that erotic nonsense. And then I am going to try my hand at feathering *you*."

And he did.

And she did.

Later they lay on the pallet under the shelter, both of them sunburned in some unmentionable places. They could not get enough of each other. Nor could he get tired of hearing the words, "I love you, you loathsome lout." Nor could she get tired of hearing, "I love you, my pretty pirate."

His father came back to the longship, much later, took one look at the two of them, and said, "I always knew I had raised a wild son, but ne'er did I expect my son to get himself a pirate bride. What a Viking!"

epilogue

The Viking's wild pirate bride . . .

It was the first wedding ever on the island of Thrudr.

Thork's family was there, of course, and all the pirate women. Bolthor and Katherine had returned for the wedding, as had Alrek and Brokk and Finn. Henry had never left. Jamie had scampered off to the Highlands, summoned home by an irate father who threatened to handfast him, by proxy, to some well-known shrewish lass. Jolstein disappeared to no one knew where.

Even Thork's uncle Eirik and Lady Eadyth had come from Northumbria, carting many crates of bees, to Medana's joy. Their son John of Hawk's Lair accompanied them with his bride, the Viking princess Ingrith. And children, lots of children. To say the island was overcrowded was a vast understatement. But it was a joyous overcrowding.

"There is naught like a black sheep come home," Lady Alinor was overheard saying. To which her husband was heard to reply, "Or a wild child reformed."

Not that Thork was really reformed. That became clear to one and all once the Christian matrimonial ceremony was completed by the beleaguered Father Peter, who'd been coaxed from Dragonstead. Thork stood under the bridal canopy—a flower-bedecked arbor near the pond—and urged his bride to come forward with a beckoning forefinger. The twinkle in his green eyes did not look at all reformed.

Tykir performed the Norse marriage rituals for the pair, with Thork's three brothers standing as his witnesses, and Gudron, Bergdis, and Solveig at Medana's side.

Medana wore a collarless, gauzy chemise that trailed in back. It would have been scandalous alone, but it was covered with the traditional long, open-sided apron of rich lavender silk, embroidered along the edges with gold thread in a diamond pattern. Her blonde hair was loose, held in place with a gold circlet in a diamond pattern, a gift from her soon-to-be husband.

Thork was finely garbed, too, all in black, except for the gold belt about his waist and the silver thunderbolt earring in his one ear. His hair was loose, at his bride's request, but with war braids on either side of his face. The braids were intertwined with green crystals, gifts from his bride.

Tykir began to chant some ancient Norse prayer, then raised his hands on high. "Odin, please bless this couple with wisdom to know when to fight with each other, and when to yield. Thor, grant them the strength of your mighty hammer Mjollnir, that they may have the stamina to meet each other's needs. Freyja, goddess of fertility, give them many children, and please gods, no wild ones."

"This is like no Norse wedding ceremony I ever attended," Medana whispered to Thork.

Tykir overheard and said, "I am making it up." He picked up a sharp knife then and asked them to extend their hands. Cutting a thin slice on each wrist, Tykir then had them press the wrists together, and he called out, "Blood of his body, blood of her body, now joined! Praise be!"

After that was the bride running. Thork gave Medana a head start, and she picked up the hem of her *gunna*, racing for the longhouse where the wedding feast was to be held. He soon caught up and whacked her on the behind with the broad side of the blade. "Just to show who will be the head of this family."

Medana turned the tables, as she was wont to do, by stamping on his foot and declaring, "Just to show who will be the head of this family."

As a bride-gift, Thork promised to stay and live on Thrudr with Medana until they could fortify it properly, construct a few longships, and, yea, build those bloody steps. Medana promised to come live with Thork after that on land near Dragonstead that his father had gifted him. It was there they would raise their many, many children, they promised each other.

There was dancing and drinking and storytelling throughout the day. In the middle of the feast, Bolthor stood up and said, "My wife has given me permission to compose a few more sagas. This one is for you, Thork."

Thork and Medana sat holding hands as the old man spoke:

"Like father, like son,
The wise men say.
Be a wild man,
And eventually you will pay.
Your sons will grow up
And cause you pain,
Just like you did when
You failed to abstain.

But listen, Thork,
On this your wedding day,
In time you will have a son
To remind you of your once wild way.

And listen, Medana,
For you will learn,
That pirate brides breed
Girls who yearn.

But wait just a moment,
Think about this,
A wild Viking and a pirate bride
Are sure to bring bliss."

Everyone clapped, even though it was a rather silly poem, but then all of Bolthor's poem were. That was their charm.

Soon, it was time for the couple to go to the hunters' hut, which had been turned into a bridal bower, complete with wine and food and soft linens on a feathered mattress. The wedding feast would continue without them.

"I've been wanting to see you all day in this

chemise and naught else," Thork whispered in her ear.

She soon complied, and he was vastly appreciative.

Then she said, "I've been wanting to see you all day in nothing at all."

He complied, too, and she was equally appreciative.

Taking her hand, Thork led her into the bedchamber and said, "I have something special to show you."

"I've already seen it."

He smacked her on her almost bare arse and laughed. "Not that."

Walking over to a low table, he picked up an ornate box and handed it to her.

Suspicious of the glint in his mischievous eyes, she opened it carefully. She put both hands to her burning face. It was another collection. An outrageous collection of various sized silver balls. She could scarce imagine their purpose, except she knew it would be wicked. Wicked good. "Are you sure this is a gift for me? Or you?"

"Both of us," he said, and with a wild Viking whoop, he picked her up and tossed her on the bed, setting the small chest beside her. A long time later . . . a very long time later . . . Thork said, "I love you."

"I love you, too, Thork. I really do."

"Why do you have that little smile on your face?"

"You can ask that?" she exclaimed, then added, "Actually, I was thinking how wonderful it is to be a wild Viking's pirate bride."

GLOSSARY

Asgard—Home of the gods, comparable to Heaven.

Below the salt—Salt was very expensive in ancient times and it was placed in the center of the high table, to be used only by those of higher rank; being placed below the salt meant the person was of lesser social status.

Berserker—An ancient Norse warrior who fought in a frenzied rage during battle.

Birka—Viking age trading town located in present-day Sweden.

Braies—Slim pants, breeches.

Byre—Cowshed.

Deadfall—Fallen trees and branches.

Drukkinn **(various spellings)**—Drunk.

Ealdormen—Chief magistrates or king's deputies in Anglo-Saxon England, later referred to as earls, appointed by the king; most often they were noblemen.

Ell—A linear measure, usually of cloth, equal to forty-five inches.

Fathom—A unit of depth measure, once said to equal the distance between a sailor's outstretched arms, equal to roughly 1.8288 meters or almost two yards.

Frankland—Later called France.

Frigg—Queen of the gods, Odin's wife.

Gammelost—A pungent cheese once a staple of Norse diet, so rank it was said to turn some warriors into berserkers.

Garth—Side yard.

Gunna—Long-sleeved ankle-length gown worn by women, sometimes worn under a tunic or a long, open-sided apron.

Handfast—A betrothal contract, usually completed by a mere handclasp.

Hedeby—Market town where Germany is now located.

Hersir—Military commander who owes allegiance to a king or jarl.

Hird—A permanent troop that a chieftain or nobleman might have.

Hnefatafl—A Viking board game.

Holgaland—A section of northern Norway.

Hordaland—Norway.

Housecarls—Troops assigned to a king's or lord's household on a long-term basis.

Jarl—A Viking social class, similar to an English earl, or could be a wealthy landowner, or chieftain or minor king.

Jorvik—Viking age York.

Jutland—Denmark.

Longship—The graceful, shallow, lightweight sailing vessels made by Vikings, known for their high speed and endurance whether in shallow water or high seas.

Lutefisk—Dried cod.

Manchet—Type of flat, unleavened bread baked in a circle with a hole in the center so that they could be stored stacked on a pole.

Mancus—A measure of weight for gold, equal to roughly 4.25 grams, or about one month's wage in those days for a skilled craftsman or soldier.

Mead—Honeyed ale.

Miklagard (various spellings)—Viking name for Constantinople or Byzantium.

More danico—The Viking practice of multiple wives.

Muspell—A fiery place in the lower level of the Norse afterlife, similar to Hell.

Neeps—Turnips.

Nithing—The worst possible insult to call a man, means he is worth less than nothing.

Norns of Fate—Three wise old women who destined everyone's fate, according to Norse legend.

Northumbria—One of the Anglo-Saxon kingdoms, bordered by the English kingdoms to the south and in the north and northwest by the Scots, Cumbrians, and Strathclyde Welsh.

Odal laws—Laws of heredity.

Pace—Distance measured by a step or stride, about thirty inches.

Pannage—Medieval term for natural, self-foraging diet of animals, like wild pigs (boars), such as beechnuts, acorns, chestnuts, and wild fruits.

Pennanular—Type of jewelry design, often of a brooch, usually in the form of an incomplete circle.

Runes—Stick-like characters in Old Norse alphabet.

Rushes—Hard-packed dirt floors were often covered with sweet-smelling grasses or straw called rushes that could be raked up when they got too dirty.

Russet—Coarse homespun, often reddish-brown color.

Scat—Animal waste.

Scathe—Harm.

Scree—A scattering of broken rocks.

Sennight—One week.

Skald—Poet.

Skyrr (skyr, various spellings)—Soft cheese favored by Vikings, similar to cream cheese or cottage cheese.

Sword dew—Blood.

Thatch—A sheltering material (roof) made of plant materials, like grass.

Thing—An assembly of free people who made laws and settle disputes; on a much larger scale it would be called an Althing.

Thrall—Slave.

Tun—252 gallons, as of ale.

Valhalla—Hall of the slain, Odin's great hall for warriors in Asgard.

Valkyries—Female warriors in the afterlife who did Odin's will.

Vapnatak—Weapon clatter; at a Thing or Althing, the men voted by banging their swords against their shields.

Vestfold—Southern Norway.

Wergild—A man's worth, often the penalty paid for killing or injuring a highborn man or woman.

READER LETTER

Dear Reader:

How did you like my latest book in Viking Series I? I hope I did Thork proud. After all, his father, Tykir, has been a beloved character, along with other members of the Haraldsson, Thorksson, Tykirsson, and Eiriksson families, for almost twenty years now.

I've said it before and will repeat again, I have good reason for loving the Vikings and their culture. My grandfather many times removed was Rolf the Gangr, first Duke of Normandy. It was a fascinating discovery when doing family genealogy research years ago to discover my Norse heritage. How many people can trace their roots back to the tenth century? I should have suspected, though, with a grandfather whose name was Magnus.

One of the sticking points for many readers in ancient historical novels is the language issue. How could the Vikings understand the Saxons or the French and vice versa? The explanation is a simple one. Old Norse (not to be confused with modern Norwegian) was mutually intelligible with Saxon English and other tongues spoken at that time. Modern Icelandic comes closest to retaining the Old Norse words.

In fact, a lot of English words are what are referred to as loanwords from Old Norse. Such as knife (*knífr*), fish (*fiski*), no (*nei*), beer (*bjr*), take (*taka*), ill (*íllr*), drunk (*drukkinn*), Russian (*Rus*), according to Wikipedia, "Old Norse Language." Or, quoting from *The Year 1000*, by Robert Lacey and Danny Danziger, "Have you a horse to sell?" would be *"Haefst thu hors to sellenne?"* in Anglo-Saxon, and *"Hefir thu hross at selja?"* in Old Norse, with the response "Obviously, I have two horses to sell" being *"Ic haebbe tvau hors"* in Anglo-Saxon, and *"Ed hefi tvau hors"* in Old Norse.

You should know that *The Pirate Bride* is the eleventh book in Viking Series I, all of which are still available in new print or e-book formats: *The Reluctant Viking*, *The Outlaw Viking*, *The Tarnished Lady*, *The Bewitched Viking*, *The Blue Viking*, *My Fair Viking* (aka *The Viking's Captive*), *A Tale of Two Vikings*, *Viking in Love*, *The Viking Takes a Knight*, and *The Norse King's Daughter*. Every time I think it's time to end this series, I wonder what will happen to Alrek, or Jamie, or Jostein, and now Starri, Guthrom, and Selik. Or how about the brooding Wulf from *Viking in Love*? Don't they all deserve their own stories?

Please visit my website at www.sandrahill.net or my Facebook page at Sandra Hill Author for news about these and my other books, contests, genealogy charts, and other good stuff. I can be reached at shill733@aol.com.

As always, I wish you smiles in your reading.

SANDRA HILL

Keep reading for

a sneak peek at

KISS OF WRATH

The next book in

the **DEADLY ANGELS** series,

coming soon

from Sandra Hill

and

Avon Books

PROLOGUE

When men turn beastly . . .

Mordr Sigurdsson, best known as Mordr the Brave, led his battle-weary men up the steep incline from the fjord to Stonegarth. His wooden castle and the surrounding village sat atop a high motte, a massive, flat-topped earthworks mound in the Frankish style, rising high above the surrounding area.

He'd already anchored his longships. Later, but not too much later, the ten vessels would be brought ashore to winter. Already, ice crusted the edges of the narrow waterway leading to his aptly named, grim estate in the far north where naught grew except boulders and hardy evergreens, which was fine with him. He obtained all he needed to subsist and prosper by trading, serving in the army of one grab-land king or another, or going a-Viking. A good life!

He and his men had been gone nigh on a year now, longer than he usually spent away from his homeland. In truth, they'd waited too long in trying to outrun winter for their return voyage, having to crack thickening ice ahead of them in many places, but that one last monastery to plunder had been too tempting. As a result, they were not only exhausted but cold to the bone with frost painting their fur cloaks and hats, not to mention beards and mustaches. Like Norse ice gods, they were. Their breaths froze into snowflakes on leaving their mouths, and below their noses, snot formed icicles into miniature tusks.

They were home now, though, and he for one intended to dig in for a long stay.

As if sensing Mordr's thoughts, his *hersir*, Geirfinn the Fearless, said on a frosty breath, "My Aud best have the fire stoked for my arrival because I intend to burrow in 'til the spring thaw."

Atzer Horse Teeth, one of Mordr's *hirdsmen* serving under Geirfinn, guffawed from his other side. "Which fire would that be? The cook fire, or the fire betwixt your wife's thighs?"

Mordr and other *hirdsmen* close by laughed, causing more frosty cloud-breaths.

"Did I not mention burrowing?" Geirfinn replied with a grin, hardly visible through his huge, walrus-like, ice-crusted mustache. "I do my best work beneath the bed furs . . . burrowing."

More companionable laughter. Ah, it was good to be home.

"First off, I want a horn of ale, or five," Mordr declared, joining in the levity. "A warm bath to wash away the battle filth."

"And lice," someone called out behind him.

Lice were ever a problem for fighting men ofttimes forced to bed down in unclean places and unable to take their customary baths. Norsemen did tend to bathe more than other men. 'Twas one reason women of all lands welcomed them to their beds. That, and other reasons, Mordr thought with silent humor at his own jest.

"Then I want a hearty meal in my great hall," Mordr went on to encourage his men onward. Many of them wore heavy hauberks of chain mail. Plus, swords and battle-axes and shields added to the weight on the climb upward. "Yea, you are all invited to my welcome feast . . . after your burrowing." He smiled before continuing, "Then a long night betwixt the thighs of my favorite concubine, Dyna."

"Dyna of the big bosoms?" Atzer teased.

"Precisely," Mordr said. "Forget a long night. Mayhap I will need a night and a day afore I am sated. I might even favor my wife, Gulli, with my attentions if she is not in her usual nagsome mood."

There was much nodding. They all understood the pain of a shrewish wife.

But, nay, Mordr realized belatedly, there was something more important than all those appetites. Most of all, he yearned to see his children, Kata and Jomar. Though only one year apart, being six and five, respectively, his little mites were naught alike in appearance or personality. Kata had pale blonde hair that would no doubt darken over time into dark blonde or light brown like his own. She was a saucy wenchling with an impish grin, always up for some mischief or other. Jomar, black-haired like his mother, Gulli, was more serious but always willing to participate in Kata's childish adventures.

Yea, that is what he had missed most about Stonegarth. His children. He pictured himself, first thing, tossing Kata and Jomar into the air, giving them huge bear hugs and playful tickles. Was there aught more glorious to a man than the giggle of a child, especially when the boyling or girling was fruit of his loins?

He'd brought Kata dozens of ribands, all the colors of the rainbow, and for Jomar, there was a miniature sword crafted of hard wood with its own belted scabbard, so small it would fit around a man's thigh. Mordr couldn't wait to see their joyful appreciation. Also, both of them would delight in an intricately carved board game of *hnefatafl* with silly game pieces—giants and trolls and such, rather than the usual king, his defending soldiers, and the opposing foemen.

His first clue that something was amiss came with the realization that none of his *housecarls*, or even any villagers, rushed to greet them. The second clue, which had his comrades-in-arms unsheathing their weapons, was no smoke rising from the roofs of his keep or any of the longhouses and outbuildings that comprised Stonegarth on the flat-topped mountain. Always there should be hearth smoke, even in the summer months, from cook fires, if not for heat. The ominous silence had them all on alert.

And then they came upon the first of the macabre scenes. In the outer courtyard lay the dead bodies of his guardsmen, frozen into stiff, grotesque postures, eyes open, mouths agape in horror. Even the blood was preserved by the cold onto their wounds in splotchy patterns. Which gave Mordr evidence that the attackers must have come just afore the more recent freeze. No more than three sennights ago.

"Was it Saxons?" someone asked.

"Those cowards would not travel this deep into our territory," another soldier replied. "Mayhap Huns."

"Nay! 'Twas Norsemen. Look at this sword. Pattern-welded in the Viking style," Atzer pointed out.

"Hordssons!" several men concluded as one.

"Those slimy outlaws do not merit the name Viking. They have lurked about for years, waiting for a chance to attack," Geirfinn said. "Damn them all to the fires of Nifhelm."

Mordr heard these remarks through the roar that was growing in his ears. "Kata? Jomar?" he cried out even as he began to sprint toward the keep. The other men began rushing in all directions, swords aready, though, from the state of the frozen corpses, it appeared the invaders had been gone for days if not weeks.

Despite his heavy armor, Mordr ran like the wind across the courtyard, up the steps, and through the open double doors leading to his great hall, where the three hearth fires were cold, the logs long burned out. Tapestries had been ripped from the walls, benches and trestle tables wantonly hacked into kindling. Along the way, he jumped over the corpses of his *housecarl*s and servants, male and female both. In the corridor betwixt the solar and the scullery, he found Dyna's body, her *gunna* torn from neck to hem, her breasts bearing dark bruise marks, as did her widespread thighs. Mordr would warrant that many men had participated in the rape, if the bloodstains on her thighs were any indication.

His wife's body bore similar signs of mistreatment when he found it in a storage room where she must have hidden, or tried to hide.

And no sign of his precious children.

With foreboding, Mordr vaulted up the steep stairs to the upper level of his wooden keep where there were three sleeping chambers. In the first one, he found Jomar, who must have been hiding, facedown, under the bed when he'd been found by the invaders. He'd been dragged out by the feet, and his skull cleaved almost clear through from the back by a broadsword. Mordr prayed gods that it had been a quick death.

He dropped to his knees and gathered his little boyling up into his arms, keening with grief. His heart felt shattered like glass, sharp slivers cutting into his soul. But he could not fall apart yet. First he must find Kata. Laying Jomar carefully onto the bed, he spread his own fur cloak over the body, as if to warm him in death.

Kata's nude, frozen corpse lay in the next chamber. No sword blow to her perfect body. Instead, from the quantity of blood pooled betwixt her thighs, he concluded with horror that she must have bled to death from her girl parts. From numerous swivings by beastly Hordsson males.

What kind of men killed women and children? What kind of men found pleasure in raping little girls? Why had they not taken women and children, or healthy males, as valuable slaves, a practice employed by even the most vile villains? The slave marts in Hedeby and Birka and Kaupang would have welcomed them in a trice. Had that been the case, Mordr would have had a chance of recovering his children, by ransom or sword.

This was an act of violence, of evil, pure and simple. Aimed at him. Monetary gain had not been the goal, leastways not totally.

Mordr stood, arms raised to tear at his own hair. The roar of outrage, "NOOOOOOOOOOOOO!" that came from him could be heard even outside the keep and beyond, into the village. Some say that was the day that Mordr the Brave became Mordr the Berserker.

CHAPTER ONE

Hell hath no fury like a Viking wronged . . .

After being restrained by his men—it took Geir-finn, Atzer, and three other burly fellows to hold him down—and after being forced to drink horn after horn of *uisge beatha*, that potent, prized Scottish brew, Mordr fell into a deep, alehead sleep. When he awakened, the rage was still in him, but he restrained it inside himself in silent, cold fury toward the Hordssons. He began to plan.

No matter what he did—walk down the incline to check on the landed longships, eat a hunk of cold boar shank, bathe his filthy body, feel the warmth of the hearth fire—images of Jomar and Kata were ever with him. And those images were not of the laughing, happy children he had left behind at Stonegarth a year ago. Nay, all he could see was their bloody, defiled bodies and sad, frozen, tormented faces.

Their deaths, all the deaths at Stonegarth, must be avenged. Thus it was that, two days later, in his great hall, which had been cleared somewhat of the destruction, Mordr raised a hand high in the air and declared, "War on the Hordssons! To the death of every misbegotten cur bearing that name!"

A loud cheer went up from the men. There were no women or children present, of course.

Within a sennight, Mordr and his reluctant followers—reluctant only because winter was not the best time for warfare and his *hirdsmen* would have preferred a springtime march to battle—had razed the sorry keep and village of the Hordsson clan. Not a single Hordsson male over the age of ten survived the surprise assault. Some women were killed, too. Mordr, even in the berserk madness that overtook him when fighting started, had no taste for killing females, but if they got in his way, they were fair targets, to his rattled mind. Never young children, though. Never!

For a year and more, he sought out Hordsson kin in other parts of the Norselands . . . Hordaland, Jutland, Vestfold, Holgaland. It did not matter if they had participated in the raid on Stonegarth, if they had Hordsson blood, Mordr decreed they must die. Then there was word of some Hordssons in the Irish lands; he traveled there and wreaked his still raging vengeance. Still others lived and died at Mordr's hands in Northumbria where a Viking king ruled that portion of Britain. After that, he moved onto the Orkney Isles.

Hundreds of dead Hordssons lay in his wake of terror. Others shook in fright and changed their names to escape Mordr's path of retaliation.

Though it had not been his aim, Mordr gained far fame for his berserk skill with a sword named Vengeance and a battle-axe named Fury. Every man with a speck of sense, even those not named Hordsson, avoided his path for fear of doing or saying something to set him off. 'Twas a well-known fact amongst fighting men that you never engaged a warrior, whether he was a berserker or not, who had no care whether he lived or died.

In truth, Mordr welcomed the road to Valhalla. Or did the Christians have the right of it? Followers of the One-God believed there was an afterlife where good deeds whilst living gained an entry into Heaven. According to their Holy Book, after death a man could meet up with those who'd gone before him. If that was the case, Mordr was lost. He'd never been baptized, and too many misdeeds would bar him from the heavenly gates. Alas, he would never see Jomar and Kata again.

By then, many of his men wearied of the vendetta and went back to Stonegarth, with Mordr's permission, led by Atzer. Mordr never returned to his home, though he had heard years later that the estate prospered as the men under Atzer took wives, had children, and drew villagers and cotters to newly built longhouses. Even his six brothers, who joined him at first from their estates scattered across the Norselands, gave up after a while. It was not their fight.

"Mayhap you need to swive a lusty maid, or ten, to calm your mind," his brother Ivak suggested before departing.

"Ivak, you think every problem in the world can be solved with your cock."

"Can it not?" his halfbrained brother asked, and he was serious.

Vikar, the oldest of the Sigurdsson brood, gave his usual sage advice, sage in his own not-so-humble opinion. "Your pride has been assuaged. Accept the *wergild* offered by King Haakon to halt your vendetta, and use it to start over again."

"Dost think this is about pride? Dost think I care for bribe coins? Dost think I could truly start over?" Mordr stormed. "I can never replace my two children."

That shut up Vikar . . . for a while.

His brother Cnut mentioned the widow whose prosperous lands adjoined his in Vestfold.

"Would that by chance be Inga No Teeth?" Mordr asked with growing impatience.

"Well . . ." Cnut said defensively, "you know what they say about all cats being the same in the dark."

"Whoever said that did not know cats, or women," Ivak interjected.

They all turned to stare at Ivak.

"I am just saying," Ivak defended himself. "Besides, there are advantages to a toothless woman in the bed arts."

They all gaped at Ivak with incredulity.

"I am just saying," Ivak repeated, this time with a grin.

"I do not need another wife," Mordr said with growing impatience.

"You could go exploring with those Vikings who seek new countries to settle beyond Iceland," said Trond.

Mordr arched a brow at Trond, who was the laziest Norseman ever born. Trond would never go exploring himself because it would require too much energy. "The only way I am going to Iceland is if there is an Hordsson sitting on an iceberg thereabouts," Mordr declared.

Sigurd the Healer made one of the most outrageous suggestions. "Methinks you should let me drill a hole in your head. Trepanning, it is called. Mayhap all your body's bad humours would be released, and you would lose this madness."

His other brothers were as stunned as Mordr.

"I like my madness, thank you very much. You come within an arm's length of me with a drill, and you will find that instrument lodged in one of your body parts, the one where the sun does not shine, lest it come up from a privy hole."

Harek, the most intelligent and most wealthy of all his brothers—he was a moneylender and tax collector—said, "If you're going to continue on this path of self-destruction, can I have Stonegarth?"

Mordr could not be angry with his brother. Harek was what he was, a greedy Viking bent on amassing enough treasure to establish his own kingdom.

"I've already given it to Atzer," Mordr told him.

His brothers left him eventually, as did many more of his followers. In the end, Geirfinn was the only one of his original *hersir*s to stay. When Mordr could find no more Hordssons to kill, Mordr, Geirfinn, and a handful of loyal comrades-in-arms hired themselves out as mercenaries to kings and chieftains of many lands. For a while, they even became Jomsvikings, but Mordr chafed under the rigid rules of that monastic-like living.

Thus it was that five years after the invasion of Stonegarth and the death of his children, Mordr found himself in a battle against a band of Saxon villains. There were only twelve men with Mordr now, but thirteen powerful Norse warriors could handle twice, mayhap thrice, that many foemen. But not today. They were outnumbered five to one, and the gods were against them, pelting rain down in cold misery. If that were not bad enough, Thor raised his mighty hammer Mjollnir, causing lightning to flash, as if foretelling doom. Already vultures—ravens of death—circled overhead, just waiting to pounce on the human carrion.

The field became slippery with sword dew, as well as mud. The air rang with the clang of metal weapon against metal weapon, the death screams of the fallen, the grunts of soldiers brandishing heavy broadswords, and his own roars of berserkness.

Mordr cleared a path through the fray in front of him, trying to get to Geirfinn, who was being attacked from both sides. When he was almost there, he saw his good friend go down from a lance thrown from behind by yet another Saxon villain. A deathblow, it had to be.

With a bellow of outrage, Mordr tossed his shield and leather helmet to the ground. Storming forward, he wielded his heavy broadsword in his right hand and his battle-axe in his left. One foeman got his head lopped off. Another Mordr speared through the heart with the sharp butt end of his battle-axe. Still another would ne'er swive any maids in the future, for Mordr firmly planted his sword Vengeance in the soldier's groin.

As he was pulling his sword back out of the groaning man's body, Mordr made a huge mistake. Ne'er turn your back on the battlefield. Someone had come up behind him, quickly reaching around and garroting him from shoulder to shoulder. Blood gushed forth, and he felt a flush of heat race across the skin of his entire body, as if he had been scalded. His arms went numb, and his legs gave out, causing him to fall forward. Soon, the sounds of battle faded as he felt his blood soaking the ground beneath him. Someone rolled him over with a booted foot and laughed. "King Edgar will give me a great boon for having felled this vicious Viking."

But then Mordr heard nothing as he sank into a dark slumber, and it was not a peaceful sleep as he'd expected death would be. It sounded like beasts gnashing their teeth all around him, just waiting for the cue to devour his flesh and bones. *Is this death then? Why am I not on the road to Asgard? Where are my Valkyries? Why am I not being welcomed into Odin's great hall in Valhalla?*

"Because thou art not in Valhalla, Viking," a voice boomed above him.

Mordr hadn't realized he'd spoken aloud. In truth, how could he speak with his neck nigh split through to his nape? He blinked his eyes open. He was still in the middle of the battlefield. Fighting was going on around him. Rain still came down in stinging sheets. Except for the circle surrounding him where a tall man stood over him. Instead of wearing a battle helmet and *brynja* of chain mesh, this lackwit wore a white robe, similar to those worn by men in eastern lands. It was tied at the waist with a golden rope, and his dark hair hung loose to his shoulder. Most amazing of all, a light emanated from the man, like a full-body halo. Mordr knew about halos, having once seen a Byzantine church mural depicting a saint, but that fellow's halo had been surrounding his head only. This must be an important saint.

"Are you a saint?" Mordr asked, oddly unsurprised that he could speak.

"You could say that," the man said, and from

his back suddenly unfurled a massive set of pure white wings.

"Bloody hell! An angel?"

The man—rather, the angel—nodded. "I am St. Michael the Archangel, and you, Viking, are in big trouble."

Mordr noticed that the angel did not say "Viking" in a complimentary way. "What do you have against Vikings?"

"You are a sorry lot of men. Vain. Prideful. Greedy. Vicious. Fornicators."

"We are also brave in battle. Good providers for our families. Yea, I know what you are going to say. We provide by plundering, but that is not so bad when you consider we are doing a good deed by relieving your churchmen of the over-abundance of wealth they garner for themselves. As for vanity, some could say that your God made Norsemen beautiful; therefore, 'tis not our fault that we are proud of ourselves."

Michael's eyes went wide before he shook his head as if Mordr were a hopeless idiot.

In fact, Michael said, "Idiot! Thou art in the greatest trouble of your life, and you dare to make excuses."

"What would you have me do? In truth, I am not sorry to have my life end."

Michael's face softened for a moment. "Your children are safe and in a happy place."

For the first time since he'd come across the ravaged bodies of Jomar and Kata, tears filled Mordr's eyes and streamed down his face, mixing with the blood on his neck. A small sob slipped from his slit neck.

"Weep not for your children, but for yourself. You are a grave sinner, Mordr, as are your six brothers."

Mordr stiffened, as much as a dead body could. "Are my brothers dead, too?"

"If they are not dead, they soon will be."

"Why?" Mordr asked.

"You know why, sinner."

Mordr did not need to think before nodding. "My berserkness. The killing. It started with the assault on Stonegarth, with the murder of my children. I had good cause to—"

"Foolish Viking! Vengeance is the Lord's, not man's," the angel said in a steely voice. Then, "Do not try to excuse your actions. Even if you could be forgiven for killing those who killed your children, and I am not sure it ever could be, there have been so many other lives you've taken. Many of them innocent of any crime."

"I understand why I must be punished, but you mentioned my brothers, as well. Why must you take all of us at one time?"

"Because you are grave sinners, each guilty in a most heinous way of the Seven Deadly Sins," Michael explained with growing impatience, "as are many of your Norse race. God in his anger has decided to use you seven as examples, and—"

"Lucky us!" Mordr muttered.

Michael cast a black look his way for the interruption.

No sense of humor.

Michael continued, "In truth, there will come a time in the future when the Viking race will no longer be. That is the will of the Lord."

Mordr's numb brain tried to comprehend what the angel told him. "How exactly are you . . . or rather, your God . . . going to use me and my brothers?"

"Ah. I thought you would never ask." Michael smiled, and it was not a nice smile. "God has commissioned me to establish a legion of vangels to fight Satan's Lucipires, demon vampires. And, at the same time, to save those humans fanged by the Lucipires with a sin taint afore they commit some grievous act, causing them to commit a grave sin." Michael motioned with his head to a sight directly behind the circle of light that surrounded him.

Mordr recalled, when he'd first emerged from his death-sleep, the sound of gnashing teeth, like leashed beasts. He saw now what had caused that noise. A band of grotesque beasts were trying—unsuccessfully, so far—to break into the halo barrier. They were huge, animal-like humans, tall as upright black bears, with scaly skin oozing slime. Their eyes were red, and their open mouths showed elongated incisors, like wolves, but longer and sharper.

"Lucipires?" Mordr asked.

"Precisely. You do not want to be in their clutches, believe you me."

Mordr believed. With typical Viking self-confidence, Mordr knew he could fight off three or four foemen, but these were not men, precisely, and they numbered in the dozens. He thought for a moment, then burst out with a chortle of laughter, which only caused more blood to spurt from his mouth. "You said you would turn me and my brothers into angels. Now there is a task! Turning Vikings into angels."

"Tsk, tsk. You do not listen carefully. I did not say angels. I said *vangels*."

"And they are?"

"Viking vampire angels."

"Huh?"

"For hundreds and hundreds and hundreds of years, seven hundred years to begin with, you would serve the Lord as a vangel."

"Seven hundred years?" Mordr exclaimed. "You mean, I would live for centuries."

Michael nodded. "Mayhap even thousands of years."

"Do I have a choice?"

"Of course. You can choose to be a vangel, or join the other side."

"The other side? Oh. Oh no!" Mordr realized that Michael meant he would be taken by those beasts, slobber dripping from their fangs, their eyes glowing like torchlights, as they tried to break the barrier to get at him. "I choose vangels. Definitely."

"So be it!" Michael said, and extended a hand over Mordr, causing him to be lifted to his feet.

Mordr put a hand to his neck and felt the skin intact. "Thank you."

"Do not thank me yet, Viking."

Mordr blinked several times. The golden halo was gone, as were the horrid beasts. In fact, the battlefield was now a clear field. No fighting soldiers. No dead bodies. There were so many questions riddling his mind, but he asked the most inane one. "Will I have wings, like yours?"

Michael hooted a short laugh. "Not yet. Maybe later. Probably never."

That was clear as mud. "By the by, what is a vampire?"

Michael graced him with another of those smiles, which were not really smiles.

Immediately, Mordr felt a fierce pain in his mouth, as if his jaw were being broken and pierced with fiery tongs. When the pain went away, as suddenly as it had hit him, Mordr felt around his mouth with his tongue and realized that he now had a long . . . really long tooth . . . on either side of his front teeth on top. With horror, he said, "You made me into a wolf? I hate wolves. They are the most devious creatures, and they smell bad."

Michael shook his head. "Not a wolf. A vampire."

Then, more pain hit him. On his shoulder blades. He reached behind him, over his shoulders, and discovered two bumps there. He arched his brows at Michael. "Please do not tell me that you put teeth in my back."

"Thickheaded dolts, that is what these Vikings are," Michael muttered. Then he told Mordr, "Do not be ridiculous. They are bumps. Where your wings *might* emerge someday."

"There is hope for me then?"

"Viking, Viking, Viking! Didst not know, there is always hope? Are you ready to begin your penance?"

Penance? Ah. He means punishment. Still, Mordr nodded, hesitantly. What choice did he have, really?

The angel took him by the hand, and Mordr found himself rising above the ground, higher and higher, spinning, through the clouds, across the skies, over countries. Where he would land, Mordr had no idea.

One thought emerged through his battered brain. *I have been given a second chance. Praise the gods! Nay, that is incorrect. Praise God!*

Michael smiled, and this time it was a good smile.

Some inheritances are better than others . . .

Dr. Miranda Hart, psychologist, prided herself on always maintaining a dignified calm. She did a half hour of yoga every morning, after all, and she gave lectures on stress management. Even so, she stared with stunned horror at the lawyer in front of her and practically screamed, "Noooooo!"

"I'm sorry, Miranda." Bradley Allison, elderly Cincinnati lawyer and longtime family retainer, clearly was not sorry. In fact, he recoiled, obviously disgusted with her reaction. "I thought you'd be pleased at this 'bequest.' The highest compliment!"

"Are you crazy?" Miranda asked, immediately realizing that she was the one who sounded crazy. And *crazy* was not a word that a mental health professional should be using. She inhaled and exhaled several times, finding her center. "You have to understand, Mr. Allison. I'm thirty-four years old. I've never been married, by choice. It's taken me eight years to pay off my college loans and establish a successful practice in Las Vegas. Not Cincinnati, by the way. I live in a luxury high-rise apartment with two bedrooms, one of which has been converted into an office. I have no desire for children . . . or a dog." She shivered with distaste.

"It was your cousin Cassandra's wish that you

adopt her five children. If you decline, there's no option but to put them in foster care. Cassandra's neighbor is unable to care for them for much longer. She has a big family of her own. I must warn you, if the Jessup children are adopted, I'm sure they will be separated."

The oldest of Cassie's children was eight-year-old Margaret, or Maggie. One set of twins was six-year-old Ben and Sam. The other twins were three-year-old Linda and Larry. Mr. Allison was right. Miranda would bet her medical degree that there would be two separate adoptions for the twins, and Maggie might not be adopted at all because of her age.

Miranda steeled herself not to care. "What about Roger's family?" Roger Jessup, Cassie's no-good husband, was in prison for assault and battery, and not for the first time, which had been news to Miranda when she'd arrived for Cassie's funeral three days ago.

"No family," Mr. Allison informed her. "Just you." By his seventy-five-year-old nose raised northward, she could tell what he thought of her. She knew for sure when he added, "Perhaps they would be better off in foster care, after all."

Miranda didn't have a maternal bone in her body, but she didn't like some old codger pointing out her flaws. Besides, she didn't consider a lack of desire for procreation a flaw.

Despite his obvious misgivings, the lawyer tried a different tack. "If money is the issue, the family home could be sold."

She waved that remark aside. "I own half the house, our grandparents', to begin with. Cassie and I both signed contracts years ago that, if one of us died first, the home belonged to the remaining cousin. Even if her husband were around, Roger has no claim on the house."

"He might try," Mr. Allison told her.

"Let him." After what she'd recently learned about Roger, she would welcome the fight. "Cassie made a good living as a nurse, but, as you mentioned earlier, there's only a few thousand in her bank account. Roger is welcome to that. Let's hope that satisfies him."

Mr. Allison nodded. "You do not need to tell me what can or cannot be done with the family home. I am very aware of the circumstances surrounding the house, young lady. Your grandfather was a good friend of mine. I drew up that contract."

Boy! Talk about pole-up-the-ass irritable! They have a syndrome name for it, in fact. Irritable bowel syndrome. Oh God! I can't believe I am making psychiatry jokes with myself. Must be the thought of sudden motherhood. To FIVE children! I need a Valium, or a fast train out of town.

"Will you or will you not be taking responsibility for the children, Miranda? It's Friday afternoon. If you're going to reject your cousin's wishes, I need to contact social services." Bradley pursed his lips and twitched his nose as if there was a foul odor in the room.

Miranda wasn't ready to make that decision, and the old fart's pressuring her didn't help at all. "Argh! What woman chooses to have five children today, anyhow?" Miranda wondered aloud, not really directing her thoughts at anyone, least of all the judgmental lawyer. "My cousin Cassie always was a ditz. Any stray animal—dog, cat, rabbit—found its way into her house. She and her family lived down the street from me in Cincinnati, and their home was like a zoo. Cassie's mother, Aunt Mary, was just the same. Apparently, Cassie extended her bleeding heart to popping out children."

Mr. Allison looked at her as if she were a species of smelly bug. "Be that as it may—"

"Who says 'Be that as it may'?" she inquired meanly.

"*Be that as it may,* your cousin died. Her husband is in prison, and even if he weren't, Cassandra did not want them to be in his custody. You might want to read this letter that Cassandra left for you before making a final decision."

"Why didn't you tell me there was a letter?" she asked coldly.

The lawyer shrugged. "I mistakenly thought you would do the right thing before reading the letter."

She took the sealed envelope from him. "Do you know what's in the letter?"

"I can guess."

Oooh, she was developing a real dislike for the man. Turning away from the lawyer, she opened the envelope and unfolded the letter, which was dated two years ago.

Hey Mir:

> *If you're reading this, I'm no longer around. Sorry we didn't keep in touch more after college, but I always felt close to you when we did talk. I love you like a sister. Remember that time we did the blood oath thing up in Willy Markle's tree house? "Sisters to the end!"*

Well, cousin, I need your help now. I have cancer. Looks like I won't make it past another year. I know, I know, I should have talked to you about this. But it's hard to admit that your life has been a huge mistake. Except for the kids, of course.

Suffice it to say, my asshole husband Roger is an abuser. The beatings started after Maggie was born. The usual pattern, violence followed by profound apologies and promises to never do it again. As a nurse, I should have known better.

Miranda stopped reading and turned to the lawyer, who was watching her from behind his antique lawyer's desk, with his bony hands tented in front of his mouth. "The assault and battery that landed Roger in jail this last time . . . was it for beating Cassie?"

He nodded. "Broke an arm, cracked several ribs, and knocked out a tooth. He also hit Maggie so hard with a belt that it broke the skin on her back." Mr. Allison glared at her, as if Miranda should have done something to stop the abuse. "Thankfully, we have a judge here in Ohio who has a low tolerance for wife abusers, and even less for men who hit children. He gave Roger Jessup the maximum of five years. With good behavior, Roger might be out in a year or so. You can see why the issue of the children needs to be settled before that."

"No one ever told me," she said defensively. "Cassie could have come to me at any time, and I would have helped."

Mr. Allison arched his unruly white brows at her in silent recrimination. *Like now?* he seemed ˌˑ ˗ saying.

Miranda returned to the letter.

> *Even knowing that I have cancer, Roger's rages haven't let up. In fact, they seem to be getting worse. For the first time, last month I called the police and had him put in jail. Aside from hitting me, he also lashed out at Maggie when she tried to intervene. He beat her with a belt. Can you imagine? The poor girl has scars. And he locked the twins—all four of them—in a closet. I fear the direction his rages might take in my absence if he did this when I was around. That is a travesty I will never allow. I should have stopped this horrible pattern long ago, for my children's sake, if not my own.*
>
> *The cancer will probably get me before Roger is released from prison. And so, dear cousin, I am asking you to please, please take care of my precious children. I know what a huge favor I am asking of you. An imposition of the highest order to your single lifestyle! Do it for love of me, please.*
>
> *Your cousin,*
> *Cassandra Hart Jessup*

Single lifestyle? Did Cassie even remotely think I am so selfish as to choose my "single lifestyle," whatever that is, over helping her? Miranda had tears in her eyes when she turned back to the lawyer.

"Where do I sign?" she asked.

For the first time, the lawyer smiled at her. "You'll never regret this decision, my dear."

Miranda wasn't so sure about that.